IGNITE

IGNITE

ERICA CROUCH

Ignite
Copyright © 2013 by Erica Crouch.

All rights reserved. This book or any portion thereof may not be reproduced or used in any manner whatsoever without the express written permission of the publisher except for the use of brief quotations in a book review.

This novel is a work of fiction. Names, characters, places and plot are all either products of the author's imagination or used fictitiously. Any resemblance to actual events, locales, or persons - living or dead - is purely coincidental.

First Edition.

ISBN: 0991789741
ISBN-13: 9780991789740

Patchwork-Press.com

*Dedicated to those still trying to find their way.
Don't worry, don't rush, you'll get there eventually.*

"THIS HORROR WILL GROW MILD,
THIS DARKNESS LIGHT."

—John Milton, *Paradise Lost*

CHAPTER 1

WARM, SLICK, AND RUSTY RED. I SHOULD BE USED TO being covered in blood by now, should be used to how it spills from their veins faster when they're scared, their heart pumping liters of it out of their body in a panic. It's not as bad as it once was. There are times when I can actually enjoy it, separate myself from the twist of guilt in my gut long enough for their eyes to glaze over and their choking to subside.

A line of poetry drips in my mind like the blood between my fingers. William Butler Yeats, one of my favorites. I whisper it aloud to the middle-aged woman, with wiry hair and gray shadows under her eyes so dark they look like bruises, as she pales of her life. "'The blood-dimmed tide is loosed, and everywhere / The ceremony of innocence is drowned.'"

She makes a small gasping noise, clutches at the tear in her throat, and passes out.

One heartbeat, two heartbeats, three incredibly slow heartbeats and she's dead.

IGNITE

Pen, can you hurry up? Azael's voice in my head is impatient. *I'm getting a little tired of playing look-out. My talents are being wasted.*

He's waiting for me from just beyond the thick walls of the asylum, anxious to reap their souls.

I sigh. *There are still two more. I feel like this is a bit overkill.*

Az laughs. *Just the way I like it.*

Gus said we only needed one of them, not all of them. They're marked as pure. We shouldn't be—

Pen, my dear sister, I like to think of Gus's instructions as more of a guideline. I'm sure he'll be thrilled about the extra souls. More company for him, and you know he can use all the friends he can get. It says a lot about his personality that we have to kill people for him to be friends with, but he's not much fun. I don't think I could bear to spend time with him, even if I were dead! It's a bit of a disservice to these souls, if you ask me.

I walk over to the last two patients sitting cuffed to the uncomfortable-looking waiting room chairs. They are dressed in blue ill-fitting hospital clothes that look like something between scrubs and a surgical gown. They have sharp, plastic medical bracelets around their wrists, identifying them and their disorders. I can't help but compare their labels to the tags on cattle, organizing them for slaughter.

The girl, who looks about nineteen, has burgundy hair that falls haphazardly around her shoulders. I read her tag: St. Luke's Memorial Hospital, Julie Owen, DOB 04/04/1990, Schizotypal Personality Disorder, Dangerous. She's older than she looks.

Her dark muddy eyes are wide and her bottom lip trembles. "Is the doctor ready?" She jerks her arm and tries to pull herself free from the chair, but she is locked in restraints, just like everyone else in the room was. They were all trapped, helpless prey in the presence of a deadly predator. It made my job much easier. No one could run.

"You don't look dangerous," I note, nodding towards her medical bracelet.

"I drowned my brother," she answers simply.

"Ah, well, I'd be lying if I said that thought never crossed my mind." I smile at her and she flinches.

I can still hear you, Azael interjects.

Good.

"Sorry about this," I say cheerfully, reaching out and snapping her neck. "See you in Hell."

The hollow crack of her spine fills the silence. I step over to the boy, letting go of her so she drops forward. Her bound wrists swing limply above the speckled carpet, the plastic restraint cuff still loosely secured to the metal leg of the chair.

"And you?" I acknowledge the boy.

"Your eyes." He stares back at me in pure terror. "Why are your eyes purple? Who—what are you?"

I shove my blue-black hair back from my eyes, smudging my pale face with the dark blood that gloves my hand. "My name's Penemuel. Call me Pen. Actually don't. Don't call me anything."

He stares back at me, silent.

"'What's in a name? That which we call a rose by any other name would smell as sweet.'"

"That's Shakespeare, isn't it?" His eyebrows pull together in confusion and his shoulders drop almost imperceptibly. I see the pulse at the base of his throat slow.

"Well look at you. I guess it's not true what they say about *Romeo and Juliet* being obsolete in the 21st century."

"No, that's true. Totally obsolete."

Azael laughs in my head. *Do you take that as a personal assault to your literary preferences?*

I look down at the plastic ID that bracelets the boy's wrist. "Jeremy Dixon, Paranoid Personality Disorder." I arch an eyebrow.

"I'm not crazy," he says angrily, tugging his shirt sleeve over his restraints.

"Keep telling them, buddy."

"You don't believe me." His face darkens. "No one believes me."

"Doesn't matter who believes you." I shift on my feet. "We've been looking for you."

His eyes glint. "I knew it. No one believed me. I knew it!" He looks almost proud. "I heard the voices and I knew. I knew!"

"If you want people to believe you aren't crazy, you might want to stop talking about 'the voices,'" I advise him. "Although, I don't know if I'm the best one to say this. I hear voices all the time."

He cocks his head, scrutinizing me suspiciously. "I don't believe you."

"I don't care," I answer on an exhale.

Tell him we used the phonebook to find him. And how we got to his parents first. I'm sure he'll be so excited to see them again!

Shut up, Az.

"How old are you?" I ask him, tilting his face up to mine and leaving my bloody fingerprints on his dark skin.

His face tightens and a scowls cuts his mouth. "Sixteen."

"Huh. Me too, technically." I twist his face in my hand and break his neck, shivering as ice creeps through my veins, and the feeling of his life falling out from under him overwhelms me. "See you in Hell."

I turn away from Jeremy and survey the damage of the room. Fourteen bodies in total, including the receptionist with the fiery hair who is spilled over the front desk and the pencil-thin psychiatrist slumped in the hallway. There is blood everywhere, sprayed across the walls like the violent strokes of an angry artist, soaking into the tightly woven carpet and drip, drip, dripping down the chairs filled with crumpled bodies.

About time.

Keep your pants on, Azael. I'll be out in a second.

Don't forget to smile for the cameras!

In the corner of the stuffy, windowless waiting room is a tiny security camera with a red light that blinks along with the ticking of the clock on the wall.

Great.

I'm sure Gus would love a copy!

Maybe he'll be so impressed with my handiwork he'll let us keep the promotion? I ask, hopeful.

Uh, yeah maybe.

Before the blood that is seeping across the carpet begins to pool under my boots, I push through the locked door of the asylum, leaving a small, red handprint on the cream paint. I stalk out into the hot, white sun and squint my eyes against the brightness. I make my way across the dead, yellow grass to the tree Azael is perched in, smirking, and cross my arms over my chest.

"Finished. Happy?"

"I will be when I finish reaping their souls. Now the fun *really* begins!" He smiles down at me sharply. "You and me, we make a great team."

"You and I," I correct under my breath. He pretends not to hear me.

"Hell is lucky to have us."

"'With mischievous, vagrant, seraphic look / And *try* if we cannot feel forsaken,'" I quote as he steps off one of the top branches.

With a quiet whoosh he lands softly next to me. "I don't know what that means."

I shrug. "It's Robert Frost."

"Whatever." He brushes me off.

His dark hair shines blue-black in the sunlight, identical to mine, but where my hair is long and tangled, his is short and scruffy. His ratty t-shirt and faded, ripped jeans hang loosely on his tall, lanky frame. He has the same violet eyes I do, only darker and more reflective.

He bends down and pulls two sharp weapons out from his sturdy boots. The first is a small scythe with a dark blue handle engraved with curses. The second is a thin silver blade with a bone-white hilt that glints wickedly in the sunlight.

"I believe this is yours," he chuckles as he turns the blade over in his hand and points it at me.

I grab the cool white handle and slide the weapon into my own boot. "Thanks."

He nods once, small and tight, and saunters off towards the front door of the asylum, twirling the scythe cheerfully. "My favorite part," he croons.

"They aren't all ours to claim," I call after him, leaning back against the thick tree trunk. "I'm not sure if it's a good idea—"

He shrugs me off, only looking over his shoulder briefly to answer. "I don't see any angels around to say otherwise, Pen."

I roll my eyes and mumble under my breath, "For now."

I look out from under the shady tree and up to the sky. Nothing. Absolutely nothing. No planes, no birds, no clouds, and most importantly, no giant fluffy white wings in sight. These deaths were not premeditated so Heaven wouldn't have gotten the call to collect the souls until it was too late. They'd have to scramble to find someone to save these souls, if anyone is even close enough to go to the effort. That makes them, innocent or not, ours. First come, first served, so to speak. But there are repercussions for taking a soul from Heaven. There always are.

Is Gus going to be pissed? I ask, stretching upwards and grabbing hold of a branch. I swing myself up into the tree and quickly climb towards the top to see what Azael has been doing. Carved into the trunk are the symbols of the damned. I trace the deep gashes with my fingers, feeling the softer wood under the rough bark of the tree. Three words are carved in sharp, curling symbols. Torment, torture, and terror.

Probably, but I couldn't care less.
What about the promotion?

Azael and I were recently promoted to level two on Hell's tier of demons. When we first fell, we were amongst some of the most powerful demons, but we've slipped down the ranks and have had to claw our way back to the top. There are no handouts in Hell, and every demon has to earn their powers—and fight to keep them.

We're Power Demons, able to interfere directly with humans through influence or action; we can kill or reap, manipulate or possess—all the fun stuff. Az and I are each other's mirror in every way, twins who share the strength of a top-tiered demon between us. I have the authorization and skill to kill whomever I want, but only Azael has the training to reap their souls. We're a bit of a packaged deal.

Unfortunately, our reliance on each other is a weakness. Every demon should be able to stand on his or her own.

Even though he can't torture people himself, he makes sure I inflict enough pain on our victims that they beg for death. He loves it when they beg. Killing them at that point, at least, becomes a merciful act. It's what Hell has trained me to do, and I'm very good at my job, but not nearly as good as Azael is at his.

Without him to reap their souls after they die, their spirits wither away, like a flower left in the dark, wilting into nothingness. He never lets them wither, though. He wouldn't want to waste a good scream; he enjoys the mournful wailing they make when he drags them to Hell even more than their begging, though I don't see the appeal. Their screams have ways of working themselves into my mind and I'm often kept awake by the memory of it.

We answer to Greater Demons, the executives of Hell who are able to divine the future and order mayhem—a plague here, a genocide there, maybe a few natural disasters like famines, floods or fires. That's something Azael tells me we should be proud of, so you're welcome, I suppose.

Throughout history, humans have been unwittingly obsessed with demons, labeling us as serial killers, dictators and madmen. Mush-mouth reporters are too blind to see what they are really dealing with. Jack the Ripper is actually the demon Zepar, one of Azael's closest friends in Hell. He loves to relive his days of ripping throats in London, teasing Az with every last detail the newspapers puzzled over.

The only reason the entire world isn't in ruins by now is because of the angels. Heaven has ways to slow down our destruction. Protection spells, guardian angels, hallowed land… Without them, there wouldn't be anything left to terrorize.

Over the millennia, Heaven and Hell have struck a sort of balance. It's contentious, always tiptoeing around the line of war, but, as the saying goes, there is no light without darkness, no shadows without a source of light. Thanks to us, there is plenty of darkness and an abundance of shadows.

I wasn't going to tell you until later, but we lost the promotion. Back down to L3.

What? My stomach drops through my feet and I scramble to think about what went wrong. Was it something I did, something I said?

There's a beat before he answers. *Yeah, remember that kid we killed in Indiana?*

Yes. I swallow hard. He was maybe only five, but Azael said he heard that his soul was one Hell had been searching for, that he was somehow going to be instrumental in a future mission. Those were all the details he had.

I still see the kid's face when I close my eyes, with his short, curly hair and freckles so bright they looked like they were painted on. I killed him fast, didn't let Az get the chance to make him scream. He wasn't afraid of us, but I still remember the look in his wide, green eyes when he saw me. Curious, trusting. I didn't want to kill him, but I couldn't walk away. Azael wouldn't have let me. At least I made it quick. No one else would have.

Well apparently we encroached on one of the higher up's assignments.

I knew we shouldn't have done it.

I thought it would have bought us bonus points! Going above and beyond, taking what's ours without apology, all that bullshit Lucifer loves.

So no promotion? I let out a long huff of breath. *I'll never have the power to reap at this rate.*

Nope. You'll have to get used to needing me as your personal reaper. You should consider yourself lucky. I am a joy to stare at. A finely sculpted model of power and beauty.

I choke on laughter. *Says the only person who doesn't have to endure staring at you.*

Very funny. Now can you shut the Hell up and let me concentrate? I can't pull an entire soul together with you distracting me.

Scything is easy for Azael and he makes quick work of it if he can concentrate. For him to properly claim a soul, he needs to mark it with darkness, if it isn't already marked, and then reach into the person's chest and untangle the gnarled soul.

Pure souls are much harder to reap because the light they emit is a blazing white so bright that it can burn a dark angel, only if handled without care.

Over the centuries, Azael has become very adept at blackening innocent souls. He loves stealing them out from under Heaven's protection. He practically has snuffing their light out down to a science, but even he still gets burned sometimes.

During the war, he reaped the soul of an extremely powerful angel that burned him so deep he still has a jagged scar that rips up his forearm. I guess that's Heaven's little 'screw you' to those who try to pilfer their souls. Speaking of which…

Don't mean to rush you, but I'm seeing some wings out here.

Not yet. Damn. How many?

I peek through the leaves and branches to get a better view. *Looks like there's only one.*

He lets out a string of curses. *There's more than that. With this many souls, there will be at least three. The others are probably hiding themselves. How close are they?*

IGNITE

A rush of air twists my hair around and into my face as two giant wings flutter right over my perch and land with a light thump on the branch above me. I brush my hair out of my face and look up to see silvery wings folding in on themselves. Behind the wings is a very young angel; he's a thin but strong-looking boy with tousled, golden blond hair that curls at the nape of his neck. He has large, bright eyes as blue and cold as a midwinter's sky just before it begins to snow.

As he shifts awkwardly on the thin branch, I can see that his cheeks are flushed a warm red. There's an innocence in his face that tells me he's a new angel. He obviously hasn't seen the woes of the Earth yet. But he is young, and he no doubt will learn.

I lean forward, tracing his tall figure with my eyes. My movement must have caught his attention, because our eyes lock on one another and surprise floods his face.

"Oh—uh, hello," he stammers, his voice sounding like a light brass horn.

Our eyes remain locked on each other and neither of us moves. Only the the wind stirs, shifting my hair over my shoulder and lifting the leaves to whisper in the uneasy silence. He takes me in, from the wicked handle of my dagger peeking out from the top of my boot, to the scars that ribbon my arms. When his gaze finally lands on the violet of my eyes, his own startling blue eyes widen and I see a dawning understanding light his face like a warm sunrise. He knows what I am, and I know what he is.

Prey and predator, light and dark... *Angel and demon*.

CHAPTER 2

GET OUT HERE, NOW! I SHOUT TO AZAEL IN MY MIND. THE angel tips his head and purses his lips. *I'm sharing a tree with one of them.*

I hear Azael let out a string of curses in response, expletive after expletive tumbling out so rapidly his words make one very long, probably hyphenated, obscenity.

How young are they starting angels these days? I speak over his profanity that clogs my head. *You would think they'd at least let their souls ripen before they pluck them out of the clouds and put them down here. Maybe toughen them up a bit.*

It's strange to see an angel so young on Earth. I know he's probably not as young as he looks—no angel is—but there's something about him that feels new and... almost unsettling. I shake the thought out of my head as Azael crashes through the front doors of the asylum. The small, blue velvet pouch that holds the souls he's reaped swings from his belt like a pendulum. The angel above me startles but doesn't say anything.

Shit. Az looks at me, his eyes alert and fierce, and spots the golden angel boy perched just over my head. Quickly, he bounds over to the tree and claws his way onto the branch next to me. I join him in a predatory crouch and let out a low, guttural growl.

The angel moves again, shuffling his feet. He shifts and the sun glints off of a large broadsword that hangs from his hip in a sturdy holster. I hadn't noticed it before, but now it demands my attention.

It looks strange on him, out of place next to his mundane jeans and t-shirt. If it weren't for the weapon, he would look like any kid on the street.

He nervously fondles the glinting handle of the sword, and I can't tell if he's anxious because of us or if it's the sharp gold and silver weapon that makes him uncomfortable. He doesn't look like he knows what to do with it, and I wonder how much training he's had, if he's had any at all.

He speaks again, uneven and unsure. "I—um, I'm here to..." he stammers to a stop and pales, his cheeks flushing.

Immediately, my apprehension disappears. This angel is no threat; his inexperience renders him harmless. I rise from my crouch and Azael follows, laughing quietly as he appraises the angel.

He's so eloquent, Pen.

Oh, so it would seem. An orator of the highest order.

The angel looks down at his feet and raises one of his hands to cup the back of his neck. In a whisper so quiet even I can't hear, he seems to find confidence. His grip tightens on the hilt of his sword with purpose and he straightens up, lets out a slow breath, and tries again. "My name is Michael and I am here to collect the souls of those who have passed. They are pure and belong to Heaven."

Shock blooms on my face. *THE Michael?*

Az tenses next to me and searches the sky before answering me. *Can't be. He's dead.* "Those souls aren't Heaven's anymore," he spits at the angel. *You saw him die, Pen. I helped trap him in Hell myself. Pull it together!*

Right. With great effort, I bury my surprise, hiding it behind a dark glower. I'm not sure it's very convincing.

Michael's gaze slide from me to Azael and back again, his eyes curious and no longer afraid. He opens his mouth to say something but I stop him before he can.

"They've been claimed in the name of Lucifer." I try to keep my voice smooth, uninterested. "We have already marked them with darkness and scythed their souls."

"I did that, actually. She just ripped them to shreds first," Az corrects with a grin.

Michael looks at me and the corner of his mouth twists into a frown. "No…"

"You weren't here to collect them," I continue, "so now they're ours."

"You snooze, you lose, kid." Azael smirks as the angel's face burns a red as bright as roses.

"They are pure. They don't belong to Hell, wh—" His words clip off when a sudden surge of air pushes down on us all.

Two more pairs of wings land on either side of him on the thick, twisting branch. Their stance is protective, their large, pure white wings spreading behind Michael, wrapping around him in an almost defensive way. They're taller than the young angel by at least six inches and it's strange to see Michael sandwiched between them.

The two angels are robed in heavy emerald gear. Loose tunics stitched in gold hang over their sturdy pants, a shade or two darker than moss, that cling to their calves closely before disappearing in their flat, brown boots. I'm not surprised that Heaven hasn't changed the uniforms for guardians since my time as an angel. Heaven loves its traditions.

Even though they look exactly like every other guardian angel in Heaven, I recognize them the moment they land. Ariel and Sablo. Fantastic.

IGNITE

Maybe this Michael is the real deal, Az. I mean, he brought our biggest fans as bodyguards.

Michael looks at me quizzically, tilting his head slightly as if trying to listen to something very far away.

Right, dumb and dumber here. Like they'll be much help. It can't be him, Pen. He looks like a child and he has no idea what's going on—probably doesn't even know the difference between a scythe and that sword he has. He must still be in training.

I study the young angel's face, trying to find any similarities to the Michael I remember. There are pieces of him there. His skin seems to glow with the soft light that the old Michael had. He's in a younger form now, but his eyes are the same.

He's fixed on me, looking out from behind his golden hair. It looks like he's trying to solve a difficult puzzle or translate an epic poem written in an undead language, but the letters shift and coil into one another, making it unreadable.

I shift forward slightly and slip the dagger from my boot. Maybe I'll carve that stupid look off his face. I twirl the blade once in my hand, but he only continues to watch me with fascination.

If it's him, he doesn't seem to remember us. But, Az, he has guardians. No ordinary angel has guardians for something as trivial as training. If that's what this is supposed to be…

"Ah, Azael, Penemuel. It's been quite a while since we've seen you two. Up to anything *good* recently?" Ariel's falsetto voice dances in the air like wind chimes.

I scrunch my face in distaste. *Has her voice risen another octave since last time?*

If it goes any higher, she may break the sound barrier, Azael retorts. *Only the dogs will hear her. Poor hellhounds.*

"It's Pen," I mutter in response to her, throwing my hair over my shoulder. I tighten my grip on the knife and point it towards the threesome.

Sablo snickers musically. It's obnoxious. "Oh yes, that's right. Pen," he corrects. "Our apologies."

Michael considers the two angels with distant interest, but he keeps glimpsing back at me. I scowl at him and when he notices, he smiles pleasantly.

What is his problem? I ask Az.

Looks like he likes you, he teases back.

Wonderful.

"These souls are ours now," Azael says, exasperated. "We were just telling your little project here that you have no authority. They've been marked with darkness and belong to Lucifer." He lets out a frustrated sigh and straightens, crossing his arms. He knows Ariel and Sablo won't start a fight. They're not good with confrontation. Not directly, anyway.

Ariel's face contorts in a reproachful frown that's far too exaggerated for my taste. Her curly, blush-colored hair falls around her, tickling the freckles on her shoulder. "But they were pure, Azael. Whatever have you done?"

"My job," he shouts back.

"Can they do that?" Michael asks, looking up at the two tall guardians that flock him. He seems genuinely curious. "Just steal them from Heaven, even though they were pure?"

I raise my eyebrows at Azael. *This kid doesn't know anything, does he?*

He shakes his head and smiles sarcastically at the three angels. *Told you. Not Michael.*

"We are no longer needed here, Michael," Sablo answers calmly. "Not everyone can be saved."

Michael raises his chin, his jaw jutting out defiantly. "So Heaven has lied? What is to become of those pure souls, souls who were promised an afterlife where—" Sablo silences him with a look.

The guardian's eyes look like they are on fire, and I wonder if his stare burns. Michael closes his mouth and his face falls in disappointment. He clenches his jaw, chewing the last of his words before he swallows them completely. His cheeks are no longer the bright red from before but are now paled with frustration. He lifts only his eyes and looks at me through impossibly thick, coppery lashes.

Who are you? My mind rings with the question and I know it will be left unasked and unanswered.

"You must pick your battles, Michael," Sablo says carefully, his voice razor sharp and warning. There's a current of anger in the air coming from Michael's bookend guardians, but their faces remain neutral.

Ariel straightens, standing even taller above Michael. "These souls were pure, but that doesn't mean..." she pauses, her neutrality shattering into panic. Her lips seal into a tight, anxious line and her eyes widen with worry. She peers over at the small bag attached to Azael's hip, her eyes sparking with greater alarm. "They—there's a lost..." She looks at Sablo. "A lost soul," she says, her voice barely a whisper. "Something isn't quite—"

The guardians lean over Michael's head and whisper amongst themselves. When they part again, Sablo looks sick. I wonder if angels can throw up? I shift back on my heels, just in case.

What the Hell was that?

Azael looks at me out of the corner of his eye and shrugs. *Maybe they want to know where I got my jeans?*

Would explain Sablo's face. 'Thou shall not steal,' and all that.

The options were theft or nudity.

Then you chose wisely.

"There is nothing more you can do," Sablo explains, placing his hand on Michael's shoulder. I think it's supposed to be comforting, but there's something about his grip that is a little too firm. I can see Sablo's sharp fingers digging into his skin, but Michael's face is set, betraying no sign of pain. "There's nothing anyone can do."

Azael laughs. "That's right, so run along little angel boy." He elbows me in the ribs, wanting me to join in.

I try to smile sharply, but it feels halfhearted. "Better luck next time."

Wow, really ruthless Pen. Azael mocks me. *'Better luck next time'—go easy on the poor boy, he's not used to our whip-smart demonic quips!*

Right, and your 'little angel boy' comment was so devastating.

"Ignore them," Ariel says in a lilting voice. "They know not what they've done."

I slide my dagger into my belt and cross my arms, satisfied that Ariel and Sablo have lost. I expect Michael to react, to snap with anger. Young angels have hot tempers, their souls so unaccustomed to strong emotions that anything they feel—happiness, anger, disappointment—is often unbridled and extreme. But there's no fire in his eyes, only cool blue. I bite my lip until it almost bleeds to hide another look of shock from slapping itself across my face.

He answers Ariel evenly. "I understand."

And with that, the two guardians lift from the branch, departing as quickly as they arrived. They make no gesture for Michael to follow and don't seem to care that they've left him alone with a pair of demons. I watch as their wings carry them farther away and not once do they look back.

Michael, however, make no move to leave. He remains perched on the branch, watching my brother and me. A patient smile spills across his lips. "I am who they say. And I'm not that young. I'm seventeen. I'm older than both of you."

"Physically, maybe," I say under my breath.

What, he can read our thoughts? Azael asks doubtfully.

"Yes, I can," he says in answer to Az's silent question. Without a sound, he swings down onto our branch so he is standing in front of me, his back pressed to the bark. He smells faintly like honey and the golden scent makes my head swim. He turns to face me directly, ignoring Azael. "You're making a huge mistake by taking these souls."

My mouth falls open momentarily, stunned. An angel would never be so blunt. He's direct, unflinching in his opinion. Angels are not even allowed to *have* opinions, at least not those that

Heaven hasn't told them to have. I quickly snap my mouth closed and shake my head, shutting out my thoughts. "There are no mistakes. Their deaths were—"

"Just?" For the first time, his voice sounds bitter. I watch his face and see him fighting his frustration into submission. He tries to speak more calmly. "No deliberate deaths are just. There's more to life than what you've been doing and maybe one day you'll see that." He looks over my shoulder at Azael and then drags his eyes back to me, holding me captive in his stare.

I don't look away. I can't.

Been there, done that, kid. Azael's voice hisses in my head like angry steam. *The angels' ways are archaic. Haven't you heard? The future favors Hell.*

Michael tears his eyes from me to stare at Azael. The way he looks at him, I'm sure he's going to say something else, but he remains silent. Without another word, he spreads his wings, ruffling the silver-tipped feathers, and disappears up through the branches. Only the fluttering of the leaves gives any indication of his departure.

I glance over at Azael and we share a look of astonishment, Az's more muted than my own.

"Did you see his wings?" he asks me.

I nod. "Silver."

"Looks like we may be dealing with a VIP angel after all. Should we roll out the red carpet?"

How could it be him? I blink a few times, trying to fit the Michael I saw today with the Michael of my memories. How is it even possible? He was destroyed millennia ago when he struck battle with Lucifer during the war. But his eyes, his voice, his presence... There was something about him that felt almost familiar.

I tell myself that it can't be him. I've persuaded myself about things much more possible than this—that I'm meant to be evil, that I made the right choice to fall from grace. Convincing myself of this, that it's not really him, should be easy. Because it's *impossible*.

I saw him die, saw Lucifer's sword strike him through the chest. I watched Lucifer trap his soul in Hell, binding them together. I've heard hundreds of unsavory limericks from Azael about "Much murdered Michael" and "Many merry men musing Michael's move from upstairs to downstairs." He never could come up with a perfect alliteration for that last one.

Michael can't be back. We would know. Right?

"I think our day just got a bit more complicated," I groan.

"Our day, our week... Hell, I'd be surprised if this bastard doesn't screw up our decade."

I reach out and touch the bark of the tree that was scarred with Azael's carving. Where Michael stood, his back pressed against the curling curses, the wood is almost completely healed. Only a thin, pale scar is left, an echo of the deep gashes from before. *Could he really be back?*

CHAPTER 3

"A NGELS CAN LIE," AZAEL MUTTERS. "RIGHT? THERE'S NO way that could have been Michael. It's impossible, absolutely impossible. Not *the* Michael."

We are walking down the side of a busy highway towards the old ruins of an abandoned New England church that we have made our temporary living quarters. The ruins are on the edge of town, miles from the asylum. It's a slow journey on foot, but Azael refuses to let us fly before it's dark enough that we won't be noticed. I kick a rock across the road with my boot and watch it scuff to a stop as he continues rambling.

"Michael's a common name, right?"

"Not with angels," I answer. "He can read our minds, Az. The only other I know who can do that is..." I let my thought trail off.

"Lucifer himself, I know." He lets out a heavy sigh.

From the corner of my eye, I see his shoulders hunch forward. The worry that creases Az's face makes him appear younger than the 16-year-old form he wears. When he looks this young, it's hard to remember the years he's lived and the battles he's fought.

He pulls distractedly at an unruly tuft of hair, and I can tell he is trying to convince himself that the Michael we saw today is not who he claimed to be. I'm halfheartedly trying to convince myself of the same thing, but the more I think about it, the more sure I become that it *was* him. The impossibility becomes less and less absurd until it becomes not only plausible, but maybe even probable.

"And you saw his wings," I continue. "Silver. Not even Ariel and Sablo are ranked high enough for silver wings."

"Because they aren't archangels," he nods, angry. "I know."

"So why would an angel as young as Michael have silver wings unless he was *the* Michael?"

"I don't know, Pen. But it's impossible. We saw him die, saw Lucifer tie what was left of him in Hell." His voice is sharp and cuts through dusk like a knife.

I let it drop as we continue down the road, walking in silence. We keep to the side of the road, staying in the shadows so we go unnoticed. A few cars speed past, their blinding headlights sweeping over us only momentarily, shrinking my pupils to pinpricks, before blazing forward into the deepening darkness of night.

The sun slips quickly down the horizon, bleaching the color from the sky as it fades from a bruised purple into a steely gray before touching the midnight blue of night. As it gets darker, I can hear the creatures of the night slowly waking up. My ears prick at the sound of scratching claws on branches and the beating of an owl's wings as it chases a skittering mouse.

A slight breeze brings the smell of tightly packed humans from downtown, and my nose wrinkles in disgust. They reek of sour sweat and it churns my stomach, which is already roiling with the thought of our inevitable punishment for the kid in Indiana and our demotion. If we've encroached on the assignment of our superiors, there's little hope that we will escape today without being, quite literally, raked over the coals.

I assume half of Azael's bitterness is over losing our promotion. He's waited so long to move beyond reaping, but a small part of me is glad we need to rely on each other. I don't know what he'd do if he could kill on his own. I'm the jar that holds his lightening, letting his rage burn me instead of everyone else. I am the only thing holding him back from destroying everyone in his path.

Azael notified Gusion, or Gus, as we call him, that we collected the soul he sent us for, plus a few extra. Gus is our advisor and boss, for all intents and purposes, and he constantly reminds us of this fact. He is also one of the top diviners of Hell. He gives us our assignments and reports our progress back to Lucifer. Azael did a quick blood ritual but didn't want to get into the details of where the additional souls came from and only briefly mentioned our encounter with Michael. One of Az's greatest talents is burying the lead and glossing over the facts.

Gus picked up enough of the details though, and sounded irritated. He told us to wait back at the ruins for him.

"Just stay there until I get a chance to divine the implications of Michael's return," he instructed. "I won't be able to visit Earth until the anti-hour so you'll have to find some way to entertain yourselves. Do you think you can manage a few hours by yourselves without getting into more trouble?" But before we could answer him, he added, "Never mind. I really don't want to know," and ended the connection.

We've known Gus for at least a dozen centuries now, and he has known us even longer. He was assigned to us when we got our first interference mission—corrupting the first man, Adam.

After Lucifer corrupted Adam's first wife, Lilith, and brought her to Hell, Heaven scrambled to replace her. The angels promised Adam he wouldn't have to be alone for long, and in a way, they were right.

At the time, Azael and I were part of the highest ranked Powers and were assigned to work with two other demons, Botis, the viper, and Naamah, the temptress, to ruin Adam. The man soon found good company with Nammah and just assumed she was the wife he was promised.

Humans still tell their story, falsely calling Naamah "Eve." Botis, as the story goes, whispered to Adam every night about the deliciousness of the apples on the forbidden tree. Adam resisted. That is, until, Naamah (or Eve, depending on your version of history) offered him the juicy fruit she had already taken a bite out of.

Well if his wife had already taken a bite of the fruit, Adam thought, then what would be the harm? Surely God wouldn't blame him for just a bite.

Poor, naïve Adam was unaware of how dramatic Heaven could be, especially when it comes to their rules. Adam never did get his new wife. At least, not the one Heaven intended.

Ever since their success in defaming Heaven's precious human, throwing him into the tarnished world of sin, Naamah and Botis have been part of a small group of high ranking Greater Demons who serve as direct advisors to Lucifer. Unfortunately, Azael and I will never get recognition for our contribution and our story with Adam will never be told. Apparently, Hell doesn't appreciate subtlety.

It was our first time in the Garden of Eden. We stood back while Naamah and Botis began to tempt Adam and got to work creating a plan of our own. I, personally, have never been one for apples. But I do have an affinity for words. One of the many reasons I fell from Heaven was because of words and my insistence that man should learn to read and write. Heaven, however, would have been happy with a bunch of bumbling, illiterate idiots running around their new world.

So, in spite of the angels, I introduced Adam to words.

I got to work carving words into the soil and curses into the bark of the trees. The more he read, the further he would have spiraled into an insanity so consuming it would only be healed by the fruit of the forbidden tree. Azael bottled spells and poisoned the dirt of the Earth, making sure the fruit and leafy greens that grew in the garden would spoil and rot to black on the inside. Adam would have had no choice but to eat from the forbidden tree if our plan had enough time to play out, because it would have been the only fruit left untouched by death.

And the best part of the plan was that there would be no direct contact with the waxy red fruit or the thick-headed human from either of us; Adam could pluck the offensive apple with his own dirty hands, thank you very much.

There was only one problem: Naamah and Botis worked faster.

We had the perfect safety net for their plan of temptation—a plan I was sure would fall through. Our success would have made our names renowned in Hell, but Adam succumbed so quickly to Naamah. Who knew that humans would be so easily sullied?

Gus had warned us that our trap would be rendered unnecessary, but we didn't listen. He divined an outcome, advised us to work with Naamah and Botis instead of planning on their failure. But Azael and I were new and cocky and we wanted to prove to Lucifer and every other demon who doubted us that we were stronger and smarter than they thought. It backfired, horribly. We should have listened to Gus.

For centuries, we were mocked about our failure, and our ranks slowly slipped. We weren't respected as demons and were assigned to fewer and fewer missions. It took us thousands of years for us to start to rebuild our reputation, but we've finally clawed our way back up to level 3 Powers. For awhile, we weren't allowed on Earth in a physical form and were only allowed to haunt the dreams of humans. We could manipulate them while they slept, twist their dreams into nightmares. Then we were allowed possessions.

In the late 1600s, we were allowed to visit Earth in our physical forms and tempt people into the shadows. We've only been killing and reaping since the early 1800s, and I really thought we would have risen in ranks again since then. But Hell never forgets.

We were nearly level 2, I remind myself bitterly.

Since then, we've begrudgingly learned that what Gus says goes. He's always right, annoyingly so, and it is in our best interest to follow his instructions to the letter. Although, the fact that he can discern the future does give him quite an unfair advantage. If we had only done what Gus had told us on this trip to Earth, we probably would have been promoted.

Always listen to Gus. I press my cool palm to my head. *How many times do you need to be given reasons to listen to Gus?*

"Azael, is it dark enough yet?" I ask, chipping away at the silence. My feet ache from all the walking we did today, and a longer walk to the edge of town in these boots seems unthinkable. I flex my fingers and feel the dried blood flake off. It's impossibly hard to wash off blood. "There are barely any cars out anymore. I doubt anyone will notice us."

"Fine," he says, sounding as tired as I feel. "But I swear, if we end up in some grainy video on the news again, it will be your turn to explain it to Gus."

"That was one time, and it was during a full moon! I promise they won't be able to see our wings tonight. It's overcast, and the roads are all but empty."

"Good enough for me," he says, not needing much convincing. He unfurls his wings, stretching them out as wide as he can, and takes off, sending a wave of air crashing down on me. I watch as he flies away towards the dark cluster of trees that circle the ruins.

I laugh to myself as my own wings open. The black feathers ruffle in the wind, whispering together softly like they are sharing secrets. I bend my knees and jump, letting the cool night's air caress my face.

There is nothing quite like the weightlessness of flight, the dizzying feeling of belonging to the sky. The dark expanse of the woods passes under me as I fly just above the treetops, like a pebble skimming a glassy lake. Small, glowing eyes stare back at me from under the leaves, shrinking into their branch as if my presence makes them nervous.

The air fills my lungs, and I gulp it in greedily, even though I don't need to. I pretend that I rely on it, like the more of it I breathe, the higher I will fly. I forget what it's like to be alive like I was in Heaven, to need to breathe instead of *pretending* to need to breathe.

The quiet beating of my wings is as rhythmic as a heartbeat, as slow and lazy as someone sleeping. I try to remember what it felt like to feel a heartbeat that belongs to me and not the person I'm killing.

Without Azael near me, sulking about our demotion or hissing snarky comments in my mind, I find myself alone with my thoughts, which somehow keep returning to Michael.

If Michael is who he claims to be—the great archangel, Lucifer's slain brother—we should have killed him, struck him down before he is strong again. Maybe now we've lost our chance. We may never see him again.

Once upon a time, Lucifer was one of the strongest angel in Heaven and, as an archangel, he belonged to the small and exclusive group of God's most powerful warriors.

When word was handed down that God would create humans, Lucifer refused to bend a knee before them. He thought they were not worthy of his Father's love, that they did not deserve paradise.

Years passed without any answer from God.

Lucifer raised his voice in protest again, saying that if God truly loved him, the angels would be enough. But again, there was silence. Lucifer's anger consumed him and he began to believe God was ignoring him, thought that he was abandoned by his own Father.

As Lucifer's power grew and the creation of mankind became more and more real, he questioned God's silence. Was it because He was ignoring Lucifer, or was it because He didn't exist? After all, no angel had seen His face—not even the archangels—but the angels didn't need proof. There was faith.

Faith, however, wasn't enough for Lucifer. When he challenged the existence of God, was brazen enough to say that he could be God himself, Michael banished him from Heaven and sent him into a realm of eternal torture. Scores of angels had fallen down with him, and war raged.

Lucifer's exile twisted the angelic morals that were once burned into his soul into a horrifying, putrid loathing. Over time, his soul died, his heart stopped, and his veins froze in the icy pits of Hell. He vowed revenge on Heaven, declared war, and said he would one day sit on the throne—a throne that has always remained empty for Him—and rule us all.

The war came to an abrupt halt after the death of Michael, after brother faced brother and Lucifer came out victorious. After Lucifer spilled Michael's blood—the same blood that once flowed through his own veins—until there was nothing left to spill. The angels returned to Heaven and, centuries later, created man, prompting Lucifer to obsess about unraveling the fabric of humanity by destroying one soul at a time.

Hell has been growing since then, as more and more humans are corrupted, and Lucifer has been preparing for a second war to finally claim the throne of Heaven. But if Michael is actually back, Lucifer will never have full power. He is not the true heir to rule Heaven.

If he manages to claim the throne, he will have immense power, but it will not be absolute. Michael will stand in his way.

Michael. He comes to me in colors—the gold of his hair, his silver wings, the red of his cheeks, the blue of his eyes that are both cool and warm all at once, both peaceful and fierce. His eyes, his eyes—I can't escape the blue of his eyes that are now ingrained in my mind.

The angel we met this afternoon wasn't the formidable Michael I remember. His face was young, not lined from war. His shoulders weren't weighed down with the weight of the world yet. He had a naïve hope to him that I know will only serve to hurt him later.

I wonder if he is still as powerful as he once was. The way he gripped his sword, apprehensive and unsure, makes me think that, if we would have put up a fight, he wouldn't have withdrawn it. I'm not sure if he even knows how to wield it, or if he would want to. It's impossible that this soft-spoken Michael is the same archangel I remember.

But maybe he's changed. I've felt his presence before, opposing mine in war. His eyes, his voice, the way he spoke unapologetically about what he thought... He has the same streak of strength that I remember. His presence is like a memory falling just out of reach. I could almost see the old Michael in this younger boy, but it was clear he didn't remember me.

And why would he? The old Michael paid little attention to anything that was outside his immediate interests. He was devoted to duty and nothing, or no one, else. I was nothing special when we first met. During my time in heaven, I made little impression and was an angel of small significance. After I fell I was just another demon in a teaming mob of violence.

But the way he watched me, kept his eyes on me, made me believe he was trying to remember, like if he concentrated he would suddenly recall the last time we met. But the memory of me slipped between his fingers like water.

It's probably for the best. The last time I saw him was the day he died. I don't want him to remember me from that day, to know what part I played in his death. It would be better for us both if he never remembered.

As much as I try to convince myself it's not him, I know it's useless. I know he's back. *He's back*. And strangely, I feel a thrill at the thought of his return, a pinch in my stomach that is like excited anxiety. As impossible as it may be, I know, without a doubt, that the golden angel boy we saw today was telling the truth.

Michael's back.

CHAPTER 4

BREAK OUT OF MY REVERIE JUST ENOUGH TO SEE THE ruins coming into view. I drift down into the dense forest, my wings setting me gently on an empty patch of dirt, and find Azael waiting for me in the grassy clearing that was, at one time, a cemetery. Crumbling tombstones create a ring around the soft, green grass. The clearing is all but empty, with just Azael and a small fire pit in the center.

"There you are. So, what should we do?" he asks, raising a sharp eyebrow.

"About what?"

"Not *about* anything. What should we do until Gus pays us a visit? We're not allowed to reap anyone or do any hell raising. 'Lay low' was what he said. 'Don't get into trouble.' How do we even do that?"

I blink at him blankly. "I don't know." It's difficult to concentrate because I keep seeing Michael's face when I close my eyes. His blue eyes watch me, amused, and I can smell the syrupy sweet scent of honey. It hangs in my mind like heavy curtains, blocking any clear thoughts.

"Wow, Pen, you're very helpful," he jeers. "Thanks for all of your *wonderful* suggestions."

I punch him in the arm and roll my eyes. "Fine, you want a suggestion?"

"I would love nothing more."

"We may have to lay low, but that doesn't mean we can't have a little fun. You still have those souls you reaped from the loony bin, right?"

"Yeah," he answers, holding up the dark velvet satchel and jostling it roughly. He sets it down on top of a tombstone that sticks out of the mossy ground at an improper angle. "What a mess you left in there, too. Enough blood to fill a swimming pool. A bit disappointed that you weren't more creative with your kills, though. The receptionist... her throat? Really? So cliche."

"What, I'm not allowed to have any fun?" I force a smile.

"Oh, no. Clearly you can have all of the fun you want."

I laugh.

"So, my sister, since you are so accustomed to having a good time, teach me your ways." He spreads his arms wide. "Show me it is possible to have fun without trouble, blood, or death. Because I've yet to experience this."

"Have a little faith."

"Bad choice of words," he says, grinning back at me.

I wave away his words and grab the cords that tie off the opening of the satchel. I swing it from my fingers, inches from his face. "Perhaps," I smile broadly, "we could do some exploring."

"Exploring?" He pushes the bag away from him and I drop my arm.

"You're not allowed to reap, and I'm not allowed to kill anyone, but Gus said nothing about reanimation."

"You need a body for reanimation. Are you hiding a corpse on you? Tucked it away in a pocket?" He crosses his arms.

"Reanimate the *memory*," I draw out the word, letting the y hang on my lips. "In my lessons, Gus is teaching me how to reanimate the soul without needing a vessel. He uses it to gather information from them that might be useful—like special skills or weaknesses they could use to their advantage later."

"And the point of this would be…?"

Nothing, I want to say. *There is no point. It's only a way to eat up the hours. It's only a way to convince you we should listen to Gus instead of ignoring his orders and finding a more violent way to keep you entertained.* But I don't say that. Instead, I offer him a suitable alternative, the next best thing to pain—recounting other people's pain. "Aren't you even the least bit interested about the memories of these souls? One girl drowned her brother."

"I heard." He sounds uninterested, bored.

"Yes, you heard about *her*. But they were all in restraints, tethered to chairs." I watch him closely as he leans back against the grave. He crosses his ankles to match his arms. I come at him from another angle, swinging the satchel around in the air uncaringly. "Remember Ariel's little aneurism back at the asylum?"

He lifts his chin, paying attention. "She said one of the souls was lost."

"You heard that?" I ask, and he shrugs. "Right, so she was seriously freaked about something. And Sablo too—you saw his face. Don't you want to know what made them give up so easily?"

He considers this, chewing his lip.

"Come on, Az," I push, bouncing up and down on my toes. "Live a little!"

Something shifts on his face, dark amusement and a decision. "Again, not the best choice of words, but sure, why not."

"That's the spirit!"

I notice him pull out a dark, metal tube from his pocket. It is old and heavy, with black carvings that string around it like the greedy fingers of weeds. Jeremy's soul is trapped within the container, locked until it reaches Hell. Azael rolls the vial between two fingers before sliding it back into his pocket for safe keeping. That's the one soul we won't get to explore, and I know it's the one he's most interested in.

The bag that holds the rest of the souls feels soft and heavy in my hands. I pull at the golden ropes until the knots fall apart and look into the shadowy bag. There's a faint glow coming off of the souls, like the dying glow of a star behind a blanket of clouds—a hazy silver-gold that is warm and clammy. The greasy souls roll over one another, reaching towards the untied opening, grasping for freedom that's just out of reach.

I plunge my hand inside and instantly the warm, slippery substance of souls wraps around my arm, grappling for escape. It feels like my hand is painted in oil, and I try to shake them off, but they hold on stubbornly, lacing tighter around my fingers and stretching up my arm with their clawing tendrils.

"Uh, a little help here?" I call over my shoulder.

Azael heaves himself off of the headstone and grabs my arm hard, scraping his scythe over my skin and forcing the wispy souls back into the bag. I read the carving on the stone behind him. The letters are shallow, only a whisper of a name. *ELIZABETH HART, 1889-1905. GONE BUT NOT FORGOTTE...* I imagine I can still see the N, even though it's erased from age.

"Thanks," I manage, pulling my arm from the bag and flexing my fingers.

He nods, cleans his scythe on his shirt, and walks back to the edge of the clearing. He sits down in front of a second tombstone that tilts backwards, as if it is trying to escape the patch of grass that splays open before it, and throws me a disparaging look.

"Pick a good one, Pen. I don't want to waste time on a respectable housewife who lost her marbles over chipped china and stabbed her husband. Make it interesting." His lips curl around his last word and he snarls slightly, settling against the grave and resting his clasped hands behind his head. His eyelids fall lazily, and if I didn't know better, I would think he is sleeping.

"Sure," I mumble, shoving my hand back into the bag.

I go back to sifting through the souls, wading through the warm, vibrating ones until I hit something solid at the bottom of the bag. Beneath the golden balminess of the still dimming white-hot souls, I feel an icy fragment the size of a small marble. The sudden, unexpected frost amidst the warmth slices through my hand sharply, hitting my bone, and I recoil from its intensity.

"Woah."

Azael opens his eyes, looking moderately interested, and sits up. "Sounds like a good one. Grab it quickly and tie that thing back up before the others spill out." He hauls himself to his feet, carelessly brushing away the dirt that follows him on his back pockets. "I'll grab the basin from inside. When you pull it out of the bag, put it in this." He pulls out a small, glass tube from the same pocket he keeps Jeremy's soul in and tosses it over his shoulder at me as he strolls into the decrepit remains of the stone chapel.

I snatch the small vial out of the air easily as I grab the soul around its small, dense body. Its tendrils reach up my arm, squirming to my elbow and pushing sharply against me in an attempt to fight my pull. When I try to pluck it from the bag, it begins to dive deeper. I adjust my grip and seize the soul tighter, choking it into submission.

When I drag it past the warmer souls, I notice the absence of other greedy tendrils that would normally be hitching a ride with this soul and searching for escape. For some reason, though, this cold soul seems to repel the brighter, warmer ones. I manage to extract it, shove it into the vial, and quickly tie off the satchel.

Triumphantly, I cap the glass vial, holding the top down with my thumb. I watch as the marble-sized soul writhes restlessly. Holding it up to my face, I can see that behind the light, buttery tendrils is a dark center. Instead of having the fading white-gold light of a pure soul, there is an underlying dirty butterscotch-brown. It's not as dark as Jeremy's soul would be—a sooty black—but it's not clean enough to belong to Heaven, either. *What is it?* I shake the vial and listen to the low pinging noise it makes as it rolls back and forth.

"Got it!"

I spin around and see Azael sauntering through the crumbling stone archway holding a large, round basin. In response, I hold up the vial and shake it again. The tendrils go wild inside the tube again and push against the corked top more forcefully. "Me too." I tighten my grip on the stopper.

"Good." Azael snaps his fingers and a small fire flares to life at the center of the stone pit. "You're the expert here, so you'll have to take the lead."

"And that must kill you," I tease.

"Just get on with it, will you?"

I chuckle and walk over to the fire, stretching my arms out so the flames lick my hand. The heat prickles my skin up to my shoulder and I revel in the sensation. It doesn't burn, just feels sharp, like a hundred tiny needles tapping on my skin, not quite piercing through. Azael steps up next to me and pushes the basin under my outstretched arm, and the dish hovers inches above the fire, cutting me off from the heat.

"You're no fun." I frown at the capped fire.

"On with the show," he prompts, his voice dipped in impatience that edges towards anger.

"Fine, on with the show," I echo, handing him the vail with the restless soul. "Keep your finger on the top. This one's feisty."

He nods and takes the tube from me, squeezing the rubber stopper tightly.

I walk around the fire, trying to think back to my lessons with Gus. What was it he had said, again? I really should pay more attention.

"There needs to be blood… and dirt, I think." I chew on my lip, recalling the list of elements the spell calls for. "Also, you wouldn't happen to have any crow feathers on you, would you?"

IGNITE

My eyes flick away from the flames that lick the base of the gently curving basin and up to Azael.

He is holding the vial up to his face, tapping on the glass and agitating the soul. When he notices me watching him, he lowers the tube and shrugs. "A couple dozen. There was a flock of them outside the asylum. You know how our dark-feathered friends love following me around. I think they think I'm they're leader." He smiles.

"Do *you* think you're they're leader?"

"I think they'd be lucky to have me." There's a beat of silence that's heavy with bitterness. *He wants to lead something, someone more than me. But he'll never get the chance if he keeps disobeying orders.* "Is there some incantation we need to say for this to work? And when are we supposed to add this?" He rattles the vial again, indicating the convulsing soul. "It looks like yellow snot. Have you seen anything like this before?" He squints at it closer and scrunches his face.

"No, and be patient. Good things come to those who wait."

"I hate waiting."

"Obviously."

"And good things."

"Obviously," I say again.

I tune out his grumbling and pull my blade from my boot, slicing my arm from wrist to elbow so a thin trickle of black blood can spill into the basin. I place the dagger back into my boot, keeping my bleeding arm held over the flame. After the bottom of the basin is completely obscured with my blood, I pull away, pressing my hand over the cut and waiting for the skin to heal. It's slow and painful, but the cut begins to fade. A few beads of blood fall down my fingers and I lick them clean.

"Where are the feathers?" I ask, looking up at Azael who is still pestering the squirming soul.

Azael pulls out three perfectly dark feathers from next to his scythe in his boot. They're bent, slightly crumpled, and some are broken—bent at strange angles—but they'll do.

I pick them from his fingers and hold them over the basin, letting my blood reach a boil before I close my eyes and burn the feathers in my hand. I open my eyes just before the feathers turn to ash and pepper into the blood. The gray ash floats across the churning black liquid before it is pulled to the bottom of the basin to drown under the thick bubbles.

"You can add the soul now," I say to Azael. "It will be trapped."

He pops off the stopper and tips the vial so the greasy soul slides into the dark mixture. It splashes in and disappears under the dark surface of the seething liquid. The mixture begins to turn a rotten shade of green and the grotesque bubbles multiply as it boils faster.

"Grave dirt," I instruct. "We need a handful for each participant." I kick my heel into the ground, scoop up a fist of loose dirt, and throw it into the basin. Azael mimics me from across the flames and throws in a handful of his own. Slowly, I circle around the large basin, never taking my eyes away from the roiling contents, and grab Azael's hand in mine.

"'Double, double, toil and trouble. Fire burn and cauldron bubble,'" he chants sarcastically.

"Very astute, Shakespeare." I squeeze his hand.

"*Romeo and Juliet* may be obsolete, but *Macbeth* never goes out of style. You have to love Lady Macbeth—she knows how to grab the power she deserves."

"All a matter of taste."

He laughs. "So sensitive about your books."

I ignore him and divert my attention back to the fire. "I'll say the incantation and we'll be pulled into the soul's memory. Gus said it will be organized like a hallway, with each room holding a different memory. Any memory touched by evil will make our amulets spark." I pull the black chain around my neck until the deep violet stone falls out and over my collar. I hold the jagged, ombre purple stone out to my brother. "Do you still wear your amulet?"

The smooth, round onyx stone of his necklace surfaces above his own collar. "Always."

"Good. To leave," I instruct, "say *Absum*." He silently forms the word on his lips and I nod. "Ready?"

He smiles conspiratorially. *Ready*, he says in my mind.

I can feel the anticipation sparking between us like electricity, and I harness the energy for the incantation. I grip his hand tighter and close my eyes. With my free hand, I hold my amulet over the basin.

"In nomine Lucifer nos postularemus animae. Memoriis mortuorum loquar."

A violent wind whips around us, and when I open my eyes, the contents of the basin are bubbling higher and higher until it stills suddenly, the liquid smoothing into a tranquil, reflective surface. It looks like a dark, nauseating mirror.

With Azael's hand in mine, I feel the world shift and fall from beneath us. The clearing disappears and we are momentarily thrown into darkness before we land with a sharp *clack* on a long, tiled corridor. I let my amulet fall back to my chest and smile breathlessly.

It worked!

Azael opens his eyes, his pupils nothing more than pinpricks, and lets a barbed smile spread across his own face.

"We're in."

CHAPTER 5

"IT DOESN'T LOOK LIKE MUCH," AZAEL COMPLAINS, HIS voice flat and unimpressed.

Brightly lit black and white checkered tiles run down the middle of the corridor with imposing, glossy black doors lining either side of the hall. The doors stretch father than the light reaches and eventually fade into shadows.

I let go of Azael's hand and step forward on the reflective tiles, the click of my boots echoing. "Would you like to try a door?"

He makes his way down the corridor slowly, stopping to point at the doors he passes. "Eenie, meenie, miney—"

I shove past him to the first door on the right and wrap my hand around the door handle, pushing into the room with Azael on my heels. The room is cold, quiet, and blindingly bright, even more so than the hallway. My eyes rage against the brightness, making me dizzy as hazy halos of light cling to my eyelashes and stretch into one another. When my eyes adjust, the light distortion fades and I can scan the room.

White walls, white floor, lighted ceiling. Empty.

"No." I shake my head in confusion, denial. "This isn't right."

"Screw up the spell, then? I guess Gus isn't the great teacher he believes himself to be," Azael says, leaning against the doorframe.

I shake my head again. "No. No, I did it right. But this... is wrong. It shouldn't be empty."

"Then what should it be?" He cranes his neck into the room and peers around the door. "Is it a hospital? I mean, it looks sterile enough to be one."

"A memory." I carefully step farther into the room, as though I'm afraid the floor will fall through. "This should be a memory," I repeat.

The soul holds life. Reanimating like I did is like opening a time capsule. I should be able to pick through each day of their life, each significant event—from birth to death—and live it as though I were there with them. Behind one door may be their first kiss. Behind another, their wedding, their parent's death, a graduation. It shouldn't be empty. *This isn't right.*

Something about this room feels wrong, but I can't put my finger on it. I turn around slowly in the middle of the room. It gives me an uneasy, hollow feeling, like something is missing. *Of course something's missing. There should be a memory—it shouldn't be empty.*

But the room feels more than empty. It's like there was something here that shouldn't have been. An intruder, a stranger to this soul that snatched whatever was once here. There's a feeling that something was taken, not just misplaced. An electric buzz in the room makes the hair on the back of my neck stand up and my stomach drop. I walk back to Azael, letting my hand skim across the plain white walls.

"It shouldn't be empty." I can't stop repeating myself. *It should be a memory. It shouldn't be empty.* There are no more coherent thoughts that form in my mind other than these. My head hurts as it spins in circles, trying to find a logical explanation for the nothingness.

"So, what happened?"

"I don't know." I run my hand anxiously through my hair, my fingers tripping on tangles. "We have to try another door."

I grab Azael by his arm and lead him back out of the room, across the hallway, and to another door. I twist the knob and lean into the room.

Empty, again.

Wrong. This is wrong.

We go down the hallway, trying each door and finding each room empty.

Empty and bright.

Empty and bright.

Always empty, and always bright.

The more rooms we find empty, the farther my stomach falls. "It's not supposed to be like this. This doesn't happen!"

"Relax, Pen," Azael says, placing a hand on my shoulder. "They were crazy. Maybe they literally lost their mind."

"It doesn't matter. The memory would still be here." The *mind* goes insane and the *mind* can forget, but not the soul. The hardware fails, not the software.

Frantically, I try another door, but the handle sticks. I shake the handle harder and try to force the door in with my shoulder, but it's locked.

"Azael!"

He runs up next to me and grabs the handle, trying it for himself.

"It's locked," I say.

"Oh really Pen? Do you think?" he asks sarcastically. "Get back and I'll kick it in."

I silently move away from the door. Azael steps back and kicks out at the handle with a violent force. The polished surface of the door cracks slightly, but it remains stuck. He steps back again and delivers a second blow. This time, the wood splinters. A third hit of his sturdy boot sends the door swinging in.

Azael holds out his arm and theatrically gestures into the room. "After you."

I move towards the door and feel my amulet pulsate eagerly around my throat. I clutch the chain and nod to Azael. "Is your pendant…?"

"Yeah," he says, pulling at the smooth, black stone that hangs around his own neck. "Is that a good sign?"

"I guess we'll find out."

I tuck the necklace back under my collar and step carefully into the room. Only the small patch of light that filters in from the door offers any illumination. Azael is silhouetted in the doorframe, his dark figure rimmed in the bright light from the hallway. He pulls the door closed behind him, extinguishing the last of the light and immediately plunging us into a darkness so absolute that I can't discern any shadows.

I squeeze my eyes closed and reopen them, but the blackness remains. I feel, more than see, Az move forward. He grabs my hand and, together, we continue to walk deeper into the darkness. The farther we get from the door, the quieter our footsteps become.

"It's not nothing, right?" His voice sounds hushed, as if it is being smothered by the dark.

"It's—I'm not sure what it is," I answer in a whisper, afraid to break the silence. "I can't see anything."

"You're pendant is glowing."

I look down at my chest and notice a faint purple glow through the thin cotton of my t-shirt. "Not exactly the best flashlight." I grip the dark chain and bring the jagged stone over my head. I hold it out in front of me so I can use it to guide us through the darkness. "Shall we?" I ask, stepping forward.

But Azael stops me short, pulling back on my hand so I am next to him again. The glowing purple stone sways erratically back and forth in my fist.

"Wait," he says under his breath. "Do you hear that?"

I stay very still and focus on finding a noise in the silence. I'm about to tell Azael that I don't hear anything when suddenly I do. My ears pick up an almost imperceptible rumble. I spin around and hold my pendent out farther, trying to find the source of the sound. I drag Azael forward with me a few steps but can't see anything. The rumbling increases slowly, and it sounds as if the entire room is vibrating.

"What is it?"

The sound continues to intensify until I am convinced the walls are collapsing in on us. I pull Azael tight to my side as the ground beneath us begins to tremble violently. A severe pressure constricts around us, and I suddenly feel like we are in a very small, confined room.

I have to yell over the commotion for Azael to hear me. "Where's the door?"

I hold the pendent between us, illuminating the sharp angles of his face. He opens his mouth like he's going to say something but before he can, a single bloodcurdling scream tears above the rumbling. The darkness explodes into chaos.

The blackness that squeezes in around me shatters with a giant crash to reveal a ruddy sky with a low, swollen and murky moon. I drop my pendant, letting it fall sharply to my chest. The floor transforms from tile into stiff, rocky orange clay. The clay continues to shift unsteadily and my boots slip out from under me, but Azael catches me before I hit the ground and pulls me to my feet.

The room is not a room at all. It's become a giant, expansive landscape of rocks and desert and everything orange and blood red.

"We have to move!" he shouts, pointing to a giant fissure splitting the ground.

I grab on to his arm and drag him with me as we jump across the swelling ravine. A second fissure rips through the clay, crisscrossing with the first and leaving us on a narrow cliff. We're not technically trapped; I could fly off of this island of rock if I wanted to, but the sky looks like it's bleeding and I don't want to move unless I have to. The rumble fades to a soft hum and the clay, finally, stills.

I break Azael's grip on my arm and walk to the edge of the ravine. Deep within the gash is a thick, boiling vein of blood. The familiar rusty smell of it allows me a moment of calm and gives me something to hold on to that makes sense. That's when another smell hits me.

Beneath the metallic scent of blood is the thick and putrid smell of death, old and ancient death, that sets my teeth on edge. I have never felt anything like this since Lucifer fell, and its unexpected presence is unsettling.

"Home, sweet home, Pen. Although, it seems that Hell's redecorated since we've left. I remember it being much colder and much more blue. But I like the change. Red is very in."

I look back at Azael and see him smiling. He looks almost cheerful, but I can't find any energy to pretend to be entertained. "This isn't Hell," I say.

"Clearly." He walks up next to me and peers down into the ravine. "But it's the next best thing. Smells like Hell."

"A bit," I say, scrunching my nose.

I close my eyes and take several deep, unnecessary breaths. With each breath, I become calmer. The nerves that spiral through my abdomen slow and my head feels lighter. The scene around me—the noise, the smell, everything—disappears.

At the edge of my consciousness, I feel a malevolent force hanging in the air, but I don't fight it. It's not bothersome. Distantly, I detect my pendant vibrating.

I relax into the sensation and notice a thick pressure on my chest. The weight of the pressure spreads through my limbs, bringing with it a wave of strange emotions, like someone else has stepped in and taken over while I'm in this state of not caring.

An intense burn seeps painfully through my veins. The pain spreads slowly to the base of my neck, where it throbs uncomfortably. The throbbing sounds like a quickening heartbeat.

Thump. Thumpthump. Thumpthumpthumpthump.

The feeling within me is foreign. I don't have heart, not anymore, and certainly not a heartbeat, but I can feel a pounding beneath my ribs. A primitive hunger begins to grow with each pulse until it becomes an unquenchable appetite. I am consumed with the hunger. It hurts, and all I can think about is trying to satisfy the need to… To what?

My throat aches with an implacable need to feed, and I roll my neck slowly in an attempt to numb the impulse. But the hunger remains, thrumming faster and more urgently.

Feed. Feedfeed. Feedfeedfeedfeed.

Blood begins to trickle down the inside of my eyelids like rain on a window and I feel my stomach clench in starvation.

"Pen?"

I ignore the muted voice. The only sounds that exist in my mind is a thick heartbeat, a strong pulsing of blood, and a distant voice—more a feeling—telling me to feed and to spread… something.

Thump. Feed. Thumpthump. Feedfeed.

I feel a hand set down on my shoulder and something in my mind snaps. Without opening my eyes, I swing my elbow back, my blow connecting to what I distantly identify as a jaw. The crack reverberates up my arm to my shoulder, but I ignore it, spin around, and pull my knee up into a rib. A loud gust of air is forced from punctured lungs, and I kick out low, striking a kneecap.

"PEN!" The voice sounds as if it's traveling from underwater. "Open your damn eyes! It's me!"

Thumpthumpthumpthump. Feedfeedfeedfeed.

I lunge forward and bite into the soft flesh of a shoulder, my teeth puncturing the skin with a soft popping noise. I feel myself sigh, but before I can drink a drop of blood, I'm thrown back from a kick to my stomach. I fly backwards and crash to the ground, my head cracking painfully on the rocky clay. The power of the blow forces my eyes open.

I gasp for air as I roll to my side in a fit of coughing, and the hunger vanishes. The world is spinning around me, bobbing up and down like a ship on rough waters. I blink a few times and focus as hard as I can on a blurry figure. It sways back and forth, fading in and out of view. *Azael.*

I see his face come into focus and it is contorted in terrifying rage. His shirt is coated with sticky, black blood and his hand is pressed to his shoulder, preventing more from spilling out.

"Pen, what the HELL?"

I lift myself up on my elbow and rub the back of my head, pressing gently on the growing knot in my skull. "What happened?" My words slur, my tongue slipping on something bitter.

"What do you *think* happened?" He pulls out his shirt collar, exposing a ragged tear in his flesh. "You bit me!"

"I—"

I sit up straighter and notice something warm slipping down my chin. I reach up to wipe at it, and when I bring my hand away, it is covered in the same black blood that is plastering Azael's shirt to him. My eyes widen to saucers and bile rises to the back of my throat. I'm wracked by another jarring cough, my tangled hair falling around my face. The cough splatters blood across the dirty orange clay, and I can't tell whether it's his or mine.

I peer back up at him. "I don't remember."

Azael looks at me with shocked fury and whispers one word, just loud enough for me to hear. "*Absum.*"

CHAPTER 6

IN A VORTEX OF HOT AIR, THE CLAY CLIFFS AND RUDDY sky slip away and are replaced by the overcast night sky that hangs above the ruins. I land, sprawled carelessly on the overgrown grass of the clearing, my joints bent in agonizing angles. I remain frozen, staring across the dying fire at Azael, and wait for him to say something.

To say anything.

But he doesn't speak. He just stands there, staring at me with a look of repulsion, as if he's going to be sick. Sluggishly, he removes his hand from his shoulder, brushing his fingers over the wound and repairing the laceration I gave him. He lets his silence say everything he needs to and I look away from him in discomfort.

I sit up, scooting backwards until my spine hits one of the cool marble tombstones that sticks out of the ground like a crooked tooth, and bring my knees in tight to my chest. I fold in on myself like origami, hoping to become some other shape

Azael won't look at like this. Maybe he'd be more pleased with a paper crane?

But no matter how I twist myself, I can't escape his accusing glare. The last thing I remember is the smell of the memory, a headache, and then nothing. I blacked out, and when I woke up, I was disoriented and he was bleeding.

I drag my hand across my mouth, convinced his blood is still dripping down my chin. My hand comes away stained black. *Azael's blood, Azael's blood, Azael's blood.* The awareness spits through me like electricity and I begin to panic. I wipe at it again and again, frantically scrubbing my skin raw.

"Enough, Pen!" His voice comes out clipped.

I can't seem to distance myself enough from his blood. Its blackness marks my chin, rests in my fingernails, and settles in the lines that swirl across my palm—all a relentless reminder of what I did to Azael. I bring my hands down from my face, pulling my sleeve over my shaking fingers, and clutch madly at the fabric until it tears. I wrap my arms around myself, squeezing my panic into submission and digging my nails sharply into my sides.

Azael folds his arms over his chest and crosses the distance between us. He kneels down next to me and scans my face calculatingly.

I bite my lip as hot tears burn the back of my eyes. The taste of his blood lingers in my mouth. "I'm so sorry."

He lets out a deep sigh and settles himself against the grave next to me. "Get it together. I've never seen a blubbering demon, and I certainly don't want you to be the first. Would give us a bad reputation. I'm fine."

I turn my head towards him doubtfully.

He pulls down his collar again, gesturing to his now unblemished shoulder. "See? Not a scratch."

"Anymore," I correct.

"I've healed from much worse. Never from a wound my own sister inflicted, however. Don't get me wrong, I'm all for bloodlust, but that was a little too on-the-nose for me."

I shift uncomfortably and look down at my lap. My jeans are smeared with orange clay and splattered with his drying black blood.

"You want to explain what the Hell happened?" he asks.

"I was hoping you could explain it to me," I say, scratching at my dirty jeans. "I don't remember. I think I blacked out."

He pulls his eyebrows together in question. "You don't remember anything?"

I shake my head. "Nothing."

"What, were you possessed?"

I look over at him in alarm. "Can demons even be possessed?"

"Hell if I know." He cocks his head sideways. "What's the last thing you remember before you went all—"

"Blood crazy? Demon Dracula?" I offer. "The smell. And then you said something about Hell redecorating."

"And then nothing?"

"Radio silence."

"So you don't remember breaking my jaw then?"

I widen my eyes in surprise. "I what?"

"Or cracking my ribs and shattering my kneecap?" His voice is flat. Not angry, exactly, but detached, like an observation. It's as if it didn't happen to him. He looks over at me and my mouth drops open. He laughs a little too harshly. "I'll take that stupid look on your face as a no. Well, even blacked out, you can still kick some major ass. I'm not easily overpowered, as you well know. I think I'll be bruised for a few days thanks to your bony fists."

I snap my mouth shut and shovel my surprise under the Earth, letting it decay with whoever's buried in the grave we're sitting on. Unraveling in front of Az like this is dangerous, so I pretend to be whole and tease him back. "I'd apologize for that, but we were due for a good fight. It must be a major blow to your ego to have been beaten by your unconscious sister."

"You were the most conscious unconscious person I've ever encountered," he objects. "I call foul. If you were possessed, you had an unfair advantage. I challenge you to a rematch when you don't have the help of bonus demon strength."

My throat tightens, strangling my words. "I still don't understand."

"Doesn't matter." He leans his head back on the tombstone, tilting his chin up to the dark sky and closing his eyes. "Gus will be here soon. Maybe he can figure it out."

"Maybe." I turn back towards the fire and watch the glowing coals, sitting forward to rest my elbows on my knees. The embers crackle sporadically, causing small sparks to jump out onto the tall grass. I catch the fire's spit in my hand and watch it fizzle out on my finger. "Do you think it hurts?" I ask quietly.

"Hmm?" Azael murmurs lazily. He doesn't bother to open his eyes. "Does what hurt?"

"Dying."

"We don't die, Pen."

"But we can be killed."

"Only by the sword of an archangel. Why are you asking me this?"

I regard the flames distantly. "I've heard that it burns. To be killed, I mean. Heaven's sword burns the evil out of you. There are stories of demons who fall to ashes after being struck."

"Ashes to ashes, dust to dust," he exhales.

"It could happen," I say, glancing at him sideways.

He looks like he's sleeping, his chest rising and falling slowly. The glow from the fire casts strange shadows across his face, giving him a haunting pallor. His cheeks look hollow, his closed eyes like empty sockets. I notice his dark hair sticking up wildly and consider brushing it flat but think better of it.

"What could?" he asks.

"We could die."

He squints one of his eyes open and considers me for a moment before shutting it again.

"Michael's back," I continue. "And he had the archangel sword."

"I really don't think we're going to have to worry about Michael killing us. At least not for another couple of centuries."

I shrug to myself. "I wouldn't underestimate him."

"Fine, but you shouldn't overestimate him either," he argues halfheartedly. "I doubt he could even lift that sword, let alone kill a demon with it."

I let the conversation drop and sit in the heavy silence. Besides the soft popping of the fire, the only noise is the quiet skittering of small animals in the woods. I watch the dying flames again and think about what it would feel like to burn from the inside out.

Fire doesn't blister my skin, doesn't curl my skin back from my bones. I've never known the pain of a real burn, but to catch fire from the inside, I imagine, would be the worst kind of agony.

'Some say the world will end in fire / Some say in ice.'

"Quoting Frost now?" Azael mutters.

"Sorry."

It's fine. And for what it's worth, the world will end in ice. 'To say that for destruction ice / Is also great / And would suffice.' Even Milton says so.

Of course. You've only read Paradise Lost *a thousand times.*

'From beds of raging fire to starve in ice...' Fire needs oxygen, and our ice will choke their flames. Hell runs cold, after all. It's the Heavens that burn.

And that's what I'm afraid of.

I roll my shoulders and settle back down against the grave, but I can't seem to settle my mind. I think back to the tree at the asylum and Michael. But instead of remembering his face or his hair, I think about the broadsword that hung from his hip.

It had a glinting golden handle with a large, round ruby secured at the top with a strong but thin silver wire carefully wrapped around it. The grip was carved with an ornate motif comprised of delicate etchings, but I couldn't make out the design from where I stood. What I did see, though, was the inscription carved in curling letters down the blade of the sword. Four simple words, laced with a subtle threat to all demons who happen upon it: "Light burns through darkness."

Message received, loud and clear.

I grab my own dagger from my boot, carefully sliding the edge of the blade so it doesn't cut through my jeans. I place the cool metal in my palm and inspect it closely. It is no match for Michael's avenging sword.

The dagger is about nine inches long, its bone-white handle short and sturdy. The hilt is carved with a thick rope that extends over the handle and knots around the top of the long, thin blade. The silver brightly reflects the amber of the fire.

I turn it over and study the engraving I have read a million times. "Not with words alone." The letters are small and pointed, but they aren't faded or scratched and neither is its message. Words are not enough; it takes action to succeed. Action in life and action in battle. I rely on words as it's a reminder I've often needed.

A loud snap from the fire sends a shower of sparks raining down on me, the embers pinging lightly off of my dagger before they die with a hiss. The flames shoot up tall around the now empty basin. I shove the tip of the dagger back into my boot and pull the dish out from the fire, tossing it behind me. The metal basin hits the grave with a loud clang, startling Az.

"We have company," I say over my shoulder.

He stretches his arms above his head. "About damn time."

The orange flames turns a searing blue as it continues to rise. I stand beside the rock-ringed pit and the fire, now reaching as tall as my shoulder, dances wildly. Azael steps up next to me.

"So do you want to tell him about your little episode, or should I?"

I glare at him. "It wasn't an episode."

"What do you want to call it?"

"Let's not call it anything. I'll tell him about the empty rooms first. He'll want to know about that. And then I'll tell him about the last door we tried." I am sure it wasn't a regular memory. It felt more like—like an implanted suggestion. Like I lost control of myself.

"So your—"

I groan. "You can have the honor of telling him about how I kicked your ass, since I blacked out."

"And how you bit me," he adds cooly.

"Yeah, that too." I look over at his shoulder again, remembering the blood. The blackness of it still darkens the pale skin across his collarbone. "Sorry about that."

He laughs. "Now *that* you're sorry for, but beating me up is fine?"

"Sounds about right," I answer.

"Okay," he nods, like he's proud. Like my not being sorry for hurting him has proven something to him. "I'll take it."

The flames pop again loudly, blue sparks spraying us both. It flares and then dies completely, revealing a tall boy in his early twenties with dark, closely cropped hair. He's dressed in a long-sleeved black t-shirt with gray jeans. The corner of a sharp tattoo peeks out from the collar of his shirt and wraps around the side of his neck, stretching to his other shoulder before disappearing again back into his shirt to spread across his chest. His violet eyes are set under thick eyebrows that are knotted in irritation, like an angry gift wrapped in a frustrated bow.

"Gus!" Azael cheers. "It's so great to see a familiar face!"

IGNITE

Gus brushes a blue ember carelessly off his shoulder and steps over the ring of rocks around the pit. "I can't say the same."

"Haven't you missed us terribly? Hell can't be the same without us!" I chime in with a smile.

He huffs in exasperation. "No, Hell definitely hasn't been the same without you two. Much less trouble. Until now, that is."

"How boring!" Azael walks over to Gus and wraps him in a tight hug. He pulls back and smirks teasingly. "Whatever would you do without us?"

I laugh as Gus fights his way out of Azael's embrace, stepping back to straighten his shirt.

"That's quite enough!"

"Oh, Gus, he's just having some fun," I say as I twist my hair into a knot at the back of my head. "We've had a very long day, or haven't you heard?"

"I have, and I think it may get more complicated still," he answers, crossing his arms across his chest. "Do you have anywhere else we can discuss this? Or do you expect me to sit around on graves all night?"

"Not one for fresh air?" Azael gasps in mock disbelief. "Well lucky for you we've got a beautiful chapel, decorated in the latest interior trends from Paris. It's called 'derelict couture.'"

He gestures grandly to a dirt path that zigzags up to the crumbling ruins of a small chapel set beyond the neglected graveyard. Gus skirts around Azael's extended arm and makes his way up the path. Azael falls in behind him, turning around to grin at me mischievously. I follow last, leisurely picking my way over the thick and twisting roots that stretch across the broken path.

"Is that what it's called?" I shout forward. "And here I've been calling it 'vacant chic.' How embarrassing."

Gus ignores our exchange and shoves open the heavy doors of the chapel, the bulky knocker beating flatly on the rotting wood. The shrill hinges creak as the doors slow to a stop. He stands in the doorway, his broad shoulders a darker shadow against the dank, unlit chapel.

He lifts his right hand and waves it indifferently, igniting the wicks of the dozen candles grouped on the altar. Several smaller candles that hang on the wall down the length of the chapel also spark with light, flickering weakly. The sudden brightness startles an assembly of bats from the vaulted ceiling, their wings flapping in a panic as they tumble carelessly out of a hole in the roof.

Even lit, the chapel looks sullen. The thick, stacked stones that make up the wall look like they are sinking slowly into the ground, and the marble steps up to the altar are cracked and sloping severely to one side. The pews are covered in a thick layer of dust and dirt, and cobwebs hang in every corner. The lower half of the stained glass window behind the altar is shattered, as if someone had thrown a rock through it. Right through Saint Peter's crotch. Broken bits of red, green, and yellow glass are scattered below the window and sparkle dully in the candlelight.

"Breathtaking," he grimaces.

"Thanks," Azael says, sidling up to Gus and draping his arm around his shoulder. "We've put a lot of work into it."

"So it would seem." Gus shakes Azael's arm off his shoulder and moves around the altar, which, miraculously, is still perfectly intact.

He pulls out a small notebook from his back pocket and lays it open on the surface of the altar. Azael follows Gus and settles in a tattered high-back chair set to the side. I walk over to the first row of pews and perch myself on top of the thick wooden half-wall.

Gus scans his notebook, snaps it closed, and looks up at us both. "There's no easy way to say this."

"Let me guess," Azael interrupts. "You've brought the erotic novel you've been writing about Lucifer and yourself instead of your proper notes. Well, don't expect us to wait for you while you run back down to Hell to grab the correct notebook. I've got places to go and people to reap!"

I look between Azael and Gus. Az has a cocky grin plastered across his face and Gus's jaw is clenched so tight that I'm sure he's cracked his teeth. I bite back my amusement.

"Michael," Gus continues, still clenching and unclenching his jaw, "has escaped."

My face falls. "So he wasn't lying? It's true?" I jump down from wall and land on the dirty stone floor with a soft crunch. "How?"

I glance at Azael and see his face set in fury, his violet eyes as bright as fire. I brace myself for him to explode. It doesn't take long.

"BULLSHIT!" Azael throws his arms up angrily, and a tall candle that sits behind him darkens, its flame whisping away into smoke. "Absolutely impossible—I helped trap him there myself! We bound him with the most powerful dark magic. Even God Himself would have had a difficult time jimmying that lock!"

"Though, somehow, it appears that He managed to do so quite easily."

"*God?*" I ask incredulously.

"So it would seem." Gus puts a fist to his chin. "Michael's soul has escaped. He has been reborn."

My head buzzes like an angry hornets' nest with Gus's words. I knew Michael was back, could feel it in my bones, no matter how impossible I believed it to be. But God? No one's ever seen Him. Only an empty throne sits in Heaven, symbolic of his ever-presence. We believe in Him on faith and faith alone. And those who lost faith fell with Lucifer.

Azael continues to shake his head. "Impossible. It's simply impossible!"

"Nothing's impossible, Azael. And, apparently, this is no exception." Gus opens his notebook again and flips through several pages loudly. "There were tests run, and they found a hole in our... security."

"The Hell hounds?" Azael asks.

"Killed. Every security measure we took was dismantled in a matter of minutes," Gus answers.

"And when did this happen?" I interrupt, walking up the steps of the altar.

"Seven months ago."

"Seven *months* ago?" I curl my fingers into a tight fist at my side. *We've been lied to for seven months?*

Azael jolts forward out of the chair and slams his hand forcefully on the altar, extinguishing a few more candles. "And why weren't we told?"

Gus sighs impatiently. "It was on a need-to-know basis."

"And you didn't think *we* needed to know?" I feel my voice rising like the bloody mercury of a thermometer in August. Hot, flat anger steams in my mind.

"Seven damn months!" Azael continues. "Seven months of him training in Heaven, while we stomp around Earth running idiotic missions. Pilfering useless souls when we could have been doing something useful!" He picks the hard metal tube from his pocket and tosses it on the table.

It rolls to a stop against Gus's notebook. He picks it up and tucks it into his own pocket, safe from Azael's tantrum. "You two were doing what you were assigned to do. You should've only been doing what you were assigned to do." He levels a gaze at Azael. "Indiana?"

Az turns away and kicks out at a small sacramental table.

"We're beyond that now," Gus continues. "You didn't need to know about Michael when it happened, but now it appears that you do." He scratches the back of his head, thinking. "There have been whispers..."

"Whispers?" I prompt.

IGNITE

He nods his head and continues. "Michael doesn't remember his past. Apparently, he's changed. Caused quite a bit of trouble in Heaven."

Azael paces furiously behind the altar, no longer paying attention. So I push Gus further. "Trouble how?" I remember the way Ariel and Sablo regarded him at the asylum. How they cut off his questions, rested a hand on Michael too heavily.

"He's not following blindly. He's asking questions, and Heaven doesn't like his particular questions," he shrugs. "When you saw him earlier... What exactly happened?"

I sit forward on my elbows, placing the heel of my hand under my chin. "We were reaping some souls—,"

"*I* was reaping some souls," Az cuts me off.

"—and he landed in a tree with me. He looked young, really young, but he said he was seventeen."

"You spoke to him?"

"Of course I did. I wasn't just going to just stand there. He had the sword with him—the archangel sword," I clarify. "I don't think he knows how to use it."

"He doesn't!" Azael interjects again, still pacing.

"Ariel and Sablo made a brief appearance," I add.

Gus nods knowingly. "They wouldn't send him alone to reap that many souls."

Azael throws his hands into the air. "Apparently not."

Neither of us acknowledge him. "He didn't seem to remember us," I continue. "And his reaction about the souls was strange, too calm for a new angel. When Ariel and Sablo left, though, he said, and I'm paraphrasing this, 'You'll be sorry.'" I waggle my fingers menacingly.

"And that's it?"

"That's it. He just left." I shrug.

"He shouldn't be much of a threat until they retrain him. That is, *if* they can retrain him. From what I hear, he's stubborn."

"That's what I told her," Azael calls over his shoulder. "Not. A. Threat."

I look over at him but ignore his comment. I brush a strand of fallen hair behind my ear and turn back to Gus. "There's more."

Gus raises his eyebrows. "Oh?"

I bite my lip. "About the souls we reaped..."

"*I* reaped," Azael corrects again. He paces faster, and I'm sure he'll burn a hole through the ground.

I wave away his comment dismissively. "Remember how you were teaching me reanimation for the purpose of collecting memories?"

"Of course. Have you gotten much practice?"

"Only once," I say, swallowing past a dry lump in my throat. "Things didn't go exactly as planned."

Azael strides up next to me, still agitated, and crosses his arms firmly. "Understatement of the year. I'd say century, but hey, it's early."

"What exactly happened?" Gus flips open his notebook to a blank page and looks at me questioningly. "Could you access the memory?"

"I—well, I did the spell as you said. Blood, the feathers of a crow, grave dirt, soul."

"And the enchantment?"

"It worked, just like you said. A long hallway with hundreds of doors lining the wall. Only, the first dozen doors we tried..." He scribbles in his notebook as I speak. "Well, they were empty."

His pen freezes and he stares at me, perplexed. "Empty?"

"Empty," Azael answers. "Adjective, from the Old English word aemettig. Two syllables. Meaning unoccupied, uninhabited, bare, desolate, clear, free, vacant. Used in a sentence: 'My, those rooms were more empty than an alcoholic's bottle of whiskey.'"

I take a deep breath before going on. "They were completely blank. White walls, white floor, bright ceiling. Until this one door."

He nods at me to continue.

IGNITE

"The handle was locked, and Azael," I gesture next to me, "kicked it in. The room was pitch dark when we went inside and seemed like it would also be empty. Dark this time, but still empty. Except my pendant started vibrating."

Gus makes a quick note. "Yes, demonic activity."

"Right. So, the pendants were vibrating, and then it sounded like the walls were too. And then, the blackness was gone. There were giant clay cliffs with two huge ravines of boiling blood. But it was still empty. We were the only two there." I shake my head. "It didn't feel like a memory, exactly. Nothing like the ones I had practiced with. It felt like, well, like something was missing, and this need, this primitive desire and pain, replaced whatever was there."

Gus's eyebrows knot together. He presses his lips into a tight, thin line but doesn't say anything.

"And then I kind of, um, blacked out, I guess," I stammer.

Azael snorts. "And by 'blacked out' she means kicked the shit out of me." He points to a swollen green bruise on his jaw. "I just touched her shoulder and she cracked me across my face, broke my ribs with her bony knee, and then shattered my kneecap with those damn boots of hers."

"Maybe she finally realized how irritating you are," Gus jeers.

"Nonsense. And besides, I can take a beating. What I don't like is being bitten into like I'm freaking Bella Swan and my immortality fantasy is finally coming to fruition. I'm no damn vampire-fetishist."

Gus's eyes widen and he looks over at me. "You *bit* him?"

"No comment about the exquisite execution of a pop-culture reference, Gus? Come on," Azael goads him, "I know you're a *Twilight* fan."

"Will you stop talking for five seconds?!" Gus snaps. He turns his attention back to me. "You bit him?"

"I—I don't remember," I say, looking down at the altar. "All I can remember is standing by the ravine and then, next thing I know, I'm lying on my side with a huge welt on the back of my head and my mouth dripping with his blood."

"Yeah and I had a huge jagged tear in my shoulder from her teeth."

"I don't remember biting him, I swear. I just—"

"Lost yourself," Gus finishes. "The empty memories, the overthrow of your senses, the lust for blood." He nods, humorless. "I've read about this before."

I push more fallen locks of my hair behind my ear and peer up at Gus.

"You have?" Azael and I ask at the same time.

"The Lilim virus."

CHAPTER 7

We stare blankly back at Gus. He shakes his head in exasperation. "Honestly, do you two even listen to anything I say?"

"Well it really depends on how many times I hear my name," Azael answers with a smile. "I can hardly show an interest in something that doesn't have anything to do with me."

"You'll just have to give it your best effort to pay attention then," Gus says pointedly.

"No promises," he mutters, slumping on his elbows so his head dips down between his shoulders.

Gus shoots him a sharp look before explaining. "The Lilim are demi-demons and the offspring of Lilith."

"Wait, Lilith has children?" I question. "How? She's a demon. It's physically impossible."

"I'm offended that I wasn't invited to her baby shower," Azael says.

Shut it, Az, I warn him, kicking at his ankles. He makes a huffing noise in acknowledgement.

Gus doesn't seem any more bothered by his comments than he already is. He ignores him and answers me. "She used to have hundreds." He looks at us expectantly. "You've learned about this. Or do you ignore my history lessons, too?"

I look at him guiltily and Azael flashes a smug smile.

"Great, I'm glad to see I've made such an impression on you two. Here's an abridged version…"

He lets his head fall back and he takes a deep breath, like he's breathing in the twenty-six letters that hang above him to piece together into a story. I lean forward to listen.

"Lilith found humans… *fascinating*. She used to be one, after all, before Lucifer stole her from Eden and brought her back to Hell with him. In the dawn of the human race, Lilith was particularly interested in men. She would seduce them, and because she was once human herself, she was somehow able to bear their children—all daughters. When her first daughter was born, it was neither human nor demon. The child was both."

"Half-human, half-demon?" I whisper.

He nods. "Lilith had inadvertently created a new breed of demons. With a foot in both worlds, Hell and Earth, her daughters were incredibly powerful. They had the strength and speed of a demon. Their only flaw was mortality. They were born without souls, but they had hearts that would beat only until their death. You must have found one that was still in the process of changing, otherwise Azael wouldn't have found a soul at all."

"If there's a soul to reap, I'll find it," Az intones, uninterested.

Again, Gus ignores his comments. "Lilith kept bearing children and eventually built up a small army of demi-demons. They threatened the purity of Earth, and Heaven recognized the danger. So the angels created the Nephilim." He looks between me and Azael. "Please tell me you remember what I've taught you about Nephilim."

It takes me a moment to grab onto the thread of the memory, but I find it. "Angel-human crossbreeds. Made by mixing human blood with that of a powerful angel."

"Good," Gus sighs, sounding relieved.

Azael rolls his eyes. *Teacher's pet.*

I jab him sharply in the ribs with my elbow.

"The Nephilim," Gus's voice echoes in the empty chapel and disrupts the flames, "were stronger than the Lilim. Their blood was pure and old, much older than Lilith's. But Hell had no alternatives to Lilith's blood. She was the only demon who could procreate with humans successfully, not that others didn't try. Demonic children not born from Lilith's blood died in miscarriages."

"How many children died?" I ask flatly. Az glances at me, a question in his eyes, but stays silent.

"The number is too high to be calculated," he answers me, unconcerned. "The children weren't the only ones who died. Humans could not handle the poison of demons. Human men were weak, and the women were poisoned by the potent demonic blood of a full strength demon. They also died during childbirth. The pain was too much for them and their bodies would give out. That is why demons can't procreate; there is nothing living within them but death. Lilith was the one exception. She was the only host who wouldn't kill the men or the children."

I close my eyes and try to imagine the deaths of the children, mothers, and men. A small part of me, buried deep in the shadows of myself that I hide from everyone, finds it disgusting. Why would Hell continue to try to mate with humans if they knew the result? How many times did they try? The deaths seem unnecessary and repulsive.

Michael's voice returns to me. *And maybe one day you'll see that.*

I shake the thought out of my head and focus on what Gus is saying.

"It didn't take long for the Nephilim to wipe out the Lilim. After seeing all of her children slaughtered, Lilith didn't want to have any more daughters of her own. So she stole the newborns of humans and killed them. It was her own small revenge on the angels who took away the only family she has ever had. She stopped creating Lilim." He brushes the stubble on his jaw. "Until now."

"Very spooky," Azael says in monotone.

"The Lilim are back." I'm thinking out loud, trying to untangle the knot of information. *Lilith had children. Lilith lost children. Lilith is creating children again.* "You said it was a virus?"

"The new Lilim are different. Lilith is stronger, and now so are her children. They can now be created by blood, not birth. Her blood is powerful enough, potent enough, that it has been transformed into a kind of virus that can effect both males and females. The infected are at the infancy stage of changing into a Lilim. The virus festers in the veins of its victim until everything pure is eaten away—the soul, their humanity... It's faster and more efficient this way. Their past is slowly erased as the virus —"

"That explains why the soul's memories were gone!" I interrupt, able to make sense of at least one small part of the strange puzzle.

He looks at me sharply and continues. "Their past is erased and their future is given one purpose: to continue to spread the virus. It is a primitive need to keep their race alive and growing. Lilith can create the Lilim by injecting them with her blood or having them drink from her vein. Once infected, they can spread it themselves. It is most commonly transmitted human to human by a bite."

I recoil slightly and glance quickly at Azael. His neck is unscarred now, but I can't forget the tear my teeth left in his flesh. *Transmitted by a bite.*

"Not every bite is successful, of course. These newborns," Gus pauses and searches for the right words in his notebook, "frequently lose control. When they feed, they are consumed completely and can sometimes kill their victim instead of changing them."

"So what is this?" Azael asks, shifting impatiently on his feet. "Another secret plan of Hell that we're kept in the dark about? Like with Michael?"

"And why has Lilith begun making Lilim again?" I scoop my own questions on top of Azael's. "Why remain dormant for so long only to resurface now?"

"I helped create the virus from her blood decades ago, but Lucifer wanted to wait to use it. I wasn't informed it was being reintroduced to humans again." Gus stops for a minute to think, consulting the small, graphite-smeared pages of the notebook. He skims the scrawled letters that I assume make some semblance of sense to him and pulls absentmindedly at his lip. "It has to be Michael," he concludes. "He is the catalyst. His presence has made the Lilim virus extremely valuable and spreading it has become more urgent. Creating the Lilim now will strengthen Hell's army."

"Michael, again? Really? How much trouble could this one kid cause?" Az's words leak out of him like piss.

"We're preparing for war, Azael," Gus is bitter and serious, his tone scolding. "His return has bigger implications than you can imagine. You know Lucifer's been focusing his efforts on reclaiming Heaven. He wants the throne, and he will build an army to help him get there. With Michael alive again, things have changed."

For once, Azael's silent and empty of comebacks, for the time being.

Gus closes his notebook solemnly. "As long as Michael lives, Lucifer cannot claim absolute power in Heaven."

"Then it's simple, really," Azael purrs. "Eliminate Michael. It would be my pleasure to kill him a second time."

"No!" The word escapes my lips before I can sew them together. Azael and Gus both look at me with raised eyebrows. I set my jaw. "I mean, Gus, you said he's changed. Maybe he won't accept the things Heaven tells him. He could be valuable. We could—"

A raised hand from Gus stops me. "It doesn't matter either way. We cannot kill him now. When he escaped, a part of him was left in Hell, and that piece still binds him there. His soul and Lucifer's are tied together; if one dies, so does the other. For the time being, it doesn't seem that Heaven is aware of this connection."

"Or he would be dead," I guess.

"They would sacrifice him without a moment's hesitation if it meant Lucifer would die. Until we can sever the connection, no harm can come to Michael."

"But he'll only grow stronger!" Azael protests.

"He is strong now," Gus says firmly. "The same power he had before resides in him now. He never lost it. It's just dormant. Don't underestimate him for a moment. If you strike now and awaken this power, there is no telling what he would do. He might cause harm to himself if he knows about the connection, become a martyr."

"So where does that leave us?" Even next to the cluster of small flames from the candles, I feel cold. I run my fingers through the flames, twirling the fire into smoke.

"You two are in the unique position of knowing information that no other non-level 1 demon knows. I am working on severing the connection between Michael and Lucifer, but progress is slow and complicated. They are woven together so absolutely..." He shakes his head. "The mark he left in Hell is complex. A part of Michael lies within Lucifer and a small part of Lucifer lies within Michael, just as you two are connected. They're brothers, but their differences bind them together more intricately than usual."

Gus pauses, his eyes darkening seriously. He glances quickly at Azael, scanning his sharply set features.

"We are on the brink of war, and if Lilith is creating Lilim again, it is nearer than I have thought. And Michael, whether Heaven has realized it or not, has become very valuable to us. And you two will be responsible for him."

"I'm sorry," Azael laughs dryly. "*Responsible* for him? What exactly does that mean?"

"It means that you will follow, observe, and protect him from harm—from others or himself."

Azael slams his hands violently on the alter again. "I'm no damn babysitter!"

I watch Gus carefully, measuring his expression as his face shifts in minute emotions. Thinking about following Michael, I feel a jolt in my veins. I could try to talk to him again, maybe even convince him to abandon Heaven for a different cause. I could fight alongside him when we overthrow Heaven. *Would he fight with me?*

"For how long?" is all I ask.

"I cannot see the future anymore," Gus says miserably. He rests his head briefly in his hands, rubbing his temples tiredly.

"Can't get it up, old boy?" Azael teases. "Perhaps *you* should be the babysitter."

"Gus, you're a diviner!" I speak over Azael. Diviners can always see the future, even if there are multiple outcomes. For him to be blind to what's coming…

"The future, it would appear, has yet to be written. Everything hangs in a balance so precious that one wrong move could collapse the world as we know it."

A choking scoff sounds from Azael. "I'm fine with the world collapsing."

"All of the worlds, Azael. Earth, Heaven, and Hell. The lines that separate the worlds are blurring, erasing, now that the apocalypse has officially begun."

My stomach twists.

"I'll break out the champagne," Azael quips.

CHAPTER 8

"CAN WE STOP THE APOCALYPSE?" I ASK.

"And why would we want to that?" Azael spreads out his arms. "It's time for the world to burn."

I shift nervously from foot to foot. "The world wouldn't be the only thing that burns." I place my hand over my ribs, imagining the sharp point of an archangel's sword piercing my skin and charring me from the inside out. "We all would."

Gus pushes his notebook around the altar distractedly. "Once the apocalypse has begun, there is little hope of stopping it. The lines between the worlds are blurring, and there's no going back now. At least, that's according to the prophecy." He shrugs lightly once, reopens his notebook hopefully, and scans a blank page. He snaps it shut decisively. "But the prophecy has been unwriting itself."

"*Unwriting* itself?"

"Pages are disappearing—as if the future's being erased. Whether or not that is because there is no longer any future, or if it simply hasn't been written yet, I'm not sure. But I've never seen anything like it before. No one has."

I look over at Azael, who has resettled himself in the high back chair. He pulls at the fraying fabric, twisting the thread around his finger until his fingertips turn white.

"So for now...?"

"For now," Gus takes a deep breath, "there is nothing to do but to wait. We bide our time, as the connection between Michael and Lucifer is severed, and we reclaim Heaven."

I feel myself getting antsy at the idea of sitting around, waiting. "And the Lilim virus?"

"It will continue to spread until the war begins. It would be in your best interest to stay out of the path of those infected, if possible. They fight for Hell but can make no distinction between enemy and ally before battle. They're too young and are only focused on spreading the infection. Which makes it all the more important for you to keep a close eye on Michael."

Azael chuckles darkly. "That won't be much of a problem for her. He seemed to take a liking to my dear sister."

My cheeks grow warm and I turn around quickly, hoping to disguise my embarrassment as anger by glaring at Azael.

"And who could blame him?" He goes on, hoping to get a rise out of me. "She's so pretty."

I will dice you into small little pieces to feed to your murder of crows, I warn him. *They'll eat their leader and you'll be nothing more than their sh—*

Gus purses his lips thoughtfully. "That could work in our advantage, actually."

I flick my eyes over to where he stands. He taps his fingers pensively on the dark wood of the altar. "Excuse me?"

"If he trusts you, which would be rare because of your status as a demon, it will be easier for you to protect him. You may even, as you suggested earlier, sway his alliance. An angel as powerful as Michael would be a significant ally in the war against Heaven."

"But," Azael interrupts, "Lucifer hates him. I don't think he would fight side by side with Michael if his life depended on it."

"His life may very well depend on it. Or at least his success." Gus's stare is distant as he weighs the options in his mind. "Neither could claim absolute control while the other survives, but I don't see that Michael, being as young as he is, would want to hold the power. He's too inexperienced. And if he does want power, if he will fight Lucifer over it, then we can put him down. No need to squander a powerful specimen just because we fear he *may* do something destructive."

"So what do you want me to do?" I ask, chewing at the inside of my cheek.

He pauses before answering cautiously. "Get close to him. Gain his trust, and when the time comes, you will either strike him down or, if you've done your job well enough, he will join Hell's army and serve his brother, Lucifer."

"And Az?" I raise an eyebrow and nod towards where he sits. He casually kicks his legs out and props his feet on top of the alter, dried mud falling off the bottom of his dark boots.

"Yeah, Gus, what about me? Do you want me to get close to him?" He bats his eyelashes dopily. "I could turn on the old charm, maybe woo him a bit. Dinner, some flowers? I draw the line at third base, though."

Gus makes a strangled noise that sounds like a tight, incredulous laugh. "We're trying to protect him and bring him to fight for Hell. We can't have him killing himself. What a waste that would be!"

Offended, Azael scrunches his face and rips more forcefully at the unraveling edge of his seat cushion.

"I think you would be better served, Azael, observing the two unseen. And, if you can handle it, you will also be responsible for tracking the spread of the Lilim virus."

"If I can handle it," he scoffs. "I can't help but feel that I've been demoted. I'm supposed to sit around and chaperone angel boy and Pen?"

"I don't need Az watching me," I protest. "Especially if he has something better to spend his time on. I am perfectly capable of handling myself. How hard can it be?"

Gus appraises me for a moment before agreeing. "Okay then, Az. You can spend your time tracking the Lilim with Lilith," Gus adds. "Lilith and I don't exactly... get along."

I raise my eyebrows. "Why, did you two used to—"

"No, no. Nothing like that," he chokes out, looking embarrassed. Azael laughs. "She's more of an act-first, plan-later kind of demon. She doesn't care about consequences or chain effects. Whereas I am the exact opposite. There's a reason we divine before doing anything of significance. But Lilith doesn't see the value."

"So you want me to follow Lilith around and be your middleman? Oh, I'm sure she'll just love that," Azael says exasperatedly. "Should I still draw the line at third base?"

I roll my eyes.

"As long as you can track the virus, I could care less what you and Lilith do," Gus says to the dusty surface of the alter.

"Sure. I'll just track Lilith as she goes around the globe, injecting boring humans and turning them into not-quite-demons. Why would I want to miss that? It sounds riveting." He lulls his head back, irritated, and pulls his feet from the altar, letting them crash to the ground with a bang. He sits forward on his elbows and stares at Gus. "And what good will tracking the Lilim actually do?"

"It should," Gus replies, "serve as a calendar of sorts. The faster the virus spreads, the closer we are to war. If I can find a trend in how the infection is spread, I should be able to determine the approximate date Lucifer is destined to storm the gates of Heaven." He sighs sadly. "Without a prophecy, or the ability to divine, it's the best option we have. And if it works, it means a promotion is in both of your futures. Top tiered demons."

I lean towards Gus and raise an eyebrow. "Level 1?"

"Level 1 Powers," he confirms.

"Fine," Azael sighs. "I'll become Lilith's BFF. Maybe she'll appreciate my company. You two certainly don't!"

I smile excitedly. "When do we start? How do I find him again? Isn't he in Heaven? I can't exactly follow him around up there…"

Gus puts up his hands to stop me. "Slow down. There's nothing you can do tonight. Michael only visits Earth during the daylight hours. He returns to Heaven as soon as the sun begins to set."

"And right when the demons crawl out of their holes in the ground," Azael growls.

Gus looks measuredly at Azael and then back to me. He reaches deep into the pocket of his jeans and brings out a thin bracelet strung with tiny clear, round beads. He slides it across the altar and I pick it up, inspecting it in the candlelight.

"This is how you'll find him. Vassago enchanted it with a tracking spell when we first locked Michael up. It was one of the precautions we never thought we'd need. But now, it should serve you well."

"He's enchanted a *bracelet?*" Azael's voice is dripping in derision. "Because, what, you both thought it'd be the perfect accessory for Lucifer, should his baby brother fly the coop? Or was it Vassago's idea?"

Vassago is an olive-colored, broadly muscled demon who can locate what has been lost or hidden. He's the one who found Pandora's box after her husband had thrown it into the sea. It's hard to imagine his thick fingers crafting something so delicate, but if he cast the enchantment, I know it will work. I slip it carefully onto my wrist, twisting my hand so the beads sparkle in the light.

"Pretty," Azael ridicules.

I shove my hand into my pocket and scowl at him.

"You," Gus says, pointing at Azael, "will use this." He reaches down into his boot and pulls out a tightly rolled up piece of yellow parchment. It's center is secured with a thin rope. He unties it quickly and unrolls the paper, spreading it smoothly on the altar. A map of Earth is drawn in faded ink across the wrinkled parchment, each continent palely painted in.

Azael heaves himself up from the chair and goes to stand next to Gus. He looks over the map with mild curiosity. "And you just happen to be carrying this around with you?"

"You'd be surprised what I carry around with me," Gus retorts. "Mark this map where there is a new attack, a new transmission. Just a small X will do. I have the complimenting map and the notes you make will appear on mine as well. Track the virus carefully, and I will be able to follow you along."

"Sounds easy enough," Azael says, rerolling the map and placing it in his own boot.

Gus nods decisively. "You know what you two have to do."

"But how can Azael find me if I'm following Michael and he's chasing the virus?"

Take a wild guess. Azael hisses in my mind.

Oh, right.

Do you think Gus will be mad if I draw obscene pictures on his map?

I put my hand up to my mouth to muffle my chuckle.

Gus looks between us, sensing our silent conversation. "Yes, you can find each other that way. Or, if that doesn't work, your amulets tie you two together. If you hold it in your palm and concentrate on one another, you should be able to communicate from greater distances apart."

I touch the chain of my necklace. "Makes sense."

"Good." Gus pockets his small notebook and walks down the listing steps of the altar and to the door. Azael and I follow behind him, Azael's boots crunching loudly on the gritty dirt as I spin the bracelet carefully around my wrist.

The three of us walk quickly down the path, through the graveyard, and back into the center of the clearing. Gus steps into the stone-circled fire pit and snaps his fingers. A small purple fire begins at his feet, slowly inching up his legs.

"One more thing before I go," he says as the fire rises to his hips. His dark eyes slide from Azael to me and back again.

"Oh, Gus, you know I'm not one for long goodbyes. I get so emotional." Azael wipes at his eyes sarcastically.

I'm about to join Az in teasing Gus, but I trap my lip between my teeth, silencing myself when I see his expression.

"This is serious." His voice is deep and weighty.

Azael stands up taller, like a soldier at attention. "Yes, Hell is very serious business. That's why no one ever smiles down there."

I jab him in the ribs with my elbow, aiming for one of the ribs I broke earlier. He groans and doubles over, folding in half at his waist. Gus looks mildly entertained, but quickly regains his composure.

"If you should fail, don't bother returning to Hell." Gus looks at us both seriously again and the purple fire brightens to a warm blue as it reaches his shoulders. Before he has a chance to say anything else—and before Azael recovers from my blow—an abrupt flare of the flames engulf him and he disappears.

The flames fall back into the stones and fade into docile embers again.

"Very dramatic," Azael says, hunching his shoulders again as he settles himself against a lopsided tombstone.

"He does love his theatrics," I agree, sitting next to him. I bump him lightly with my shoulder. "So tomorrow?"

He kicks his boot on the ground, rattling the rolled parchment, and looks over at me. "Well, technically just later today." He smirks and I stick my tongue out at him. "But fine, let's call it tomorrow."

I take a deep breath and raise my face to the sky. The clouds have cleared, opening to a crisp dark blue sky dotted with millions of shining, flickering stars. There are still hours left in the night, but my chest tightens in anticipation of the coming day.

When the sun rises, I'll find Michael. But for now, I must rest.

CHAPTER 9

WHEN I WAKE UP, THE SKY IS JUST TURNING A PALE GRAY. I can see it through the holes in the cathedral ceiling. Last night, I slept stretched out on one of the thin, musty cushions that line the dark wooden pews.

I sit up stiffly, rolling my aching neck and stifling a yawn. I lean over my shoulder to the pew behind me and see Azael, still in a deep sleep. One of his legs is draped carelessly over the back row of his pew while his other has fallen to the floor, his bare foot a shock of white against the dark stone. His arm is thrown over his face, shielding his eyes, and his mouth hangs open.

Rolling off the creaking seat as quietly as I can, I make my way to the door of the chapel and out into the graveyard. I sit on one of the cool stone steps outside and watch as the orange light of the day slowly seeps across the sky.

The last heat of summer seems to have ebbed away overnight, leaving room for the brisk chill of autumn. *Summer isn't the only thing leaving*, I think as I lean back against the outer wall of the chapel.

IGNITE

Today is the first time in decades Azael and I will go our separate ways. I've grown so accustomed to having him by my side every day that I can't even remember what it's like to be on my own.

Will I be different without my brother? Sometimes I feel that, when I am with Azael, a part of him is reflected in me. His dark humor rubs off on me, and I find myself more willing to joke along with him. We are two halves of one whole; neither of us is complete in the absence of the other. So what will it mean when I am forced to define myself?

It doesn't really matter, I remind myself. I'm not on some coming-of-age adventure where I'll come to some new understanding of the purpose of my life. It's much too late to change the path I'm headed down. Besides, my goal is clear, as is the significance of my success. I'm to befriend Michael, protect him, and, if at all possible, bring him to the dark side. Even just thinking that, I feel like I should be twirling a mustache and stroking a menacing white cat that sits forebodingly in my lap.

As the sun breeches the tree tops, I stand up and walk back into the chapel, running my fingers through my knotted hair.

I go back to where Azael sleeps, following the grumble of him snoring. He's rolled over to his stomach, his face smashed awkwardly into the foam cushion. I grab his shoulder and shake him awake.

"Rise and shine, sleeping beauty. It's another beautiful day on Earth. Temperatures will be in the mid-60s, with a clear sky and a slight breeze."

He groans and rolls over, muffling his ear with his fist. "Tired. Sleep."

I shake him again. *I think it was you who said last night that you have, 'places to go and people to reap.'*

He rolls back again, nearly falling off the narrow bench, sits up, and stares at me through squinted eyes. His hair is pushed up in strange shapes and he has a line down the side of his face that rested on the cushion's seam.

"Well don't you look gorgeous," I tease.

He makes a face at me and pushes his hand sloppily through his hair. "Someone interrupted my beauty sleep."

"I'm sure you'll survive. But I won't if I don't get something to eat soon! Do you have any food left?" I bend down to see if I can see inside the knapsack he has tucked under the pew. He swings his legs down, blocking my view.

"Enough for breakfast."

"Great, I'll take two eggs, over easy, bacon on the side."

"You'll take scrambled, and we're out of bacon," he counters.

I stick out my lower lip in a pout. "Fine, but make it quick. I feel like I'm starving." My stomach growls loudly to emphasize my point.

"Could be worse. If you were human, you could *actually* starve," he laughs. "They may have been modeled after us, but they are so much weaker. Eating should be recreational, not essential."

"Shouldn't some of this stuff have evolved out of them by now?"

"These little insects are slow on the evolutionary race. I'm sure they'll get there eventually. That is, if they even survive long enough to do so," he says as he scoops the backpack off the floor and yanks it onto his shoulder. He stands up, pulls on his boots, and walks grumpily out the door, down the path, and into the clearing to the fire pit. I grab a dented skillet from behind one of the large angel statues at the edge of the graveyard and follow him.

I spark a fire with a snap and throw the skillet over the flames, setting it on a small metal grate that bridges the pit. Azael sets the backpack down on the grass and takes out a small carton of eggs. He opens it, removing the last of the eggs and cracking them each, one by one, onto the skillet. The yolk breaks as the eggs land in the pan with a sizzle.

Azael sits down next to the fire, putting his hands out in front of him to warm them. "Kind of nippy today, no?"

"Kind of," I agree. "Much better than that heat, though. I can't stand summer."

"Typical demon response. Missing the icy depths of Hell?"

I roll my eyes. "Are you saying you like the heat?"

"I'm simply saying that I would like to feel my fingers when I'm forced to wake up at the ass-crack of dawn to make breakfast."

"Always the gentleman."

He bows his head. "Wouldn't be right any other way."

"And no, I don't miss it."

"Hmm?" he says, looking over at me. "Miss what?"

"Hell. You just asked me— ah, never mind. But I don't miss Hell particularly. I just don't like the heat. But I love Earth's colder seasons. Do you remember last time we were here during winter?" I ask, and he nods. "All of that snow. It never snows in Hell! It's always cold but that's all it is. Cold, empty, icy. It's so much more interesting on Earth."

"If you say so," he says, returning his attention to the eggs. He shuffles the pan impatiently. "I hate the snow. Too wet."

"Well I liked it. I wonder if it will snow again?" I look up at the clear sky that is now a light blue.

"It's not cold enough," he answers.

I frown in disappointment. "Maybe it will be soon."

"I hope not," he says around a yawn. "I can't stand all those snow angels people make. Very inaccurate. And it's insulting that there are no snow demons."

"Isn't that what Jack Frost is supposed to be?" I ask, raising an eyebrow. "A demon who brings fierce snow storms?"

"That's the stupidest thing I've ever heard."

"Maybe I'll be Jack Frost," I add, smiling. "I'll follow you around pelting you with snowballs!"

"Or you could just rip my head off, spare me from that soggy nightmare with a nice quick death," he quips.

"You are absolutely no fun this morning," I say as I kneel down next to him, bumping against his shoulder.

"See what happens when you don't let me get a solid eight hours?"

"Oh, rest assured. I've learned my lesson."

He turns and smiles sleepily. "Good."

He pulls the pan off the fire, the eggs a dark yellow, burned brown around the edge. I pull out two chipped plates from a backpack and hold them out to him, watching as he slides the eggs out of the skillet and onto the plates.

"Bon appetite," he says, tossing the pan back over the fire.

I pull the eggs apart, popping small bites into my mouth. "A little runny," I say around my fingers.

"What is this, *Top Chef*? Just be grateful we still had something left to eat."

I cock my head at him in confusion.

"It's a TV show where people compete to make the best dishes. You know what, I don't have to explain this to you!" He shovels his eggs into his mouth quickly, hardly chewing.

I smile. "Now I know you've been out of Hell for too long."

He shakes his head, downing the last of his breakfast. With the hem of his t-shirt, he wipes the empty plate clean and then slides it back into his backpack. I quickly finish the last of my breakfast and hand him my plate to place with the other.

"Thanks," I mumble, my mouth still partially full.

He raises his eyebrows. "Very ladylike." The plates click together as he shoves mine into the pack, hoists it onto his back, and offers me his hand. I take it and he pulls me roughly to my feet. "Did you pack your bag last night?"

"I did," I answer. "Not much to pack, though. Just a couple of shirts, a few bruised apples, and a water bottle. I'm going to have to stock up on some more food soon. Did you?"

He nods. "Of course. Packed it to capacity. Bag of souls, supplies, change of clothes, and a second scythe. Do you want one of the plates?" He shakes the bag on his shoulder, rattling the dishes.

"No, I'll be fine." I smile at him. "I'll miss you."

"That's awfully sentimental of you," he teases.

I shrug. "Like you won't miss me?"

He glances over me quickly and purses his lips. "Fine, maybe a little."

We both stand awkwardly. Azael shoves his hands deep into his pockets and looks back towards the chapel as I kick idly at the ground. Neither one of us is very good at goodbyes.

"So..."

Azael takes a deep breath and looks down at the grass I'm kicking up with my boots. "So," he repeats.

"I guess this is goodbye? For now?" I bend my head so he is forced to look at me.

He lifts his chin and smiles, a little sadly and a little crookedly. "For now."

Boldly, I step forward and wrap my arms around him. *Good luck.*

He places one of his hands on my back and pats my shoulder uncomfortably. *I don't need luck.* He pulls back from the hug, his eyes sparkling devilishly. *I'm a spectacular specimen of demonic prowess. I never fail.*

I roll my eyes. *And unfailingly humble. But still—*

I know. He pulls up the second strap of the backpack, adjusting it so it rests between his pointed shoulder blades. *Good luck to you too.*

I don't need it. I stick my tongue out at him.

He just smiles back at me, unfurls his dark, black wings, and lifts quickly out of the clearing. His wings push cool air down onto me, tangling my hair in the wind and flattening the grass that once stood tall around me.

I bring my hand to my forehead, shading my eyes to watch as he leaves. He flies quickly and chases the fading gray of dawn, outpacing the sun. When he's out of view, I turn around and walk back up to the chapel.

Standing at the large doorway, I survey the small, crumbling shell of the chapel one last time. We've only been staying here for a week, but I still feel a slight twinge of loss as I swipe the last few candles off of the alter and place them into the open backpack that leans against it.

I shoulder the dark green backpack, turn around, and make sure I haven't left anything behind. I don't see anything under the pews or hidden in the choir loft so I walk out of the hazy chapel and back into the brisk, cloudless morning. I close the doors behind me and walk down the root-ridden path.

When I reach the top of the graveyard, I lean against a small mausoleum and spin my bracelet around my wrist deliberately. I roll each clear bead in my fingers, close my eyes, and think of Michael.

Golden hair, blue eyes, silver wings, white smile.

As I'm picturing Michael, a background begins to appear behind him, like lights rising on the scenery of a play. I can see him standing in a misty forest, thick with pine trees. The more I focus on Michael, the clearer the location becomes.

I open my eyes and grin. *There you are.*

CHAPTER 10

It doesn't take me long to find Michael. The closer I get to him, the sharper I can see him in my mind. He's smiling, looking past me and swinging his sword playfully. He steps out with his foot and slices the air with his sword, and I can almost hear him laughing musically as he does so. From what I can see, he appears to be alone. And I hope he stays that way.

As the woods of tall maple trees slowly transition into forests of thick, green pine trees, my bracelet becomes warm. I let my feet skim the willowy tops of the trees when I see that I am close to Michael. I land next to a small, twisting stream where the pine trees are thinner, my feet hitting the ground with a dull thud and my boots splashing in the shallow water. I curl my wings back into myself and look around.

I haven't been to the Pacific Northwest in over a century. Civilization has been consistently pushing deeper and deeper into woods and forests, but this area has been left unblemished by a bulldozer. It smells different up here too, like wet earth and crisp leaves. Even when it's not raining, the air is damp with mist that brushes my face like a whisper and cools me down.

It's very peaceful, and I wonder why anyone would want to live in a city when they could live somewhere like this. Who needs buildings and roads when you have trees and streams?

I reach down and touch my bracelet again, twisting it once to see Michael. This time, he's sitting down on the dark dirt of the forest, leaning against the thick trunk of a massive pine tree. I drop my hand again, shift my backpack on my shoulders, and listen closely.

There is a steady dripping sound of yesterday's rain sliding down branches and splashing on rocks, into the stream, or onto the soft ground. Periodically, there is a loud chirp from a bird that flits from branch to branch, answered later by a bright melody from its unseen companion. Behind these noises is a quieter humming sound. I follow the humming, walking soundlessly under branches and over flat, slippery rocks. I keep walking until I come up to a grouping of thinned trees that lets sunlight come streaming down onto a small patch of ground that is covered in dry, coppery pine needles.

I pull apart two heavy green limbs of a gigantic fir and see Michael sitting alone. His eyes are closed, but he has a warm smile spread across his face and he is humming brassily. He looks so serene that I can't help but watch him a while longer.

His hair is bright and golden against the deep emerald and brown of his surroundings, a beacon in a sea of shadows. He is wearing jeans that are covered in dark grass stains and a long-sleeved gray sweater. I push the branches farther apart and lean forward, trying to see him more clearly, but when I do, one of the branches cracks.

I let go of the tree and hide myself behind the greenery. Through the closed branches, I see Michael open his eyes, straighten his back, and look around.

"Hello?" he calls, his voice as golden as his hair. "Is anyone there?"

He has his back turned towards me and is looking into the shadowy woods over his shoulder. I take a calming breath and step out from behind the tree, brushing the drooping green branches out of my way.

"Do I count as anyone?" I ask, eyebrow arched.

He whips his head back around towards me. Still sitting, he has to crane his neck up to see me. I give him a smile that I hope isn't too sharp and hold out my empty hands, like I'm approaching a wild animal. Any sudden movements and he'll bolt. He looks me over apprehensively and his eyes fixate on the handle of my dagger that sticks out from my boot.

He grabs the hilt of his sword with one hand and scrambles to a standing position. Clumsily, he pulls his sword out of his belt and holds it out in front of him. It's not pointed at me, though. Instead, its tip drops to the ground with a small bounce.

I look from the sword back to him skeptically. "Really?"

He stares at me for a moment and then he shifts the sword so it is centered on me, clutching it with both of his hands. His posture straightens as he squares his shoulders. "Really."

I step towards him cautiously, still holding my hands up. "If I wanted to kill you, I could have done it by now." It's laughable how easy it would have been. I can practically see the entire scene—me slinking up behind him, snapping his neck, grabbing his sword and skewering him to the tree. He would have been dead in under sixty seconds. "Where are your bodyguards, anyway?"

The sword wavers, lowering slightly from my chest to my abdomen. "Ariel and Sablo?"

"Do you have other bodyguards I don't know about?"

He considers me and drops one of his hands from the hilt of his sword. "I gave them the day off."

Or, more likely, they had more important things to do, I think to myself. Something big must've caught their attention if they're letting Michael off of the short leash they keep him on. But they're still probably watching him. I glance up through the tall trees and into the sky before looking back at Michael. *Maybe news of the Lilim has reached the pearly gates.*

"And do you regret that decision now?" I say, taking another careful step towards him. One more step and his sword would hit my stomach, so I stop, lowering my hands slowly.

Michael examines me again. He glances between me and the point of his weapon. *Do it,* I want to say. I don't know why, but I want to push him, see if he'd even be able to kill me. I'm nearly positive he wouldn't be able to, but I'm not willing to risk my life on nearly.

I shift on my feet. "Do you mind lowering that?" I ask, gesturing to his sword. He focuses on my dagger again before his eyes flick back up to my face.

"I'll drop my weapon if you drop yours."

"I'm not even holding—oh, all right." I bend down and take the blade out of my boot. He raises the sword back up to my chest anxiously, his knuckles white. I roll my eyes. I wouldn't be able to kill him with my dagger, only stun him. But he doesn't know that.

He keeps his eyes trained on my dagger and I imagine the sword piercing through my chest over the spot where my heart would be if I make any quick movements. I go slower, my movements languid like I'm submerged in water, and hold up my free hand in submission. I toss the blade over onto some pine needles and it slides until it hits the trunk of the tree I had been hiding behind.

I straighten and nod towards his sword. "Your turn."

He hesitates for a moment before lowering his sword again and leaning it against the base of his own tree, the point stuck firmly into the dirt. He doesn't take his eyes off of me as he does so. "Where's your brother?" he asks.

"How do you know he's my brother?"

"Oh please." He crosses his arms over his chest. "I may be new at this but I'm not blind and I'm not an idiot. Where is he?" he asks again.

"Gone," I say simply. "We're not attached at the hip, in case you were wondering. We don't always have to be together."

"Are you sure?" He tilts his head as if he is truly curious, but I get the sense he is mocking me.

"Maybe I gave him the day off," I retort. "Like your two buddies."

He looks away from me and mumbles, "They're not my buddies."

"Oh? You three sure looked chummy last time I saw you."

I put my hands in my back pockets and watch, amused, as he kicks at the ground with his thin, blue sneakers. There is a long pause before he answers.

"Not everything is what it appears to be."

"No," I say, studying him thoughtfully. "Apparently not."

"What are you doing here, anyway?" he asks, looking back at me. "If you're not here to kill me, then what—"

"I'm not allowed to have interests outside of killing people?"

He quirks one side of his mouth up into a crooked grin. "From what I've heard, usually no. And the last time I saw you, you seemed to be pretty thrilled about killing those people in the hospital."

"Yeah, well then I guess I'm an anomaly." I glance back at my dagger. "If it helps you at all, those souls we reaped kind of bit us in the ass." I bite my tongue and look back at him but he says nothing. He just continues to watch me patiently. "Look, if you want me to leave, I can just go," I say, gesturing over my shoulder.

He wavers for a moment, glancing back at his sword and then tilting his face up to the sky. *So they are watching him.* When he lowers his face again, his jaw strong and his eyes level with mine, he lets out a small sigh.

There's something about him that feels so lonely. I chew on the inside of my cheek, waiting for him to say something. If he wants me to leave, I'll have to find a way to follow him without being noticed. I still have a job to do. It would be much easier if he lets me stay, if he *wants* my company.

"You don't have to go," he finally replies, his eyes a steely blue. "I mean, unless you want to go. But I won't make you." He looks at me closely, his eyes stopping at a spot just below my ribs. "Besides, I don't think you'll hurt me." He walks over to his sword and slides it back into his belt.

Pulling at the hem of my shirt, I look down at my ribs to see if there's a stain or a tear or something distracting. But there's nothing, so I cross my arms and look at Michael again.

"If you're so sure I won't hurt you, why do you need that?" I wave my hand towards his hip. The sword glints forebodingly in a stream of light that seems to be falling just around Michael, leaving me in the shadows.

"Oh this?" He touches the sword, considering it. "Well, I wouldn't want to lose it. It seems pretty important."

"You have no idea what that is, do you?"

"I know it's beautiful." He removes his gaze from the sword and peers up at me. "Have you seen it?"

I shake my head. "Not up close, no. But, I've heard stories of its... destruction, I guess you would say."

His eyebrows draw together. "Oh." With a slow, deliberate motion, he pulls the blade back out of its holster and places it so it rests delicately in his hands. He closes the distance between us and holds it out for me to admire. "See?" He regards the great weapon eagerly. "Beautiful, isn't it?"

I inspect the blade closer. The giant ruby at the top of the handle is larger than I thought it was and much more round. What I thought was silver wire that held it in place I now see, in the silver-gold reflection, is electrum. The tableau that is carved into the gold of the handle is a gruesome scene from the war. It shows a barren land scorched by fire with a giant angel standing in the center, arms opened wide to Heaven as a sword pierces through his chest. Someone must have altered the sword after the war to include it.

I lean back involuntarily from the weapon. "Sure, beautiful."

He seems to notice my discomfort at the sword and slides it into his belt again for safekeeping. "You don't like it." He leaves his hand resting on the reflective handle.

"You could say that." I take a deep, uneasy breath.

"Why?"

I meet his eyes and see nothing but curiosity. I expected him to mock me, knowing that with that sword he could end my life faster than I could call for help. I thought I would see a blaze of arrogance behind his eyes as he realizes the power he holds over me, that I am weak and he is strong. But I see none of that.

"You really don't know," I say, surprised.

He remains wordless, blinking at me innocently with his lips parted. His eyebrows are drawn together and under them his bright eyes are confused.

"That is an archangel sword. You at least know that much, right?"

I should really not be telling him this, I think.

But he nods, so I continue, against my better judgment. "The sword of an archangel, which you are—or, were, or still are? I'm confused about the logistics of this resurrection—is one of the only weapons that can truly kill a demon. Other weapons can only injure us, temporarily of course, or send us back to Hell. I've been slain on Earth more times than I can count, but I can always come back. But that," I glance briefly at his belt again, "can kill us. Permanently."

He drops his hand from his waist, leaving it hanging awkwardly in the air.

"I've heard," I go on, unable to stop myself, "that it burns the evil out of demons until they are nothing more than ash. It's supposed to be the most painful thing anyone—angel, demon, or human—could ever experience."

With a twist, he turns his belt so that the sword is hanging behind him, nearly hidden from my view. "Sorry."

"Sorry?" I scrunch my nose and frown.

"I didn't—I mean, I wasn't going to kill you. And you might've thought..." He trails off, shifting his weight from one foot to the other. "I didn't know it could do all of that. I've probably killed demons before with this."

I trip on a laugh. *"Probably?"*

He's quiet for a minute, watching me. I look away from him, deciding to study the patterns in the bark of the trees that surround us, fencing us in together. But I can still feel his gaze on me.

"Why did you tell me?"

I don't know, I think to myself. But out loud, I answer, "You would have found out anyway." I face him again. "I might as well be the one to tell you."

He squints his eyes. "You're very strange, you know?"

"I'm sorry, I'm the strange one?"

"Yes," he says, nodding his head. His hair bounces carelessly across one of his eyes, and he brushes it away to look at me. "They've been telling me demons don't feel anything. Except maybe a twisted pleasure when other people are in pain or something. I can see you've killed a lot of people, innocent people..." Again, he stars at a spot just under my ribs, and I pull my arms tighter around myself. "But you seem different. You don't enjoy it the same way other demons do. The pleasure you feel isn't as deep. It's like you have to force the excitement."

And just like that, I'm cut open, turned inside out, and displayed for him to study. My boat has sprung a leak and I'm drowning in the lies I've told and lived. But before he gets a chance to prod too deeply into the fiction that is my life, I stitch myself back together and plaster on a sardonic grin.

"And the data pool from which you formed this opinion is what? Two demons? Me and my brother, or have you run across others?"

"I've seen enough to know that you're different."

I pause. "Should I be offended?"

His face is overtaken by a brilliant, white smile. "I wouldn't be. I meant it as a compliment. Especially since you're not here to kill me."

"Great, so can I have my dagger back?"

He looks over my shoulder and at the dagger at the base of the tree. Without answering me, he walks over and scoops it off the ground, brushing a few pine needles off of the blade. I follow and hold my hand out to him, palm up. But he doesn't hand it back to me. Instead, he studies the small weapon with fascination, turning it over in his hand.

"This is beautiful, too."

"Excuse me?" I ask, letting my hand fall back down to my side.

"Is this made from bone?" He looks up from the dagger at me. I shrug at him and cross my arms over my chest. "And this inscription—" He traces the small engraving with his finger, reading aloud. "'Not with words alone.' What does that mean?"

I rock back slightly on my heels. "Have you ever heard of the saying 'Actions speak louder than words'?"

"No."

"Of course you haven't," I sigh. "It's an expression. Basically, it means that what you do is more significant than what you say. I often need that reminder."

He looks back down at the dagger. "But aren't words just as important?" He grips the blade tighter. "What you've done isn't the only thing that defines who you are. Words are just as powerful as action. They can inspire action in others, can't they?"

"Words without action," I answer cautiously, remembering what Azael's told me at least a hundred times, "are empty and meaningless."

He nods, seemingly to himself, and hands me back my dagger. "Of course," he says softly.

I kneel down and slip the blade back into my boot. When I stand up, I find myself looking straight into Michael's chest, which still smells heavily of honey, just as I remember. Has he gotten taller? I raise my chin to his face, which is drawn pensively.

"Penemuel."

"It's Pen," I correct.

"Right, sorry. Pen." He says my name slowly, shaping it tenderly in his mouth, committing the three letters—two consonants, one vowel—to memory. "May I ask you a question?"

"Haven't you just asked one?"

He sputters in confusion. "I—what?"

"Never mind. Go ahead."

"Have we met before?"

I furrow my brow. "You must have very poor short-term memory."

He stops me, shaking his head emphatically. "No, no. I know I've met you. But, did we meet *before*?"

"Oh." Before you died; before you were reborn as a golden, Bambi-eyed, naïve seventeen-year-old angel boy. "Yes."

"And?"

"And what?"

"What was I like? Was I kind?" He looks at me, hopeful.

"You were an archangel. I wouldn't have described you as kind, necessarily," I say. His face falls slightly. "You were strong and powerful. Loyal to Heaven until death."

He's silent for a moment before he speaks again, his voice low. "Were you there?"

"When you…?" I let the unspoken word hang in the dewy air between us. *Died*. He nods once, locking his eyes fiercely on mine. "I was."

"Could you tell me what happened?"

I back away from him. "I really don't think you want to hear."

I step back again and my ankle twists, skidding on the slippery pine needles. Before I have a chance to catch myself, Michael has one warm arm wrapped around my back and the other cradling my head. His face hovers inches above mine, his eyes deep and pleading. He rights me and removes his hands, stepping back respectfully.

"Please," he says, his voice small. "I need to know."

"Fine." I tense my jaw anxiously. "But can we find somewhere else to talk about this before I break my neck on these damn pine needles?"

"Sure." His face brightens. "I've got the perfect spot. You don't mind a bit of a hike, though, do you?"

"A hike? You know you have wings, right?"

He adjusts his shoulders, as if the weight of his hidden wings makes him uncomfortable. "I prefer to walk, if that's okay with you."

"Of course you do. All right, lead the way."

"It'll be worth it, trust me," he says, taking off into the woods.

I follow closely behind him. "We'll see."

CHAPTER 11

MICHAEL HOLDS BACK SEVERAL BRANCHES FOR ME AS WE go deeper into the forest, walking up a sloping hill. For the most part, we walk in silence. He keeps looking up through the trees and whistling back to the singing birds, answering their songs with one of his own. We jump across a yawning gully and he lands clumsily, his feet slipping on the loose, wet soil. I regard him mildly but don't offer help.

When we make it to the top of the hill, there is a wide, fast-moving stream. A thick trunk of a fallen tree bridges the cold, spraying water.

"It would be much easier to fly," I say, looking into the dark water. Large, sharp rocks poke through the rough surface and I make a face, imagining cracking my head on one of them.

"It's not about what's easy. It's about having some fun." He smiles, grabs onto one of the thick, twisted roots, and swings himself up onto the tree. Peering back at me, he holds out his hand. "Come on, you can trust me. I won't let you fall."

I ignore his hand and jump onto the tree next to him effortlessly. "Thanks, but I think I can handle myself."

He drops his hand and smiles more broadly. I turn away from him and walk confidently across the soggy tree. I glance over my shoulder to make sure he is still following me and hasn't been swept away in the water. He catches my eye and I immediately look away.

When we reach the other side of the log, I jump off, landing on the sludge of the bank. I pull my boots from the silt, wading forward slowly. I hear Michael land behind me with a splat. He starts laughing musically, and I think he's laughing at the sucking sound my boots are making in the mud, but when I turn to face him, I see he is sprawled on his back in the silt. He sits up and shakes his head, his hair flinging drops of mud in a halo around him.

I laugh once. "It looks like you're the one who needed the assistance."

He pulls himself out of the muck, his jeans dripping with mud and covered in gritty sand. His sweater sticks to his chest, and he has a smear of grime on his cheek. My fingers twitch, wanting to reach out and wipe away the dirt, but I ball my hands into fists to keep them by my side.

"You've got a bit of mud—" I motion to his cheek. He reaches up with a filthy hand and tries to wipe it away but ends up spreading more of it across his face. "Yeah, that didn't really help."

"Give me a minute," he says, walking to the bank of the stream.

He kneels down and leans forward, putting his cupped hands into the water. He brings up a handful of water and splashes it across his face. The mud runs down his neck and under the collar of his sweater as he continues to pour water over his face. He rubs his hands together under the water and washes the rest of the dirt off his arms. He shakes his hands dry and stands back up carefully. His clothes are still caked in mud that is now starting to dry stiffly in a lighter shade of brown, but his hair is mostly clean—except for the dirt that clings to the end of his curls.

I look him up and down, arching my eyebrow and pressing my lips together in a thin line.

He shrugs at me, clearly not bothered by the filth. "I think that's as good as it's going to get for now." He walks forward, moving around me carefully. I stay in my place, watching him walk on and away from the stream. "Are you coming?" he calls back.

"Yeah," I say, unsticking my boots from the soft mud and stepping onto solid ground again. "Where exactly are we going?"

Without looking back at me, he answers, "You'll see. We're almost there."

Only the sludge squeaking in his shoes tempers the hushed woods as we fall into silence again. I pull my amulet out from under my maroon shirt and grip the stone tightly in my hand. I picture Azael.

Hey, Az, you there?

Michael looks over his shoulder at me, stumbling slightly on the uneven forest floor. "What was that?"

I tuck the pendant back under my collar. "Nothing."

He looks at me quizzically but lets it drop.

We walk farther, winding along an overgrown game path until he stops so suddenly that I nearly run into his back.

"There," he says, pointing in front of us.

I follow his gaze. In front of us, the dense trees open up to frame a small, reflective teal pond that feeds into a thin, trickling creek. A frothy white waterfall slips between a notch in a precarious overhang carved into a small mountain. The waterfall splashes over the rocks at the bottom and cascades into the pond.

The ground around the pond is covered in small, smooth pebbles, not like the muddy bank of the river we crossed. Moss hangs like soft, green drapes on several branches that reach out towards the water like thirsty fingers.

I've never seen something so peaceful. I take an unintentional step forward, trying to absorb the loveliness so I can remember it later.

"I found this place when I was exploring the woods." Michael's voice drifts above the rush of water. "It's become one of my favorite places. When I'm here, I feel like I don't have to do anything or be anyone. I can just…"

"Be yourself," I finish for him.

I turn to him and see that he's watching me, his arms crossed over his muddy chest. His eyebrows are drawn high above his bright eyes, surprised. I spin away from him and take another tentative step towards the pond, the heels of my boots clicking delicately on the smooth stones. I stoop down, skim my hand through the water, and am amazed by its warmth.

"It's warm," I say dumbly.

"It's fed by an underground hot spring," he explains.

Michael joins me by the pond, slips off his shoes, and pulls his sweater over his head. I look over at him furtively as he dips his sweater in the water, letting the dried mud wash off. His chest is broad and strung with tight muscles that stretch down his abdomen, coming to a sharp V at the top of his waistband. He removes his sweater from the pond and wrings out the water, the muscles in his shoulders and arms flexing.

"You're staring," he says as he stands up and lays his shirt flat on the stony bank. I look away quickly but can feel him smiling at me. "Can you swim?"

"Of course I can," I answer sharply.

"Good. There's a cavern behind the waterfall. It's private, and there's plenty of room for both of us."

"Private?"

He nods and points up to the sky. "No one can hear inside. I've enchanted it."

I rise and look towards the waterfall, trying to see what's behind it. But if there is a cavern back there, it is completely hidden from where we stand. Now I understand why this is the one place he feels he can be himself. I glance at Michael, who is only dressed in his muddy jeans. His sword hangs casually off his belt, glinting forbiddingly in the filtered light.

He brings his arms in front of him and dives gracefully into the pond with a small splash and when he resurfaces he's smiling. He waves to me. "Come on!"

I pause for only a moment before I zip my boots off, take my dagger and slide it through my belt. I place my boots next to Michael's sweater and drop the backpack from my shoulder. I rest my hands on the edge of my shirt hesitantly before I pull it off and throw it towards my boots. Standing on the edge of the pond in my dark jeans and a thin black tank top, I let my toes skim the warm water.

I bend my legs and launch myself into the pond. The sound of rushing water suddenly replaces the chirping of the forest. I arc out of the water, throwing my heavy, wet hair behind me.

The pond is deeper than I thought it was, and I have to tread water to stay afloat. I spin around and see Michael watching me with a weird expression. I skim my hand across the surface of the pond and send a wave of water towards him.

"Now who's staring?" I mock.

"Fair enough," he laughs, a small smile twisting at the corner of his mouth.

He submerges under the surface again and swims over to the waterfall, his arms pinwheeling easily through the water. When he gets to the bottom of the warm, churning water of the fall, he turns around and waits for me. He pushes the wet hair back from his forehead, uncovering his bright eyes. I swim over to him quickly, and when I reach him, I have to blink away the water that clings to my eyelashes. I feel them slide down my cheek like tears, and I wipe them away.

"I'll give you a boost up," he says "But be careful. The rocks are slippery."

This time I don't protest to his help. He places his hands delicately on my waist, his long fingers careful to avoid my dagger, and easily lifts me up, guiding me behind the waterfall so I can reach the edge of the cave. I grab on to the cool, damp rock and pull myself up, tucking my legs under myself so I can stand.

The cavern is a little taller than I am, and I reach up to run my fingers along the rough stone. There are dozens of small, glowing jars deeper into the cave, but it is otherwise empty. I turn back to the waterfall, which rushes down in a thick curtain, hiding me from the rest of the world.

I look down between the waterfall and the rocky surface of the small mountain the cavern is set in and see Michael squinting through the spray. Reaching down, I offer him my hand. He bobs up in the water and grips it tightly as I help lift him into the cave. He slides forward on his stomach, rolls onto his back, and sits up, leaving his feet dangling over the edge.

"Thanks," he says, running a hand through his glistening hair.

I clear my throat. "No problem."

I turn around again, away from Michael, and walk deeper into the cavern towards the lights. The thin opening of the cave ends in a medium-sized round room. A short ledge is carved into the rock around the perimeter of the room, forming a sort of slender bench.

Michael skirts past me, careful not to touch me, and walks into the room. He is too tall for the cave, so his shoulders are hunched slightly forward and his head is ducked. He sits on the edge of the bench and motions for me to join him.

I enter the room, scrutinizing the collection of glowing mason jars.

"A little trick I learned," he explains.

"Is it fire?" I ask, leaning closer.

"It is," he says, watching me carefully. I sit down on the ground in front of the jars and lean back on the bench. "Now will you tell me what happened?"

"For an angel," I answer quietly, "you are rather morbid."

He leans forward on his elbows and looks down at his hands that rest folded between his knees. "No one will tell me what happened. It was my death. Is it really too much to ask for an explanation?"

I remain quiet for a moment, pulling my necklace out to hold in my hand and slowly twining the chain around my fingers. "It's not too much to ask," I allow. "I would want to know if it were me. Although, if I were killed, I wouldn't be able to ask any questions afterwards."

Michael lowers his eyes to the golden glowing jars. "I know not everyone gets a second chance at life. That's why I have to know what happened in my first—so I can live this one better."

No one gets a second chance at life, I think to myself. *No one but you.*

"I need to know what happened," he continues, raising his eyes to meet mine. "Please."

The faint sound of the waterfall drifts back into the cave. I hold his stare, sitting in silence for a several of his loud heartbeats before I finally nod.

"I know you don't remember me, but I clearly remember you," I begin. "And I remember that day."

He watches me attentively.

I close my eyes, evoking the memory. "Lucifer killed you," I say, my voice tight.

"My brother," he says quietly.

Slowly, I open my eyes and look at him across the glowing jars. The bright blue of his eyes is now dark and reflective, reminding me of the warm pond below the cave. I nod my head again.

"Yes, your brother."

CHAPTER 12

"When God set about creating man, Lucifer was cast from Heaven."

He nods. "By me, I've heard."

"Right. He refused to bend a knee to humans, believed that God was making a mistake by creating man—something with free will. He was jealous, angry that we weren't enough. He was convinced it was his destiny to lead the angels, to save them from whatever fate man would condemn us to, and for that he was banished to Hell. Many angels fell with him."

"How many?" He leans forward and his face appears to be glowing in the squirming flames of the mason jars.

"One third of all angels in Heaven."

He's silent for a moment as this sinks in. Finally, he asks, "Did you fall?"

"No," I answer, fiddling with the cold chain of my pendant. "Not then. I didn't think humans would be so bad, so I remained in Heaven. But not for much long after..." I shake my head. He doesn't need to know that yet. "Trapped in Hell, though, Lucifer had plenty of time to let his anger fester. He fell from grace, was disrobed of his angelic title, and labeled a demon. The first demon."

Michael's eyes fall to the collection of jars. A serious silence hangs between us, tension sparking in the small room of the cave like electricity.

"What he did," I go on, "really wasn't so bad when you think about it. He said that he wouldn't honor anyone over God, and for that he was to face endless suffering? He spoke up for something he believed in. It started out pure but then—" I shake my head, letting the words die in my mouth. *Pure motives mean nothing when they distort under ego.*

Lucifer thought he knew more, could rule better, than God. His good intentions warped into a play for power. He overstepped his bounds, grew more and more arrogant in his claim for the throne. Heaven could never let a threat like him stay amongst the angels; he's lucky he was allowed to live. But which fate is worse: death, or living in exile? Revenge soured him into something almost unrecognizable.

"It didn't take long for Lucifer to escape his chains. I don't think God ever intended to have him imprisoned in Hell forever. I think it was meant as penance, that the angels hoped he would change his mind. Obviously, he didn't. After a few decades, Lucifer was able to walk the Earth again. At this time, there still weren't any humans, but his freedom threw a wrench in Heaven's plan.

"No angel wanted to start a species in a hostile environment; they wouldn't survive a day with Lucifer stalking around. So plans were made to destroy him. But he was the first of his kind, and Heaven had never had to kill a demon before. They didn't have the means to destroy him. That was when the seven archangels' swords were cast. Jophiel, Chamuel, Gabriel, Raphael, Uriel, Zadkiel and you were given great swords that would slay any and all evil. Almost all of the swords were lost or destroyed in battle, which is why yours is so unique. It is the lone survivor."

He looks down at his sword, adjusting it on his hip. I flinch, but bury it under my words before he notices.

"You were the most powerful of all of the archangels and led Heaven's army in battle. The fighting raged on for years. Each year, more and more angels fell from grace, abandoning a cause they no longer believed in." I pause. "And that's when Azael and I fell."

I watch him measuredly, carefully gauging his reaction, but he doesn't say anything.

I take a steady breath. "When an angel falls, they begin to die. Their heart stops beating, their soul begins to wither away. Eventually, the heart and the soul are completely eaten away by the poison that replaces our blood."

I look up at him, watching as he processes everything I tell him. His forehead creases, as if he doesn't believe me, so I remove my dagger from my belt and pull the blade across my hand, splitting the skin. Black blood begins to pool in my palm, and I wince at the feeling of holding my own blood. I let it spill out of my hand and fall to the ground next to me as I place the dagger back at my hip and ball my hand into a fist, waiting for the flayed skin to heal.

"My eyes used to be a light green, almost translucent." The words slip from my lips before I can pull them back. "Azael's were a mossy green," I say to the ground. "But the moment we fell from grace, our eyes changed to this violet."

He lifts his eyes and looks across the cave at me, holding me in a gaze that neither of us is willing to break. The fire from the jars dances wildly in his darkening eyes, as if the flames live inside of him.

"I could imagine you with green eyes," he says softly.

I clear my throat, pulling my eyes from him, and continue. "Azael and I fought in hundreds of battles. We were repeatedly told lies—from both sides— to persuade us to fight. There was so much senseless violence. We fought with and against our friends and saw them die in front of us. I had to kill angels I had known since before Earth knew light. My hands will never be clean of their blood." My voice sounds strangled so I stop, tightening my fist. "The one thing we never saw, though, was compassion."

There's a long beat of silence, and he shifts in his seat, uncomfortable. I think he's going to say something, but only his silence speaks to me.

"No angel is perfect," I begin in a whisper. "And Lucifer was far from perfect, but there was no forgiving his faults, no understanding. I couldn't fight for Heaven when their definition of good was so narrow that it excluded any instance of weakness. When it punished doubt. Being righteous does not always mean being right. It simply means trying to do what you think is right."

I twist the dark chain of my necklace and look at Michael. His eyebrows are drawn together and his lips are pursed. I can't tell whether what I've said upset him or confused him, so I close my eyes. But I can feel that he's still watching me.

"I laid down my sword for Heaven and pledged my allegiance to Hell with Azael. We fought together, side by side." I open my eyes but keep them lowered to my lap. "The war seemed like it was coming to an end. Heaven continued to lose angels to Hell, and those who remained loyal soon grew weary of the fighting. Less and less forces arrived in battles, and Lucifer's growing army was conquering Heaven with relative ease. Hell had no moral contract to constrict our fighting, and we became more powerful with each win."

"How many angels died?" he asks solemnly.

"Scores of them, but no one knows for sure. There wasn't anyone counting the losses," I answer angrily. "There was no dignity to the angels who died. The dead from both sides were left where they had fallen."

His face is drawn.

"I can stop," I offer. The worst of the story has yet to come, and I'm worried that he won't be able to handle it.

"No," he says quickly. "I need to know."

I study his face, trying to read the dark clouds of emotions that pass over him, but I can't decipher his thoughts.

"The final battle was the most violent of all," I say carefully. "The last of Heaven's forces arrived, bringing the fire of Heaven to Earth. The land burned. The archangels who still had their weapons—you, Gabriel, and Raphael—sliced their way through the throng of demons that surrounded them. Azael and I held back the other angels as the more powerful demons charged the archangels. The only way we could differentiate enemy from ally was their eyes. Violet was safe, but everyone else was a threat.

"I remember throwing a knife into the stomach of an angel with amber eyes that was wielding a bow and arrow. Her name was Amitiel, an angel of truth, but I used to call her Ami. We weren't exactly close, but I didn't want to kill her…"

Michael's gaze falls to the flames. There's an ache in my core and I want so badly for him to say something, to know what he's thinking. He should yell at me, tell me what a monster I am for killing an angel I knew—*angels* I knew. Maybe even a friend. But he doesn't, and somehow his silence is worse than any insult he could throw.

"She collapsed and I retrieved my knife, and then there were others—some I knew, others I didn't. An angel with a slingshot, another with a spear…" The deaths all play across the back of my mind like a movie, and try as I might, I can't look away. "After I killed them, I turned to make sure Azael was safe, but I couldn't find him. I kept calling out to him."

It feels like I'm back in the throng of battle. I can feel the heavy wings pulsing around me, knocking me off my path as I run in search of him. I remember my throat, raw from screaming, and the heat I couldn't escape.

"For those five minutes we were separated, I was convinced he was dead. I was ready to give up, just let myself be killed, but somehow... I survived. And then I saw him. He was climbing up a steep, rocky cliff with his scythe held in his teeth.

"You and Lucifer were locked in battle at the top of the mountain. Lucifer slashed out at your abdomen, but you were able to avoid the worst of his strike. Your face was set in angry determination, even as you became drenched in your blood. I was frozen where I stood, motionless in the midst of chaos. I couldn't look away from you." My cheeks burn and I let my hair fall around my shoulders. "You never wavered, never hesitated. Until Azael made it to the top of the mountain."

"Azael," he repeats.

"He walked forward, positioning himself so that he was standing almost directly between you and Lucifer. I don't know if he knew what he was doing—if he was sacrificing himself, distracting you, or if he thought he could help Lucifer kill you. Probably a bit of each, knowing Az. He's reckless in battle. He never thinks about the consequences of his actions. Never plans..."

I stop for a moment, remembering how angry I was at what Azael had done. Never for a moment did he consider me when he climbed up that mountain. He didn't even say goodbye when he left me during battle.

He should have at least said goodbye.

"You drew your sword back to strike," I go on, "and I let out a horrible bloodcurdling scream that stopped some of those fighting around me. Everyone turned to stare at what I was looking at, and I couldn't stop screaming."

I pause again as the anger fades and I remember the horror I felt in that moment. I was terrified that he was going to strike Azael and I would have to watch as he turned to ash in front of me. I tighten my grip on my necklace, the sharp stone cutting into the soft flesh of my palm. I lift my eyes, looking at him, mystified.

"But you didn't strike," I whisper. "You looked at me."

Just like you are looking at me now, I think to myself. His eyes hold the same mixture of surprise and concentration.

"In that brief moment of hesitation, Lucifer grabbed his sword, held it high above his head, and brought it down so forcefully into your chest that its tip sliced through you completely, the end of it reaching out of your back, coated in the reddest blood I had ever seen. The blade pierced through your heart." Michael flinches, but I continue. "You collapsed to the ground, the sword still stuck in your chest. The sky went black, and when the darkness lifted, the angels were gone. But you remained, crumpled on the top of the mountain.

"I ran up the mountain to Azael, not believing he had truly survived. But he had. He laughed at me, thought I was losing my mind, and he kept reassuring me that he was fine. And he was, for the most part. He had broken bones, bruises, and horrible gashes covering his body, but he would heal. He *did* heal." I run a shaky hand through my hair.

That moment still makes me sick, even after all this time. The anger at his recklessness, the fear that I would lose him forever, and then the flood of dizzy relief that he was alive. It all happened so fast, but it replays in my mind in slow motion and makes me nauseous.

"Lucifer told him to reap your soul. I stood there and watched, horrified. I didn't fight for Heaven, I no longer belonged to the angels, but somewhere, inside the pit of my stomach, it felt wrong."

"Wrong," he echoes.

I nod and lick my lips. "He pulled your soul from your chest and was burned terribly by your light. He still has a scar running up his left arm, if you look closely, from where your soul wrapped around him."

Reaching forward, I grab his wrist in my hand and trace the path of Azael's scar up his forearm slowly. I freeze, suddenly aware of my touch and how still he has become, and I look up to meet his eyes. I can hear his heartbeat in his chest. It's faster, slightly uneven.

With a sharp intake of breath, I let go of him and sit back against the rocky bench, pushing myself as far away from him as I can. *Stupid.* I wrap my arms around myself.

"Lucifer took what was left of you to Hell. Azael went with him, conferring about how best to keep you caged. I had no part in the process. They believed that I was too fragile and undone by what I had seen to be of any help. And maybe they were right, in the moment. I had just left Heaven to stop a war I didn't believe in, and my brother then played an instrumental role in the success of Hell. *I* unwittingly played a part in Hell's success." I drop my necklace. "No one has ever thought me too weak to handle anything since then."

Michael rests his hand on his chest, his broad fingers spread out over his heart. When he removes his hand, he looks at me. "Pierced through the heart."

"Yes."

"Somehow I knew."

He points at a thin silver scar that curves over his chest. It is so thin that I didn't notice it before. I lean towards him, across the jars of light, studying the scar. It is positioned right over his heart, which beats defiantly in his chest now. *He should be dead.* I look up into his eyes and see that he is watching me closely.

"Pen?"

A coil wraps around my insides. "Yes?"

"Everyone is allowed a moment of weakness."

"Not me." I sit back on my heels. "I can't allow myself to be seen as weak."

"Why?"

I bite my lip, drawing a thin trickle of blood. "Vulnerability and uncertainty are dangerous and often exploited."

He shifts forward towards me. "I hesitated."

"For a split second," I say harshly, "you hesitated. And that's all it took."

"And then I was killed."

Because of me, I add in my mind.

"I may not remember what I was thinking in that moment, but I don't blame you, or your brother, for my death."

I look at him guardedly. "Maybe you should."

CHAPTER 13

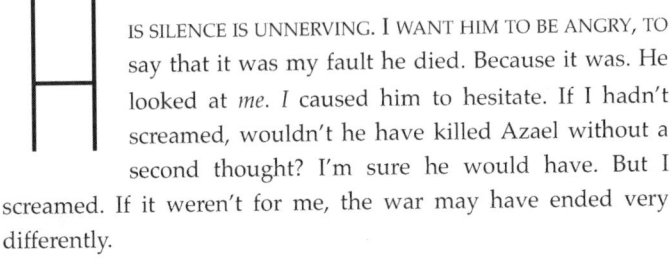

HIS SILENCE IS UNNERVING. I WANT HIM TO BE ANGRY, TO say that it was my fault he died. Because it was. He looked at *me*. *I* caused him to hesitate. If I hadn't screamed, wouldn't he have killed Azael without a second thought? I'm sure he would have. But I screamed. If it weren't for me, the war may have ended very differently.

I stand up restlessly, my hands balled into tight fists at my sides, and move to the front of the cave.

"Where are you going?" he asks, rising as if to follow me.

"I just need some air." I look back at him. "Just—just give me a second, okay?"

Reluctantly, he sits back down, his hands resting on his slowly drying jeans.

I walk unsteadily through the narrow passage from the warm, glowing room to the opening of the cave. It's much cooler out here, with a soft spray from the waterfall misting the floor and the walls, making the rocks slippery. I look over my shoulder and can just barely see Michael's silhouette. He is leaning forward, his head resting low in his hands. He's upset.

Of course he is, I think. I just told him how he died. I admitted to him that I was the reason why he died. I may as well have driven the sword through his chest myself. Hearing about how he died, learning what part I played in his death, couldn't be easy.

I sit down on the ledge of the opening and let my legs dangle over the sharp rocks. The sun is moving lazily across the sky as the early afternoon drags on. I straighten my leg, breaking the solid curtain of water with my foot, and try to contact Azael again.

Az. C'mon, are you there?

I wait anxiously, worried that I won't be able to reach him. We've never tried to communicate from this far away. And if I can't get through to him…

I may really be in this alone.

Right as the panic begins to set in, I hear a faint answer.
Pen?

Azael! Relief floods through me. *I'm so glad to hear from you.*

See, I knew you would start to realize my worth as soon as I was gone. I'm so under-appreciated. Nobody knows what they have until it's gone!

I smile to myself. *I'm glad to see that you haven't changed in the hours we've been separated. I would have thought some space may have matured you.*

Me? Mature? He scoffs. *Never. I'll forever stay a Lost Boy.*
Where are you, anyway?

Hicksville, America, it would seem. I don't know really, I've been tailing Lilith across Texas. And let me tell you, the apocalypse could not come soon enough.

Are you wearing a cowboy hat? Because I've always seen you as more of a saloon girl.

I would make a superb harlot. But I think I may be too deep in the South to play up the old west theme.

No honky-tonk pianos for you to sit upon?

None! It's a shame, really. It's all guns, trucks, and beer down here.

Well, guns are sort of old west. Not so much with the trucks...

He laughs dryly. *So, did you find what you were looking for?*

Yeah, I found him.

And how is dear Michael? He drawls.

I tug at my necklace, sliding the stone up and down the chain, making it hum. *He's... he's alone. Ariel and Sablo are nowhere in sight.*

Convenient. It's too bad Gus was specific with his instructions. 'Protect him.' And how's that going?

He's safe. He wanted me to tell him about how he died.

There's a pause.

Azael?

And did you tell him?

I did.

How'd he take it?

I glance towards the back of the cave. *As expected, I would say.*

Ah, so he's threatened to seek revenge on me, make you watch as he fillets me with his broadsword, and then kill you? The little beast.

No, I mean, he didn't seem upset that we were involved. In fact, he said he didn't blame us for what happened.

Awfully big of him. But I would like some credit!

I don't know if I believe him. I kick my feet out and into the waterfall again, letting the warm water bounce off my legs and splash me.

Then watch your back. Hey, listen, I've gotta go. It looks like I'm going to a rodeo tonight. Plenty of idiots to feed on there.

Have fun.

Oh yeah, I'm sure it will be more fun than a barrel of monkeys!

Actually, I heard that clowns hide in barrels at rodeos. To distract the bulls.

Well if that doesn't sound like it crawled right out of a nightmare...

IGNITE

I laugh. *You'll fit right in.*

Fingers crossed! I'll update you later if I have anything of importance. Like if I happen upon the world's largest ball of yarn or some other stupid attraction. You'd be surprised how many there are out here. It's nauseating. Good luck with Goldilocks.

Thanks and good luck— I hear a click, like a phone hanging up, and realize he's gone. I let the necklace fall back down, the cool chain resting on my collarbone. I take a steadying breath, kick my leg through the waterfall once more, and roll over to my knees.

When I look up, I see Michael standing a few feet away from me. I freeze.

"Eavesdropping?" I ask. "How long have you been standing there?"

"Who were you talking to?"

I stand and cross my arms defensively. "How long have you been standing there?" I ask again.

"Long enough. Was it Azael?"

I bite my lip, trying to come up with a convincing lie, but it would be pointless. He's heard Azael's voice before. "Yes, it was Az."

"Is he coming to get you?" He steps forward into the small patch of sunlight that filters in past the water. His bare chest is bathed in the orange light of mid-afternoon. "Are you, I mean, are you going with him, wherever he's going?"

So he didn't hear everything. He doesn't know I'm staying. My shoulders relax slightly. "No, I'm staying. Or going. I don't really know, but I'm on my own for now."

"Sounds lonely."

"I'm fine. I can handle myself."

He smiles. "I believe I've heard that about you."

"You make me uncomfortable," I blurt out without thinking.

"That's awfully blunt of you," he says, raising a surprised eyebrow. "Shouldn't you be the one who makes me uncomfortable? After all, you believe yourself to be the catalyst to my death. If that were true, wouldn't you be a danger to me in this second life?"

"Not the catalyst," I correct. "The catalyst was the start of the war. What I did simply guaranteed your death. And maybe I *should* make you uncomfortable."

He comes even closer, reaching out his hand. I think he's going to touch my cheek, but instead he reaches over my shoulder and runs his hand through the stream of water. "Do you know why I hesitated?"

"No. Do you?"

"No. But I'll find out." He removes his hand, smirks at me, and then dives through the waterfall into the pond below.

I lean over the edge of the rocks and call out, "What is that supposed to mean?"

His musical laughter floats up over the soft roar of the churning water.

I back up, run a few steps, and launch myself gracefully off of my perch, breaking through the waterfall with a twist. I hit the warm water of the pond with a splash, flipping twice under the water. I stay below the surface of the water longer than any human could, letting myself drift to the dark bottom. I begin to drift back up to the surface but I grab onto the tangles of weeds, holding myself on the rocky bottom of the pond. I look up to the surface.

The water sends ripples across the sky as Michael's legs tread in the water. I can see him turning around, looking for me to resurface, but I keep ahold of the weeds. He sticks his head under the surface, squinting through the water. When he sees me, he submerges himself completely, blowing air from his mouth and sending a stream of bubbles floating above him. He swims to the floor of the pond and stands in another tangle of weeds. The tip of his sword clanks lightly on the small, round stones.

I stay seated on the ground, wrapping the weeds around my arm securely. He motions to them. He mouths, "Are you stuck?"

and I shake my head no. He tilts his head, puzzled. I make no move to explain. I just want to stay under the water, submerged in a muffled world where I am not expected to talk to anyone. Especially him.

Michael's cheeks expand animatedly, like he's imitating a puffer fish. I think he is joking, trying to make me laugh, so at first I ignore him. His eyes widen and the veins in his head, neck, and across his chest begin to bulge. He thrashes his arms, trying to swim back to the surface, but his foot is caught in one of the thick knots of weeds. He bends down and pulls at his leg, trying to free himself.

The harder he pulls, the tighter the weeds twist around his legs. With one last exaggerated yank, he seems to run out of energy. His eyes start to roll backwards in his head, and I realize he isn't joking. He shouldn't have to breathe!

With my free hand, I grab my dagger and cut through the weeds I've wrapped around my arms. I swim over to Michael, pushing through the thick tangles of slippery weeds with my thin fingers, and saw at the green plants that anchor him to the floor of the pond. Sharp barbs on darker black weeds rip into my knuckles as I drag the blade back and forth, trying to cut through the stringy roots as fast as I can. I look up at his face and can only see the whites of his eyes.

Shit.

When I cut the last of the weeds, he begins to drift back to the surface, but he isn't swimming. His limbs float lifelessly around him. I push myself off the floor of the pond and grab onto his waist, towing him behind me back to the surface.

I hit the surface of the water with my arms wrapped around an unconscious Michael. We bob in the water and I shake him, trying desperately to wake him. His lips are no longer a light peach; they've turned a cold blue. Even his skin has lost its glow, his cheeks their rosiness. He looks gray. He looks like Hell. It's not right to see him drained of his light.

I pull him next to me as I swim over to the shore, hardly noticing his weight. When I hit the shallows, I stand up and tug him out of the water and onto his back. I bend down and rest my ear to his chest. After a pause that seems to drag on painfully long, I hear his heart beating feebly.

Not dead. I tell myself. *He's not dead.*

I clasp my hands together and press down on his chest with the heel of my hand.

One. Two. Three. Four. Five.

He doesn't move.

I do it again.

One. Two. Three. Four. Five.

Still nothing.

I hover closely over his face, waiting for his eyes to open.

"Come on, you stupid angel."

One. Two. Three.

"This cannot be how you die!"

Four. Five.

"Don't do this—" I curse under my breath. "I won't be the reason you die again."

He remains motionless.

"I'm supposed to keep you safe," I say through gritted teeth.

I lean closer, plugging his nose with my fingers and pressing my mouth to his. I breathe into him, his lungs filling and chest rising with my breath. I sit back and look at his face.

When he doesn't move, I don't wait to start compressions again.

One. Two. Three—

And then he sits up, choking and sputtering on swallowed water. He turns away from me and throws up, gasping for air after all of the water is emptied from his lungs and stomach.

I sigh in relief, rolling off my toes to move back from him and sit by the edge of the woods. I give him space, but I watch him closely, making sure he's really okay.

He coughs a few more times, drags his hand across his mouth, and then turns to look at me. The color is gradually returning to his face, and I let out a small breath I didn't realize I was holding.

"Did you just save my life?" he asks incredulously.

"I think I almost killed you again," I say, curling my knees up to my chest.

"But you saved my life. I thought I was going to save yours. When you didn't resurface, I thought…"

"I'm a demon. I don't need to breathe. And neither should you. Why didn't you just cut yourself free with your sword?" I ask angrily.

He pauses, pushes himself up on his elbow, and looks down at his hip, where his sword still hangs. "I guess I forgot it was there. I couldn't breathe, and I was getting dizzy. I would have died." His eyes flick back up to me. "You saved me."

"You need to stop saying that," I say, looking away from him, uncomfortable.

"You did though!"

"Well then, let's call it even," I say flatly. "You spared my brother in your first life, which I effectively ended, and I saved your second life."

"For the record, *you* didn't end my first life. Lucifer did."

I roll my eyes.

"But if it makes you more comfortable, fine." He smiles at me gratefully. "We're even."

"Don't patronize me," I say, insulted.

He draws his face in confusion, the ends of his mouth turning down in a slight frown. With great effort, he tries to stand. He stumbles clumsily on his feet, attempting to regain his balance. I lower my knees, my body tense and ready to catch him if he falls, but he puts his hands up. I sit back but don't relax. He looks clammy, his torso pale and still very damp from the pond. Even though his cheeks are rosy again, I'm worried the color is too bright to be healthy and he may be flushed from a fever.

When he steadies himself, he walks over to me and sloppily lowers himself to the ground. He hits the pebbled bank jarringly, scattering loose stones, and winces. I watch his face contort in pain for a moment before it slackens with relief.

He turns his head and looks at me, sincerity printed across his face like ink on a page. "I'm not trying to patronize you."

I regard him suspiciously.

"You should learn to trust people more," he advises. " I'm not trying to trick you, but you keep looking at me like I'm going to do something awful."

"From my experience, it's only a matter of time before someone does. It's in my best interest not to trust anyone," I say. "I've learned that the hard way, and it's not a lesson I'll soon forget."

He considers this. "Letting yourself be vulnerable can be hard."

"No, it's not that vulnerability is hard." My voice comes out harsher than I mean it to, so I take a breath. "Vulnerability is dangerous."

"But sometimes it's the only way you can get to know someone," he says, evaluating me through wet blond hair that has fallen back over his eyes.

His cheeks blaze a brighter red, and he has a strange look in his vivid blue eyes. He looks delirious. I reach towards him, push back his hair, and rest my cold palm on his forehead.

"Pen?"

"Shut up," I silence him.

I move my hand across his forehead and then down onto one of his cheeks. He watches me as I lean in towards him, pressing my hand on his other cheek. The heel of my hand grazes his lip. His skin is warm, but not feverish. Self-consciously, I remove my hand and curl it in my lap.

"You're vulnerable now, aren't you?" he asks hoarsely. His throat must still burn from choking on the pond water he swallowed.

"I thought you had a fever," I explain.

He lowers his chin so his eyes are even with mine. "Couldn't I have killed you, if I wanted to?"

I look at his sword and then up to the thin scar over his heart. "Maybe you are delirious."

"Why won't you answer me?"

"Fine. You want an answer?" I look down to his sword which still waits, forgotten, at his hip. I try to imagine him picking it up and piercing it through me. But I can't. The image doesn't make sense. "You don't seem the type."

"To kill?" he asks.

I nod.

"But I have before, haven't I?"

"Yes. Before." I look away from him, over to the waterfall at the slowly sinking sun. The orange of the sky is bruising into a light purple edged in blue. "But you don't seem to be the same Michael as before. And when I saw you again, I thought you would be. I thought you'd be *exactly* the same." Angels never change. Not really. But he's... "You're different. You seem—"

"Weaker?" he asks, deflated.

I shake my head. "Kinder."

He had asked me earlier if he had been kind in Heaven. But he was far from kind, which is why I'm so surprised by him now. The way he speaks to me, how he treats me, it's not only foreign to me, but it's uncharacteristic of the Michael I knew before. No one seems to be insignificant to this new Michael. No one's opinion is wrong or invalid.

I chew on my lip. If I were to be completely honest, I would tell him that he is also stronger. He may not have the brute strength and assuredness he had when he commanded Heaven as an archangel, but he has a different kind of strength now. A strength that doesn't require force or persuasion. He's genuine and good, a leader people would be proud to follow into battle.

But the change I notice most in him is his strength of conviction.

He fights back now. He questions the past. He doesn't simply accept things the way that they are. When I look at him closely, I see a spark in his eyes that I haven't seen in over a millennium.

Michael could bring about a revolution.

Michael could change the world.

And who am I to stop him?

CHAPTER 14

WE SPEND THE REST OF THE AFTERNOON RELAXING BY THE water, waiting for Michael to regain his strength. He keeps picking up the small pebbles that are scattered across the ground and skimming them over the smooth surface of the pond. They bounce all the way across the water until they hit the bottom of the waterfall and disappear in the spray.

I lean back and lie down on the bank, my bare feet resting in the warm water of the pond. I look up through the canopy of trees to the sky, which appears to be fractured through the spindly green branches. I feel Michael lie down next to me and I glance over at him briefly before looking back up at the sky. He raises his arms and folds them under his head.

"It's amazing how different everything looks from down here," he says.

"What do you mean?" I turn my head and watch him.

The slowly setting sun casts a soft light across his face, illuminating his smile, and I can see the broken sky reflected in his eyes.

"From Earth, everything seems so big and infinite. It's not like that from Heaven. Earth looks miniature and insignificant from up there. I think that's why so many angels are indifferent."

"Indifferent?" I ask, surprised. "Angels aren't indifferent." Certainly not when it comes to Earth, when it comes to their precious human race.

He shrugs, his head bouncing lightly on his arms. "Maybe not before, but they are now. They're more preoccupied with themselves than anything down here. They don't even seem to care about what happens on Earth. Haven't you noticed?"

I consider what he says, trying to imagine the angels sitting around, watching Earth with disinterest. I can't seem to connect the thought to an image, though. When I was an angel, there was nothing more important than the creation of humankind. I find it hard to believe that they would have given up so easily on humanity after a couple hundred centuries.

"Look at all of the wars that are left unchecked," Michael continues. "How many people die from things as insignificant as disease? How many people kill each other without any provocation? The world is tearing apart at the seams, and humans are self-destructing. They're praying to angels who just don't care."

"I think Hell can take a good portion of the credit," I say in defense. "That's our job. We're the ones who start the wars and spread disease. We're the ones who corrupt the good into madmen."

"Are you, though?" he asks, glancing sideways at me. "Humans were built with the capacity for evil. They're complacent with whatever happens as long as *they* survive. I bet they'd do just fine at ruining this planet on their own."

I look back through the trees again. "That would make us obsolete."

"Demons?"

"Demons and angels. If angels don't care anymore, and demons don't have any work left to do, what then? Do we just wait for them to implode and start over again with a new species? Speed up the process maybe?"

I think about the Lilim virus. While it originated from a demon, it is spread by humans. It's humans who let the virus live on, infecting anyone they can. How long would it take for a virus like that to spread throughout all of the world? Would humans eventually become extinct? Maybe they are adept to end the world after all.

"You can't think everyone is bad," I say. I can't imagine Michael—God's favorite angel—having such a negative disposition towards mankind. It's... backwards.

"I don't. I think that everyone has goodness in them. But this goodness doesn't erase the capacity for evil."

I feel him look over at me, but I keep my eyes glued to the sky

He continues. "Being good is hard. It takes a conscious effort to do the right thing, especially when doing the wrong thing is so simple." He takes a deep breath and looks back through the branches that stretch out above us. "Giving in to evil is like falling asleep. You can just close your eyes and submit to the darkness. The shadows will spill forward and steal all of the light from you, like a well of black ink spilling over fresh parchment. It's an unending night, and it's very tempting to just sleep forever."

The image of parchment drowning in ink fills my mind. The ink rolls across the paper and spreads out like a starless night sky. No wonder people are so easily tempted to evil. Who would choose hot, bright noon to the cool blanket of night?

"*Everyone* has goodness in them?" I repeat, skeptical.

"Everyone," he confirms. "Some people just forget that they do. If they only opened their eyes, they would see." He rolls onto his side, propping his head up on his hand, and looks at me. "You have goodness in you."

I laugh disbelievingly. "Oh, do I now? And where would that be? I have no heart, no soul. Where is my goodness hiding?"

He looks at my chest. "No heart?"

"Or soul!" I remind him, forcing cheeriness into my voice that's so sweet my stomach hurts.

"I don't believe that."

I grab his hand that is resting on his hip and place it firmly on my chest. I hold it there for a few minutes, letting him feel the hollowness. He watches my face, anticipating to feel a heartbeat. But there's nothing. I let go of his wrist and drop his hand.

"No heartbeat," I say, rolling onto my back again. "No heart."

He pauses for a moment, his face sad. "You don't have to have a heart to be good. Or even a soul, for that matter."

"Isn't that where the term 'heartless' comes from?" I smile bitterly up at the trees, avoiding his gaze. "Or 'soulless monster'?"

He's quiet.

"That's me all right: a heartless, soulless monster. Cruel with compassion. I can kill someone without even blinking."

There's a long silence that stretches out between us. It joins us on the bank of the water, wedging between us like a wall built from everything that is left unsaid. It's painted with crude graffiti that reminds us both what we're supposed to be. Enemies.

He ignores the graffiti.

"Can you see me, Pen?" he asks seriously.

The invisible wall crumbles and I turn to look at him, confused. "What do you mean? Of course I can see you. You're sitting right next to me."

"No." He calmly shakes his head and takes a deep breath. He leans forward and looks at me meaningfully. "Can you *see* me? Because I can see you. And I know that, below your tough exterior, you are good. Because I can see it." His gaze flicks over my ribs again before he looks back into my eyes. "It's there. You just have to be brave enough to see the good in yourself."

I turn farther away from him and mumble, "You must be suffering brain damage from lack of oxygen."

"You don't have to believe me now, Pen," he says. I hear him shift and lie back down on the bank. His movements sends small ripples through the water, letting it lap lightly at my ankles. "One day, you'll wake up. You'll see what I see and then you'll know that you are good. There is light in you."

I'm agitated by his naïve hopefulness. What I am and what I've done cannot be undone overnight. The last of my light was extinguished long ago. I've been a lost cause since I fell from Earth. All of Heaven has given up on me, told me that I am evil through the core. Why should he believe any differently? Why should I?

"Right," I whisper. "Don't hold your breath."

"I don't think I'll have to," he answers back quietly. "Besides, I should probably refrain from holding my breath for a while. Last time, it didn't work out too well for me. Although, you did kiss me."

I can hear the grin in his voice and I want nothing more than to slap it off his stupid face. "I did not kiss you!"

"If you say so."

I consider arguing the point more but I decide to let it go.

We're both quiet for a few minutes. The silence is filled by the soft noise of the waterfall splashing distantly into the pond. I close my eyes, listening. I hear the water, birds singing their last songs of the day, and the soft sound of Michael breathing. The sound is comforting, lulling me into a hazy daydream.

"Pen?"

I snap my eyes open, mildly annoyed. "Michael?"

"What were you like as an angel?"

"Angelic," I say sarcastically.

He laughs. "I mean it. I can't remember what you were like —I can't remember what I was like either, so don't take it personally. If you don't want to answer, you don't have to. I was just curious."

"Curiosity killed the cat," I warn.

"What cat? I don't understand..."

I roll my eyes. "Okay, what was I like as an angel? Let's see. Azael and I weren't important in Heaven. We didn't have special titles, talents, or anything like that. Just two faceless angels in the crowd. I wrote a lot, transcribing prophecies, documenting different fates, that kind of thing. Azael worked with souls. He would match up two souls who were destined to be together, according to the fates I wrote. *Soul mates*, he called them. I don't know, we were just typical angels. White wings, uniforms. Azael wore blue like all of the angels who worked with souls, and I wore gold like the rest of the scribes. We were ordinary. I wasn't anything special."

"I find that difficult to believe."

"I was hardly the powerful archangel you were. I was insignificant. My fall from grace didn't upset the order of things in the least."

"Every loss upset the balance. Every angel that fell was significant," he says severely.

"How do you know? You can't even remember fighting in the war. You can't remember the disinterest Heaven showed when the lower level angels fell, the complete lack of compassion for the lives lost! No one even batted an eye. Not even *you*."

He's quiet, but when I look over at him, I see the muscles in his jaw are tense. I've gone too far.

I curse under my breath. "Sorry," I say quietly, backpedaling.

He doesn't say anything. His face is set in a stoic mix of anger and despair. *So much for trying to win him over for Hell*. The last thing I need to do is upset him and have him ask me to leave. I can't destroy the bridge I've tentatively begun constructing.

I take a deep breath, trying to calm myself down. "I met you before the war."

His jaw relaxes and he looks over at me. "You did?"

I nod. "A few times. I don't think you were ever able to remember my name. You didn't really concern yourself with angels like me. I was trivial in the grand scheme of things. Like I said—nameless, faceless, insignificant."

"I remember your name now," he says. He watches my eyes intently. "Pen."

"Very impressive."

He gives me a small smile. That's progress. "I know you told me what I was during the war. But what about before the war? What was I like then?"

"Serious," I say quickly, not needing to think about it. "You were always a no-nonsense kind of angel, war or not."

"And were you nonsense?" he guesses.

"Everyone was nonsense."

"Was there anyone that I—" He struggles to finish his thought and blushes.

"Were involved with?"

He wants to know who he left behind when he died. If there's anyone in Heaven missing him more than usual.

"No one in particular," I answer. "Like I said, you didn't like distractions. But you did have an impressive string of lovers. Every angel was pining for your attention, for one night with the great archangel."

He looks down, embarrassed. "And you?"

"I was not on the string," I say, startled.

"Oh—no, I didn't mean—I just wanted to know," he stammers. "What I meant to ask was were you ever... involved with anyone?"

Now I blush. I turn my face back up to the sky, watching the light seep out of the day. "I was alone. Like I said, I wasn't anything special."

I was always alone. I had a friend or two periodically, but eventually they would tire of me and move on. Azael didn't have many friends, but he always had company. He was strong, handsome, and rebellious—a dangerous mix that many angels unwillingly fell for.

Despite the fact that Azael was always surrounded with admirers, he still found time for me. I was his sister, and he tried his best to not leave me alone for too long. But at the end of the day, even though I knew I could rely on Azael, the only person I could ever trust completely was myself.

I feel Michael watching me. I sit up and let my long, dark hair shield my face from him.

"Don't you have somewhere you need to be?" I ask, suddenly wanting to be alone again. I'm tired of answering questions. "Like a curfew or something?"

He looks up at the sky and pushes himself into a seated position. His shoulder grazes against mine lightly and I pull back.

"Soon, yes." Tentatively, he reaches a hand out and pushes my hair behind my ear. I flinch. "Sorry," he says. "I just couldn't see your face. I thought I may have upset you."

"It takes much more than that to upset me. I'm a big girl."

"I just wanted to make sure."

"I'm not yours to worry about," I say sharply. "You don't have to worry about hurting my feelings or something. In case you haven't noticed, I'm a demon. We're enemies."

"You aren't my enemy," he says, hurt. "I thought we were getting along."

"Yeah, well, maybe you thought wrong." *Because we can't be friends. We can't be anything.* I'm amazed at how quickly he could forget that.

He looks out towards the water and then back at me. "I'm sorry."

"Stop apologizing!"

"I—" he stops himself. "I'll just go then."

He stands up, walks over to where his sweater is laid out, now dried on the stones, and slips it over his shoulders. He pulls it down roughly as he slides his feet back into his thin sneakers. Cautiously, he looks back over at me.

"I'm coming back tomorrow. I was wondering…" He looks up through the trees, appears to be counting the clouds, and then glances back to me. "Will you still be here? Or are you leaving to join Azael?"

I look at him and see the unasked question in his eyes: Will I be alone again?

I have to be here, I think. *You're my assignment.* "I—I don't know. I have nowhere else to go."

He inclines his head. "You are welcome to use the cave overnight if you want. It's not exactly the most comfortable place to sleep, but it should stay pretty warm."

I look at him measuredly. I don't offer him a thank you. I simply say, "Fine."

"I'll see you tomorrow then," he says, his face brightening slightly. "Sleep well."

And with that, he unfurls his great silver wings and lifts into the darkening sky. I crane my neck up, watching his wings until he vanishes behind the clouds.

See you tomorrow, I repeat in my head. I touch the bracelet around my wrist and feel it get cooler, the warmth of the beads disappearing with Michael.

After the last of the clouds pull apart like thinning cotton, I jump to my feet and grab my shirt from the shore. I ball it up and shove it into a large pocket of my backpack that rests on a squishy patch of moss, moving my boots away from the water with my bag. I kick my backpack so it is hidden under the caging roots of a large tree and stand, unsure of what to do with myself.

It's been so long since I've been able to do what I want to do. I'm always on an assignment or on Azael's time, where he tows me around town telling me who to kill so he can collect their souls. I never have any real time to myself, even though I'm so often alone.

I don't ever have to worry about being bored with Azael, and Michael has proven to be interesting company as well. I fiddle with the pendent of my necklace, letting the large stone twist around the chain. I consider calling Azael again, but he's busy. I smile, picturing him at a rodeo in boots and spurs. *I hope he's having fun.*

I walk over to the edge of the water and stand on my tiptoes. I spring into the water again and resurface soundlessly, floating on my back across the pond. My hair fans out, circling around me like a dark halo. I wait for the sun to disappear completely from the sky and the stars to come out. One by one, they appear, like bright silver lights turning on.

The stars are so large and lustrous. They look much closer than they do in the city. From the pond, the sky appears to have an edge, a small rim of pink that sinks below the forest. The willowy tops of the tall pine trees that surround the pond block some of the splattering of stars from my view, but I can still see their glow.

I almost believe that I can reach out and pick the stars out of the sky and hold them in my hands. I imagine stealing a small constellation of the glinting lights and putting it in one of the mason jars from the cave. I would love to carry the stars with me.

I remember what they looked like from Heaven. They're nearly as bright as they are here, illuminating the darkness with an almost eerie silvery light. But they don't look as big in Heaven; they don't seem to be as dreamy and mysterious.

There were nights in Heaven that I would sit and look down at the stars. Sometimes, Az would join me, but he didn't find them nearly as interesting as I did. I seemed to be the only one who cared about them at all.

From Heaven, something about the stars seems disingenuous. I could never figure out exactly why, no matter how long I watched them twinkle, but they always appeared mechanical and fake, their shine a little duller. Something about the stars is missing in Heaven. Maybe that's why no one gave them any attention. Their beauty was imperfect.

I'm still amazed at how much purer the stars are from down here. It wouldn't seem that they would be, what with Earth being so far away from the glitter of space, but they are.

Michael would love to see these stars. I wonder if he's ever seen them from Earth? If he thought the sky looked infinite during the day, he should see it at night when we're not caged by clouds.

I roll over in the water, off of my back and onto my stomach, and swim over to the rocky wall of the cliff. Without Michael here to help me up, I can't reach the ledge behind the waterfall. The water beats down on my shoulders, pulling heavily at my hair as I grab onto the slippery rocks and climb up to the opening. I slide forward onto the cold, uneven floor of the cave.

I lean out from the mouth of the cave, holding on to a handhold in the wall, and look around the waterfall. The forest is dark and quiet. The tall trees are illuminated by the bright stars and the large, buttery moon, but the woods behind them are shadowy. It's empty though, and I am alone. Only the small, blinking eyes of animals look back at me.

I go to the back of the cave and lie down on the rough, carved bench. The bench is hard and narrow and the tool of whatever carved it decades, maybe even centuries, ago has left deep grooves that sprawl across the surface like thick brushstrokes. Its uneven surface slopes periodically into my bones and then recedes abruptly away from me, leaving me suspended between the carvings. It won't be the comfiest place I have ever slept, but it won't be the worst either. It's not like I have a lot of alternatives.

Shifting from my back onto my side, I curse myself for not bringing my t-shirt to use as a pillow. I rest my face on my cold hands, watch the glowing amber of the collection of mason jars, and let my eyes droop with tiredness until they close completely.

The last thing I see before I fall asleep is the soft, coppery halo of light around my eyelashes.

Exhaustion seals my eyes closed like glue, and everything becomes dark and still.

CHAPTER 15

IT STARTS WITH A SINGLE FAMILIAR SCREAM THAT echoes from deep within the forest. Fighting every instinct, I run towards it. The low hanging branches, which are thick and shadowy in the darkness, whip violently into my face. The scream hitches, ending abruptly, and suddenly the woods are quiet again.

I stop, bracing myself on the back of a large tree, and try to catch my breath.

Listen, I tell myself.

I focus on the sounds around me and try to make sense of the strange shadows that curl devilishly in the moonlight. There is movement, quick and soft. I hear a dull thud, peer around the tree, and see something small and thin slide off of a large sword that glints wickedly in the moonlight. A body. The figure falls limply to the ground. A tall, broad shadow stands above the crumpled figure.

Patience. I count to ten in my head, waiting for the shadowed figure to leave, but he doesn't move.

I let out a soft huff of my breath, visible in the crisp, cool night, and run in the direction of the shadow. Faster, I throw myself into a full sprint until I reach the clearing, where I come to a stop. I draw my dagger quietly from my belt and wait.

The shadow remains still, unaware of my presence. I go to take a step forward but a second shadow glides up behind the first and I stop. This shadow is narrower than the first but equally as tall and strong.

I step forward, my dagger raised threateningly in front of me. "Turn around," I demand. "Let me see your faces."

The two figures ignore me. With their bare, muscled backs turned to me, I see them lean in towards one another and whisper between themselves, but I can't make out what they're saying. I circle around them carefully, keeping my dagger held high. Their heads are bowed low, and I cannot make out their faces.

Suddenly, the sharp and rusty smell of blood washes over me. But there's something different about this blood. It doesn't have the same intoxicating sweetness it usually does. Instead, it smells bitter, like garbage or rot. I freeze, look down at my feet, and see thick, dark blood sliding slowly across the ground until it seeps under my boots. I draw my eyebrows together in confusion.

Black blood?

I follow the viscid, black stream and find that it is spilling rapidly out of the chest, up the neck, and across the face of a thin, pale girl. There is so much blood caked to her face that I don't recognize her right away, but she seems familiar.

I know her...

I raise my eyes back to the two men standing in front of me. Both of their chests are bare and their skin, one tan and the other pale, seems to be glowing in the moonlight. Their faces are masked in shadows.

The first shadow is holding a large sword in his hand, the black blood sliding down the shining blade, obscuring a thin inscription. He whispers to the second, "Take her soul."

"Who are you?" I yell. "Show me your faces!"

Again, I'm ignored. They move carefully and slowly, like phantoms.

The second shadow bends down to the body and reaches into her chest. I see that he has a long welt along his forearm, and I lean closer. His dark hair shines blue-black in the silvery light.

No, it can't be.

His hand searches inside the chest. "There's nothing here."

"Look again," orders the first shadow.

There's a pause. "Nothing." He stands up, raising his face and looking right through me with large, violet eyes.

"Azael!" My voice sounds hollow. I'm frozen in place, staring at him in disbelief.

He doesn't respond, doesn't acknowledge me at all.

The first shadow crouches down next to the body. I watch him, confused. He leans into the spotlight cast by the moon and I see that his hair is a tangle of gold. I throw my hand over my mouth, stifling a scream.

Michael.

He reaches out a large hand and tenderly brushes the girl's face.

"Such a shame," he says. "Her soul would have been valuable."

"Not surprising, though," Azael says cooly. "She lost her soul long ago. At least she didn't burn up completely. Her body could still be useful…"

I inch closer to Michael, watching his face fearfully. I kneel in front of him and scan down to the girl's pale chest, where there is a large, grotesque wound. The skin around the gash is charred as if it were burnt. I look back up at Michael's hand, which is resting on the blood-smeared cheek of the girl's face.

With the dark, bloodied hair out of her face, I realize why she is so familiar. Her nose is small and pointed, and she has large, round, violet eyes that stare up at the stars unseeingly. Her lips are cracked, split in the middle with a small cut. Bile rises in my throat.

It's me, I realize, choked with panic.

I wake up to the sound of another scream. This time, I know immediately it is my own.

I continue to scream until my throat is raw, keeping my eyes stitched shut even as two strong hands wrap around my shoulders.

"Pen!" The voice sounds worried. "Pen, you're fine! You're fine. It's just a dream!"

The world is shaking. No, not the world. Just me. My eyes fly open as another scream escapes, my body shuddering violently when I sit up.

Everything is the soft, hazy color of morning and I struggle to make sense of my surroundings. I can't breathe right, not that I should have to breathe at all. But I am hyperventilating, my breaths coming too fast and panicked. I try to focus on small details of my surroundings, which are blurred and dizzying.

I'm not outside. I'm inside rocky walls. For a moment, I think I'm in a tomb, buried deep beneath the Earth. But there's too much light for that. I squint my eyes, trying desperately to focus. I see more rock walls and the soft glow of a collection of jars, and I can hear the sound of falling water.

The cave.

That's right, I'm inside the cave, sitting on the carved, stony bench. I feel two hands around my arms, holding me steady, and

I throw myself forward into the chest attached to the arms attached to the hands.

"Azael!" I choke on subsiding panic that bubbles up in my throat as a sob. "It was horrible!"

Warm arms wrap around me protectively. "It's okay, Pen. You're awake. But I'm not—"

I cut him off. "I died. Az, I saw myself dead." I let silent tears slip down my cheek and onto the dark cotton of his shirt, which is already damp. My throat burns and I realize I must have been screaming for a while. I pull back, wipe my cheek, and look at his face.

But it's not Azael's face. It's Michael's, creased with concern.

"Sorry," he whispers hoarsely. He still holds on to my hand. "I didn't intend to, I mean... You were screaming and I..."

I break free of his grip and push myself back against the sharp wall of the cave, distancing myself from him as best as I can. I curl in on myself, pulling my knees to my chest and wrapping my arms around my legs.

"When did you get here?" I ask defensively.

"I thought I'd bring you breakfast," he answers, gesturing towards the center of the cave.

Next to the cluster of mason jars is a small bag of food. The smokey smell of bacon wafts over to me.

"I saw you didn't have anything to eat and thought maybe you'd be hungry. But when I got to the pond, I heard you screaming. I flew up here as fast as I could. I thought you were being attacked, but you were only sleeping. You looked so scared, and I thought that maybe if I woke you up... What happened?"

"Nightmare," I answer flatly.

He nods, understanding. "It sounded like a bad one." It's not a question. I glance at the sword that hangs off of his waist. He watches my face carefully. "I have nightmares, too."

I relax a little, letting my legs straighten. "You have nightmares?" I ask, surprised. Angels don't usually dream—of anything. "Of what?"

"I can never remember them. But they must be horrible. I think they may have something to do with my first life. I wake up frozen with a fear so consuming I can't move or breathe and my heart burns. I'm worried one day I won't wake up from them, and maybe I'll live in the nightmare forever." He blushes and shifts uncomfortably.

"Demons don't have nightmares," I say quietly. "We *are* the nightmares."

"Didn't you say yesterday that you were an anomaly?"

Why does he remember that? "I guess it's more true than I thought."

"Do you want to talk about it? Your dream, I mean?"

I fold my legs on the bench in front of me. "No."

He studies me for a minute and then shrugs. "Well if you do, I'll always listen."

"You don't have to."

He smiles. "I know I don't have to. But I will." He leans forward, grabs the paper bag off of the ground, and pulls out two styrofoam containers. "I don't know what you eat, or what you like. I've never had this kind of food myself, so I just picked one at random."

"How did you pay for this?" I ask, taking one of the containers he hands to me.

"A girl at the counter said she'd pay for it," he shrugs, opening his food.

I roll my eyes as I open my own container. *Of course she did.*

Inside lies a large, greasy breakfast sandwich. One doughy bagel hugs a saucer of egg with two crispy pieces of bacon sticking out the side. Next to the sandwich, a flat oval of hash browns sits inside a thin, paper sleeve.

"Thanks," I say, picking up the bagel sandwich. "These are delicious. You'll like them."

He looks pleased with himself. "I think this is the first time you thanked me for something."

I bite into the sandwich and chew. "Mmh," I mumble noncommittally.

He picks up the sandwich, mimicking me, and bites into it. His eyes widen as he chews the hot bagel, egg, and bacon, his cheeks stuffed.

I swallow my bite and look at him. "And?"

He nods and takes another large bite. "This is amazing!" he says, his mouth full.

I laugh. "I know," I say smiling. "Just wait until you try their french fries."

CHAPTER 16

"I WAS THINKING," I SAY, AFTER I SHOVE MY EMPTY sandwich wrapper back into the bag, "that today I could train you."

"Train me?" He drags his hand across his mouth.

"How to fight."

"I don't want to fight," he says, touching the handle of his sword tentatively.

"Doesn't matter. You'll have to fight eventually. And it would be better if you actually know what you are doing when the time comes."

"And if that time never comes?"

"The time will come," I say with absolute certainty.

He doesn't know how precarious the situation is between Heaven and Hell. If he will fight with Hell, he needs to know how to properly handle a sword. He will be useless to us if he dies in the first battle. And if he doesn't join us...

I stand up from the bench and move over to the mason jars. I unscrew the lids one by one and blow out the small flames, extinguishing the light in the cave. Only the thin, watery light that passes through the waterfall brightens the gloominess of the cave.

"It's raining. We can't do much in the rain."

"Of course it's raining," I say with an exasperated sigh. "This is the Pacific Northwest. It's always raining. Don't tell me you're afraid of a little water?" I bite my tongue, remembering the lifelessness in his face yesterday when he almost drowned. The blue lips, his quiet heart. "We can go somewhere else if it starts raining too hard."

He nods his head. "It's fine. The rain is fine."

"And training?"

"It doesn't seem like I have much of a choice, does it?" He lowers his eyes to his sword, his shoulders slumped.

"Not really."

He looks at me through the hair that has fallen over his eyes. For a moment, it looks like he's going to say something, but he thinks better of it.

"It's really not that bad," I assure him.

I rise, kicking a fallen mason jar out of the way. It clinks across the uneven surface of the floor until it hits the wall. I step over to Michael and hold out my arm, offering it to him. He grabs me gently, his long fingers wrapping around my thin hand, and I help lift him to his feet.

"Thanks." He bends his head, his mouth level with my forehead.

His hand lingers, his thumb brushing once across the back of my hand absentmindedly. I quickly tear my hand away from his and hurry to the front of the cave. I don't look over my shoulder at him, but I can feel him watching me.

"I have to get my t-shirt and my boots before we leave," I call back to him. "Follow me."

I throw myself out of the cave and through the waterfall. I fall for a moment, but before I land in the dark blue pond below, I open my dark wings and lift on the air. A lazy drizzle of rain falls through the gray clouds. I look up and let the cool rain wash over my face and wake me up. My feet skim across the surface of the water as I fly over it and onto the bank.

Michael lands soundlessly next to me, his wings open wide. I glance up at him, squinting through the rain. Thick raindrops slide down his blond hair, which shines brightly against the silver of his wings. More drops cling to his pale eyelashes. He blinks and the rain falls off of his eyelashes and down his cheek, making it look like he's crying.

I turn away from him and walk forward, grabbing the strap of my backpack from under the tree. I reach inside to find a clean t-shirt and pull out a dark blue long-sleeved shirt. I shove my hands into the thin sleeves, the fabric clinging to my wet arms.

Struggling to get my other arm through the shirt, I drop the backpack. I bring the shirt over my head and pull it down my chest and over my black tank top, settling the thin fabric at my hips. I slip my feet into my boots and zip up the sides, spinning around to scoop up my backpack again. But it's gone.

Instead, when I straighten up, I find Michael standing with the green backpack, one of the thin straps thrown over his shoulder. He smiles at me. "Looked like you needed some help. I can carry it if you would like."

"It's really not that heavy. I think I can manage it," I say, holding out my hand. He slides the strap off of his shoulder, hanging the loop around one of my hooked fingers.

"Thought I'd at least offer," he says cheerfully.

"Thanks. I got it."

I settle the worn backpack between my shoulder blades and unfurl my wings again. Michael's wings, still outstretched, rustle lightly in the rain. His feathers brush together softly, whispering like the pages of books being turned too quickly.

"There's a small clearing of sorts a little ways from here," he offers. "Would that be a good place to train?"

I rip my gaze away from his wings to meet his eye. "Should be fine. You're not going to make me hike, are you?"

A bemused grin lights up his face. "Would you prefer to hike?"

"Absolutely not. Just—lead the way," I answer, circling my hand in the rain and motioning to the stormy clouds.

We lift into the sky together, our wings creating small cyclones of rain that spin around us. He flies in front of me, away from the pond, and I watch the silver of his wings become slick with the raindrops. It shines brilliantly, hypnotizing me.

Miles of thick, green pine trees blur below us before he turns his head over his shoulder and says that we're nearly there.

Gradually, his wings beat slower and he lowers into a small, barren clearing, similar to the one I first found him in. The ground looks like it is the bottom of a dry creek bed. It is covered in a thick layer of pine needles that keep the cracked ground from becoming muddy. I land behind him, turning around and surveying the clearing.

To my surprise, a lining of tall, thin aspen trees grow around the clearing. Their large, yellow leaves and willowy, white trunks are shockingly bright against the dark background of brown and green pines. Michael stares at me as I walk out and place my hand on one of the trees, smiling.

"I haven't seen these trees in so long," I say in a hushed tone. "They're my favorites."

"What are they called?"

"Aspens, I think."

"They're great to climb. And I like their leaves."

I scrunch my face. "They don't look like they're good for climbing. They're too narrow."

"Which makes it more difficult for *humans* to climb, not us."

He comes up and places his hand next to mine on the tree, his fingers lightly brushing against mine. Under the large branches of the tree, we are nearly shielded from all of the rain, but his face is still dewy with raindrops. He looks behind me and I see my black wings reflected in his pale eyes. I study his wings, slick and silver, and start to tuck my own away, self-conscious.

My wings, the color as black as coal, are nothing compared to his expansive, metallic wings. His are a sign of power while mine are only a mark of the darkness inside me. When I was in Heaven, I had soft white wings, but after I fell, they became dirty, the pure white darkening slowly over time. The more people I killed, the darker they became.

He takes his hand off of the tree and stops me from hiding my wings. "Wait," he says. "I want to see them."

I still, letting his hands brush through the glossy black feathers. I watch his face carefully, trying to decipher his silence. He tilts his head to one side examining them closer, and a fat raindrop falls from a golden curl that is looped around his ear. I follow it as it drips down his neck and stops at his pulse.

"It's amazing," he says.

"What is?"

"Your wings." He runs his fingers over the feathers again, ruffling them. "They are the same color as your hair."

I step back and fold my wings closed. "Yours aren't."

He frowns.

"The same color, I mean. Your hair is gold, but your wings are silver." I shift on my feet. "When your wings are open like that, you look… You're like a wishing well full of shiny coins."

"A wishing well?" His eyes are curious.

"Oh, it's a human thing. Urban legend, I think. Maybe folklore? I'm not sure what it's officially classified as…" I'm rambling. I bite my lip and try to explain. "People throw their coins into a well and make a wish. Supposedly, a wishing well wish should come true."

"Like a prayer."

I shrug. "In a way."

"And do they come true?"

"I think it depends on the wish."

We're both silent, and he curls his wings into himself, letting them disappear.

"What would you wish for?" he asks. "In a wishing well?"

"I—I probably wouldn't wish for anything."

"Nothing at all?" he asks disbelievingly.

"I have nothing to wish for."

He studies my face and nods. "I would wish that you would get your wish."

"But I have no wish," I say.

"One day you will. And when that time comes, I wish that it will come true."

I roll my eyes, let the straps of my backpack slip off of my shoulders, and walk out from under the canopy of trees. "Go for it," I say, striding into the center of the clearing and into the rain. "But now it's time to train."

He laughs. "I *do* make you uncomfortable, don't I? I'm sorry." He stands in front of me, smiling stupidly and opening his arms wide. "I'm all yours. Teach me."

I pull my dagger from my belt and hold the blade against the hollow of his throat. He freezes, the corners of his mouth falling out of his smile. The light rain continues to fall on his face, but he doesn't blink. "Lesson one: never let your guard down."

I lower my blade and he lets out a long breath.

I back away from him. "Attack me."

"I'm sorry, what?"

"Attack me," I repeat.

"But…" He looks between the hilt of his sword and me. "I could—"

For a split second, I am arrested with fear. My nightmare comes crashing back to me, slamming into my ribs and stealing my breath. I remember seeing myself slide off of Michael's sword, crumpling to the ground. My stomach knots in fear as the vivid image of my lifeless, bloody body swims in my vision. I was dead. No soul, Azael said, but at least I didn't burn. It was in a clearing just like this…

I close my eyes for a moment and shake my head, banishing the memory. *It was only a nightmare.*

I reach behind me and snap a thin branch off of the tree. It breaks off and I slide my blade over the bark to scrape off the small twigs and clinging wet leaves. I hold it up to inspect; the tip is pointed like a stake and about as long as his sword. It weighs less, but it should be a good enough substitute. I toss it to him. He holds it out in front of him warily.

"Attack me."

After a moment of hesitation, he clenches his jaw and charges me, holding the stake out in front of him. He thrusts it towards my chest, but I duck quickly and avoid the hit. He swings it again, cutting through the rain with a whipping sound, and tries to knock me with the length of it, but again I dodge his strike.

I grab on to the makeshift sword and whip it around violently. He holds on to it tightly, swinging around behind it. I roughly push on the stake, throwing him across the clearing where his back strikes loudly against the trunk of a tree and knocks the wind out of him. But he manages to stay on his feet.

I shift my weight onto my back foot, holding my elbow steady as I throw my wrist forward, letting go of the dagger so it spins quickly and sticks into the white trunk of the tree, not even an inch above his left shoulder.

He looks over at the dagger sticking out from the tree and his eyes widen.

"Lesson two: never go for the obvious attack. You could learn a little subtlety. And lesson three: precision and speed are more valuable than power."

"You could have hit me!" His voice is tight.

"No, I couldn't have."

He grabs the bone handle of the dagger and unsticks it from the tree. He stares at the tip. "Yes, you definitely could have."

"I have never missed a target I throw at. If I wanted to hit you, I would have hit you. But I didn't, so you live to see another day."

He chuckles nervously. "Right."

I meet him in the middle of the clearing and take back my dagger. "Drop the stick," I order, "and draw your sword." He hesitates. "You're not going to attack me again. Not right now. But you need to know how to fight with an actual sword. Trust me when I say that fighting with that branch won't get you very far in a battle." I toss my heavy, wet hair over my shoulder and wait.

He throws the branch to the side, the tip sticking into the ground. Carefully, he draws his sword out of his belt.

"Always draw your sword before you engage," I tell him. "And faster than that. It takes longer to draw a sword than it does to get hit by one."

He nods, replaces his sword, and draws it again. This time, he grabs the golden handle and pulls the sword from his belt much faster, the metal of the blade ringing. "Better?"

"Better," I confirm.

He holds the sword in both of his hands, his gripped knuckles white. His shoulders are raised and he stands stiffly.

"Relax," I advise him. "Lower your shoulders and learn to hold the sword with one hand. You won't get a large enough range of motion if you hold it like that." I hold my own dagger out in example.

He relaxes a little and lets go of the sword with his left hand. He holds it in his right hand, the blade bouncing in the air. Raindrops fall onto the blade, pinging softly.

"You have to hold it with confidence. Grip it securely, but not so tight that your knuckles turn white. The blade shouldn't be bouncing like that."

He does as I say and the sword levels.

"Good." I lower my dagger and walk closer to him, carefully avoiding the tip of the sword. "Turn your body to the side. There's less area to strike if you stand like that. You don't want to give your opponent a large target."

He wavers.

I move to his side, place my hands gently on his hips, and position him. "Like this. And keep your legs shoulder-width apart." I kick my foot between his feet, widening his stance. "This will help you stay balanced. Also, it's easier to move quickly when you stand like this."

He looks over his shoulder and down at me. "How do you know all of this?"

"I've fought with a sword before."

"Who taught you?" he asks.

"No one. I taught myself." I roll up my sleeve and show him a series of scars that crisscross my left wrist and forearm. Some of the scars are thin and delicate, while others are longer and rougher.

I have scars from swords, others from daggers, and a few from razor-sharp teeth. One of the scars wraps around my wrist like a ribbon—a faint reminder of a blessed golden whip.

"A bit of trial and error at first," I tell him. "But trust me, once you're hit for the first time, you learn to move faster. When your life depends on it, you fight with all you're worth."

He drops his sword and turns to face me. His fingers brush across my wrist carefully, tracing my scars. My breath catches and is pulled back down my throat by whatever is clawing my stomach.

"Have you had to fight like your life depended on it?"

"Yes," I say, forcing my voice to stay calm. "In the war, every day I fought was for my life and Azael's."

"Oh, right." His eyes meet mine for a brief moment before he turns and positions himself so he is standing like I told him to again, his back pressed up against me and his sword held level. He looks back at his outstretched arm. "Is this right?"

I step back and move around him so I can see his complete stance. "Keep your elbow bent and close to your body. Don't stretch out your arm—you won't be able to strike quickly." I explain. "Extend your sword, not your arm."

He bends his elbow and holds it closer to his abdomen.

"When you strike out," I continue, "try not to lift your feet from the ground. The higher you lift your feet, the easier it is to be knocked over." I stand in front of him and demonstrate. "The more the sole of your foot remains on the ground, the more solid your stance is. Your attacks will be stronger. Try to slide your feet instead of lifting them." I swing out, sliding my feet across the pine needles and slashing through the rain.

He copies me, sliding his feet forward and thrashing his sword through the air.

"When you block a strike, keep your blade close to you. You don't need to be stretching out and exposing your chest. Missing one block can be fatal. Protect yourself."

"Keep it close. Okay, got it."

"Never, and I cannot stress this enough, *never* charge."

"Why?"

"I can't tell you how many people I've seen charge someone wielding a sword and impale themselves. It's about precision, remember. You have to be careful and focused, not stupid and hot-headed."

He nods seriously. "Never charge."

"*Never*," I say again. "Hold your opponent at bay by either pointing the tip of your sword at their heart or their throat." I grip my dagger in my hand and point it at him. I let the sharp end pause at his neck before I lower it to his chest, remembering the small scar that is hidden beneath his shirt, marking his strong, beating heart.

His eyes widen anxiously, so I lower my arm back to my side.

"Don't let it bounce down. Always keep it ready to strike. And as soon as you see an opening, you have to take it. Kill them."

He watches me.

"If you dodge an attack, your opponent's torso will almost always be open to you." I demonstrate what it would look like if I missed a strike, my shoulders turned towards him, my chest vulnerable to an attack. "Allowing you to deliver the final, winning blow."

He drops his eyes to his still outstretched sword, considering the weapon. "I couldn't do that."

"You can," I say forcefully. "And you will."

He shakes his head, dropping his sword so the tip hits the ground.

"Look at me," I say, and he raises his bright blue eyes to meet mine. I take a step towards him, closing the distance between us where the rain continues to fall, drenching us both. "If you are engaged in a fight, you do not hesitate. You do not consider your morals. War is not the time to waver. You save yourself. You *fight* for your life. Do you understand?"

He pauses. "War?"

I raise my voice. "You protect yourself at all costs. Promise me."

"I understand," he says quietly. I look at him harder. "I promise."

I slip my dagger back into my belt. "Good."

I turn from him and walk back under the canopy of branches, hiding from the rain as I pull my fingers through my knotted hair.

"Why do you care?" His voice stops my fidgeting.

I swivel around and stare at him. He is standing in the center of the clearing, rain pouring down on him and sticking his hair to his face. His sword is lowered to the ground, no longer held at attention.

"What?"

"Why do you care? If I fight for my life?"

I lean back against the tree and shove my hands deep into my pockets. He's my assignment, mine to protect. It's my job to make sure that he is safe and ready for battle, should the time come. *When* the time comes. Isn't that why I want him to fight for his life?

Yes. That has to be why. But a small part of me, a part that I am trying to keep quiet, says that there's another reason. It's screaming at me, but I tune it out. *Don't think about it.*

I shake my head, ignoring the uncertainty that cycles through my mind. "No one should fight halfheartedly. It isn't admirable."

"Demons care about what is admirable?"

"Some," I say quickly. "Not all of us fight dirty."

He squints his eyes, watching me through the rain. "Is that all?" he asks.

I stay silent.

He holsters his sword and walks over to me, coming so close that I have to crane my head back to look up at him. The smell of honey clings to him, bright and sweet in the rain. "Is that the only reason I had to promise you? You want me to fight for my life because it is the *admirable* thing to do?"

"Yes." My voice sounds strained in my ears. "That's all." I lower my chin and look away from him, clearing my throat.

"If you say so," he says. He steps back from me and I look up to see that he is staring towards the top of the trees. "These really are great for climbing."

"So you've said."

"Care to join me?" In a quick motion, he slides his sword out of its holster and leans it against the tree.

Before I can answer, he jumps high into the air and grabs on to the lowest branch, pulling himself up so he can stand on it. He reaches above his head again, grabbing on to two more branches, and continues to climb up the tree through the large yellow leaves.

I stand, watching him climb gracefully up the narrow branches for a moment before I join him.

CHAPTER 17

I SHIMMY UP THROUGH THE THIN BRANCHES OF THE tree, following Michael as he ducks behind golden leaves, nearly the same color of his hair. My own hair swings around my arms, a dark, wet black against the white trunk. My clothes are heavy with rainwater, but luckily the rain can't reach us through the leaves.

"Pen?" he calls down to me.

"Michael?" I imitate him.

"You decided to join me after all?"

I look up and see him sitting between two forked branches. He smiles at me and I look away, feeling awkward under his stare. "Well, I've heard that these are great to climb. And you know what they say about trees. They're nature's stairways to Heaven. And with an angel sitting so high on one, well it must be true."

"People say that?" he asks, curious.

"Hell if I know. But I just said it. Isn't that what counts?"

He laughs. "So if this is the stairway to Heaven…"

"Why is there a demon climbing up it so quickly?" I finish for him, huffing as I pull myself through two intersecting branches. His feet dangle a few branches above me, so I continue to climb, my hands tearing on the rough bark.

"Not what I was going to ask," he says, watching me, amused. One corner of his mouth is lifted in a lopsided grin. "What I was going to ask was, if this is the stairway to Heaven, where is the gate?"

I grip another branch and, with one last effort, pull myself up so I am sitting on a thick, round limb, facing Michael. "You're going to have to tell me, angel boy."

He smiles again, his teeth a pearly white against his peach lips. "I don't see it. We must've taken the wrong set of stairs."

"Oh rats, I guess we'll just have to try one of the other million trees in this huge forest. One of them is bound to be the correct steps!"

He laughs and looks over to me. I pull my sleeves down over my hands, covering the scrapes across my palm. I press the wet fabric of my shirt on the cuts and they sting mildly. I suck air through my teeth in a hiss.

"Are you hurt?" He leans towards me, trying to inspect my hands, which I have folded in my lap.

"It's fine. I'll heal in a second."

"Let me see," he says. He reaches his arm out and opens one of his large hands.

"I'll heal. It's not a big deal."

"Please, let me see," he repeats, moving his hand closer to me in insistence.

Silently, I push my sleeves up from my hands and rest them in his, my palms open to the sky. Small, red cuts are scratched across both of my palms like dozens of tiny paper cuts.

"See?" I say, pulling back my hands slowly. "Just a few cuts. Nothing I can't handle. I've had a lot worse."

He holds on to my wrists, trapping my hands in his. He brings his other hand and lays it gently on top of mine. A warmth spreads from his palm to mine, and when he removes his hand again, the cuts are gone, the skin smooth and perfect.

"You shouldn't have to wait," he says, releasing my hands.

I bring them into my lap again, fidgeting with my sleeves. "Guess I won't have to."

"You're welcome."

"I didn't say thank you."

"Sure you did." He smiles again, broad and sincere. "In your own way."

I stare at him in annoyance. "You are truly vexing."

"Vexing?"

"Bothersome, irritating," I wave my hand in the air. "Vexing."

"Am I really that bad? I brought you breakfast. And I healed your hands—"

"Which would have healed in a few minutes anyway," I interrupt.

"I thought you were starting to like me," he says, watching me intently.

I change the subject. "Can I ask you a question?"

"Didn't you just ask me one?" His smile broadens, teasing me the same way I teased him the other day.

"I'll take that as a yes, if you don't mind," I continue. "I was wondering why Heaven keeps you on such a short leash? I know how important you are to them and all, but why the curfew? What's the point?"

"You think I'm important," he says, ignoring my questions.

"To Heaven," I clarify, blushing lightly. "But I don't understand the curfew."

"The curfew is to protect me. That's what they've said, at least. My defenses, as you've seen, are not what they apparently used to be. And that's during the day. At night, when more demons walk the Earth freely... Well, I'd imagine my skills would be even weaker."

"Night isn't suddenly a free-for-all," I tell him, leaning my shoulder against the trunk of the tree. "Demons can walk during the daylight now. We're not confined to the dark."

"But some still prefer the darkness, right? I mean, there are substantially more monsters at night than during the day."

I sit up straighter, perched rigidly on my gnarled branch. "Monsters?" My voice slides up an octave unintentionally. Is that what he sees me as?

"Not you, obviously," he says in a rush. "I don't think— you're not a monster, Pen."

"Aren't I, though?"

"No, you're not. You are kind. You just taught me how to protect myself, how to fight with a sword. A monster wouldn't be helping me. They'd be hurting me."

I pause, closing my eyes to him. "The only reason I know how to fight is because of all of the practice I've had, all of the people I've killed. You know what I am and what I do." I open my eyes again and look at him seriously. "I am a demon. There is nothing deeper to me than that. You think that somewhere, buried deep inside of me, there is goodness. I'm telling you there isn't. You've felt that I don't have a heart, and I've told you I have no soul."

"And I've said that I don't believe you."

"Stop, Michael. Listen to what I'm saying." I take a deep breath. "I kill people, and I enjoy killing people. I love the power I have."

"Because it's the only thing you've known how to do for hundreds of centuries!" He looks at me pleadingly.

"Exactly!" I yell back. "*Hundreds* of centuries. Do you think everything I've done during that time can just be forgotten or forgiven?"

"You were betrayed by Heaven. They hurt you, not just physically. There was nowhere for you to go, except into the waiting arms of Lucifer, who was more than willing to adopt lost souls and train them to carry out *his* plans." He stops suddenly, his eyes sad and serious. "But this isn't you. I don't believe you enjoy it as much as you say you do."

I look away from him.

"I think," he continues, "that it's all an act to protect yourself. What would happen if they knew you didn't belong?" He waits, and when I don't answer he nods. "That's what I thought. So you pretend to revel in the spilled blood, you do what you're told, you complete your assignments with enthusiasm. Because they're watching you closely, and if, even just for a moment, they think you're different, that'd be it. If they knew you didn't belong, they'd kill you, right?"

I'm silent again. They'd do something much worse than kill me.

"You want to fit in, stay with Azael. But what he does, and what you've done, isn't who you are inside. You don't belong in Hell."

"You don't know me," I groan.

"Imagine the life you want to live."

I give him a look, and he backtracks.

"Sorry, poor choice of words." He pauses and tries again. "Imagine your future. Centuries from now, do you still see yourself in Hell? Is that where you really belong, or is it somewhere else?"

"Somewhere like Heaven?" I ask sarcastically.

He shrugs.

"You don't know me," I repeat again. "Michael, you've met me before. You don't remember, but it wouldn't matter even if you did because you didn't know me back then either. Not really. Since you've been back, you've seen me, what? Three different times? And suddenly you have this complete understanding of who I am? Of *what* I am and where I belong?"

"I am an angel, and so are you." I make another face at him, and he shakes his head, insisting that it's true. "You've fallen, sure, but you are still an angel. I can feel who you are, your true spirit. I can see the soul you believe you've lost. It's still there inside of you." He shifts forward so he is inches from me. Slowly, he reaches out and places his hand on my ribs, right at the spot he keeps staring at. Is this where he thinks my soul is buried? When he speaks, his breath tickles my ear. "When you're far enough away from Hell, you'll see that you have light in you. I can *feel* it."

But I can't. I grab his wrist and remove his hand from me. Reluctantly, he sits back down. My eyes meet his and we hold each other's gaze, neither of us able to look away.

"I can't go back to Heaven." My voice sounds as dead as I feel inside.

"You're just lost, Pen."

"And you're here to find me?"

He's silent.

"To save me?" I guess again. "Newsflash: I *can't* be saved. And who says I even want to be?"

Even as the words come out of my mouth, I question myself. Can I really never be saved?

I try to imagine the next few centuries in Hell, going through the same motions day after day, year after year. I'll have to push down what little of Heaven is left in me, put it in a small box, locked up tight, and hide it somewhere I will never be able to find it again. If I do that, will I lose myself completely? Maybe one day I will be exactly like Azael. But is that what I want?

What option do I have? I can't go back to Heaven—not after everything I've done. So, without Hell, where would I belong? Where would I even go?

"I'm not here to save you. I'm here to remind you of who you are. You can save yourself. You're more than capable."

"And if I can't be saved?" I raise an eyebrow.

"Everyone can be saved if they want to be," he answers simply.

"Did you ever think, just for one minute, that perhaps you are on the wrong side of this war?" I ask angrily. "That maybe Heaven isn't as pure as they think?"

"I have," he says quietly.

"Exactly, you're too—" I stop. "Wait, what?"

"I question what I believe in everyday."

I stay quiet, shocked, and wait for him to continue.

"Pen, I know that the world is not black and white. But that seems to be the only options for Heaven and Hell. You're either good or you're bad. You can't be both. But what if we are? There are gray areas, and both sides are blind to it. They refuse to even acknowledge its existence." He sighs. "No one is only good or only bad. We have a bit of both inside of us all. We're flawed. Imperfect. And why is that a bad thing?"

He catches me off guard. An angel—especially an angel as important to Heaven as Michael, an angel who was once the most devoted proponent of Heaven—should not be questioning the laws of Heaven.

I remember Gus saying that he was causing trouble, but I didn't know this is what he meant. If he mentioned this to any of the other angels, what would they think of him?

Angels only see in black and white, not shades of gray. There is lightness and darkness, with nothing in between. Because if there were, what judgment could they pass? How would they determine where they belong? Could someone with evil inside them walk amongst the angels? Would someone with some goodness left be banished to Hell?

I consider what he's saying. It's something I've mentioned to Azael once. It was shortly after we had fallen, and I tried to tell him that he doesn't have to belong wholly to one side. He was darkening quickly, and I felt like I was losing a part of him. The part of him that would come and watch the stars with me, even though they bored him. The part of him that *cared*.

Naturally, he brushed it off, said that of course there is only black and white in this world. "There are only two sides to a coin," he told me. "Not three." But it's not as simple as that. People—and angels and demons—are complex and indecisive. Nothing they do is absolute.

IGNITE

There have to be gray areas. Why else would I want to spare Michael's life? I was the one who suggested that, instead of killing him, we could shift his allegiance from Heaven to Hell.

I don't want to have to kill him. But I should. As a demon, I should want to see him strung up, begging for mercy that he would never see.

If the world was only black and white, I would be exactly like Azael, ready to watch the world burn. It's the gray in me that wants to save it. It's the gray in me that prevents me from belonging fully to either Heaven or Hell.

No one is perfectly dark or perfectly light. I've always thought this, but ever since I mentioned it to Azael and had him scoff at the idea, I've bitten my tongue. I have had to accept things the way they were for not only my own safety, but also Az's.

Darkness bleaches at the corners, and lightness becomes dirty. There are flaws to even the smoothest black stone, even the purest diamond. Aren't these flaws the things that make us individuals? Don't flaws distinguish one stone from another, one diamond from another? Without these differences, these mistakes, the world would be masked in dull sameness.

The rain above Michael and me hits the leaves loudly, splashing down the branches and onto the ground. It's raining harder, as if the weather around us is suddenly aware of the seriousness of our conversation. How appropriate.

"It's not a bad thing," I admit. "Flaws are inescapable." I shake my head. "What I mean is, we are our flaws, but they don't have to define us as either good or evil. It's possible to be both."

"Yes!" He gestures wildly, rocking back on the branches. "But with the way things are run now, our flaws do define us. The seven deadly sins—envy, gluttony, greed, lust, sloth, pride, and wrath—don't they exist in everyone? The force Heaven exerted in the war against Lucifer, was that not wrath? It's not fair that we pass judgment on others so easily without first looking inside ourselves. Are we too proud to admit that good is not absolute?"

He speaks so quickly that he seems out of breath, but that doesn't stop him.

"Pen, if the world was only black and white, how did the angels fall?" He looks at me meaningfully. "Hell is comprised of fallen angels, who Heaven thought held pure light. But they weren't as pure as they were believed to be. They had something deeper inside of them, some blackness that sullied their purity into gray. And it's not bad that they weren't perfect. No one is. But Heaven couldn't accept this. They abandoned them because the darkness scared them. It was wrong." His voice sounds bitter, and he shakes his head.

I nod slowly. "So what does this mean for you?"

He looks up at me in question. "I don't understand."

"Will you fight with Hell? You don't believe in Heaven, in goodness…"

"No, I do believe in goodness," he corrects, his eyebrows knotted in concentration. "I believe in goodness above everything, but I don't believe it's simple. I don't agree with the narrow parameters in which Heaven considers what is good."

"And Hell?"

"Hell…" He rolls the word around in his mouth.

"Would you fight with Hell?" I prompt. This is my first chance to convince him. He seems completely at odds with Heaven, and I wonder if he would want to see the angels dethroned like Lucifer does. "If a war was to rise, between Heaven and Hell, which side would you fight on?"

He considers this for a moment, and I'm surprised. I didn't think he would hesitate, but he does. He must have really lost faith in Heaven.

"You could fight with me," I suggest. "With Hell."

I wonder if the angels can feel that they're losing him like I felt that I was losing Azael before we fell. Do they know? Do they care?

Finally, he answers. "I cannot fight for the darkness to conquer the light. It is a cause I do not believe in. In a war between Heaven and Hell, I wouldn't fight."

I lean forward. "What do you mean, you wouldn't fight?"

"I don't believe I belong fully to either side. I may not agree with the antiquated beliefs of Heaven, but I do still believe in good, and I know that I couldn't fight for Hell."

I peer down through the branches to the orange pine-covered ground below us. He doesn't belong to Heaven or Hell. Do I? I am not worthy of Heaven anymore; I've fallen too far. But do I belong to Hell? I'm cunning. I'm a skilled fighter, and I'm smart. But does that make me evil?

Of course it does, a small voice in my head sneers. It sounds a bit like Azael, but I know it's not him. I grip my amulet and hear nothing from him. These thoughts are my own, angry and bitter. *Think of everyone you've killed. How you reveled in their blood! You are a monster. Don't let this golden boy tell you otherwise. He's playing you. What would he say if he knew about the child from Indiana?*

I look at Michael thoughtfully. A part of me wants to believe that what he's saying is right, that there is goodness buried deep inside of me. I feel hope that I can be better than who I am now, that I won't be trapped in the life I've been living.

At least part of what Michael said is true. When I fell from Heaven, it was because I had nowhere else to go. There was Heaven or Hell—good or evil, nothing in between. There was no middle ground, no compromise.

I lost my faith in what was good, and so did Azael. He was furious with the war and the way Heaven was using us—lying to us. I saw him withdrawing from the battles, and I knew I was losing him. He wasn't going to fight with Heaven; he was going to fight against them. He would have left me.

But I needed Azael. I had no one else. So I fell with him when he abandoned Heaven. I see much of Azael reflected in myself, and the longer we are out of Heaven, the darker that reflection becomes. He took to being a demon so easily and with an enthusiasm I had never seen in him before. And he was good at it, too. At first it was frightening, but it is something I have grown used to over the centuries.

Azael was made to be a demon. It's where he belongs, where he is comfortable. But I've never been fully comfortable in Hell. Not like Az. There are times I question if I'm cut out to be a demon, if I belong in Hell, and Michael is doing nothing to silence these worries.

But if neither Heaven nor Hell, where would I go?

I belong with Azael, I remind myself. *And he belongs to Hell wholeheartedly. So that means I do, too. Right?*

"I think I understand," I say shakily. "There are times that I feel like I don't belong."

"In Hell?"

"Anywhere," I shrug. "I don't think I belong anywhere."

"You can belong with me," he offers. He smiles crookedly at me, his eyes sad. "We can be misfits together."

I give him a small smile of my own. "And what a pair we are."

He pauses and shifts forward on the branch, bringing his face inches in front of mine. My breath hitches in surprise. Hesitantly, he reaches forward and curls my wet, heavy hair behind my ear, his hot fingers sliding across my cheek, leaving my skin blazingly warm. I remain perfectly still.

"Pen, I believe in you."

"Believe in me?"

"In your strength and courage. I believe that you'll wake up and see how great you truly are one day. You are good, and I'm going to keep telling you that until you believe me, even if I have to say it a million times."

"Why are you being so nice to me?" I ask skeptically.

"Because you deserve to be treated with kindness, and I get the feeling no one has been kind to you in a very long time."

I lower my eyes.

"And why are you being nice to me?" he asks.

I look up at him, confusion raging inside of my head. "I don't know."

He watches me closely, his bright eyes lifting to mine. "Don't hit me, okay?" he says slowly, leaning close enough to whisper in my ear. He's standing on a branch below me and his face is nearly even with mine.

"Why would I hit you?" I ask, pulling my eyebrows together, baffled.

"Because I'm going to do this."

With a rush of air, he closes the distance between us, leaning forward so that I my legs straddle his hips. He gently places his hand on my cheek, his thumb brushing over my cold, damp skin.

For a moment, I am disoriented by his nearness, his face inches from mine, his eyelashes stretching between us. His breath whispers across my skin, and before I pull away, he slides his hand under my chin and tilts my face up to meet his, pressing his soft lips onto mine.

A small gasp escapes my lips as I watch with wide, surprised eyes as he lets his fall closed slowly. I freeze under his touch, too dizzy to move. It feels as if the rest of the world is falling away beneath me, but I grip tighter on to the branch and know that I am here, that this moment is real. I keep my eyes open, watching him as his eyelids flutter. His lips send a strange warmth spreading through my veins, like the ice inside of me is melting.

I'm perfectly still, afraid that any movement, however small, will shatter the fragile moment. I'm alarmed at the heat in my veins, at the fogginess of my mind, but I don't move away.

He does.

He pulls back from my face, a shy smile on his lips, and instantly the ice returns to my veins.

"I'm sorry," he whispers. He looks down self-consciously, shifting backwards to sit on his branch.

I stop him, roughly grabbing his elbow. My eyes dance across his face, conflicted. Without a word, I pull him back to me and brush my lips lightly across his. Now he freezes.

I run my hands up his arms and onto his shoulders, kissing him with a controlled urgency, needing the warmth to return. Hesitantly, he circles my neck with one of his arms, his hand reaching up into my tangled hair. His other arm presses against the small of my back, holding me close to him. His heart beats fast in his chest, strong and sure. The ice begins to thaw again as he kisses me with a building confidence.

He smiles against my lips and my self-control vanishes. I wrap my arms around him tighter, keeping him closer and closer still, unwilling to let go. There are no fireworks, no music. I only see light, white and pure, and hear beautiful, complicated lines of poetry. Unwritten poetry, primitive poetry, poetry about love that can change the world. I wonder if he can hear the poetry, too.

A flush creeps up into my cheeks, like when I take someone's life, but this is better. I don't lose a small part of myself when I'm kissing Michael. Instead, it feels like I found another piece of myself that I thought I had lost forever. I don't have to detach from the sensation. I feel alive in a way I never have before. It's like a light switch being turned on for the first time in a long-abandoned, dark room.

"What in me is dark / Illumine, what is low raise and support." It's a line from *Paradise Lost*, a line I never paid much attention to, but now I find a solace in Milton's words, an understanding. The words ring in my mind and slide through my veins as Michael continues kissing me, raising me from the shadows and supporting the heaviness that weighs me down.

He's gentle but sure, knotting his arms around me. I can feel his heartbeat in my chest, echoing emptily and making me believe for a moment that it's my own. In this small moment, perched high up in a tree above the Earth and tangled in his fevered embrace, I feel the sparks of hope ignite. And Michael is there to fan the flames.

I can be good.

I don't have to be evil.

Maybe I'm even worthy of kindness.

I break away from him slowly, placing my hand on his chest, and search his eyes. My movements feel languid and the noises around us sound muffled. All I hear clearly is his heart beating quickly in his chest, his labored breathing, and my own short, shallow (and altogether unnecessary) breaths.

"What was that?" His voice, when he speaks, sounds rough, like it did after he nearly drowned in the pond just the other day. It's like we are underwater again. Is he drowning now?

I shake my head, biting my lip. It feels like *I'm* drowning. "I don't know. I was hoping you could tell me."

"You kissed me back." He laughs lightly and presses his forehead against mine. "You kissed me back," he repeats in an almost silent whisper.

"You should see the stars," I tell him suddenly. "I want to show you my stars."

CHAPTER 18

"I'VE SEEN THE STARS." HE KEEPS HIS FOREHEAD RESTING against mine and brings his one hand up to cup the nape of my neck. With his other hand, he twines his fingers with mine and circles his thumb across the back of my hand, drawing strange patterns I can't identify.

"Not my stars," I insist. "You haven't seen what they really look like. You've seen them from behind, in Heaven."

"And what are your stars like?"

"Magical," I sigh. "When the sun sets, they blink on like Christmas lights. They're cool and bright, dusted across the sky in beautiful patterns. Some are more gold, their light warm and hazy, while others are a sharp silver. When you look up into the night sky from Earth, it looks limitless. You're dwarfed in comparison to this wide open universe. It's not the same from Heaven."

He nods. "The stars are hollow, tinny."

"From above, but not from below. They're dreamy."

"Dreamy," he echoes, closing his eyes. "Earth is so different."

"I want to show you my stars," I say again.

"I can't." He sits back, raising his face to mine. "Not tonight, anyway."

"Because of your curfew."

"That, and there's something happening in Heaven. I'm not exactly in the loop up there, but it's something big. I may not be able to come back for a couple of days," he says.

I let out a breathy, halfhearted laugh. "You don't owe me an explanation. And I think I'll survive a couple of days without you." I drop his hand gently and knot my own fingers together to keep from reaching back out to touch him.

"I have no doubt you'll survive. I'm more concerned about myself."

"Ah, worried about cabin fever while locked behind those pearly gates?"

"Sure, let's call it that." He shrugs, taking a moment to find the right words to share. "I'm alone up there. Isolated, really. I have no friends, no one to talk to. Actually, that's not entirely true. I have lessons every so often. History, mostly."

I make a face and he laughs.

"I know. It's very dull. But it's the only time I'm not by myself."

"You are alone in Heaven?"

He nods once, small and quick. "Almost always. It's like they don't want me up there. But I don't think I'm ever completely alone, even when I'm by myself. I feel them watching me all the time."

He glances up through the branches and into the cloudy sky that hangs heavily over us before looking back at me.

"They don't trust me and I'm not sure why. I haven't done anything wrong." His voice is sad. "I think my presence makes them uncomfortable. Just being back, not fully belonging. Maybe they're afraid that Hell has done something to me that they won't be able to undo. I'm different, and they don't know how to handle me."

"Haven't they been training you? Isn't that what you were doing when Az and I first saw you at the asylum?" I ask, leaning into him.

"Yes, but I've proven to be a disappointment to them. They've tried training me to become an archangel again, the Michael I used to be, but I ask too many questions. The wrong question, it seems. I can tell that the things I ask—it is upsetting to them. But I have no one else to ask."

"I'll answer any questions that I can," I offer. "But I haven't been in Heaven in a very long time, so I don't know how much help I'll actually be."

He gives me a ghost of a smile. "You've already been very helpful. You told me how I died."

I study his face. His eyes are bright, and his smile is lopsided, one corner of his mouth raised higher than the other. But even though he is smiling, he looks wounded, upset at Heaven's distaste for him. He doesn't like being a disappointment to anyone, let alone the angels.

"They really leave you by yourself?" I ask.

"No one wants to be near me. That's why they let me come down to Earth by myself, I think. They're probably relieved when I'm gone. But when I'm not, when I'm in Heaven, they still keep me separated from everyone else. They just lock me away in a room. Lately, I've asked for books to be left for me so I have something to do other than stare at the walls and wait for the door to open again."

"You can't even leave your room?"

"Not without an escort. Ariel or Sablo, usually. I can't tell if they're meant to make me feel safe or make the other angels feel safe. Either way, they hate it."

"They hate most things," I agree. "Including me. They always have."

"I don't hate you." He smiles at me conspiratorially. "What did you do to make them hate you so much anyway? They wouldn't stop talking about you two after we left."

"They're not overly fond of pranks. I, on the other hand, am quite enamored with a well played trick. As is Azael. Though he is known for taking things a bit too far."

"That sounds about right. They're not much fun."

"*Angels* aren't much fun in general," I point out. "It's the demons who are up for a good time."

He raises an eyebrow.

"There's a saying—go to Heaven for the climate, Hell for the company. I, personally, prefer Hell's climate, but maybe I'm the only one. Az doesn't seem to like the cold very much. But he tolerates it."

"I didn't know Hell was cold," he says.

"Didn't learn that in one of your history lessons yet?" I grin. "It's completely frozen. A barren land of icy blues and grays with rivers of blood pulsing under the ice. Peaceful and still, in a gruesome way."

I look over at him, perched between the thin white branches of the tree. Even in the overcast gray of the late afternoon, Michael shines golden. I try to imagine him in Hell, but the images clash. Something so bright and warm doesn't belong in the cold darkness.

He leans back, resting one leg on the branch in front of him with the other dangling below him. He looks so comfortable, so at ease, sitting up here. On the ground he seems unsure and a bit clumsy. But far above the Earth, he breathes more easily, relaxes more.

"You don't like Earth very much, do you?" I ask suddenly.

He turns his head, resting his cheek on the rough branch to look at me. "I think it's fine. It's better than being locked up in Heaven. And it's so full of life. Everything seems to be growing and changing."

"It's just, you seem more relaxed up here."

"We're still on Earth right?" He cocks an eyebrow up at me and twists his mouth into a teasing grin.

"Technically, sure, but we're not *on* Earth. You like to be higher up, I've noticed. Or hidden away." I think back to the cave and his small, secret room, tucked behind the veil of a waterfall.

"It's different than I imagined it would be," he says. "Earth, I mean. In my lessons I thought it would be more solid. More concrete. But everything seems uncertain and precariously balanced. Like a house of cards. If I'm not careful, I could topple everything over. I feel like I shouldn't be here, like I'm upsetting the order of things."

"You're an archangel, so you feel more than a typical angel," I explain. "You can sense things, see things others can't."

Briefly, his eyes land on a spot just below my ribs and he nods.

"But the Earth is fine. Well, no, it's not exactly fine, but you being here shouldn't disrupt—" I stop.

He's right.

His presence *has* disrupted the order of Earth. The Lilim virus has resurfaced. Gus said that the future has been erasing itself. And it's all tied to Michael's return. So if everything Michael does or touches changes the future, what effect have I had?

An archangel and a demon should be trying to kill one another. That is the order of the worlds. They shouldn't be talking like friends, and they definitely shouldn't be kissing.

Oh, Hell. Oh holy, flaming shit.

I kissed Michael.

My cheeks burn hot with shame. I think immediately of Azael and what he would say if he knew. There would be derision, and of course he'd make some snide comment. I can practically hear his voice.

Pen and Michael sitting in the tree. K-I-S-S-I-N-G. You sure do go above and beyond the call of duty, don't you?

IGNITE

I practically lobbed that one right over the plate for him. But underneath his jokes and behind his jeers, there would be disgust. There would be the anger of betrayal burning hot in his dark eyes. A demon and an angel! It's unnatural; it's wrong. I don't know how I feel about Michael, but there is no question of how Hell would feel about us. I would be a traitor, executed immediately and shown no mercy. If I'm lucky.

If not, I would spend eternity being tortured, ripped apart, almost completely destroyed, and then pieced back together only to be torn apart again. And repeat. And repeat again. Heaven's reaction wouldn't be much different.

Gus gave me an assignment, I try to convince myself. *He told me to get close to Michael, whatever it took. So what if this is just what it took?*

But I'm having a more difficult time lying to myself. It's more than that—so much more than that. This is a thought, a wish, a stupid dream that's haunted me since I first saw Michael, since he first spoke to me. He asked me what I was reading, and I couldn't answer because I wasn't reading anything. I was *writing*.

He asked if he could see, so I showed him my notebook, and he read page after page of me, spilled out in ink. After just a minute, he closed it, glanced over me and said "Thank you." We had never spoken again unless it was him handing down orders, or me reporting fates.

This moment has been played and replayed in my mind more times than I can count. If this was an assignment, I wouldn't be so conflicted. When I look at him, I don't see a target. I see *him*; I see *Michael*—the only angel who asked about my writing, who didn't mock me for keeping my nose tucked inside the pages of a book. If I were doing my job, I wouldn't feel anything towards him. But I do. I *do* and I can't crush the part of me that is glad.

"Pen?" Michael's face is pinched with concern. "Are you okay? You don't look so good."

I laugh shakily. "Just what every girl wants to hear."

"I didn't mean it like that—"

I cut him off. "I'm all right, just a little dizzy."

"Should we climb down?" He looks overhead through the thick cover of leaves. "I think it stopped raining."

I swallow a lump in my throat. "Yeah, sure, let's climb down."

He slides off of his branch, placing his feet on a limb below, and then hesitates. "Do you need any help?"

"Big girl," I remind him, pointing to myself. "More experienced than you."

He scrutinizes my face closely, nods, and then begins to climb down the tree wordlessly.

I watch him lower towards the ground, and the farther he descends, the less I can see him. Soon enough, he is completely blocked behind large leaves that bridge between the white, twisting branches. I take a few breaths, trying to calm down.

I need to distance myself from him. I can't do this—I can't be vulnerable. He's changed something in me, and it's terrifying. Even now, without his lips on mine, my veins feel warm, thrumming with heat. The ice inside of me doesn't seem as piercing, as painful as it did before. It's melting away, transforming me from the inside out. His kindness is disorienting, and his blue eyes... I shake my head, trying to erase his face from my mind.

Stop. STOP.

With another deep, steadying breath, I begin to climb down the tree, my feet gingerly touching down on the branches. When I can see the ground, I jump, falling the rest of the way down the tree. I land on the hard ground in a crouch and then stand up. I look at my hands and am pleased to see that they aren't as scratched as they were after the climb up.

Michael is standing there waiting for me. He lifts up the sword that he left lying against the base of the tree and re-holsters it into his belt. I touch the dagger that hangs at my hip, reassuring myself that it's still there.

"How will I find you again?" he asks. "I'm assuming you won't still be here when I come back, whenever that will be."

Whenever that will be?

"Um…" I fiddle lightly with the bracelet on my wrist, feeling the warm, round beads slide across my skin.

He steps closer to me and takes my hand in his. He touches the bracelet. "This is interesting," he says curiously. "I hadn't noticed it before."

"Yeah, it's, uh, just a bracelet Az gave me," I lie.

"It's warm," he says. "Is it special?"

I pull my hand away from him. "It's from Azael."

"Of course." He places his hands at his sides, nodding understandingly.

"How about I find you," I offer. "Whenever you get back."

"How would you do that?"

I waggle my fingers in front of him. "With powerful, secret demon magic."

A small smile begins to spread across his face. "And if I want to find you?"

I hesitate. I have to give him something, but what? "Oh," I say, bending down to my backpack. I pull out a scrap of paper from the bottom of the bag and a black pen with runny ink. I sign my name on the paper, blow on the ink to dry, fold it in half, and hand it to him. "You can use this."

He takes the scrap and opens it. "It's just your name."

"You can use it to track me if you need to. But you *shouldn't* need to, because I can find you."

"How does it work?" he asks, tucking the scrap of paper into his pocket carefully.

"Right, you don't know any tracking spells. This one's simple, but relatively effective. It only works if the person you are looking for signed the paper. If you write my name yourself, my location won't be clear. You just take the paper, look at the name, and say 'Monstra mihi nominavit.'"

"*Monstra mihi nominavit,*" he repeats slowly, his tongue tripping over the foreign Latin words. "What does it mean?"

"'Show me the named.' If it works, which it should, you will see the location of whoever you are looking for. It's a bit of a one-hit-wonder, though because after you use it, it will burst into flames."

"Theatric."

"Just the way Hell likes it."

"But I should be able to find you?"

"Easier than a GPS," I confirm.

"GPS?"

"Never mind. Yes, you will be able to find me."

He smiles wider. "I'll find you."

I remain quiet.

He leans forward and gently presses his lips to my forehead, his hand resting on my shoulder. I close my eyes and fight the urge to tilt my chin up and meet his lips with my own.

Don't, I warn myself.

He steps back, still smiling brightly at me. Happiness rolls off of him in waves, and I am knocked breathless. I offer him a tight smile back as he unfurls his wings. He watches me intently, as if he's afraid that if he looks away I'll disappear, so he stares at me, memorizing my face.

"I'll be back later."

"I know," I say, hugging myself.

"Be safe, Pen."

"Not in my nature, Michael."

He tilts his chin down. "Then do it for me."

I look back at him in silence. His blazingly bright eyes are pleading. I nod once, small and quick.

"Thank you."

I turn away before I see him lift out of the clearing, but I can feel the cyclone of air his wings creates. I feel a tightness in my chest at knowing he's gone and I am suddenly aware of the emptiness of the forest without him.

Stop caring.
Stop caring.
Stop. Caring.

But I can't. Something about Michael has changed me, and I'm worried I won't ever be the same. Worse, I'm worried I won't want to be the same.

CHAPTER 19

AZAEL ONCE ASKED ME WHAT I HATED MOST ABOUT humans. After the incident at Eden, he created a list a mile long of everything he hated. I think a large part of him was jealous that humans had more of a choice than angels or demons did. They were influenced by both sides of Earth, pulled in one direction or the other, but ultimately it was their decision who to listen to. They could chose Heaven, Hell, or a bit both.

Az never had a choice like that. He had a fate, a destiny that was already written, and despite what he did, he would always end up where he was supposed to be. Ultimately, everything he did to try to change his story failed.

When he thought he was rebelling against Heaven by falling with Lucifer and joining Hell, he was really just following his fate. He was always destined to fall. It wasn't rebellious; it was expected.

I know that's what upset him most. He had no free will—just the illusion of choice. But his decision was never a surprise. Maybe now that fate is erasing itself, he'll finally get the chance

IGNITE

to write his own destiny. Now that choice won't only be an illusion for him, he could see what I see if he looks hard enough. Being good or being evil aren't the only two options we have. It's possible to be both, and maybe I can convince him of this.

When he would push the issue, force me to pick something that annoyed me about humanity, I would always answer the same: their emotions.

Human emotions are confusing, and Heaven and Hell have been trying to unravel the mystery since Adam. So, it seems, has man. There is no logical explanation for many of the things they feel or what they do in response to that feeling. Emotions are instinctual. They don't need to be learned.

In Greek mythology, emotions were destructive to the world. When Pandora opened her box, out crawled rage, revenge, and spite, ready to tear apart the seams of functional society.

Ancient doctors believed that emotions were controlled by the body's organs. Fear, these doctors thought, was produced by the kidneys. Remove the kidneys, remove fear. Anger, likewise, surged out of the liver like poison. Happiness came from the heart.

Maybe they had that part right. Happiness, love, and affection must lie in the heart. That would explain why I feel so detached from these feelings. I find it hard to imagine falling in love with someone. What would it feel like to have your heart stutter in another's presence? Would it hurt, like a dizzying pinch, or would it be enjoyable, something you crave?

If I still had a heart, I would want to know what falling in love feels like. I would want to experience it for myself.

I've read about falling in love in hundreds of books and thousands of sonnets. Poetry describes love as sudden, unexpected, and overwhelming. It's like a light suddenly appears next to you, warm and bright, showing you everything you couldn't see in the dark. That sounds a lot like Michael. Bright, warm, illuminating.

Emotions are irrational, uncontrollable, and, until a few moments ago, I believed they were a condition only humans could suffer from. But now I think I'm wrong.

I've never been ruled by emotion before, and I'm surprised by how deep these feelings root themselves. I feel different somehow, lighter on my feet. And it terrifies me. I'm not accustomed to happiness, not true happiness, anyway. iIt takes me a minute to identify that happy is what I am feeling. How can someone without a heart be happy? But I am. Happy.

And scared.

I don't understand how I can experience two such strongly opposing feelings at the same time. My emotions fight within me, tumbling over one another, wrestling for dominance. One minute, I'm smiling, imagining a future which, if Michael is right, could be filled with brightness and joy instead of darkness. The next minute, I'm terrified, arrested by the fear of losing my current life. This fear penetrates into my bones and makes me feel like I am made of glass, ready to shatter at any moment.

To give up Hell, I would be giving up a life that's been all I've known for centuries. I would have to start again with nothing and no one.

Because that is what it would mean to trade Hell for something else—for something *more*. I would lose Azael and I would lose my home. I would be completely and utterly alone. Unless I had Michael.

The more I think about it, the more I wonder if I made the right decision to turn my back on Heaven all those years ago. It was a decision I made so quickly, without much consideration. I just knew that I couldn't lose Azael. I was willing to lose almost anything if it meant I could stay close to him.

Something about Hell hasn't ever sat quite right with me and I've never really settled into my role as a demon. At least, I've never been as comfortable as Az has. It never came as naturally for me as it did for my brother. I thought I was able to hide my discomfort with what I've done, but Michael knew. How did he know? I've played my part so well, let it almost completely consume me. If he was able to see that I don't lose myself the way Azael does in evil, who else can?

Over the years, I've carefully built a wall around myself, taller and taller, so that no one could see me for who I really am. No one has ever cared enough to look too closely. But somehow, after just a short time with me, Michael has scaled the wall and gotten a glimpse, however fleeting, at the real me.

The ultimate question is whether or not I am willing to embrace the real me. If I abandon my life in Hell, what do I have? Where would I go?

Heaven is obviously out of the question. I burned that bridge centuries ago, and I don't think there's any penance I can pay to rectify my past mistakes. There are so many questions spinning around in my head that I become dizzy.

I may be losing everything I am familiar with, but maybe I would be gaining something better, something that is completely mine. Something new and untouched that I can define on my own. A path that I can forage for myself. I smile to myself as a line of poetry dances through my mind.

Two roads diverged in a yellow wood...

It's time for me to travel down the road not taken. I don't fit in with angels or demons, but perhaps there is someone else out there as conflicted as I am. Like Michael. And maybe there are others.

My head is pounding as I turn over my options in my head. Heaven, Hell, Heaven, Hell, *other*. The words spin so quickly in my mind they start to blur together. I have no one to turn to for advice. Michael is gone, for now, and if I even hinted to Azael that I was considering shedding my demonic title, he'd flip. He wouldn't let me out of his sight, and I would be forever under his thumb, following his lead. He was the reason I became a demon, and if he had his way, he would be the reason I would stay one.

Azael's darkness is absolute and impossible to ignore. Next to him, anything I am—dark, light, or something in between—is dull and unimpressive. I'm tired of being in his shadow. I can't continue to make my life choices revolve around him. He's my flesh and blood, but he isn't the sun my Earth revolves around.

I'm done holding back my thoughts; I'm done biting my tongue.

As I fly across the expansive forests of the Pacific Northwest, headed towards the rocky cliffs of the Appalachian trails, hope begins to bloom in my stomach, its roots reaching out and growing into my veins. The warmth seeps slowly through me, and I find that I'm smiling to myself, unafraid of who sees me.

Salvation comes at the strangest moments and in the most unsuspecting forms. Salvation is a second chance that I never expected, and this second chance came from someone who has now lived twice. I only hope that I am brave enough to accept this chance that has been placed before me. I'll have to take another leap, be vulnerable, and put my trust in someone else to catch me. This courage could set me free.

It feels like the black clouds of my past are finally behind me and I have the strength and courage to move forward into a future that will be decided solely by me. It feels like I've been sleepwalking since I fell from Heaven, and now Michael's shaken me awake.

I won't be forced down a path by fate or ruled by fear. I won't let anyone, or anything, stand in my way. This is my decision, and while it may be one that I one day come to regret, today I embrace it.

Embrace it fearfully, that is. I don't think my apprehension will fade so quickly.

It's going to take a while for me to unlearn what I have been taught in Hell. Fear's been my life—causing fear, typically. It's not as pleasant when the tables are turned on me.

I remember what Michael said about how being good isn't easy. It takes work, a concentrated effort to do what is right. And for me, this effort will be doubled, as I am forced to redefine what is right and what is wrong. Screw the laws of Heaven and Hell; I'll make my own.

Perhaps I can convince Michael to run away from me, flee the restrictive grip of the angels and demons, and figure out where to go from there. I've battled horrible things before, and I'm sure to battle horrible things in the future, but with Michael, this threat feels manageable, defeatable, even. I may not have faith in Heaven or Hell, but I have a new faith in myself and a growing trust in Michael. I recognized earlier that he had the power to change the world, and maybe I do too.

I know it's going to be difficult, but I'm determined to turn over a new leaf, so to speak. I'll put in the effort, and I'll have Michael next to me for help, just as I'll be there for him. He won't let me fall asleep again, drift back out into the dark waters of evil. He'll be my lighthouse off of a cold black ocean, reminding me what I'm fighting against. Or what I'm fighting for.

Acres of land spin below me as I fly on, leaving the afternoon sun of the west for the twilight streaked sky of the east. Farms and cities rush by with people mulling about in miniature.

I pull my amulet out of my shirt and think of Azael. I can't tell him about my change of heart.

Bad choice of words, I think to myself dryly.

I hate lying to him, but I've painted myself into a corner. I won't let him hurt Michael, and I refuse to let him rope me back down to Hell. So my only option is to keep up my ruse and hope he buys it. And why shouldn't he? As far as he knows, I have no motives to lie.

Azael, I say, focusing my energy into my pendent. I slide the rough stone back and forth across the chain, which buzzes quietly.

Pen. His voice is quiet and clipped.

Am I interrupting something?

Not anymore. Just had a bit of a problem with a rogue 'Lim.

Giving them nicknames, now?

Ah, that would be dear Lilith's doing. It's catchy, don't you think? Sounds a bit like "limb," which is always the first thing they try to bite! They love calves and a nice chewy bicep. Get it? When they spread the virus, they make this weird sound in their throat that sounds a bit like croaking. You know, before the bone crunching and muscle munching sounds.

I scrunch my face in disgust. And that is when I know something is truly different inside of me. This gore, days ago, would have excited me, at least to some extent. I would have hung on every detail of the virus spreading, the humans slowly decimating their own race. But now, it makes me queasy. So much waste...

Fantastic, but I think I prefer Lilim over 'Lim. So I take it the tracking is going well? Have you heard from Gus?

Azael scoffs. *I am not Gus's messenger.*

I wait.

Okay, fine, this time maybe I am his messenger. I've been communicating with him through the map. I've sent him beautiful illustrations I've done just for him. A melting horse, two fornicating women. Very raunchy, and I'm getting pretty good, too. They're much more realistic than I used to draw. I don't think he appreciates them though.

I can't imagine why.

I think it's because he has nothing to draw back to me. He's barely able to craft a verbal insult, let alone a pictorial one. I bet he can't even draw well!

Has he said anything useful? Like when this will all be over? I sigh quietly, hoping he can't hear.

You'll have to be more specific with 'this.' This task? This war? This world?

Don't be a prick. I just need a status report. Is that too much to ask?

He laughs. *Progress is... progressing. And fast, it would seem. He's still not set on an exact date, but I think it's soon. I can feel it, can't you? It's escalating much faster than anyone anticipated, as things are wont to do with angels and demons. And I can't wait to get my hands on some of those angels and pluck the feathers from their wings like chickens.*

I remain quiet.

C'mon, Pen, get excited! It's not too often that we get the green light to go full force at some angels. It's about time, too! I say we grill them over the flames of the dead. Torture them, make it nice and slow.

I shake my head. *Gus must be so pleased you are coming up with these creative plans. I know how he loves your innovation.*

Exactly my thought! OH! I forgot to tell you the best part. We've officially been promoted. Or, I have, specifically. Yours is more... tentative.

Another tentative promotion?

They can track my progress as I go, so they know I'm kicking some major ass out here. I can practically hear the cocky grin in his voice. *You, on the other hand, are working on a cumulative score. No one knows how well you've done your job until D-day. Speaking of which, how's it going?*

It's going... I try to think of something convincing to say, some detail to prove that I'm doing what I've been told to do. *I taught him how to fight today. And he told me he's not convinced Heaven's got it right. I asked him if he would fight for Lucifer. Not straight out, like that, just offhandedly.*

And little Michael said...?

He considered it. I think I can convince him. I swallow a lump in my throat.

That's my sister.

I hesitate for a moment, trying to grab on to a small shard of courage to ask him what's been weighing on my mind for the last few days. *Hey, Az, remember when we first fell and I asked if you thought there was a middle ground between Heaven and Hell?*

He scoffs. *Yeah, it's called Earth.*

No, what I mean is... I take a breath and try to come at him from another angle. *There can't only be pure goodness and pure evil, right?*

We've been over this, Pen. He sounds angry, his voice flat and cruel. *There are only two sides to a coin. Heads or tails, good or evil. There is no third side—when you flip a coin it doesn't land on its edge. There is nothing in between. It's one or the other.*

Well what if—

He cuts me off. *Enough nonsense. Let's get back to me before I lose interest in this conversation completely.*

I bite my tongue and stay silent. He's not hearing what I'm saying; he doesn't want to listen. I have to force back my disappointment with his dismissive tone and pretend not to be bothered by it. Az can't know how important this is to me—how desperately I want there to be a third side to a coin, a middle ground, a gray area.

So do you know what it means when we get a promotion?

Darker wings? I guess. *Larger weapons? A fruit basket?*

Muffin basket, actually, he jokes back. *And on top of that, added skills. I don't need you to kill people for me anymore.*

What?! Even though I knew the time would come where he would have full powers, a shock pierces through me. I never thought it would be so soon.

That's right. We can now be sold as separate items, making us both drastically more valuable! I can kill now. And Hell, it feels amazing. No wonder you went so crazy in that hospital waiting room. I don't see why you hold yourself back so much. I can't even begin to tell you how many throats I've ripped. I can fillet a human like no other.

So I'll be able to reap?

IGNITE

I can almost feel him roll his eyes. *Fine, ignore all the cool things I can do now. Yes, when you get your promotion, you'll be able to reap souls. They figured that it would be beneficial for us both to be able to kill and reap. That way they can send us on more solo missions. Spread our wings, so to speak.*

So to speak, I repeat.

Are you jealous?

No, I'm not jealous, I say a little sharply.

No, you're not jealous at all. Definitely not. You don't sound the least bit bitter.

I'll be promoted soon, and then you'll be the one moping around because I won't need you anymore. I'll have my own collection of souls to carry around.

Except I won't. I'll never be promoted, and I'll never be able to reap a soul. Because I'm a traitor. It's not official yet, and I haven't technically done anything traitorous against Hell, but the thought is there, as is the plan.

In some ways, it's a relief to hear that Azael has been promoted. He doesn't need me anymore. I can let go of him and know that he'll be fine. He won't be looked down on for being only a half-powerful demon. He can do it all now. But this also makes him more of a threat to me. I never had to worry about keeping my eye on Az before, and now suddenly he seems dangerous.

I won't have time to mope. I'll be too busy ripping my way through Heaven!

Right.

So you see, I'll have bigger and better things on my plate than to worry about you encroaching on my territory.

I hear a loud explosion from Azael's side of the conversation.

Az?

Silence.

Azael?!

Holy Hell, that was awesome! He's laughing like a lunatic.

What was that? Are you okay?

Of course I'm okay, Pen. Who do you think I am, some amateur? That was just a propane tank blowing up. The hazards of Lilim fighting a bit too close to a barbecue. The fireworks are fantastic. It's just the meat shower afterwards that I find a tad unpleasant. I'll have to wash their flesh out of my hair. Do you know how hard it is to wash flesh out of your hair?

My stomach flips uncharacteristically. *Not personally, no.*

Consider yourself lucky.

He's so flippant about those affected by the virus. He doesn't care at all. He's worried more about his hair than the people who were blown up in the explosion. And suddenly I understand that all of the good that was left in Azael is gone, frozen over time in the depths of Hell.

That's why he can't even fathom that there is something between good and evil, that both tendencies can exist in all of us. That's why he won't listen to what I'm saying.

I hear him laugh again as a second explosion erupts on his side. With a sinking feeling, I realize that it is hopeless to save him. There's no convincing him; the evil in him will never thaw and give way to something better.

If I leave Hell, he will never follow me.

Oh trust me, I consider myself very lucky to not be covered in chunks of human flesh. Az, I'll talk to you later, all right?

Yeah, sure. He sounds distracted.

Just, be safe... I say, hoping he can hear me.

Not in my nature, he hisses before severing our connection.

I know it's not.

I tuck my necklace back under my shirt, adjust the straps of my backpack on my shoulder, and allow myself to let go of Azael as I see the tops of the mountains coming into view. I imagine saying goodbye one last time, and I picture what it will be like walking away from him.

He'll be better off without me. I have to tell myself that. I have to believe that's the truth.

CHAPTER 20

WHEN I LEFT THE PACIFIC NORTHWEST, THE FINGERS OF fall had just started to spread across the forests. The autumn palette of oranges, golds, and reds was slowly beginning to encroach on the greens of summer, like the woods were starting to rust. But there are no traces of summer left in the ridges and valleys of the Appalachian. Even in the darkness, I can see the rich colors of the leaves that cling desperately to the trees.

The October air is crisp and dry, the sky clear and bright. I've missed the mountains. This weather invites more hikers during the days, but they typically remain on the designated paths. And those who don't stay on the paths, those adventurous or stupid enough to explore the overgrown trails on their own, are easy to avoid. After all, the mountains are huge and offer hundreds of hiding places, and there is no one more familiar with these hiding places than I am.

None are as beautiful as Michael's cave, I think.

I don't plan on staying out here too long. Tomorrow, I'll go into the closest city and find someplace decent to stay.

Somewhere more human, less animal. Maybe I'll use some of the emergency cash I have stolen away in my backpack to rent a nice, fluffy hotel room with room service and a hot shower. I would kill for a hot shower.

But for tonight, the woods will do.

I land on a high bluff of one of the tallest ridges of the mountain, my feet connecting solidly to the rocks below with a crunch. I lean over the cliff and stare down to the tops of the trees below me. The colorful tawny leaves are splattered across the trees like the drunken brushstrokes of a careless artist. The color stands out brightly against the cold gray of the mountain side.

I walk away from the bluff and into the thick covering of trees. The ground slopes down and the rough granite turns into tightly packed dirt. Roots of trees that border the narrow trail twist above the dirt and create a set of large landings, sectioning the path off into strange steps. Without these natural stairs, the path would have been too steep and I would not have been able to climb down without slipping.

I run down the hill, hopping from one step to another, until I reach a small shack meant for hunters or campers. The wood of the cabin is old and dry, and it lists horribly to one side, sinking into the uneven ground, but it doesn't look like it's rotting. The roof has no noticeable holes, and the windows, surprisingly, aren't broken. I walk up to the creaking, wooden-planked entrance of the cabin and peek in one of the grimy windows. It's empty, so I reach to the front door and go in.

The inside of the cabin smells musty and like animals, but it's better than sleeping outside in the dirt. It's a one-room shack with a tiny fireplace on one wall, a wooden pallet for a bed pushed below a small window, and a rickety picnic table in the center of the room. There are two windows next to the front door and two small windows looking out of the back of the cabin that offer a dirty view of a valley below this ridge.

There are still some logs stacked in the fireplace, charred black on their bottom. I light them with a wave of my hand and swing my backpack onto the picnic table. It lands with a thud and I straddle the splintered bench, digging through the pockets of the bag.

I only have one more clean t-shirt left and one tattered sweatshirt. Sitting at the bottom of the bag is a bruised apple wrapped up in a cloth napkin. It's the last of my food so I'll have to hike down into the city early tomorrow if I want breakfast. I pull it out and shine it on my shirt before biting into it. The apple is bitter and juicy, and underneath its soft skin, it is beginning to brown. I finish it too quickly and toss the core into the fire.

I sit on the picnic bench for a few minutes, watching the flames lick lazily against the blackened stones of the fireplace as I distractedly spin my bracelet around my wrist. The beads are clear and cold, reminding me how far away Michael is.

When I'm around him, I feel almost like my old self again. He has an energy about him that is bright and inviting, like a fire in the middle of a snowstorm. Maybe he holds the flames of Heaven inside of him, I think, just as I hold the ice of Hell inside of me.

But I won't for much longer. One day soon, I'll be warm too. And tonight is my first step. I'll take the time to peel away the layers of my past, step out of the shadows, and wade into the light. I'll bury my old life in these woods and walk away, but I won't forget. I have to remember my mistakes if I have any hope of learning from them.

I stand up from the table, grabbing a dirty t-shirt from my backpack, and walk over to the pallet bed. I ball the shirt up, setting it at the head of the bed, and lie down. My shoulders dig painfully into the hard frame and I try to shift myself into a comfortable position, but there isn't one.

Somehow, this wooden bed is more painful than the uneven bench of the cave. At least in the cave there was the comforting glow of the mason jars and the lingering scent of honey. All I have here is a gloomy cabin that smells like animals, dirt, and sweat. Even the fire doesn't do anything to cheer up the shack.

I stare up at the ceiling, willing myself to fall asleep, but my mind is too loud.

I try closing my eyes, but when I do, I picture the way Azael will look at me when I betray him. His sharp, dark-featured face fades away into Michael's, his eyes bright and hopeful.

We can do it. I hear his whisper swirl in my head. *You've woken up. You see what I see.*

I imagine reaching out to him and placing my cool hand on his cheek. *I'm almost there,* I tell him. *I may still need some convincing, a reminder.*

He smiles and leans forward as if to kiss me again.

I open my eyes and roll over, facing the back windows. I'll see him again soon. And when I do, I'll tell him that I'm different. I'll tell him how he's changed me and that I want to run away with him. Run away from Heaven, from Hell, and from the war. We'll run until we can't run anymore.

I take a deep breath, close my eyes, and touch my bracelet again. *We can do it, Michael.*

I'm on the brink of sleep when I think I hear him answer me. *Pen?*

His soft voice relaxes me and I fall over the edge of sleep, landing dreamlessly into unconsciousness.

CHAPTER 21

The sound of Azael's needlelike voice wakes me up.

You like poetry, don't you, Pen? How about a little Percy Bysshe Shelley.

It's early, Az. I throw my arm over my face, shielding my eyes from the hot sunlight that streams through the window of the shack.

He ignores me and begins to recite the lines of a poem dramatically. "Horror covers all the sky / Clouds of darkness blot the moon…"

I sigh.

"Prepare! for mortal thou must die / Prepare to yield thy soul up soon."

Why the sudden interest in literature?

I thought you would appreciate it! He sounds mildly offended.

Sure, I love it. Just maybe not at this ungodly hour.

Great choice of words. This hour is indeed Godless.

Har, har.

I peer out from under my arm and look around the empty cabin. The fire is dead, the logs reduced to ashes. By the angle of the sun outside, I realize it's not as early as I thought it was. I sit up, swing my legs over the bed, and stand up stiffly, stretching my arms and rolling my shoulders.

Remind me never to wake you up again, he complains.

It's fine. But did you have something else to say, or did you just want to share with me the fact that you've learned how to read? I tease.

Wrong-o, dear sister. He tsks. *I heard that poem from Lilith. She sings it as she makes her way across the globe, creating one Lilim after another. The virus is spreading at an impressive rate, and I would like to think that I am the reason it is so successful.*

I'm sure Lilith would love to hear that. I laugh. *So you still can't read, then?*

I'll have you know I can read at an advanced level. Tolstoy, Kipling, Shakespeare, all the so-called greats! None of whom can compare to John Milton, though. You know my fondness for Paradise Lost.

Indeed I do.

Even though most literature bores Azael, he's always been attracted to *Paradise Lost*. He's read it more times than I can count. In fact, I think it's the only book suggestion that I've given him that he actually read himself.

I used to read to him while he trained or as he drifted off to sleep in our frozen room in Hell. He didn't like to read, didn't understand why it wasn't a waste of time, and would usually end up losing or destroying any books I lent him. So I would read to him, making sure my books stayed safe. Even more often, I would quote scenes of dialogue or poetry at him and he would deflect my words with a scoff or an eye roll.

One of my favorite stories to read to Azael was *Romeo and Juliet*. I thought the sudden, consuming love—a love that was impossible and forbidden—was fascinating and tragic. Azael, on the other hand, hated it. He was a much bigger fan of

Shakespeare's *Macbeth*. Murder, mayhem, an evil plot... It was right up his alley.

But there was something about Juliet that I found almost familiar. I could never quite identify what it was. I could relate to her on a strange level, and I felt her story strike me through my chest. Her loss became my loss, like in most books I read, as I threw myself completely into the story.

I couldn't explain to Az how books were a kind of rare magic. Words have a power of their own. They build worlds, create lives, shape futures. You can delve into these foreign worlds just by opening the cover of a book and escape from it as quickly as you could shut it again. I was able to travel through time and space just within the pages of a novel. I could be a hero, a villain, or someone driven mad by romance.

For days, I would surround myself with the delicate parchment, fingering my way through chapters of adventures I would never experience first-hand. I would emerge with another stack of books or sheets of sonnets, my fingers dark and bruised-looking, stained with blue and black ink.

He clears his throat. *"The mind is its own place, and in itself / Can make a heav'n of hell, a hell of heav'n." Milton could not be more right! Heaven was my Hell, but Hell is my Heaven.*

I stay silent.

Anyway, this all brings me to my point.

You have a point? I say in mock surprise.

Two points, actually. Point number one: It's getting closer. The war, that is. Gus says that they've nearly severed the connection between Michael and Lucifer, so when the time comes, you'll be able to either bring him with you back to Hell or kill him. I personally am rooting for the latter of those two options. I say goodbye and good riddance to the glowing bastard. I don't want to fight next to him. You couldn't pay me enough!

How soon? Will they be severed, I mean?

According to good old Gus, they should be split by tomorrow night.

That's great! I say, forcing enthusiasm. He'll be free from Lucifer. I don't let myself smile about this fact, however, because I know that this freedom comes at a cost, as most freedom does. He won't be safe anymore. Every demon will be after him if he doesn't join Hell. And he won't. Neither will I.

Hold on to your seat, Pen, because if you thought that that news is good, wait until you hear what I have to say next.

I sit down on the picnic tabletop and grab the splintered edge. *Consider my seat held.*

The second point I needed to tell you was that Lucifer has been taking notice and is impressed. Gus has been reporting back to him every day with the new data I've given him, and it's helping with the whole disappearing future thing. Sort of. We're getting a clearer date...

Did you get a gold star?

Better. He takes a pause. *I'm second in command.*

Second... I shake my head, confused. *In all of Hell?*

Soon to be all of Hell and *Heaven! When we reclaim the throne of Heaven, I will be in charge of Hell, oversee the demons that prefer the basement to the attic. I'll be ranked even higher than an L1 demon, with special quarters in Heaven.*

My mouth hangs open in shock. I try to grab at something to say but can't think of anything coherent.

Don't be worried, he continues. *I plan on making you my number two. Which, if you're doing the math, would make you overall number three. Bronze—that's not too bad, right?*

I—

Listen to Milton, Pen. "Better to reign in Hell, than to serve in Heaven." Do you see how poignant that is? Are you appreciating my grasp of literature now?

I guess congratulations are in order.

We'll throw a party after the war. I expect you to give a moving speech that speaks in wonder of my accolades.

I'll get started on that right away.

IGNITE

I put my head in my hands. He'll rule Hell, and I won't be there for it. For a brief moment, I reconsider my decision about Michael. If Azael will be in charge, maybe I should...

No. I've made my choice, and nothing is going to change that. Azael won't control my future anymore. I may not have any guarantee of what my future will be without him, but I'll have the possibility of something better. And sometimes the possibility of something different is better than the promise of sameness.

You must! Because if it does not meet my expectations, I'll have the strength of an army behind me to express my dismay.

I wonder how soon Lucifer will reconsider putting you in charge, I joke. *Probably moments after you make your first decision.*

I can tell you one thing: Expect casual Fridays! He laughs to himself, and I swear I can hear someone else talking to him. A higher female voice that's as thick as smoke and smooth as velvet. It must be Lilith.

Az, I have to go. I need to—

I couldn't care less, I've got things I've got to do. He says something else. It's muffled, clearly not directed at me, and I'm wondering what Lilith has made of him. Azael, I think, will be perfectly fine without me. He won't even have the time or energy to miss me. *I'll check in later if there are any updates. Remember Michael.*

Michael? I ask, dazed.

Convince him. Or don't. You don't have much time left either way.

And then he's gone, my head filled with only my own thoughts again, which are loud and tumultuous.

Lucifer will overthrow Heaven and Azael will rule Hell. At this point, these two facts are inevitable. I'm coming to understand that Hell has grown far too powerful for Heaven to defeat. The demonic army is expanding at an alarming pace—the demons and fallen angels are stronger than they have ever been before, and with the added strength of the Lilim, Heaven stands little chance.

I want to call Michael, to talk to him and share my worries with him. I want to tell him that I believe in him, too, like he believes in me. I want to take his hand and flee the darkness, and if we aren't able to find any light, we'll make our own. I want to make sure he knows that I know I can save myself, I just need him to stand by me. I'm still not strong enough to face this entirely alone.

The fact is, Michael makes me *feel* again. I'm not sure what I feel yet. I'm still trying to untangle the confusing knot inside my mind.

But I can't talk to Michael, and I have no idea when I'll see him next. He didn't tell me when he'd be back, and all I can do is sit and wait. I hate being useless; I hate being still. I'm antsy and have the urge to do something—anything, really. I just need to move.

So I move.

I jump down from the tabletop, take my balled up shirt from the pallet bed, and throw it in the open backpack, which I zip up quickly and throw over my shoulders. I rush out of the cabin, pulling the door closed behind me, the hinges whining pathetically.

I run down the mountain and into the mist that hangs between the peaks, following the twisting trail as it winds between tall trees and overgrown wildflowers. My boots crunch loudly on fallen twigs and leaves, keeping rhythm with the puffs of my breath.

As I near the bottom of the mountain, I hear other people's voices. I slow my run down to a brisk walk, and when I round the corner, I see a man in his mid-forties with two small girls. They all have bright, rosy cheeks, twill pants, and matching sweatshirts on, keeping them warm in the autumn chill. They are also wearing strange, flat packs on their backs. A plastic tube strings out from the bottom of their packs. One of the girls chews on the gummy end of the plastic tube and then sucks water through it. The other girl is holding a narrow container that holds a sliced green apple and a dollop of peanut butter.

They hear me as I come around the tree and I smile at them. The two girls wave happily, and I rush past them, getting ready to run the rest of the way down the path, but the man calls out to me.

"Hey, are you all right?" he asks.

I stop and turn around to look at him. "Yeah, I'm fine. Just camping. Enjoying the weather and all." I hold out one of my arms and gesture around to the vibrant-colored leaves. Hoping that will be the end of our conversation, I spin on my heel and continue on.

He calls out again. "You sure? You're awfully young to be out here by yourself. Is there anyone else with you? Are you lost, maybe?"

I shift my backpack between my shoulders and look back at them. "I'm older than you think. I am meeting someone though, so I have to go…"

"Well, if you're sure." He watches me carefully, unconvinced.

The older of the two small girls steps forward and holds out the plastic container that is clutched between her tiny, tan hands. "Wanna slice?"

I consider the apples for a moment before shaking my head. "That's okay. I had an apple earlier."

The girl giggles. "I hate apples."

"Me too," I confess, smiling.

She laughs again, and I turn around, walking away from the three. I distantly hear the older man tell the girls to roll up their socks to protect themselves from ticks. When I'm convinced they won't be able to see me anymore, I break out in a sprint again.

Unfortunately, it's too sunny today and too crowded in the woods for me to fly.

CHAPTER 22

I T TAKES ME THE MAJORITY OF THE MORNING TO MAKE IT out of the mountains and into the nearest city.

I marvel at the amount of people mulling about on the sidewalks, rushing from store to store, into waiting cabs and parked cars. It's amazing that a city this busy can rest so closely to someplace as peaceful as the mountains. I wonder how many of them have ever even been into the woods before, let alone seen more grass than the narrow strips of green that make up the sad, tiny parks that are wedged between towering office buildings.

As I walk deeper into the heart of the city, I remember that Azael used to call cities like this concrete canyons. There is no phrase better to describe the way the massive steel, concrete, and glass buildings rise out of the sidewalks and stretch up towards the sky. It's beautiful in a very cold, manmade way. This is a different kind of mountain range but the buildings seem equally as tall and gray as the natural ones that are just miles away.

These buildings line both sides of the pothole-riddled, narrow street that is congested with traffic. Cars honk their horns impatiently at each other and at passing pedestrians that weave between the stopped traffic. A few blocks from where I am, I see the large, lit awning of a hotel.

Finally, some place decent to sleep.

Azael and I were stockpiling money over the last few months from people we conned and pockets we picked. I have a few fat wads of cash at the bottom of my bag that should let me stay in a decent room for a couple of weeks, but I don't think I'll need to stay here that long. I'm hoping Michael will be back in a few days.

I push through the glass and gold revolving doors and walk up to the front desk. A woman with dark red hair twisted up into a neat bun paces behind the desk with a small headset pressed into her ear. I lean forward and rest my arms on the tall, marble counter. She lifts one finger to me, asking me to wait.

"I understand, sir. I'll send maintenance up right away. Yes, sir. Well, the fans cannot hold anything over a couple of pounds, which is why it fell when you... Okay, of course. Our apologies. We will send a complimentary breakfast to you tomorrow morning. Of course. Yes, sir. Thank you for staying at The Aria. Let us know if there is anything else we can do to make your stay more enjoyable."

She presses a finger up to her ear, pulls the microphone away from her mouth, and smiles at me tightly.

"Welcome to The Aria. My name is Nicole," she says, pointing to her name tag, as if proving to me that what she's saying is true. Sure enough, in thick, black marker, her name is scribbled across the golden tag that is pinned to her shirt. I raise my eyebrows and nod. Satisfied, she drops her hand, but not her fake smile. "How can I help you today?"

"I need to book a room."

She looks down at the glowing screen of her computer. "Sure. How many beds?"

"One."

She types, her fingers punching the letters of her keyboard with a loud clack. "King or queen?"

"King." I excitedly imagine sinking into the soft foam of an expensive mattress. After weeks of roughing it, I'm ready for a real bed. I'm sure Azael and Lilith are living it up as they cross the globe, infecting more Lilim. Why shouldn't I?

"Perfect." She hits more keys, nodding. "How long will you be staying with us?"

"Uh, can I book it for the week?" That should be more than enough time. Michael could be back any day now.

"The week or the week plus the weekend? Our weekend rates are double."

I pull my backpack around and stick my hand deep into one of the pockets, feeling the cash. "Just the week, thanks."

"Of course. No problem." She prints off a small receipt and holds it out to me, circling the cost with a red ballpoint pen. "And how will you be paying today?"

I bring out the stack of cash and place it on the counter. Her eyes widen. "Cash," I answer. "This should cover it."

She hesitates a moment and her eyes rake over my tangled hair and dirty clothes, like she's seeing me for the first time. She purses her lips. "How old are you?"

I reach into my backpack again and pull out another thinner stack of cash, sliding it across the counter to her. "Old enough."

She reaches out and picks up the money, flipping through the green bills with excitement. The paper whispers together, tempting her further. With a look over her shoulder, she pockets it, and returns to the computer.

"Of course, my mistake. You look old enough to me." She doesn't look at me when she says this. Instead, she fans out the rest of the money, her eyes scanning the bills quickly before she closes it again, tapping the stack on the counter to make them line up. "Great. Everything seems to be in order." She reaches down, picks up a gold and red plastic card from behind the computer, and slides it back across the counter towards me. "Top floor. Enjoy your stay at The Aria. Let us know if there is anything we can do to make your stay more enjoyable."

I grab the card from her fingers, waving it once in the air in a small, sarcastic salute. "Sure thing."

My boots click loudly on the gold-colored marble floor as I make my way over to the bank of elevators that ping periodically, their shiny doors sighing open and closed. I hit one of the buttons between two elevators, it lights up, and I step back and wait.

The doors open with a chime and a group of people surge out, some clutching suite cases and others bundled in large downey coats. I press myself back against the wall and wait for all of them to stream past me before I go into the mirrored elevator and press the button for the top floor.

A generic song plays over the speakers of the elevator as it smoothly ascends. No one joins me in the elevator as I go higher and higher so I lean back against one of the walls and watch myself, reflected on every surface of the small space.

My face is pale, but relatively clean, and I have dark circles bruised under my deep purple eyes that flick anxiously from one image of myself to another. My hair is a mess of black and blue knots, and I brush my fingers through the tangles, trying to tame it.

Finally, the doors slide open and reveal a small corridor with tall, teal walls and wide, hardwood planks. I glance at the number on my card. 13. I lean out of the elevator and look up and down the hallway. Rooms one through six are to the left, and seven through thirteen line down the right side.

I step out of the elevator just as the doors begin to slide closed, clutching my room key in my hands. I pivot on my heel and walk down the empty hallway, dark doors passing by on one side as bright windows blur past me on the other side. A few rooms have a crack of light peeking out from the bottom of their doors while others appear to be empty. Even though the doors are thick and soundproofed, I can still hear the muffled sounds of TVs, showers, and conversations through the walls.

Room 13 is at the end of the long hallway, facing the length of the corridor instead of the windows that look out and over the busy streets of the city like the other rooms do. I step up to the mahogany door and slide my keycard into the slot. A small green light turns on, and the door clicks loudly, opening up for me.

I go into the room, squeezing through the door into the dark room, and grab the "Do Not Disturb" sign. I hang the plastic sign on the handle and close the door behind me, sliding the chain through the door and locking the deadbolt for good measure before I go farther into the room. There is a panel of light switches next to the door and I flick on a few, bathing the room in a warm, buttery light.

When I turn away from the door, I'm nearly knocked off my feet by the luxuriousness of the room. I'm not accustomed to such fine items and I'm worried that if I touch something I'll break it. There is a small bar with several crystal champagne glasses turned upside down on the black marbled top. The walls are a deep gray and the floor is covered with a soft, feathery white rug. In front of me is a large bed with a black cushioned headboard adorned with dozens of crisp, plump pillows and a fluffy white comforter. Vintage-looking wooden nightstands sit on either side of the bed with silver wall lights shining down on them.

Three tall windows line either side of the room. The windows on the left show the same view as the ones in the hallway—the street below, bustling with people flitting from one place to another. The windows on the right side, however, offer a picturesque view of the distant mountains. They sit like shadowed giants on the horizon, guarding the city as the sun slowly sets behind them.

I walk over and look out one of the large windows, leaning against the frame. My room sits above the other tall buildings of the city, and I'm glad I have this unobstructed view of the mountains. Without a reminder that there are still places on this Earth that aren't crowded with people and paved over, I would go crazy.

I stare out at the mountains, trying to memorize the rocky silhouette and store the memory away for later. I'll keep this image ingrained in my mind the same way I've kept Michael's secret pond and hidden cave with me. I need these reminders of the beauty of Earth, of the life. This world is not worthless. There are things worth saving here, regardless of what Azael thinks.

With great difficulty, I remove myself from the window, walk over to the doors of a mirrored closet, and toss my dirty backpack inside. Before I touch anything else, I desperately need to shower. I don't want to leave dirt on the pristine bed or track more mud over the white carpet.

I make my way back towards the front of the room and stop at a tall door that is set into the wall midway through the room. I slide the door open and step inside the bathroom, pulling the door closed so I can trap the steam of my shower in with me.

Glittering black granite makes up the majority of the bathroom—the vanity, the floor, and even the lower half of the walls. Two clear, large bowls sit on top of the vanity with ornate golden faucets fixed above them. A huge rectangular mirror is also framed in gold above the vanity and reflects the large shower and bathtub on the other side of the room.

A giant glass door opens into the shower, which is tiled in smaller glittering black squares. The shower head is flat and square, hanging in the center of the shower. When I reach in to turn it on, cool water falls out of the head like a waterfall. The water slaps on the floor as it warms up, steaming the glass of the door.

I take off my boots and strip off my dirt-covered clothes, tossing them in a pile in the corner of the bathroom. After the glass door is almost completely fogged over with steam, I step into the shower and let the water slip over my head and down my shoulders, washing away the thin layer of dirt that seems to cling to my skin. I tip my head back and close my eyes, letting the hot water hit my face.

The complimentary hotel shampoo and soap smells like lavender and lathers soothingly in my hair and over my body. I pull together some of the bubbles in my hands and blow them across the shower, laughing to myself. It's amazing what a decent shower can do to my mood.

After I lazily rinse the foam off of me, I cut off the warm water, reach through the shower door, and grab a heavy white bathrobe. I wrap myself in the robe, wring out my hair, and step out of the shower and onto the cold, slippery tiles.

The mirror has completely fogged over during my shower, and I swipe my hand across it, clearing off a small circle so I can see myself. Wide, violet eyes stare back at me, surprised, and my cheeks are red from the hot water, but my skin looks brighter now that it isn't coated in dust and dirt.

I roll up the sleeve of my robe and examine the scars I showed Michael the other day. Thin, delicate, and pale scars lace up my arm and onto my shoulder, wrapping around the back of my neck at the nape of my hair. These scars are so familiar I can almost remember where each one came from.

The thin scars came from whips, sharp, golden, and dipped in holy water. They burned my skin, tied me down, and nearly bled me out. There are other scars too, thick and jagged. One at the crook of my elbow I remember receiving from the serrated tip of an arrow; another that slashes across my wrist is from the hot blade of a dagger.

There are scars from sharp teeth, from when I was an angel still fighting against the snarling demons of Hell. Those scars are small and perfectly round, like white freckles up the inside of my arm, from wrist to elbow. I count them. There are nineteen in total, but they are so pale that they're nearly impossible to see from far away.

I cover my arm with the robe again and leave the bathroom, moving from cold tile to plush carpet as I go over and hop onto the tall, squishy bed. The mattress sinks under me, warm, fluffy, and so comfortable I don't think I'll ever be able to leave it. I lean over to grab the phone that rests on one of the nightstands. A small framed menu lists room services and the numbers for each service. I dial the number for the hotel restaurant.

The phone rings once before a man with a thick, drawling southern accent picks up. "The Aria restaurant. Are you making a reservation or placing an order for room service?"

"Room service," I say slowly and clearly, hoping that my enunciation will rub off on him.

"I can take your order, miss. What'll it be?" It doesn't.

"Chicken. Whatever kind you've got."

"Oh, well that's a fair amount, miss. We've got grilled chicken, chicken parm, spinach-stuffed chicken, barbecue chicken, lemon-basil chicken, chicken strips—"

I cut him off before he lists every chicken dish ever made. "Chicken strips are fine."

"Great choice, but it's from our kids menu. Is that all right with you, miss?"

"That's fine. Just make it a double order."

"Sure enough, sure enough." I hear him typing through the phone. "What would you like for your side? Your options are salad, vegetables, french fries—"

Again, I cut him off. "French fries."

"Would you like your fries curly, thin cut, wedged, chipped…"

His voice continues to list the innumerable styles of french fries they make, and I roll my eyes, bringing the phone away from my ear. I just want a simple dinner. This shouldn't be so complicated. I bring the phone back up to my ear, and when he breaks for a breath, I quickly answer, "Surprise me."

I hang up before he has time to give me any more options about how I would like my food.

A small, silver remote rests next to the phone so I scoop it up and turn on the wide, flat TV that hangs from the wall in front of the bed. With nothing better to do, I flip through a few dismal nightly news programs until I hear room service knock on my door. I jump down, still wrapped in my thick bathrobe, and run to the door barefoot. I unlock the door and yank it open, leaning out to take the tray of food from a man dressed in a crisp, red and black uniform.

"Add a tip to my room bill," I tell him with a smile.

He nods and I close the door to him, running back to my bed to eat.

The chicken strips are crispy and delicious, as are the french fries. I sip at the complimentary fizzing drink as I polish off my dinner and watch the end of a strange cartoon about a boy and his magical dog. I lick my fingers clean, set the empty tray on the floor next to the bed, and scoot myself under the covers. I pull the blankets up past my shoulders and bury my head into the feathery pillows, sighing contentedly.

A hot shower, a full meal, and a soft bed. Maybe this is all Heaven needs to be.

I smile as I drift off into sleep, my thoughts dancing around Michael.

Goodnight, Michael. I think to myself.

Goodnight, Pen.

I open my eyes for a minute, thinking I heard his voice in the room. I sit up, pushing the blankets down so I can look around the room. But I'm alone, and I can see the locks in place on the door. It was just my imagination.

I lie back down and resettle myself.

Don't worry. You can sleep. I'll chase away any nightmares. His voice is golden and musical, just like I remember it.

I'll chase away yours, I sleepily answer in my mind. *Next time I see you.*

And I fall asleep.

CHAPTER 23

DAYS DRAG ON QUIETLY AND UNEVENTFULLY. I SHOULD be glad for the peace, but instead it makes me nervous. It's like the calm before a violent storm. I can feel the electricity in the air and I'm just waiting for the lightening to strike, the fire to spread, and the chaos to begin.

The news gets bleaker and bleaker each day. There's a mass shooting at a mall, a movie theater, a school. The murder and suicide rates are soaring. Almost every country in the East is at war—uprisings, bombings... Eventually I have to turn the television off. I can't stomach the news anymore; it only makes me anxious.

Azael checks in periodically.

How do you say "Leave me alone" in Japanese? What about "Go to Hell"?

Is it bad form to say "Bon appetit" instead of "Bon jour" in France? I just think it would be better to be upfront with them. Let them know it's not going to be a good day, but they'll have a good appetite.

IGNITE

Have you ever been to Florida? You're not missing much. Unless you enjoy the juxtaposition of alligators and the elderly, who, coincidentally, are both equally as wrinkled and leathery.

I sent Gus another one of my masterpieces. Lilim Cubism, very avant-garde. He doesn't seem to appreciate the fine arts.

I'm convinced all of West Virginia has been infected at this point. It's the only explanation for some of the things I've seen.

But he never says anything of real significance, so our conversations are limited. Occasionally, he will ask about Michael. He doesn't ask about specifics though. He just wants to make sure I'm still in contact with him. I assure him that I am, and he usually lets the subject drop. I try not to ask him anything too serious, and he returns the favor, saving me from having to fabricate too many lies.

The majority of my days are spent avoiding the news by watching horrible daytime television, messing around with the strange gadgets and jets on the bathtub, ordering an exorbitant amount of room service, and pacing back and forth in front of my bed. I'm nearly convinced that there will be a hole in the carpet by the time I leave.

I have nothing to do until Michael comes back, and I'm going stir crazy. There are too many things to think about—some things are out of my control, but they still clog up my mind.

Azael, I fear, is becoming more distant and detached from the barbaric things he does and the people he kills. I think he's completely forgotten what it was like to have a soul. The Lilim virus is spreading at an alarming rate, and I can feel a shift happening beneath my feet. Even though I'm not in Hell, I can sense the dark excitement in the air, like a heavy cloud, all around me. I wonder if I'm the only one that has noticed it.

None of this is within my control. Logically, I realize this, but I can't stop thinking about it, worrying about it, planning for it to happen. But how do you plan for something when you don't know when it will happen or how? You can't. So I pace back and forth, spinning my dagger around in the air, and worry. The only thing I can do is be ready for when the time comes and hope Michael will come with me when I run—wherever I run to.

I wait for Michael, sometimes thinking I can hear his voice. I have fake conversations with him, telling him stories from my past and dreams I have for my future. Talking to him is easy. I can forget my worry and be distracted for at least a few minutes. We don't talk about the war, about the Lilim, or about anything dark or scary.

I think, I imagine telling him, *that you would have loved the 1920s.*

I hear his chuckle. *Oh, and why is that?*

The music, the passion. There was this new sense of freedom, of liberation. The whole decade felt like one long, drawn out New Years celebration.

Were you on Earth during the 20s?

Of course! Chicago, mostly. Everything, it seemed, was alcohol, bright lights, and loud music. Maybe not everywhere, but definitely in Chicago. Azael befriended some prominent gangsters and had a rousing good time tearing up the town.

He did?

Oh yes. He and Al Capone were the best of friends. Al and Az: the two smartest bootleggers in all of America. The police could never quite pin them down because whenever they came too close, I would throw them off the trail. All it took was a smooth, smokey voice, maybe a rolled down stocking, and those cops couldn't even remember which way was up.

So you worked with the smugglers? What was it like?

I didn't interfere much with 'the business.' That's what they always called it, 'the business.' Mostly, I was on Azael's arm, or spending my time at speakeasies, dancing. I flop down on the bed, throwing my arm over my head and close my eyes, remembering the glitter of the decade, the brassy music, the smoke.

What did you look like? I imagine him resting his head on his hand, listening intently.

IGNITE

Cropped, jaw-length dark hair with a silky wave, ivory skin, blood-red lipstick, and coal eyeliner. And like any respectable flapper girl, a short, gold sequined dress, t-strap shoes, and a flask full of gin secured to my thigh. I smile, remembering the way I shined in the dress, spinning on the dance floor to loud, gravelly jazz music.

I would have loved to see you dance.

You would have danced with me, I tell him. *I would have made you.*

You wouldn't have had to make me, I imagine him saying back to me. *I'm sure I would have been more than eager to dance with you.*

I roll my eyes. That's exactly something Michael would say, were I really talking to him. *Azael never danced*, I say. *He only sat with a drink in his hand, his fedora pulled low, hiding his eyes, and a cigarette between his lips. He enjoyed watching the girls who spun around him, their fringe fanning out in front of his face. A total bore.*

He can't dance?

He can, but, surprisingly, he wasn't into the flashy style of the 20s. He can waltz really well, though. One of the best waltzers I've ever danced with. He thrived in England during the late 1800s. Every girl who hadn't already pledged to marry had their eyes on him. Hell, even some who had *already pledged marriage. But a Victorian dance such as the waltz has no place in 1920s Chicago. Thankfully, neither did the corsets.*

He laughs.

His voice is clear and calm in my head, and I swear he is in the room with me. I touch my bracelet every few hours, letting the cool beads slip across my wrist, and remind myself he's gone. His voice lives in my imagination, in my memory, not in this room. But he'll be back soon.

From my window, I watch the days pass. The mornings are bright and busy, filled with people, cars, and the loud thumping noise of bass music. As the blue sky bruises into blackness, I expect the streets to begin to empty and the lights to fade. But they don't. Instead, the sun is replaced by glowing signs, marquees, and streetlights.

Even in the middle of the night, people still rush along many of the streets, jumping in and out of yellow taxis and ducking into neon-lit bars and restaurants. Only the unlit, narrow alleys that run between the dark office buildings are vacant. A few teenagers stand at the front of some alleys making out, pushed up against brick walls, wrapped around one another next to large, green dumpsters. How romantic.

On the fourth day of being cooped up in my hotel room, I decide I need to get out and do something. I'm tired of waiting around and wasting time worrying. I need to run, or fly, or at least smell the cold air of fall. I wait until the day fades into early dusk to leave my room. I figure if I go to the more corporate side of the city, I will be able to avoid the crowds. Most of the office buildings seem to close by six, and there are no restaurants outside of the heart of the city, so it is unlikely that anyone will be walking along those streets.

I pull my hair back behind my head in a messy knot and put on a newly cleaned long-sleeved shirt and a pair of tight, frayed jeans. Earlier this morning, I had room service deliver a rugged leather jacket I'd ordered from one of the boutiques across from the hotel, and I throw that over my shirt, too. It's grown colder outside, my windows frosting over at the corners, and while the weather doesn't have any particular effects on me, I find it's best to blend in and pretend to be bothered by the cold. I tug on my boots, zipping them over the torn edges of my jeans.

Briefly, I consider leaving my dagger behind but end up tucking it securely into my boot. It feels strange to be without it, so I bring it with me more out of habit than necessity. I grab my room card off of the nightstand, shove it into my back pocket, and leave the room, flipping off the lights just before the door slams closed behind me.

Silently, I walk through the hall, step into the waiting elevator, and ride down to the lobby of the hotel, keeping my head low. The lobby is practically empty. Most people have either already left for an evening out in the city or holed themselves away in their room for the night. I push through the revolving doors and out into the cold, dark evening, slipping into the flow of people.

I follow the sidewalk until I see an empty alley to disappear into and fade away from the crowd. I fall out of step and slide into the shadowed shortcut from the busy commercial blocks to the corporate block of the city. Just as I expected, it's empty.

Smiling to myself, I look up to the sky, expecting to see an expanse of stars staring back at me. But I can hardly see any. The bright glow of the city pollutes the sky and turns the edges of the deep night a strange orange, extinguishing the lights of the stars. I sigh. I know the stars are there. They're just masked behind the city's brightness. I can unmask them if I can just get far away enough from the city and its glaring marquees.

I wonder if this is what Michael thinks when he sees me—that my light is just masked by pollution and if I just get far enough away from that pollution, I'll shine brighter. If I am distanced from Hell, I'll be able to see my light for myself. How much distance will it take?

I come out of the alley on a vacant street and run down the middle of the road, throwing myself into the air as my wings open wide and soar up into the sky, flying towards the dark mountains. As I leave behind the steel and cement of the city for the dark green, reds, and browns of the mountains, the stars become visible.

Small stars blink on, one by one, and they sparkle delicately below larger stars. Their silvery blue lights wink at me, welcoming me back.

It feels good to leave the busy city for the open, empty mountains. I fly above the peaks and through the valleys of the mountains, looking down at the trees that are now just beginning to drop their colorful leaves. The cold wind whips my face and brings light tears to my eyes. I spin around wildly, enjoying this moment of freedom and letting go of all my worries. This could be one of the last times I can do something like this, to really let go.

Recently, I have had the same feeling Michael has been having. My perfect house of cards, I fear, is about to collapse. It just takes one mistimed moment, one shaky hand. For now, though, I am able to forget about the uncertainty and just fly.

After a few hours of circling the sky outside of the city, I decide to go back to my room and check in with Azael again. He still thinks I've been spending my days with Michael, so I'll have to come up with another story to tell him. An excuse to feed him to buy myself time.

I fall out of the sky slowly, folding my wings behind me as I land on the empty street. The streetlights lining the road are dark, their lightbulbs either shattered or burned out. I don't mind, though, because I can see fine in the dark. I walk down the middle of the street, aimlessly kicking at gravel loosed from the paved road.

This road is much more narrow than the road in front of the hotel. It is only one lane wide, forcing traffic during the day to flow in the same direction, and there are no metered parking spaces. Instead, there is a short, wide parking garage at the end of the block.

IGNITE

A loud crash of metal garbage cans echoes behind me. I look over my shoulder and don't see anything, so I keep walking. But then I hear something else, another loud sound that breaks through the darkness. The noise is high and twinkling, and by the smell I can tell its beer bottles falling against the sidewalk, the glass shattering. I stop, turn around, and wait. I scan the buildings lining the street and squint into the alleys that stretch between the offices.

An alley I just passed a few buildings back has a shattered beer bottle broken at its mouth, the green shards of glass sparkling on top of a murky amber liquid that spreads across the sidewalk. Shadows dance wildly in the alley, but I don't move. I wait in the silence. My amulet pulses once, glowing faintly above my shirt, and I regard it suspiciously before tucking it below my collar. If it's Azael, he'll have to wait.

A group of men comes stumbling out of the alley, leaning on each other to keep from falling face first onto the sidewalk. Each of them has a bottle of beer clutched in their meaty hands, and they hoot loudly at one another.

The five men are large and muscled, dressed in stained sweatshirts and hats with logos, none of the brims facing the same way. I guess them to be in their mid-twenties. They all sway together as they fall off the curb and spill out into the road, like a tipsy ballet.

Even from here, I can smell them. They smell like a brewery—warm beer and something stronger and drier. The sour smell of sweat also clings to them and I wrinkle my nose in disgust.

I'm about to turn around and keep walking to the alley that lets out nearer to the hotel when one of the men spots me. He is tall and wide, thick as a tree. He whistles loudly and shouts something vulgar at me. His friends laugh, raising their bottles and taking a long swig. He breaks away from the pack, steadying himself as he takes a few steps in front of them, pointing at me with his hand that's clutching his beer.

"You there. Pretty girl." His words slur.

I sneer and turn away from him, but I don't walk fast. I won't run away from them. They are nothing. Just a bunch of drunk frat boys.

"Hey!" he shouts angrily. "What, are you too good for me or something?"

I keep walking.

"You're a bitch." His friends bark out an entertained laugh and clink their bottles together.

I stop, turning slowly on my heel to look at them all.

They notice I've stopped and the leader of their boozy pack steps forward again, striding up to me. His eyes are dark and slightly glassy, but they hold a sharpness to them, an understanding. He's not as drunk as he's pretending to be. He knows what he's doing.

I look past him at his other four friends. One of them bends over and throws up on the street, wipes his hand across his mouth, and laughs, taking another swig. They're all completely drunk, their eyes swimming with alcohol, but I can tell they're not harmless.

The one in front of me, however, appears to be the most dangerous of them all—and he's lucid. Something about him seems mildly threatening, his posture challenging and confident. He's foolishly brazen.

I look at him, my eyes hard and my jaw clenched.

"Well what have we here?" He walks around me, pushing his body up against mine. He circles his arm across my shoulder and grips tightly, pinning me to his chest for a moment. His forearm presses against my windpipe, and if I had to breathe, I wouldn't be able to. It's a threat, a show of dominance.

I don't flinch, even when I see the excited, smug grins of the four other men who watch me. None of them step up to stop their friend. If anything, he seems to be encouraged by their stares and squeezes tighter around my throat.

He lets go and stands in front of me, inches from my face. "What's a pretty little thing like you doing out so late all by yourself?"

He reaches his sweaty hand out towards my face and I swat it away.

His eyes blaze with anger, but he beats it down. "No one is out this late unless they're looking for trouble. You looking for trouble?" He no longer slurs his words; they are crisp and sharp with rage.

The desire to kill him boils up inside of me, hot and urgent, but I ignore it, taking a short breath. *Think of Michael.*

I stare at him for a moment before I answer. "I think you are making a mistake."

He ignores me. "Because if you are looking for trouble, I've got good news for you: you've found it." He spreads his arms wide and tosses aside his beer. "Aren't you lucky."

"You should leave," I hiss. I look over his shoulder to his friends again. "All of you should go, now."

They laugh stupidly, snorting and huffing for breath. One of the four men behind the first guy calls out, "I don't know, Danny." A boozy hiccup bubbles up in his throat. "She seems pretty tough. Maybe we should just beat it."

Everyone laughs except for Danny, who continues to watch me hungrily. "Shut up, Mark. I know what I'm doing." He leans forward. "You've got really strange eyes, girl. What's your name?" His sharp gaze rakes over me, sliding greedily up my legs and resting on my chest before it jumps up to my face.

I recoil slightly from his hot, putrid breath but stay quiet. The stone of my necklace pulses again. I close my eyes and picture Michael's face. Before Michael, I wouldn't have hesitated to kill these men. But now, I have pause. I don't have to kill away my problems. That's what Hell has taught me to do, but it's not what I should do. I'll just turn and leave, spare these idiots. But before I can step away, Danny grabs my wrist, crushing my thin bones in his tight fist.

"No, I don't think so. You won't be going anywhere."

"I think I am." I pull my wrist free, and his eyes narrow into slits.

"Mark, Kyle, grab her wrists. Alex, Liam, grab her ankles. Pin her down." He smiles at me threateningly. "I'm gonna teach this girl a lesson."

The four others behind him throw down their bottles. One burps before they all stumble forward, their meaty hands reaching out to grab me. The same hunger I saw in Danny's eyes flashes in theirs.

Before any one of them can trap me on the pavement, I have my dagger out from my boot, gripped tightly in my hand. I hold the razor sharp blade out in front of me, pointing it at Danny's wide neck. I'm thankful I didn't leave it back at The Aria. I want to twist it in his fat, bulging veins and make him scream.

"Last chance. Walk away."

A chorus of derision sounds from the four drunk men. Danny just stares unbelievingly at me, sizing me up. He takes another step towards me.

"That was a mistake, sweetheart. There ain't no way we're letting you go now."

"*Isn't*," I correct under my breath, rage coiling around my gut, ready to spring.

He lunges at me and I swing out, slashing my dagger across his throat.

They should have just walked away. I told them to walk away.

He staggers once, grabbing at the wound, and I thrust my knife under his ribs, into his heart. I push him off of my blade and let him fall to the ground, dead. The four others stare at me, blinking stupidly.

"Leave," I growl. "Now!"

"Danny!" One of the men walks forward and looks at him. Behind him, the other three watch. "You killed him! You'll pay for that, you little—" he yells at me, fury thickening his words and snapping the others out of their daze.

IGNITE

All at once, the four men run towards me, surrounding me. They grab at me, tearing my shirt, pulling my hair, and crushing my arms in their grasp. I feel bruises begin to blossom on my wrists and I forcefully pull them free. I kick out at the first body to wrap itself around me.

Unseeingly, I drag my blade across the air, sending blood flying and another body to the street. A second meaty man wraps me in his arms, cracking my ribs painfully in his tight embrace. His hot mouth slides over my shoulder, his dull teeth skimming my veins. I kick out backwards, my boot slamming into his knee with a wicked crack. He shouts out, dropping me clumsily, and I turn around and stab him in the neck.

I pull my dagger back and it is slick with blood that slides down the blade, over the clean, white handle, and up my arm. My shirt is ripped and stained with more blood, but it's red, not black, so I'm fine.

The last two men descend on me together, knocking me down to the pavement. I hit the ground hard, my elbow cracking on the street, and one of the men lands on top of me, pinning me down. He makes a growling sound, his teeth snapping at me like a rabid dog. I push my arm across his neck, keeping his hot, wet mouth away from my face. His face turns beet red as he fights against me, and I kick out, trying to roll him off of me. But he's heavy and he stays on top, groping at me with calloused hands.

He throws one of his sweaty hands over my mouth. "Shut up!" he orders.

I bite down hard on his palm, causing him to cry out. I drag my blade across his throat while he calls for his friend, and he falls limp on me as his warm blood spills over my face. I turn my head to the side and choke, pushing him off of me with great effort.

I sit up slowly, my dagger gripped tightly in my scraped hand. I look around for the last of the men and see him running away, towards the alley they climbed out of. He turns back to look at me, his face drawn in terror. I raise my arm and throw my dagger with all of my strength, despite the painful protests of my injuries. I won't let him get away.

The blade cuts through the air, spinning so fast that it blurs, and finds its target, burying itself in the last man's chest, right over the heart. I never miss my target. With a soft yelp and a throaty gurgle, he falls down, dead.

I force myself to my feet, my bones bruised and broken, making it painful to stand. I walk over to the last man and pull my dagger from his chest. A dark red stain is spreading across his dirty, white shirt and pools in a thick puddle beneath him. I turn around and survey the damage I've done.

The five men are sprawled across the street, bloodied and still. I limp to Danny, looking down to his slack face. His eyes are open and glassy, all of the rage spilled out of him with his blood. His shirt is sticky with it, dark and ruby red, and I'm glad.

I don't have the same joy I usually do when I kill someone though. I'm not reveling in the gore and wasted life. This is different. It's a deeper kind of frustrating satisfaction that makes my chest ache. I've removed monsters from the streets—permanently. And that should make me happy, regardless of my allegiance. Shouldn't it?

But behind this strange feeling is something else that I try to ignore. It's almost like terror, but it's not as piercing. It feels more blunt than sharp. My eyes burn in anger, and I kick out at him, my boot cracking his ribs.

"Bastard," I say, my voice tight and quiet.

"Pen?"

I freeze, not believing what I hear.

The sound of footsteps makes its way down the street, coming closer to me.

"Pen?" The voice is sad and golden and I must have been killed because this can't be real.

I turn around slowly, scared of the face I know I will see.

Michael stands a few feet away from me, his silver wings still open wide behind him. He looks at me, his icy blue eyes both worried and hurt. He glances down at the dead bodies, his gaze bouncing from one man to another, landing on all five briefly. I watch him, holding my breath, and when he looks back up at me, I see he is disappointed.

Something in me breaks.

I drop my dagger to the ground and it hits the road, the blade scraping against the rough pavement. I look behind me at Danny one last time and then back to Michael. I take a tentative step forward.

"I…" My voice fails and I snap my mouth shut, staring up at him with wide, startled eyes. I wrap my arms around myself, the blood on my hands seeping through the ripped elbows of my jacket.

"I just came to see the stars," he says simply. "You… you wanted me to see the stars."

CHAPTER 24

EVERYTHING AROUND ME IS TOO STILL, TOO QUIET, AND too harsh. I'm frozen where I stand, lips parted, eyebrows knotted together. Every shallow breath I take hurts as my broken ribs pinch into my side.

Michael stands a little bit down the road, watching me intently. I stare back at him as a panic so absolute swells up around me. It's like the world beneath me has fallen off its axis and we're about to drop out of orbit. My knees are weak and I feel like I'm going to pass out, but, by some miracle, I don't. I remain standing, trembling so violently that I have to wrap my arms around myself. Somehow, I find my voice again, however weak.

"Wh-what are you doing here?" I ask shakily. "How did you... It's after your curfew."

"I snuck out," he explains, stepping forward and drawing in his broad wings.

I continue to stare at him in shock. "H-how?" I ask again.

"It was easier than I thought it would be. The angels—they're distracted."

"Why... why are you here?" I'm so dizzy and covered in too much blood. I just want to fall to the ground, to shrink away from Michael until I completely disappear, but my knees are locked. I'm frozen in pain and terror, surrounded by blood.

Blood blood blood. It's inescapable.

"I came to see you," he answers carefully. "You said you wanted me to see the stars."

I tear at the bottom of my lip with my teeth. This is not what's supposed to happen. This isn't how I thought I would see him next, coated in blood and surrounded by five slain humans. Monsters, really, but he doesn't know what happened. He didn't see the glint in their eyes that I did.

My chest is tight, and I clutch at it desperately with hands covered in slick, red blood as the corners of my vision blur into darkness for a moment before returning to normal again.

"I—I didn't mean to."

I back away from him, tripping over the body of the first man, Danny. I fall back onto the road, splashing in a shallow pool of blood. I catch myself with the heel of my hand, scraping the thin skin across the rough asphalt.

Michael steps forward, as if he's going to reach down to help me, but he pauses, his arm halfway extended to me, unsure of what to do. Cradling my hand to my stomach, I look back up at Michael.

"I didn't mean to," I repeat pitifully.

I'm not sure if I'm trying to convince him or myself.

He watches me, concerned, ignoring the bodies scattered around me, and seems to make a decision. He leans forward and offers me his hand. I hesitate before I take it.

Gently, he helps me to my feet, and when I let go, I leave a small red handprint across his large hand. I'm going to be sick.

"Sorry," I mumble, desperately trying to wipe my bloody hands clean on my jeans. Instead, I manage to coat my hand in even more of it that stains my jeans a burgundy so dark it's nearly black.

He doesn't make any move to clean his hand though. He just continues to watch me, leaning his head down so he can meet my eyes.

"Are you okay?"

I stare back at him blankly. "Okay?"

"Are you hurt?

"Am I..." I trail off unbelievingly. I run my hands down my shirt, smearing more blood as I straighten it to lay at my hips, and answer him, my voice high and shrill. "I'm sorry, are you asking me if *I'm* okay? You do see the five men that are lying in the street, right? Or did you miss them? Maybe I'm hallucinating."

"I see them," he assures me. "There's not much I can do to help them now. But if you're hurt, I can help you. If you'll let me." He steps forward, his face inches from mine. "I'll ask again. Are you hurt?"

I shrug, hugging myself to stop the tremors that shake my bones. "A few cracked ribs, bruises. I think my wrist is broken, and maybe my elbow too."

"Which arm?"

I hold up my left wrist for him. He takes it delicately in his hands, his long fingers carefully skimming over my paper-thin skin. A warmth trails after his fingers, and I can feel the splintered bones fusing back together. His hand slides up to my elbow and I feel a warmth begin to spread there, too. He lets go, and I roll my wrist once and extend my elbow, letting the bones snap back into place.

"And your ribs?"

"They're just cracked."

When I speak, I feel a sharp twinge in my side, the fractured bones of my ribs piercing me with each breath. I concentrate and try not to breathe as deeply, but the pain is excruciating, and I can't hide my agony from Michael. He sees it, clear as day, played out on the twisted features of my face.

"I don't care if they're 'just cracked.' Please, Pen. Let me help you. You're hurting."

I consider him for a moment, but I'm too tired to argue the point.

Slowly, I slip my jacket off of my shoulders, letting it fall to the ground. It's ruined anyway, ripped at the elbows and across the back, stained just as badly as all of my other clothes. I keep my eyes on his as I raise my shirt to just below my chest, exposing the green and blue expanse of bruises that stretch above my ribs like a morbid patch of flowers.

He places his hands on my hips and slides them up my side, spreading a warm sense of relief through my ribs that elicits a soft sigh from me. I watch as the bruises slowly lose their color, the blue fading into the green before the green disappears into yellow which vanishes completely.

When he reaches my shirt, he stops, his long fingers wrapped around my side and stretching to my back. Before he takes them away, I notice that his hands are trembling slightly.

"You're freezing," he says, watching my face.

"I told you, it's a common misconception that Hell's hot. It's completely—" I take a shaky breath. "frozen."

My ribs don't snap anymore, any my words come easier.

"The same ice of Hell runs through my veins," I tell him. My voice sounds uneven, and I can't tell if it's from him touching me or from my remaining injuries. Probably a combination of the two.

He drops his hands and leaves them hanging awkwardly at his sides.

I lower my shirt again, looking down at my feet self-consciously, and take another breath, this time slower and deeper. It's easier to breathe now, not as painful. Instead of the pinching of my ribs, I feel the heat remaining from Michael's hands, like he left a permanent mark on me.

"Thank you," I say seriously.

"You're welcome."

He's quiet for a moment before he reaches out and takes my hand in his, guiding me around the fallen bodies, out of the street, and onto the sidewalk. He leads me carefully, as if he's worried I'll break. We lower onto the curb together. Silently, I look out at the street, still clutching Michael's hand.

He lets me cling to him unquestioningly. I must look incredibly broken for him to be treating me so delicately. I'm covered in blood, scratched, and bruised, and my hair is tangled and falling out of the knot I tied it in. There's blood on my hands, my face, my body...

My eyes are still open wide, like giant saucers, and my dry and cracked lips are parted. I probably look terrified, like I'm about to run away or scream or breakdown. I can't seem to bury my distress. I'm still in shock about the five men—men I didn't want to hurt, men I hadn't meant to kill—and about Michael's sudden appearance.

"Are you all right?"

I'm not, not really, but I nod anyway.

"What happened?" he asks.

"I just wanted to fly, to stretch my wings. When I was on my way back to where I'm staying, these five men—" I feel a sharp pain pierce through my chest and stop short, falling forward and curling in on myself. I rest my chest on my knees and suck in air, panicked. It's like something in me is broken, unhinged.

I've never felt this kind of fear before, never known what it was like to experience pure panic about something. Not like this. The last time I felt something even close to what I'm feeling now was in the war when I thought Michael was going to kill Azael.

But this isn't Azael I'm worried about now. It's me.

Michael leans towards me, alert with worry. "Pen?"

I put up one hand. "Wait," I say through a hysterical hiccup. "I'm fine. Just, wait."

He does. He's patient, resting his hand on my back until I calm down.

I sit up again and take a deep breath. "They attacked me," I say hollowly. I don't look at him, don't want to see the way he's looking at me. Will there be pity in his eyes? Disgust?

He repeats what I said, slowly forming the words with a confused tongue. "Attacked you? How?"

"Four of them were drunk, but the main guy, Danny," I spit his name, "he wasn't. He knew what he was doing, he understood, and he was enjoying it."

Finally I look over at him. He's silent, watching me with his lips pressed in a hard line. But there's no pity in his eyes, no disgust—at least none directed at me. All I see is concern with a flash of something hotter underneath. Anger?

"Danny told the others to… *pin me down*."

Michael tenses, his hands curling into tight fists. I look away, bile rising to the back of my throat.

"Needless to say," I continue, "they never got the chance."

"Because you stopped them." His voice is deep and even.

"Killed them," I correct. "They never got the chance because I killed them. And they'll never get the chance with anyone else again."

"If I was just a few minutes earlier…" He stands up suddenly, his posture rigid with anger.

I blink, taken aback. "You would have stopped me?" I ask in a whisper.

He looks back at me. "No. I wouldn't have stopped you. I would have *helped* you," he says fiercely, predatorily. He kneels in front of me, looking into my eyes, his hands resting lightly on my knees, like he's afraid if he touches me—really touches me—I'll crumble. "I know you don't need anyone to save you. You are much stronger than even you realize. But I wasn't here, and if anything had happened to you…"

Impulsively, I grab his hands in mine. He looks down at my small, scraped hand in his and knots our fingers together.

"I may not need you to save me," I say in a whisper, "but I think I still need you." Heat rises to my face and I swallow hard. I just admitted something I hadn't meant to. Not yet, anyway.

This is not where I want to have this conversation, but the adrenaline that is coursing through me is making me reckless. I'm scared and excited and shaky, and all I can do is talk. All I can do is bleed for him, tell him a truth I have been trying to deny for far too long.

He tilts his head, not understanding what I'm telling him. "Why would you need me?"

"There's something about you," I say, unable to stop myself. Well, there's no turning back now, no hiding. "I'm stronger with you next to me. I feel like my darkness is more manageable with you, like I'll even be able to defeat it one day. I have hope that things can change, that *I* can change. I may be heartless—"

He shakes his head. "You're not heartless," he says quickly. "When you care too much, it's easier to ignore your heart, pretend it's not there. It's safer to ignore it so you can protect yourself from being hurt."

"Michael, remember when you told me that choosing to do the right thing, choosing to be good, was like waking up?"

"Of course I remember. I remember every moment I've ever spent with you, Pen. In this lifetime, anyway. I remember *everything* about you."

I search his eyes and find a peace inside of them I hadn't realized I was searching for. In his eyes, I see the blue of the pond, the brilliant shine of the stars. It's him I've been waiting for this entire time, and I finally found him. And he found me. I lean into him, resting my hand on his warm chest, and kiss him. Around his lips, I whisper, "You woke me up."

He places his hand at the nape of my neck, under my hair, and pulls me closer to him, wrapping me in his strong embrace. I hear his voice in my head, bright and brilliant. *You woke up.* I push away from him and he looks up at me with surprise.

"What the Hell was that?" I ask.

IGNITE

"What do you mean?"

"I heard your voice in my head."

He smiles, raising his eyebrows. "Just like you've heard my voice in your head yesterday, and the day before, and the night before that." His fingers curl absently around fallen pieces of my hair and he tucks it securely behind my ear. "Remember? You told me about Chicago. You wanted me to dance with you."

I look around in confusion, as if I can find an explanation sitting next to me on the sidewalk. "That was really you?"

"Well it wasn't Azael. You had to have known that." He looks at me with concern. "You did know it was me, right?" His face falls slightly.

"I thought you were a dream. I didn't think I was really... How can I talk to you?" I scramble to remember what I've told him, what I've shown him. He knows secrets about me that I've never told anyone, not even Azael.

"I don't know. I thought it was something you had done."

"It wasn't." I shake my head and whisper, "It's impossible."

He gently rests his hand on my cheek. "It's a miracle," he says softly.

I try to ignore the nervous electricity that spreads across my skin from his touch. I look down at his chest where my hand rested just moments earlier and see a bright, red handprint. My handprint.

Suddenly I am snapped back into the dark reality of the night. My focus on Michael blurs as I look past him and back out at the street.

The men.

Michael hears me, his face growing grave.

I stand up and walk away from the sidewalk and into the middle of the street. It feels like I'm walking through a nightmare, like what's in front of me isn't real. But it is real. Everything is much too real.

As Michael wordlessly steps up next to me, I look down at the vacant faces of the five men, stained red with their own blood. The real monsters aren't in Hell, I think. They're here on Earth, walking unnoticed in the crowd. They're family, friends, neighbors. The monsters are the people you least expect.

"I can't." I shake my head back and forth, causing more of my hair to fall down and into my face. I push the tangles out of my eyes with bloody hands as I'm flooded with panic again. "I mean, I can't reap their souls. I don't have—it was always Az." My throat is dry. "Their souls will die if they aren't reaped. Not that they don't deserve it."

Michael looks down at the men, his jaw tight and his eyes hard. "I can reap their souls." He's quiet and serious. "I at least know how to do that much. I'll take them."

"To Heaven?" I hiss. "Is that really where they belong?"

"It's not. But what choice do I have?" He looks at me, his lips set in a tight, thin line. "I have a job to do, don't I? A responsibility to not let their souls just…"

He shakes his head and clenches his jaw, chewing his resentment so he can do his duty. He doesn't want to help them, doesn't think they deserve to be saved. And he's right—they don't. But he still believes there is goodness in everyone, and he won't let go of that notion, no matter how lost a person is.

He crouches next to Danny's body, resting his hand on his chest. "I have a job to do," he says again, as if he is trying to convince himself.

His hand seems to glow as it sinks into his chest. Michael closes his eyes in concentration, his eyebrows drawn low and his lips parted. I want to look away, to be sick, but I can't. I watch in horror as he leans forward, searching the far corners of Danny's chest. Danny soul doesn't deserve to be saved. He especially doesn't deserve Heaven.

When Michael finally pulls his hand back out, it's empty. There's no slippery soul twining itself around his hand, no silver wisps squeezing through his fist.

He looks at me in alarm. "I can't find it."

I kneel down next to him, my jeans soaking up the blood that is settled in a small pool around Danny's body. "Can't find it?"

"He has no soul," Michael says, shaking his head.

"He—what?" I lean forward and rest my own hand on top of his chest, trying to see if I can sense something within it's deep caverns.

"He has no soul," he says again, mystified. He turns around and reaches into a second chest, searching just as he did in Danny's. "This one's gone, too."

He makes his way around to each of the five men, coming up empty every time.

"Gone. They're all gone. You didn't do anything..." He stands and reaches his hand up, running it through his unruly hair, thinking. His hand leaves a trail of deep crimson, staining his blond hair in streaks.

"I told you I can't reap souls. I certainly can't *destroy* a soul. Not with only my dagger," I say, gesturing to the blade that still sits in the street covered in drying blood. I pick it up and wipe it over my jeans, trying to clean the blade as best as I can before I slip it back into my boot. "It takes a much stronger weapon to destroy a soul like that than I have. Are you sure you're doing it right?"

"Yes, I'm positive." He crosses his arms across his chest, spinning around in a small, slow circle in the middle of the road. "None of them has a soul. I've never felt anything like it. There's something about them. Like their souls were..."

"Poisoned," I finish for him, my voice hushed. "Like their souls were already dead and gone before I killed them."

He looks at me questioningly. I grab at my amulet, which is heavy and sharp in my hand. It pulsed when I saw them. It was a warning that I ignored. *How did I miss this?*

"I've seen this," I go on. "The early stages, anyway. With Azael. One of the souls we stole from the patients at the asylum was changed."

"Changed?"

I take a deep breath. "When you enter a soul, you can experience memories from its life. But this soul had no memories; it was like they were erased. The soul was being eaten away by a demonic virus." I swallow past a lump in my throat. "The Lilim virus."

He stirs. "It sounds familiar, but I don't know anything about it."

"The virus originated in Lilith's blood. She gave birth to children that were half human, half demon. Demi-demons. Now it is spread from person to person," I explain. "It is transmitted through a bite. The virus festers in the blood until everything pure is eaten away. It destroys memories, poisons their blood, and eventually, the soul. All it leaves is the heart."

"And the purpose of this virus?" he asks in a low voice.

"To change humans into demons," I answer. "It's the start of the war between Heaven and Hell. It's a sign of the apocalypse, the end of the world as we know it."

He's very still, standing frozen in his place. All of the color is drained from his face. In a tiny whisper, he echoes me, disbelieving. "The apocalypse." He pauses, a realization dawning on his face. "Did I cause this? Me being back... Is this my fault?"

He lifts his eyes from the road to me. They are desperate and dark, pleading me to tell him it's not his fault. I knot my eyebrows together and bite my lip. I can't give him what he wants. Not this time. His face falls, darkening behind a cloud of guilt, and the corners of his mouth pull down.

I hear his thought, hopelessly sad, in my mind. *This is my fault.*

CHAPTER 25

"MICHAEL?"

He's very still. He stares through me like I'm made of glass.

I step up to him, reaching out to touch his face, to bring him back to me. "Michael? Can you hear me?"

His eyes are distant and foggy. He can't hear me. It's like I'm not even there.

I cup his face between my cool hands. *Michael. Please, Michael. Say something. You're scaring me.*

He blinks and refocuses on my face. "We have to stop it. The war, the virus, everything."

I let my hands slide off of his face and onto his shoulders. "We can't. It's too far gone."

He shakes his head. "No, it can't be. We have to do something. This is my fault. I have to—"

"There's nothing we can do. We'd be killed without a moment's hesitation." I look at him seriously, desperately needing him to understand. "Michael, we can't stop any of it from happening." I take his hands in mine.

"So what are we supposed to do?" His voice is sharp and angry, but not at me. He doesn't tighten his grip on me when his voice rises. Instead, he looks up to the dirty sky, his face drawn. He knows that this is out of my control, too, and it makes him angry. Angry at everything—at the world, at our situation, at its inescapability.

I know how he feels. Powerless. It's a feeling I've had over the last few days, trapped in the middle of Hell's plan. I'm powerless against the Lilim virus, powerless at fighting against the end of the world, even powerless when it comes to saving Azael, my own brother. It is the most hopeless feeling in the world because there's no way to fight it. It's like quicksand—the harder you struggle, the faster you'll sink.

"We wait," I say simply. "We bide our time." I look at him meaningfully. "And when the moment is right, we strike."

His eyes soften.

"We destroy the virus, and we dismantle Hell."

"You would do that?" he asks, leaning back from me. "You would betray Hell for me?"

"I would do a lot for you," I say slowly, realizing as I'm saying it just how true it is. "But this isn't only about you. It's about me, too, and about what I believe is right. And this, what I've been living for the past hundred centuries, is not what's right. It's not what I believe in anymore."

"You don't?"

"I don't think I've believed in Hell for a while. I just needed someone to remind me, challenge me." I shrug. "No one in Hell questions what we do anymore. And it was like that in Heaven before I fell. We stop wondering why we are doing what we do and just focus on what we're told. We do what we are supposed to do without thinking. But you reminded me to look closer at what I am, at what I do."

IGNITE

He doesn't say anything. He just grabs my hand and pulls me to him, threading his arms around me and kissing the top of my head. I tip my head back so his lips can reach mine.

"I've never met anyone so brave," he says.

"I'm not brave."

And it's true—I'm not. Every choice I've made up until now has been cowardly. I fell from Heaven because I was afraid to lose Azael. I've lost myself in slaughter and let my veins freeze over with Hell's ice because I was afraid of what would happen if anyone knew I didn't believe in what Hell stands for. I'm anything but brave.

"Yes you are. You're brave and strong and smart." He smiles down at me. "I knew from the moment I met you that there was something different about you. I was meant to meet you. I was meant to land in that tree. It was fate."

"I don't believe in fate anymore," I tell him.

"No?"

"No. Before you returned, the future was written, marked in black permanent ink. But lately, the future has been erasing itself. Pages that were once filled with fates and destinies are empty. It's no longer predetermined. We are writing our fate right now."

"And how will our story end?"

I smirk. "We'll just have to wait and see."

He places his hand on my lower back and pulls me closer to him. He bends down, places his lips next to my ear, and whispers, "I'm falling for you."

"What?" I freeze.

"The more I listen to you, the more I fall for you. You see things differently. " He kisses the soft skin just below my jaw and then looks back into my eyes, which are wide and surprised. "There's no one else like you."

I don't say anything, and I don't need to because he continues.

"It's really not fair, you know. You've bewitched me. I've never felt something so completely. I'm absolutely consumed by the thought of you. When we're together, it's like every nerve in me sings for you, begging me to touch you, to be closer. And when we're apart, it's nearly unbearable. It's like I'm missing a piece of myself, and its sudden absence reminds me of just how important that piece was. How that piece allowed me to not only survive, but *live*." He smiles. "With you, I'm whole. With you, I'm alive."

My head spins, and I say the first coherent thought I can grab hold of, however inadequate it is. "Are you worried I've cast some curse on you?" I ask, raising an eyebrow.

Stupid, I think. *Stupid, stupid*. Here he is, proclaiming his feelings for me, and I cannot return his words. It's not that I don't feel the same, because I do. My nerves sing for him too, desperate and loud, because they have to be heard over the doubt in my mind, the distrust that I've been ingrained with.

His words are like the lines of poetry that I carry around with me. The prose that stick in my mind and pierce through my chest. I want to memorize what he's told me, because they're words I never thought I would hear. But he's said them to me, brave and unashamed, and I'm too weak to return them.

I'm a coward. The words are stuck in my throat, fighting to escape, but I'm too careful to let them out. I'm still hesitant to reveal the emotions I've spent so long ignoring, denying.

"Oh no, I know it's not a curse." He pauses. "Pen, do you know what it's like to be in love?"

I rest my head on his chest. "I'm a demon, what do you think?"

He laughs.

"Do you, Michael?"

He runs his hand gently through my hair, thinking. "In theory."

My cheeks burn and I stay silent, letting him hold me as I watch the dark sky start to lighten into a steely morning.

"We need to leave here," Michael says, letting go of me.

IGNITE

I step back and nod. "I need to get rid of the bodies. I can't just... I can't leave them." My chest tightens again with anxiety as I look at the faces of the men. I know they're dead, but I can still see their furious expressions, Danny's eyes glinting in excitement. I should have known they were Lilim. They were much stronger than any human. They could have killed me. "I need to burn them."

"I'll help."

"No, I need to do this."

Michael stays quiet, watching me as I go up to the men one at a time, lift them over my shoulder, and walk them into an alley on the far side of the street. I struggle to carry them, my muscles straining under their weight, but I keep moving forward, gritting my teeth and pushing against the pain. I have to rise onto my tiptoes to drop their lifeless forms into the empty, green dumpster. They hit the metal bottom with a dull clang, and I bite my tongue, trying to keep from throwing up. I have to stop several times, propping myself against the gritty wall of the alley to catch my breath and steady myself. I set my ruined jacket in last.

After they are all stacked in the dumpster, I look inside. They lie on top of one another, their elbows bent awkwardly, their eyes open and foggy.

I'm surprised when I feel hot tears sting the backs of my eyes. They're in the trash, where they belong. I won't cry, won't waste my tears on the loss of their atrocious lives. But I can't help thinking about what they were like before the virus.

They didn't ask for this, and for all I know, they were good. They probably have family, friends, people who will miss them. I blink quickly and look away, trying to swallow my tears as I reach my hand in the dumpster. I whisper, "Ignis," and blanket the men in the blue fire of Hell, turning them to ash. I let the lid slam closed, hiding them from me forever.

When I turn around, I see Michael watching me. He nods his head and holds out his hand to me. But I don't take it. I tie my arms around myself and fall against the rough brick wall of the alley. I slide down the wall to the dirty ground, paralyzed. He walks over to me and I look up at him.

"I should be crying, right?"

He's silent.

"What's wrong with me?" My bottom lip trembles and I trap it between my teeth.

Michael bends down in front of me and wipes at my cheek. He pulls his hand back and shows me a single tear on his thumb. "You are crying, and there's nothing wrong with you."

I shake my head. "You—you never saw the stars," I say, breathless.

"Shh." He stands up and pulls me off of the ground so I am with him, wrapped in his strong arms. He removes his jacket and sets it on my shoulders. "I don't need the stars tonight. I have you." He looks up at the brightening sky and then back at me. "We need to go before the sun rises much higher. You're covered in blood. It'll probably be best if no one else sees you looking like this."

I glance down at myself. His jacket hides the worst of it, but my jeans are also stained, as are my hands, and I can feel dried blood sticking to my cheeks.

"I'm staying at The Aria Hotel. It's just a block from here, that way," I say, pointing across the street to another alley with a bloody finger. I stare at it for a moment, amazed at how the blood swirls into the small lines of my fingertip, before curling it back into my fist and tucking it below the long sleeves of Michael's jacket.

"Then let's go."

He grabs my hand, lacing his fingers through mine. Together, we walk through the now empty street and into the adjacent alley, rounding the corner and staying close to the closed shopfronts lining the sidewalk.

He keeps his arm around my shoulder protectively, and I bury myself into him, hiding myself from the few pedestrians that still linger outside of the last open bars, slouching against splintered door frames. I peer up through my tangle of blue-black hair and see a small group of women stumbling towards us, their makeup smeared from a long night out in the city. They'll run right into us with the way they're walking, but they don't see us yet. They're typing away on their small phones, talking amongst themselves in lilting whispers.

"Shit," I hiss, nudging Michael with my elbow.

He looks over at me, his eyebrows raised in confusion, but then he looks down the sidewalk and sees the women. Without even having to think about it, Michael swings me off of the sidewalk and into the opening of the alley closest to The Aria. He looks at me briefly, his eyes telling me to trust him, and pushes me up against the brick wall, twining himself around me until we are knotted together, completely entangled. His lips, my lips; his body, my body. Where he ends I begin. I only have a moment to realize that we look just like the teenagers I saw from my window, passionately kissing next to a large, green dumpster. It's much more romantic than I gave it credit for.

The women pass us, their heels clicking on the gritty sidewalk. I can hear one of them whisper about us, telling her friend to "check out the two in the alley," but they don't notice the blood I'm covered in. Michael's hiding me with his body, with his hands, with his lips. When we can no longer hear them, Michael peels himself away from me, a small smile painted across his bright face.

"That was close," he says, smirking.

I shake my head and grab his hand in mine as we slip out of the alley and pass the last few dark windows of boutiques before we reach the canopied entrance of The Aria. I keep my head down as we slide through the revolving doors and into the dimly lit lobby. This early, there is no one standing behind the front desk and we are able to sneak through and into a waiting elevator unnoticed.

"Top floor," I say. He hesitates for a moment, looking at the unlit buttons in confusion. "Top button."

Michael hits the button and it lights up, closing the door. We rise through the hotel in silence, still tangled up in one another, unwilling to let go. I keep my eyes on the floor of the elevator. I don't need to see myself reflected in the walls and door of the elevator, covered in blood and standing next to Michael. I don't want to see that.

When the doors open on the top floor with a ding, I grab his hand and pull him after me through the hallway and to my door. I panic for a moment, thinking I left my keycard in my jacket that I destroyed, before I remember it's in my back pocket.

I slide the keycard into the slot and when the light turns green, I drag him into the room with me, closing and locking the door behind us. Michael is pinned between me and the door, his back pressed against the thick wood. The room is dim, only lit by the lights from the street, but I can see him smile at me.

"Nice room," he says softly. "It sure beats the cave."

I step to the side, allowing him to enter the room. "I suppose."

He still has a hold of my hand and I follow him as he walks back to the bed, his fingers trailing lightly across the unmade sheets. He walks to the windows that look out to the mountains. The stars are gone from the sky, hidden by the light of the rising sun. I frown.

"I didn't realize how close the mountains were," Michael says.

"That's where I stayed the first night. Up on top of the mountains in a small cabin."

He turns to look at me. "Were the stars beautiful?"

"I'll show you tomorrow," I tell him, squeezing his hand.

He nods once and then scrutinizes my face. "Are you really okay?"

I don't lie to him this time. "Not really, but I will be." I drop his hand and slide out of his jacket, hanging it in a small, mirrored closet. The door to the bathroom is pushed open, but before I go in, I look back at him, suddenly worried. "Don't go anywhere."

"Where would I go?" he asks.

"I don't know, I just have this feeling that when I come back from my shower you'll be gone. I don't want you to leave."

"I won't."

I look at him closely, my stomach squeezed with anxiety. I don't want him out of my sight. The men's faces keep flashing before my eyes.

"I'll be here," he reassures me.

My vision darkens until the only thing I can see are their faces.

Angry.

Hungry.

Excited.

Snarling, snapping teeth.

I hear Michael exhale and realize he can see them too. "I won't leave," he promises again.

I squeeze my eyes shut and nod, trying to believe him. I push my fingers through my hair, bite the inside of my cheek, curl around myself—anything to keep from falling apart. It does little good. My own hands remind me of their groping, grabbing hands.

I can feel them all over me—on my wrists, on my waist. I can feel one of them rake their teeth across my shoulder again, dull and warm. If I hadn't hit him at that moment, he would have bitten me.

I take several short, sharp breaths and open my eyes again, dizzy. Michael comes across the room in a few large strides, grabbing my shoulders. He hugs me to him, as if he can block out their faces.

"It's okay," he soothes me.

"It's really not."

I crush my eyes closed again, but I still see them. By the way he tightens his grip on me, I know that he still can, too. He sees the flash in their eyes, the threat in their postures. He can see Danny licking his lips, his eyes greedily devouring me. I bury my face into Michael's chest.

"They're gone," he promises me.

"I know. I killed them. I'm lucky." My voice is strained. "I wonder how many before me weren't."

I start to sink down the door frame, but he holds me up. He helps me into the bathroom and sets me on the side of the bathtub, opens the shower door, and turns the water on full heat. I watch him, frozen and unwilling to move. He kneels in front of me and unzips my boots, setting them to the side.

I look up from his shoulders and at the mirror across from the shower and tub at my reflection. I'm worse than I thought. I have a thick cut that spreads from my jaw to my mouth. Smeared blood is dried on my face, in my hair, and on my shirt. It reminds me of my nightmare where I saw myself covered in so much blood I was unrecognizable. Except this blood is red, not black.

It's not mine, I remind myself. *Not mine.*

"Pen?" Michael stands up, blocking my reflection.

I don't look up at him, I just stare ahead blankly.

Distantly I hear the shower running, but it sounds muted. I feel myself being lifted onto my feet and led into the shower. With my clothes still on, I am guided into the hot water, Michael's hands on my hips holding me up. He brushes his large hands over my face, washing the blood from my cheek and neck.

His fingers carefully clean the cuts on my face. I feel the dull sting of the soap for a moment but don't react because I feel them fade away under the water, the skin healing itself. I look down at the ground and watch as red water swirls and disappears down the drain.

Michael sets his fingers under my chin and tips my face up to his. His eyes search mine, and I try to focus them on him through the water but he's so blurry. I squint and try to concentrate harder. The blue of his eyes pierces through the haze.

"Do you see me?" he asks.

I nod mutely.

"You see my face. Not theirs. Just look at my face."

I nod again and blink away more of the blur. Other parts of his face slowly come into view. His golden hair. His strong, angled jaw. His peach lips and the blush that heats his cheeks. I see Michael's face, not Danny's.

I stay still under the shower, letting the water wash me and my clothes clean. Michael stays with me, talking to me calmly, and I continue to watch his face, my eyes following him languidly.

"You're here with me," he reminds me every few minutes. "Not them."

His words slowly start to piece me back together until I can see him clearly again.

"Michael."

He is bent down, rubbing at a bloodstain at the bottom of my jeans. He looks up at me and smiles. "Look who's back."

"I don't deserve you."

He stands up. He's so tall that I find myself staring at the hollow of his neck that curves just above his collarbone. I don't remember him being this tall.

"And you don't deserve someone like me," I say. "You deserve someone who's good and kind and not insane, not broken. Someone who can return your feelings completely because they have a heart." I bite my lip. "I can only give you so much. My feelings can't be a bottomless well. I'm not capable of —of *love*, of—"

He cuts me off. "I don't want someone else," he says, folding my hand into his. "And I don't need you to give me anything."

The wide shower head sends a stream of water over us, beating down on our shoulders. I blink through the water. It's like we're back in the rain again. "You deserve someone better."

"You're wrong. Maybe I don't deserve you, but not for the reasons you think." He runs his free hand up my arm. "How many times do I have to tell you that you are good? I want *you*, Pen. No one else. I told you that you're brave, smart, and strong. But you're also beautiful, and whether or not you can admit it, you are good. Do you hear me? Regardless of how much darkness you've seen, goodness still lives inside of you, just as it does in me. *You are good!*"

I shake my head, ready to protest, but before I can, he silences me with a kiss. He traps my face within his hands, holding me gently, like I'm sculpted from ice. And in a way, I am. But under his touch, I warm. The ice cracks.

I kiss him back harder, showing him I'm not as breakable as he thinks. Heat courses between us, traveling out from his touch. The warmth dances across my skin and penetrates into my veins, the blood coursing like fire following a rivulet of gasoline until I'm entirely consumed. I walk him backwards and shove him against the shower wall, sliding my arms up his chest and around his neck only to tangle my hands in his wet hair.

I want you. I don't want anyone else. His golden voice is soft in my head, whispering like smoke from a snuffed candle. I gasp, breaking away. His eyes are bright blue and water clings to his coppery eyelashes. He stares at me unwaveringly. *It's you, Pen. It will always be you.* I trace his lips with my finger, daring him to say it out loud.

"Pen." My name falls from his mouth desperately.

He grabs my waist and spins us around so I am leaning against the cool tiles of the shower. He kisses me again sweetly before letting go—too soon, my head sings—and stepping out of the shower. He never turns his back to me as he makes his way over to the bathroom door, and the smile never leaves his lips.

"I'll be waiting out here," he promises. "I'm not going anywhere. I won't leave you, I swear on my life."

I watch him, my lips parted and my head dizzy, as he steps out of the room and pulls the door closed in front of him. The door clicks lightly into place and he's gone. I let my head fall back on the shower wall and I close my eyes.

This boy will be the death of me, I think quietly, letting out a long breath.

CHAPTER 26

WHEN I COME OUT OF THE BATHROOM DRESSED IN A long, clean t-shirt and loose pajama pants, the sun is still rising slowly in the sky. It shines weakly through the window that looks down onto the city, and it casts a soft pink light throughout the room. I tiptoe over to the bed, pulling off my necklace and hanging it on one of the lamps above the nightstand. With Michael, I feel the need to distance myself from Azael, and I don't want him to be the one to wake me up again.

I find Michael waiting for me in the pillowy bed. He's asleep, lying on top of the white comforter, his dark jeans dry and his feet and chest bare. His legs stretch down the length of the bed and his hand is thrown over his head, resting above his damp, golden curls. I see his shirt crumpled on the ground in front of the closet, still wet from the shower. His eyes are closed and his mouth is opened slightly, his breath whistling quietly.

I slide into the bed next to Michael and slip under the covers, my damp hair fanning out on the pillow beneath me. I watch him sleep, his tan chest rising and falling in a gentle rhythm, the corded muscles expanding and contracting.

"I'm falling for you, too," I confess to him, knowing he won't hear me. "And I'm terrified." Hesitantly, I inch nearer to him, but not so close that I'm touching him.

He yawns and turns towards me, his eyes opening sleepily. "Pen," he says, his voice thick.

"Yeah, it's just me," I whisper back. "I didn't mean to wake you."

"I don't mind." He reaches out his arm and shifts me closer to him. "I told you I wouldn't leave."

I roll over so my back is pressed to his chest and his arm is draped over my waist. This is new to me, this kind of closeness, and I feel my nerves buzzing just below my skin. I lace my fingers through his and let my eyes close.

"You're so cold."

"I'm sorry." I start to let go of his hand, but he grabs on tighter.

"It's not a complaint, just an observation. I'm burning up—you feel nice." He brushes his lips against my neck. "Stay."

"Oh," I say simply, my head spinning from his touch. "Okay."

He wraps his arm around me, pulling me even closer to him. "Goodnight, Pen," he breathes in my ear.

"Goodnight, Michael," I whisper back. "Sleep, and I'll chase away any nightmares."

"How can I have a nightmare when I'm already in the middle of a dream?"

I roll my eyes. "Goodnight," I say again, settling against him.

We fall asleep together, tangled in one another's embrace as the sun continues to rise unhurriedly into the city's steel sky.

5:23PM.

That's what the red numbers of the clock blink when I finally wake up and rub the sleep from my eyes. Michael still has his arm draped around my waist, but it is no longer soft and relaxed. He grabs me, my waist trapped against the tense and unmoving muscles of his abdomen.

"Michael?" I shake his arm, trying to wake him up, but he doesn't let go. He just grabs me tighter, crushing me against him painfully. "Michael!"

I squirm in his arms until I break free of his grip, sit up, and turn to face him. His face is pinched, contorted in either pain or fear—I can't tell. His eyebrows are knotted together fiercely, the muscles in his jaw clenched tight. He is covered in a light sheen of sweat, all of his muscles hard and rigid under his hot skin, and I run my hand over his chest. I can feel his heart pounding furiously beneath my hand.

Michael, wake up. Listen to my voice. You're just dreaming. I lean forward and kiss his eyebrows, feeling them relax under my lips. *Wake up. You're fine. I'm here with you.* I place another soft kiss at the corner of his mouth.

He twitches once under my touch, the muscle at the top of his arm bouncing.

I press my cold hand on his hot forehead. *Please wake up. Come back to me.*

His eyes fly open, his pupils huge and wild as they flick around the room anxiously. He doesn't see me at first, and he starts to push himself up on the bed, against the dark cushioned headboard, but I hold him down, resting my hands gently on his shoulders. He claws at his chest, closing his eyes against whatever pain he's feeling, so I place one of my hands over his, stilling his searching fingers.

He closes his eyes and in a strangled sound says, "It burns. Please, it *burns.*"

I move my hand under his, my icy fingers pressed over his warm, hammering heart.

"Relax. You're okay. I'm here."

"You're—" His eyes open again. He looks at me for a moment, confused, and then his eyes soften as his shoulders lower. "You're here," he breathes.

I feel his heartbeat slowing under my palm, eventually returning to a normal rhythm.

I take a slow, deep breath and smile shakily. "I'm here. It was just a nightmare."

He reaches up and hugs me to him, burying his face in my hair. "Thank you."

After a moment, I remove my palm from his chest and bring my arms around him too, hugging him back. He doesn't seem to be in pain anymore. It's like it evaporated when he looked at me.

"You saved me from my nightmare," I say. "I'm just returning the favor."

He lets go and leans up against the headboard, pulling me to sit next to him. Our arms brush and I rest my head on his shoulder.

"What were you dreaming about?"

"I don't remember," he says, knotting his fingers in the sheets. "The only thing I can remember is hearing your voice call my name. And then a horrible fire in my chest."

I glance over at the small white scar that sits just over his heart and reach out to touch it. I set my hand on it and he shivers. "The burning's gone now?" I ask.

He nods, watching my hand closely. I let it slide down his chest to his abdomen, lingering a moment before pulling it back into my lap and knotting my hands together.

"I wouldn't have known you were having a nightmare if you hadn't told me before… Your arm locked around me, and I had to break free. You weren't moving." I shake my head. "You were so still."

The muscle in his jaw tenses. Through his teeth, he asks, "Did I hurt you?"

He looks away from me, waiting anxiously for my answer.

"No, you didn't hurt me."

He lets out a breath I didn't notice he was holding.

"You only scared me," I tell him. "My nightmare was so different."

"I remember." He leans his head onto mine and picks up my hand to hold between his. "You were screaming and thrashing out. It was like you were being attacked."

My breath catches.

"But you didn't have any nightmares last night," he says softly.

"No," I acknowledge. "I didn't. I had you."

He turns my hand over in his and studies my scars, tracing the small, delicate reminders of war.

"I still wonder about your nightmare. You never told me what you dreamed. You began to when you woke up and thought I was Azael. You said something about seeing yourself dead."

I sigh. "I did."

"What happened?" His fingers freeze and he looks over at me through coppery eyelashes.

I tuck my feet under myself and remove my hand from his to clutch at the blankets as the nightmare comes rushing back to me.

"I was in the forest." I twist the sheet between my fingers, fidgeting against the memory, and close my eyes. I feel Michael take both of my hands in his again, and even though I know he can feel them tremble, he doesn't let go. He places his other hand on top of mine to stop the shaking, holding them securely in his own.

"If it's too much—"

IGNITE

I shake my head, seeing my nightmare replayed on the backs of my eyelids. "It's not." When I open my eyes, I can still see the forest, the moonlight, the shadows. But I also see Michael here, in this hotel room, in the sunlight of the late afternoon. The fear isn't overwhelming when I can ground myself here, when I can ground myself in the now. "I heard a scream, and I ran towards it, up into a clearing. There was a shadowed man standing above a figure that had fallen to the ground, dead. He had stabbed her with a great sword. I couldn't see the person on the ground or the face of the shadowed man."

I pause and he squeezes my hand reassuringly.

"A second shadow joined the first and was told to take her soul."

"Her?"

"The figure, the dead girl. But when he went to look for her soul, he said he couldn't find it. She didn't have one."

"She was infected with the Lilim virus?" he guesses, but I shake my head no.

"I told them to show me their faces, but they couldn't hear me. When I walked around the clearing to face them, I saw that the second shadow was Azael. The girl had a large wound in her chest and was covered in dark, black blood." I swallow around a lump in my throat. "When the first shadow bent down, I recognized him."

"Who was he?"

I look at him and into his impossibly blue eyes. "You."

He stares back in disbelief. "It was me?"

I tear at my bottom lip with my teeth. "When you pushed the matted hair out of the girl's face, I recognized her too."

"The girl was you." His eyes light up with understanding.

I nod.

"You dreamt that…" He pauses, the corners of his mouth pulling down in a frown. "That I killed you? And told Azael to take your soul?"

I'm silent.

"Oh," he says quietly. "That's why you wouldn't tell me."

"I couldn't."

He turns sideways so he can look at me, still holding on to my hands. "I would never kill you, Pen. I would rather die myself than hurt you, than see you hurt."

"Don't you dare sacrifice yourself for me," I say forcefully, shaking my head. "Do you know what kind of burden it is to carry the life of someone with you? Someone who placed more value in your life over their own, decided that your life was worth *sacrificing* theirs for… It's unbearable. It's a burden I wouldn't be able to handle." I look at him carefully, searching his face. "Especially if it was your life I carried with me, if it was your sacrifice."

"If you were to be hurt, if I lost you…" His voice fades. He leans forward, places his hand on my cheek, and rests his forehead against mine. "I would be lost without you."

"When I had that dream—Michael, I didn't know you then."

"But you know me now. You have to know I would never…"

I trap his lips with mine. "I know. And I could never hurt you." *Never.* The finality of the word echoes through my head. Strangely, I find that I'm not scared by it. I'm not afraid to tell Michael this, that his life is important to me. I rely on his breaths, his beating heart, and I could never take that away from him without losing myself. I will never hurt him.

He sits back and smiles. "Really?"

"Really," I say seriously. I look around the room. "Speaking of which, where is your sword?"

"I left it in Heaven," he says. "I didn't think I would need it for anything. So I brought that instead." He gestures to his crumpled shirt in front of the closet. Peeking out from under the dark green cotton is a small serrated blade. "It's much less conspicuous."

"I didn't even see it," I say surprised.

"That's the point."

IGNITE

I laugh and slide out of bed, walking over to the closet and picking up the blade by its smooth, black handle. "You know, you really shouldn't leave this on the floor. I could have cut my foot on it."

"I'll have to be more careful where I leave my weapons," he says with a light laugh. If he were Azael, I would expect some sort of unsavory innuendo regarding weapons and swords and where it is best to keep them, but this is Michael, and all I receive is his smile.

"A little responsibility goes a long way," I mock, walking over to the nightstand next to him and sticking the tip of the blade into the wood.

He reaches up and catches my arm, pulling me towards him, but I put up my hand, blocking his kiss.

"I need to get dressed." I look down at his chest. "And so do you."

"The stars?" he asks excitedly.

"You like hiking, right?" I quirk one side of my mouth up in a slanted smile.

"More and more every day." He jumps out of bed and lifts me up, spinning me around. "And I can't wait to see your stars."

CHAPTER 27

We leave The Aria while the sun is still sinking into the sky and walk down the same street we did last night. It's not quite dark yet, so some of the offices are still open, but most of the people on the street ignore us, clutching briefcases in one hand and pressing cell phones to their ears with the other as they hurry down the sidewalk towards the parking garage.

I flex my fingers in the cold air and Michael slides his hand into mine without a second thought, the warmth of his hand gloving mine. It's so strange to feel my hand in Michael's. I'm used to holding Azael's, his bones sharp and his fingers long, cold, and calloused from battle.

Michael's hand, though, is warm and soft, his skin new and unscarred. Without meaning to, I find myself wondering how long it will stay that way. With the way Azael's been raving about the forthcoming war, I fear it won't be too much longer.

I marvel at the way Michael holds my hand. It's new to me and so unlike holding Azael's. Who would have thought a simple gesture could mean something so drastically different when shared with someone else?

When Azael and I hold hands, it is to guide the other where we want them to go or to drag them along behind us. Sometimes we would even hold hands to protect each other. His grip always felt like a warning to those we fought, saying, "She is mine, and I will destroy anyone who says otherwise." I feel the same sense of possession over Azael, and my grip is equally as fierce. After all, he is my brother, and the need to protect each other binds us together. It's helped us survive. It's not like that with Michael.

The way Michael folds my small hand into his is almost intimate, like we can't stand to be parted from the other's touch for even a moment. Our fingers laced together are not fighting for possession, for dominance. Our grip isn't even about protection, really, though I do want to keep him safe. But that's not why I hold on to him, and that's not why he holds on to me.

The pressure of his hand on mine is reassuring, a reminder that I am not alone because he is here, next to me. I can feel his pulse in his fingertips and it travels up my own arm into my chest. He's alive, he is here, and we are together.

Tied to Michael like this, I'm not telling the world "He is mine." The way we touch each other, cling desperately to the other's hand, tells the world "We belong to each other."

I squeeze his hand in mine and we run faster down the street together, my amulet bouncing against my collarbone as we weave between men and women dressed in stiff suits who step out of our way with annoyance. When we get past the crowds, I turn and look behind us to see shoulders of gray, black, and blue wool jackets bounce away from us, hunched against the cold.

"We'll fly from here to the mountains," I say, looking up at Michael. His nose and cheeks are flushed red from the cold. I wonder if my face is as rosy as his and try to imagine how shocking the red looks against my pale face. "And then we'll walk. I don't want you to see the stars until it's completely dark."

"As you wish."

We run a few paces, still clutching each other's hands, and jump, our wings sprawling out behind us as we lift higher into the darkening sky. I look back down to the ground at the shrinking people and see that no one noticed our wings, let alone us flying miles above them in the sky. They're so focused on the tiny glowing screens they hold between gloved hands that they don't look up. I wonder how much of the world passes before them unnoticed. Do they look up at all? Do they know what they're missing?

Michael and I fly over the sky-scraping city, watching as the tall buildings bordered by busy streets ebb away, the buildings shrinking and growing farther apart from one another.

Eventually, the urban cement of the city softens into sprawling, rural farms, the ground patched in shades of yellow, red, green, and even swatches of lavender. The streets become wider and emptier until eventually it tapers off into one winding road that slips between rolling hills before disappearing into a carve in the mountain.

I point to a green bridge that hangs above the road, feeding one mountain to another.

Let's land there, I tell him.

He nods and we turn towards the bridge, setting down on the green metal mesh that cages the walkway. The chain of the cover rattles against metal supports as I stand up, looking out over the road.

Between the two shelves of the mountain, I see the edge of the sun drop behind the sharp peak of a distant ridge. I glance up at the sky and notice a light dusting of stars begin to appear across the quickly darkening sky like freckles.

I grab Michael's hand again and pull him roughly across the bridge. We jump down and into the woods, onto a narrow and steep dirt path that curls its way away from the road and under the canopy of trees.

"No cheating," I say over my shoulder. "Don't look up."

He laughs and puts his free hand over his eyes, blocking his view. "I wouldn't dream of it."

I pull him up the path and through the trees, making sure he doesn't twist an ankle on the exposed roots. I run a little farther down the path and it levels, no longer rushing us up the side of the mountain.

It's darker in the woods, hidden under the thick branches and colorful leaves. The moonlight shines through the backs of the leaves, exposing the intricate veins of the foliage, but I can't see the stars anymore. I want to keep them hidden from Michael until we get to the top of the mountain, and the trees provide the perfect veil to the glittering sky. A gentle breeze whispers around us, lifting my hair and shaking the leaves, making it look like they are waving at us.

I turn back to Michael and remove his hand from his eyes. "You can look now."

He brings his hand down and brushes a curl of my hair behind my ear. "You're right. It is beautiful."

I roll my eyes. "You can't even see them yet." I let go of him and start walking up a sloping path, making sure to stay under the arches of the trees. "Come on."

He chuckles and follows after me, his shoes crunching across acorns and small twigs that litter the ground. "What is your favorite thing about Earth?" he asks.

"Snow," I answer without having to think about it.

"I would have thought it would be the stars, what with the way you've been speaking of them."

"Stars belong to the sky." I look back and smile. "You asked what my favorite thing was about *Earth*. It's snow."

"I've never seen it," he says. "But I've heard it's beautiful. It's just like rain, right?"

"It's better than rain. When it snows, it's like the sky is dropping tiny white crystals that stick to everything—roads, trees, people, anything that's still long enough to be covered in a dusting of snowflakes. And right after it snows, there's always this moment of absolute silence where everything seems like it is sleeping, tucked under the thick blanket of pure, white snow."

"Maybe next you'll show me snow," he says hopefully. "After the stars."

"Could be a while," I answer. "It has to be really cold to snow. And it's not that cold yet. Maybe in a month or so…"

He's quiet as we continue to walk, the back of his hand brushing against mine, sending sparks of electricity up my arm.

"Snow is very particular," I go on. "Everything has to be just right, but it's worth the wait. Az hates it. You wouldn't though. There's nothing else like it." I smile to myself. "You'll see."

"Good things are always worth the wait," he says meaningfully, glancing at me sideways.

I bite at my lip and let his words hang in the air and lift through the trees, carried away by the wind.

We make the majority of the hike up the mountain in silence. Michael hums occasionally or whispers lines of poetry that he doesn't think I can hear. I didn't know he knew any poetry. I know he mentioned that he would keep books with him when he was locked away in his room, but I thought it was just a way for him to pass the time. I didn't think anything he read would leave much of an impression; Heaven doesn't place much value on mortal literature. They're all about the sacred texts written by powerful angel historians and scribes. For him to remember lines of poems he's read, to recite it here for the shadows of the woods with such reverence, is surprising.

I look down at my fingers, remembering the dark stains my books would leave on their tips after days of reading. My mouth twitches, fighting a smile. I wonder if Michael's fingers were ever stained from the ink of the words he memorized.

He doesn't try to start a conversation as we walk, and neither do I. I just stay quiet, listening to him closely, attempting to pick up the lines he's reciting.

It's not an uncomfortable silence. Being around Michael is so easy that it's scary. I've never been comfortable around anyone but Azael before. But even around Az I have to mask my real self. With Michael I can just be me. There are no pretenses, and I don't have to try to be anything I'm not. It's as effortless as breathing, as weightless as flying.

Michael seems equally at ease. He runs his hands across trees we pass and looks around in awe at the twisting branches that stretch deep into the dark woods like lonely fingers seeking a companion.

A small part of me expected him to be nervous at night. I thought he would be searching the darkness for shadows that move a little too quickly or intelligently, waiting for something to jump out and attack him. But he doesn't seem jumpy, doesn't seem worried at all. He's relaxed and unconcerned as we follow the dark, secluded path.

It's confusing. For the entirety of his short, new life, he had been fed lies about what was past his bedroom door, what was beyond the gates of Heaven. It wasn't long ago that he was worried about the monsters he thought stalked the night. He'd lived on a curfew that he believed would protect him from these monsters, and now he's here, walking through the woods in the middle of the night, alone with a demon.

I'm surprised he is so quick to throw away what Heaven has told him. He doesn't seem to have an alliance to anyone but himself. Maybe he really doesn't belong anywhere.

"Just a little farther," I say to him, breaking the silence.

He looks at me, his eyes bright and excited. "Really?"

I nod. "The trees end where the dirt thins out and the rocks of the mountain begin. That's just around this corner up here. You'll have to close your eyes again."

Immediately, he snaps his eyes closed and holds out his hand out for me. "No cheating," he promises.

I smile as I take his hand in mine, guiding him out of the woods and onto the hard surface of a flat shelf of the mountain that falls away in a sheer drop. Beneath the ledge lies a cropping of trees that hugs the bank of a thin stream that snakes its way down a second mountain. I let go of Michael's hand.

"Stay here for a second. Don't move."

I inch farther out on the flat rock, closer to the edge, and look up at the sky. An inky blackness is settled across the sky with millions of stars peeking through like found diamonds.

Part of the sky is lighter, a strange maroon color that cuts through the blackness like a ripped seam in the dark. More stars, gold and silver, peek through the tear, shining even brighter. It's perfect.

Michael still stands at the edge of the rocks, his heels settled in the soft dirt of the woods, waiting with his eyes closed. I go back to him and take both of his hands in mine, slowly walking him out onto the ledge of the mountain. He follows me without hesitation.

"You're very trusting," I laugh. "I could be walking you right over the side, leading you to your death."

His grip tightens on my hands, but he smiles. "From the way you are leading me, I think you would be the first to fall. Plus," he adds, shrugging his shoulders, "I think my wings may be of some help should you lead me over the edge."

"Touché." I smile. "Okay, you need to lie down. The best way to see the stars is to look straight up at them."

He drops one of my hands and carefully lowers himself to the ground, his hand searching around him before he lies down. Without letting go of his other hand, I lie down next to him, close enough that the entire lengths of our bodies are touching. I squeeze his hand once and take a deep breath.

"Open your eyes."

I know his eyes are open when I hear him gasp. He shifts next to me, turning his head from side to side, swallowing the expanse of stars with wide, mystified eyes.

I point up at the sky. The stars are large and shining perfectly, as if they knew we would be watching. They're putting on their best show to impress Michael.

"That is called the North Star," I tell him, indicating the largest and brightest star in the sky. "No matter where you are in the world, if you can find this star, you can find North. And there," I say, sliding my finger across the sky to point at a dimmer set of stars, "is the constellation Cepheus, or The King. It was named after King Cepheus, husband of Cassiopeia and father of Andromeda. He was an Argonaut in Greek mythology."

"A what?"

"The Argonauts," I explain, letting my arm fall back down next to me, "were a band of heroes who, in the years before the Trojan War, sailed with a man named Jason on a quest for the Golden Fleece. This fleece, as the story goes, was needed for Jason to claim the throne. The heroes all sailed on a great ship called the Argo." I look over at him. "Every great hero needs a great ship."

"You like mythology," he observes.

I shrug, turning my face back to the sky. "I've lived through mythology. There are stories about all of us—angels, demons, what happens after life. In fact, you make cameos in a lot of mythology. The Greeks loved Archangels, especially you. It's interesting to see what humans tell themselves about our existence. It's even more interesting how close they often come to the truth."

I continue to gaze up at the stars above us trying to identify more constellations. It doesn't take long before I start to see the patterns in the sky of strung-together stars. The Big Dipper, Andromeda, Orion The Hunter...

"Beautiful," Michael murmurs.

I look over at him and see he isn't looking at the stars. Instead, he's watching me.

"You're not even looking."

"Sure I am. And what I see is beautiful." He smiles. "I don't think I'll be able to look away."

I squirm, still uncomfortable with being complimented. I'm not used to being noticed or told that I'm anything special. Because I'm not. "I'm only beautiful if you don't look too closely. If you know what's inside of me, that pretty outside shatters."

"I'm close, and I'm looking," he whispers, his breath warm on my cheek. "I see what's inside of you. You," he says, reaching out carefully with his hand to brush my hair back from my face, "are beautiful."

For a moment, our eyes lock, and I feel like he can see through me. Like I can't hide anything from him because he sees it all. All of the darkest corners of my mind, the shadows that loom in my memory... he sees them and he's not afraid. No one's ever seen me and not been afraid. Not unless they were like me.

His kindness sets me on fire. His absolute acceptance of the parts of me that are broken shouldn't be possible, but it is. I can see it in his eyes. He ignites me, sets me ablaze, and if I don't look away, we'll burn together, turn to ash and blow away on the wind, joining the stars in the sky.

So I look away. I roll my eyes, brushing off his compliment. "Just look at the stars, all right?"

His shoulders shake with laughter as he turns his face to the sky again. I keep stealing furtive glances at him, making sure he's watching the sky and not me.

When I'm convinced he's more enraptured with the stars than me, I tilt my head to the side and rest it on his arm. He shifts under me and curls his arm around my shoulder, his thumb brushing over my arm sending pulses of electricity through my nerves.

"Why do you love the stars so much?" he asks.

I pause, considering his question. "They're poetic," I say finally. "Did you know that most of the stars we see are already dead?"

He shakes his head.

"Their light is burned out by the time it reaches us." It reminds me a little of me and Michael. By the time he found me, almost all of my light was extinguished. I wonder how much longer it would have taken for my light to burn out completely.

"Sad," he whispers.

"No, *poetic*," I remind him. "They're like the lanterns of ghosts, swinging in the sky, reminding us that there's more out there. That there's more than just our life. There's something bigger."

He turns his head to look at me but stays quiet.

"They may be dead," I go on, "but they've shared the last of their light in their dying moments with us. And that's poetic."

"I would have never thought about it that way," he says in a hushed voice.

I turn my head and lock eyes with him. "You like poetry," I guess.

"What I've heard, yes, I have liked. Do you know any poetry?"

"Plenty. Robert Frost is one of my favorites."

"I don't know him," he says, frowning.

I clear my throat. "'How countlessly they congregate / O'er our tumultuous snow / Which flows in shapes as tall as trees / When wintry winds do blow.'"

"Was that Frost?"

I nod. "It's from a poem called *Stars*."

He smiles. "Any other poets you can recommend?"

"E. E. Cummings is great. Always made great use of parentheses and hated capital letters," I say with a laugh. "So is

William Blake. And then, of course, there's Wordsworth, Poe, Thomas, Shakespeare, Byron, Whitman…"

He raises his eyebrows.

"I don't know if you're ready for this conversation. There are hundreds of poets that I love. I'm a bit literature-eclectic. I'll read just about anything I can get my hands on, and I love it all."

"I know some Byron. I'll try to find something from Blake, though," he says. "Maybe he has a poem about the stars."

I think for a minute. "Many of his poems have a line about stars. I'm sure you'll find one."

He looks up at the stars again and I see them reflected in his eyes. "You were right, by the way, about how different these are from Heaven's stars. There are so many more of them. And they look… real."

"I remember I thought the stars looked mechanical from Heaven," I say. "Like they were manmade."

He nods. "That's exactly it. These ones are so much more pure, more genuine."

I was worried that he wouldn't see the stars the same way I do. I thought maybe he wouldn't notice the difference and appreciate the beauty of Earth's stars that I saw. But I can tell by the wonder in his smile and the amazement that lights his face that he does.

"Thank you," he whispers, his breath smokey in the cold night, "for sharing your stars."

"They're your stars too," I tell him.

His smile grows and he props himself up on his elbow, leaning over me. "Our stars," he says, his eyes hazy with desire.

Carefully, he lowers his lips to mine. A heat spreads through me, spiraling out from my abdomen, as his lips move against mine so slowly it's agonizing. I thread my arms around his neck and pull him closer to me.

"Pen." He murmurs my name, his voice hushed and gravelly with desire. He says my name again, even softer, "Pen," and his eyelids flutter closed.

IGNITE

I ache to be nearer to him, to fill the emptiness I feel in my chest, and to thaw the ice in my veins. He runs his hands up my sides and into my hair, leaving a trail of heat on the bare skin his fingers brush against. We burn where we touch, consume one another completely. Softly, he hums against my lips, sending small vibrations radiating through my body. I close my eyes and knot my fingers in his hair.

Brazenly, I tease his mouth open above mine and feel him gasp. My cool breath fills his warm mouth and we breathe together like we are starved for oxygen only the other can provide. I give him the air I don't need and he breathes me in desperately, and for a second time his lungs fill with my breath, his chest rising and falling on my accord.

We kiss slowly, deliberately, trying to commit the shape of each other's mouths to memory. I touch his cheek, my fingers sliding to his jaw before traveling down to his neck and strong, corded shoulders. His body is hard against me, strung with tight, toned muscles, but his lips are soft, so soft. We hold on to each other like lifeboats but still we manage to drown in the kiss. Under the sea of stars, with Michael, I cannot imagine ever needing to come up for air.

Quietly, like a soft caress in my mind, I hear his golden voice. *'She walks in beauty, like the night / Of cloudless climes and starry skies.'*

I sigh against him, recognizing the poem.

'And all that's best of dark and bright / Meet in her aspect and her eyes.'

Byron, I say, almost surprised. *You* have *read his poetry.*

It wasn't until I met you that it had any meaning. He leans on his elbows and lifts away from me, his eyelids heavy and his cheeks flushed. "Now I understand."

I search his eyes. They're deep and glossy, the bluish steel of a midnight sky that burns cold. In his eyes, I find the courage to tell him what I was too afraid to say to him last night. At least, what I was too afraid to tell him when he was awake.

"I'm falling for you, too." My voice comes out in a soft whisper that swirls between us. "I've tried to fight it, but it seems pointless. I can't stop thinking about you, and I'm not sure I even want to."

"Pen." He says my name like a prayer. "My heart is yours."

I rest my hand on his chest and feel his racing heart. It stutters once under my touch. "But I have nothing to give you back."

"I don't need anything back. I have you, here, with me. That's all I need." He hesitates before adding, "You're all I need."

A tightness in my chest releases, like a heavy weight I didn't know I've been carrying has suddenly been lifted, and I let out my breath slowly. I feel warm and feather light, the coldness inside of me melting away, making me feel like I could float. But he holds me with him, anchored securely on the ground.

I can't find any words to offer him, so I show him what I can't say with another tender kiss. Like our last kiss, it starts slowly, his lips moving against mine softly as he reaches up and touches my cheek.

Then a fire spreads, and his lips move faster, more insistently, and my hips swirl under his. I arch up to meet his body with mine, shifting us so he is on his back, and I am pressed against him from above. Again, the world falls away beneath us. Michael is all that is real.

My pendant hangs down from my neck, the large stone resting on his chest. I feel my hands trembling slightly, shaking as I slide them up his arm so they can rest on his neck. He reaches up with a hand and undoes my hair, letting it fall around us like a small, dark curtain, hiding us from the stars for just a brief moment. We both smile as we roll again, Michael hovering over me.

Pen, where are you?

I freeze under Michael, and he lifts his head, looking around. "What was that?" he asks, confused.

I look at him, eyes wide. "Azael," I croak.

IGNITE

Pen? Are you there?

Michael sits up, his legs straddling mine. He watches me quietly, his lips swollen and blushed from our kiss.

I grab the stone of my necklace in my fist, crushing my eyes closed. What horrible, horrible timing Azael has. I don't sit up when I answer. *Az?* I steady my voice and try not to sound as breathless as I feel.

FINALLY! I tried to call you earlier this morning, but you weren't answering.

Yeah, I was sleeping, sorry.

And they say there ain't no rest for the wicked. Shows you how much they know!

Who is this "they"?

You know... the collective they.

I take a few breaths and open my eyes, looking at Michael. He tilts his head to the side, listening. I mouth "Can you hear him?" and he nods.

What do you need, Azael?

Don't be cranky, I've got big news.

I wait.

He continues. *Where are you?*

Um, I'm near the Appalachian mountains. Why? And by "near the Appalachian mountains," I mean sitting on top of one with an angel straddling me. Horrible, horrible timing.

This is news I can only deliver in person. I'm close, like really close, so I'll see you soon.

I sit straight, accidentally pushing Michael off of me. *Az, can't this wait?*

If it could wait, do you think I'd go out of my way to tell you tonight? No.

I'm dizzy and disoriented. Panic rises within me as I search out in the sky, looking for dark wings. But I wouldn't see him yet, right? He can't be that close...

I will see you soon, sister. He hisses and it sounds like a vague threat.

With a snap, I can feel that he's gone. I shiver.

"Pen?" Michael leans forward on his knees and rests a hand on my shoulder.

"You have to hide," I say hollowly. "Azael's coming."

CHAPTER 28

THE EASINESS OF THE NIGHT SHATTERS APART AS I REPEAT in my head, *Azael's coming*.

The sky now looks dark and jagged to me. The purple vein of stars looks like a bruise and the stars themselves appear eerie and cold. *Ghost lights*. The edge of the woods seems thick with shadows, and I'm paranoid I'll see a pair of violet eyes staring out at me accusingly.

I push Michael all the way off of me, scrambling to my feet and dragging him up to stand next to me. "We have to hide you. He can't—it wouldn't be good if—if he sees you he will—" My head spins and my stomach twists, winding tight like spaghetti being twirled by a fork. I bounce nervously on my toes and clasp my hands together to stop them from shaking.

Michael is unnervingly still and calm. He takes my hands in his and speaks slowly. "He'll never know I was here."

I bite my lip anxiously. He'll know—Azael always knows. But I nod anyway. "You have to hide."

He places a small kiss on the top of my head. "I will," he says, stepping away from me and walking towards the woods. "Tell Azael I say hi."

I laugh weakly and turn back to the wide sky as he is swallowed into the shadows of the trees. I search for a pair of dark wings on the horizon but still don't see any. I close my eyes, listening. I hear a restless breeze skim over the trees and through the valleys of the mountains, the wind whistling tentatively to the darkness, but I can't hear Michael anywhere in the woods. I touch my bracelet absently and feel that it is still warm.

He's still here, I reassure myself. *Stay close.*

When I hear a response, it's not Michael's voice. *Close to what?*

A surge of air pushes against me and my eyes fly open. "Azael."

"Sister," he says, a barbed smile spreading across his sharp face. "What am I to stay close to?"

I hesitate. "Nothing. I just meant..." I falter, my tongue tripping over itself. "You're cutting it close. I was about to leave."

He watches me skeptically, his eyes narrow. "Then I guess it's a good thing I made such excellent time."

With effort, I plaster what I hope will pass as a genuine smile across my face. "So, what's the big news?"

"Ah, yes. Down to business." He flexes his hands and holds up a single finger. "First, as you know, I am second-in-command. And, because I am such a swell brother," he says with a grin, standing a bit taller and puffing his chest out, "I have made you my number two. When I lead the army of Hell across the fiery threshold of Heaven, you will be by my side, wielding one of the most powerful weapons anyone has ever seen."

I arch an eyebrow in interest. "What weapon?"

"Be patient! I'm getting to it. That's the second order of business. Hell is forging their own archangel swords. Well, they're not exactly *archangel* swords... I guess they would be

Greater Demon swords? I don't know. I'm still working on a name for them."

I lean forward, waiting for him to go on. A smile crooks the corner of his mouth and he knows he's got me interested.

"They're more powerful than Heaven's weapons—darker and stronger. Generally, more badass," he brags. "Now, I haven't technically seen one yet, but even Gus sounded excited about it, and you know his aversion to weapons! All he ever carries around with him is that damn notebook. You can't quite kill someone with paper cuts, can you?"

I stay quiet.

"Right. Now to the good stuff about the swords. Get this." He steps closer to me, his eyebrows raised high and his eyes smoldering darkly. "They'll kill angels, archangels, and even demons. If it lives, it'll kill it. Hell, I even think it'll kill what's already dead!" He smiles arrogantly.

"Impressive."

"Really? Impressive? That's all you've got for me?"

"You're right." I shake my head and place my hand over my chest where my heart would be. "Goodness me, Azael. This is the kind of news you should deliver to a lady while she is seated, lest she faint!" I fan my hand in front of me theatrically, batting my eyes.

"Much better. A little too 'overwhelmed debutante' for my taste, but I can appreciate the improvisation. It felt sincere, like it was coming from your gut."

I stick my tongue out and move my hands to my hips.

"All right, third order of business." He pauses dramatically and leans in close to me. In a slicing hiss, he whispers, "It's time." He steps back, as if giving me room to appreciate what he is saying.

"Time for what?" I ask.

"For the love of—Pen, how short is your memory?"

I stare at him blankly, my mind somewhere deep in the woods with wherever Michael is.

"Gus says that it's time to come back to Hell. Leave this horrible world for something a bit more pleasant. It's nearly the day of reckoning, and as the new leaders of Hell, we need to go finish preparations. Sharpen a few blades, torture a few weak souls who refuse to fight, shake a few hands, maybe even get a portrait of us commissioned. You know, leader-y type things."

"Now?" My hands drop from my hips, hanging loosely by my side.

He shrugs. "I'm going to be leaving tonight. But you still have to complete *your* job. How is little Michael, anyway?" His lips curl back from his teeth. "Have you seen him lately?"

I nod, swallowing around a lump in my throat. "Of course. I saw him today."

"And have you convinced him?"

I cross my arms over my chest and kick at the ground with my feet. "I'm working on it."

"Well you've run out of time. One way or another, you're done. When will you see him next? Tomorrow?"

"I suppose." I bite my tongue, fighting the urge to look over my shoulder into the woods.

"Then tomorrow's the day. You either convince him to join us or you kill him. And when you kill him—which I have my money on, so don't let me down—make sure to bring back a present for Lucifer. Maybe his heart or that pretty little head of his."

I set my face in stone, not letting his words affect me. One mistimed flinch and Azael will know. *He always knows*, I think to myself desperately. *Somehow Az always knows*. I take a deep breath and fidget with my fingers, curling them around one another so tight that my bones could break. I half hope one of them does. "What if I don't see him tomorrow?"

"Then wait. He'll be back. I'm sure, if you've done your job, he's entirely enthralled with you. My pretty little sister."

He steps towards me and tugs at a loose strand of hair. I pull it away from him and tuck it back behind my ear. Azael smiles at me and grabs my chin, holding my face between his long, thin fingers. For the first time, I truly notice how cold they are. I must have become accustomed to Michael's warm hands holding me —his touch soft and gentle, not rough and pinching like Azael's.

Az tilts my head up so he can look down into my eyes.

"I bet you've completely blinded him." With a slight sneer on his face, he lets go. "He'll follow you anywhere if you just ask in the right way."

I scowl in disgust. "Just what are you asking me to do?"

"I think you know," he laughs darkly. "Tempt him. Persuade him. I learned a lot during my time with Lilith. Lessons, I think, you would be smart to learn. I'm sure she'd be willing to teach you when you come back home."

The only way I can fight down my disgust is by biting the inside of my cheek so hard it bleeds. I focus on the bitter taste in my mouth instead of the churning acid in my stomach.

"I don't think you're aware of the power you have in your beauty. It's a weapon not everyone has at their disposal. So *use it*. And if he resists, then…" He drags his finger across his throat. "End him."

I beat down a wave of nausea with clenched fists. "If that's what you think is best."

He pats me on the head condescendingly. "That's a good Pen. So agreeable tonight." He turns around, spreading his dark wings as wide as he can, ready to take off. I stare a hole into his back, waiting for him to leave. But he pauses and looks back at me. "It's strange."

"Hmm?" I try to soften my face into disinterest.

He folds his wings behind him quickly and turns around, stepping up so he is inches in front of me. He smells like cool peppermint and warm blood. It masks the sweet smell of honey that lingered on the rocks from Michael, and I'm glad he's oblivious to the golden scent.

"You never agree with me," he says, eyeing me suspiciously. "Nothing is ever this easy with you."

"Do you want me to fight you on this?" I tilt my head. "To waste time arguing about something when… when I agree with you?"

"You agree with me?" he asks slowly, pulling the words apart until the letters hang on to one another by only a thin thread.

"What is there to disagree about?" I ask innocently. "I will convince Michael. And if I can't, then the only option left is to kill him. It's my job."

I watch him and see that it's not good enough. He needs more convincing. I bite the inside of my cheek again and force the next words out through gritted teeth.

"I've been wanting to snap that angel in half since we first saw him," I lie as convincingly as I can. "He's an insignificant little pest who wouldn't be able to hold his own in a battle against one angel, let alone fight an army of angels. I only hope I get the chance to kill him soon."

"But he likes you?" Azael asks.

This is all a test, and I just have to find the right answer. I feel like I'm going to be sick and it takes all I have to keep standing.

"Yes. And he believes that I return the feelings." I shove a sharp laugh out from my mouth, and somehow I manage to make it sound crueler than I could have believed possible. "As if I could feel anything for someone so insignificant and weak." I'm going to pass out. "He's… *pathetic*." The words nearly choke me.

Azael searches my face, his dark eyes unyielding and superior. Finally, he smiles at me. "I couldn't agree more."

I let out a soft breath as he turns back around. For the first time, Azael couldn't see the truth. He looked into me and was satisfied with my lie. Maybe he just doesn't want to acknowledge the truth. I'm relieved, but at the same time, I'm overwhelmed by sadness.

We've lost each other, and this realization feels like a large stone slowly sinking to the bottom of an empty sea. This very well may be the last time I see him if I am to truly abandon Hell and run away with Michael. So before he can reopen his wings, I grab one of his sharp shoulders and spin him to me, wrapping him in a tight hug.

"What the Hell is this?"

"Shut up. It's called a hug." I say, squeezing tighter and closing my eyes. "Just... be careful and good luck and everything."

He hits me once on the back with his hand, and I know it's all he can muster. Uncomfortably, he pushes me back from him, an arm's length away. "Yeah, uh, that's nice."

I laugh and he rolls his eyes at me.

"You've been spending too much time with that haloed freak," he says.

"Maybe," I allow.

He smiles again wickedly. Behind his eyes, I see deep determination. He's going to burn the world down, and he's going to enjoy every moment of it. Hell has received a powerful leader.

He opens his wings, hiding himself from me behind large, glossy black feathers. "I'll see you in Hell," he says menacingly as he lifts off of the mountain and back into the sky.

I watch him as he flies away, his wings sliding in front of the glowing stars, extinguishing them for a moment before they spark back to life.

Goodbye, Azael, I think, settling down on the ledge of the cliff so my feet can dangle over the side. *And good luck.*

But I know what he would say to that. He doesn't need luck.

A soft scraping from the behind me draws my attention away from the sky and I look back to see Michael climbing out of one of the trees on the edge of the woods. He climbs down slowly and silently, not even looking over at me. His feet connect with the packed dirt of the ground with a dull thud.

"Michael," I say, smiling.

Finally, he turns to look at me, his face flat and emotionless. "Pen."

My smile falters slightly, but I fight to keep it. "I should have guessed you would hide in a tree."

He's shadowed under the branches but I can see him clearly enough to notice that his eyebrows are drawn low.

"Michael?"

He shakes his head and looks away from me.

"Michael, what's wrong?" I stand up and walk towards him slowly. For some reason, I get the feeling that we are balancing on a razor's edge, and I'm trying carefully not to fall.

He holds out one of his hands to stop me, and when he faces me again, his eyes are bright with hurt. His expression is pinched in betrayal and he looks at me like I am a stranger. Deep beneath my ribs, I feel an ache, and I want so badly to smooth away his worries, but I'm frozen where I stand.

"Everything you've said." He takes a few quiet breaths and shakes his head again. "Everything you've done."

I take another step forward but freeze when he puts up his hand again.

"Stop. I don't want you near me right now. I need you to stay far away." He agitatedly drags his hand through his hair, the muscles of his jaw clenching, crushing words he's unwilling to share with me. He looks at me hard and, in a voice as soft and sad as a whisper, he sighs, "Everything we were was a lie?"

His voice breaks, and just like that, I'm pushed over the edge, falling helplessly into the abyss.

"No, Michael," I say, rushing forward, pushing away his hand that is stretched out in protest. "We weren't the lie." I reach forward to touch him, but he grabs my wrist and sets my hand back down at my side.

"Don't."

I knot my fingers together to keep from reaching out to him again. I feel ill. "You can't really think that what I said to Azael was true."

"Is what *he* said true?" His voice is sharp and accusatory.

I can only answer him with silence.

"Was I just an assignment?"

I have no good answer for him. "Michael…"

"Stop." He looks away from me. "The only thing you *need* me for is a promotion, am I right? Because I'm just a job to you. You needed to convince me to join Hell. Isn't that what you're here for?"

I shake my head, but he's not looking at me. "No. No, you know that I'm not here for that. That's not why I need you. Maybe at first, but—" I see his face darken, "Not anymore. You have to know that."

He closes his eyes, squeezing them shut and blocking me out.

"Look at me. Michael, look at me!"

He snaps his head towards me and stares down at me unkindly. "The day you trained me… When we were up in the tree, you asked if I would fight for Hell."

I look at him desperately.

He just shakes his head in disgust. "Well you can tell Azael you've done your job. You did your best to persuade me. To *tempt* me. But I'm sorry to say that you've failed."

I drag my teeth across my lip painfully and taste the sharp metallic of my own blood. "The reason I could find you, that first day in the forest, was because you were assigned to me. My bracelet," I say, holding it up for him to see, "allowed me to find you."

"The one Azael gave you?" he asks angrily. "Or was that another lie?"

My mouth falls open, and I can't stop shaking my head. *No. No. No.* "You may have started off as an assignment… But you mean more than that to me." I search his face and see him slowly fading away from me. "*You are not an assignment.*" I can't stop repeating myself, but he's not listening. I need him to hear what I'm saying—to believe me.

"Then what am I to you, if not an assignment?"

I pause and hesitantly place my hand on his arm, but he shakes me off. "I don't know," I answer honestly. Because he deserves the truth.

"I don't know anymore either, Penemuel." He spits out my name so harshly it feels like a slap across the face.

"It's Pen," I say weakly, my voice catching.

But he doesn't correct himself. He just continues to stare at me, setting his mouth in an angry line. Betrayal hardens him into something terrible.

"I had to lie to Azael, Michael." I'm pleading with him, desperate to break through the wall he is building around himself. I once built a wall of my own, and he was able to reach me. Now I need to reach him. "You know that. He wants to see you dead. He would have killed you himself. You're not even supposed to be here! It's the middle of the night. What do you think he would assume if you were here? That I convinced you, at best, or that I…" I trail off. "I lied to protect you—to protect *us*."

"I don't think there is an 'us' anymore."

I step back, stung. "Don't say that."

"I don't think there ever really was an us to begin with." His voice is distant and low, a horrible mixture of despair and fury.

"Please," I shake my head again, reaching out to him, but he fights me off, pushing me back from him. "You're not an assignment to me," I repeat helplessly. "You're Michael—not an assignment. Do you hear me?"

He flinches but remains quiet, so I go on.

"I will give up everything for you, turn my back on Azael, on Lucifer, on Hell all together. I wanted to tell you tonight that I was going to run away, but I never got the chance. I wanted you…" My voice falters, catching in my throat. "I wanted you to join me. I thought we could start over. That I could be something better than what I am now. Because you showed me that I could be more than this. That my fate isn't sealed. *You* made that possible."

He crosses his arms, unmoved.

"Because you gave me hope," I say, my voice soft and trembling. "I didn't lie when I said—when I told you that I was falling for you. Michael, you have to believe me!"

"I can't tell who you're lying to anymore." His words slice through me like a knife, the pain nearly doubling me over. I know he can see the agony in my eyes, but this time he doesn't stop himself. Uncharacteristically, he continues to tear me apart, splitting me open until I am completely exposed. "If it's me, Azael, or yourself."

"I'm not lying to you, Michael. Please!" I fight back hot, angry tears and suffocate on my words.

"And to yourself?"

My voice is so small and quiet, I'm surprised he can hear it. "Please believe me."

He shakes his head. "I can't."

Please…

No.

The last thing I see is Michael's face, hurt and angry, a single tear sliding down his cheek. And then he's gone, up through the trees and into the sky, flying into the stars until he disappears in their light completely.

I collapse to my knees, the soft ground pressing into my jeans. It feels like there is a hot blade sticking through my stomach, and I am convinced this is what it feels like to be killed by the sword of an archangel. The heat travels outward, burning me up and stealing away my breath. I touch my bracelet and the clear beads are cold and lifeless, like me.

Michael is gone, and I don't think he's ever coming back.

Please.

His answer still echoes in my mind. *No.*

CHAPTER 29

DON'T WANT TO MOVE. I DON'T WANT TO THINK. I JUST want to forget everything. Not only from tonight, but from the first time I saw Michael. But I won't forget because I can't forget. Every moment of my life is as clear in my memory as it was the day it happened. This will be no different. Michael will remain seared in my memory.

This is so much worse than my nightmare because it is real. There is no waking up and there is no escaping it. I have to live through this pain and endure it because the curtain of death will not fall on me. It will never fall on me.

I knew his return would mean trouble, but I had no idea of the extent his presence would have on me. I thought he would destroy the order of things, the balance of the worlds. If I had known it would be me he would destroy…

I wouldn't have thought it possible to experience pain like this. It feels like there's a hot knife slowly slicing through my chest, and every time I breathe, that knife twists deeper. I've read poems and stories about people dying from broken hearts, but they've always seen overdramatic. It's a fallacy that hearts can be broken. Hearts can't break—they can only be crushed. But I don't even have a heart to be crushed. So what is this blazing pain that stretches its hot fingers out from my chest, engulfing me in invisible flames?

My chest aches, and I clutch desperately at my amulet, pulling the chain tight around my neck to distract myself. I tug on my hair, bite my cheek, do anything I can to hold back the hot tears that are threatening to escape.

Nothing helps.

I can't look at the stars. I don't want to see them shining just as bright as they were earlier tonight. Unchanged, unaffected, unaware. It's me that has changed, that has been affected, that is aware of what has happened in the last few minutes. But their sameness makes me angry.

How can they remain just as they were? Shouldn't they look different? When Michael was with me, the stars were beautiful. They should not be just as beautiful in his absence. It isn't right.

A poem comes flooding back to me, uninvited and unwelcome.

> *Nature's first green is gold,*
> *Her hardest hue to hold.*
> *Her early leaf's a flower;*
> *But only so an hour.*
> *The leaf subsides to leaf.*
> *So Eden sank to grief,*
> *So dawn goes down to day.*
> *Nothing gold can stay.*

The last line of Frost's poem echoes in my mind, mocking me. Michael's gone. His golden hair, crystal eyes, silver wings. Gold, blue, silver. *"Nothing gold can stay."*

I stumble out on the flat rock of the cliff and throw myself over the edge, spreading my wings and flying above the tops of the twisting trees that reach to the sky like they are trying to grab me and pull me back down to Earth. The colorful leaves streak below me, blurring into a muddied hue that makes me sick. I have to keep moving, but more importantly, I have to get away from here. I won't sit on the ground reliving his goodbye.

I'm not pathetic.

I'm strong.

I'm a demon and this weakness is unacceptable.

This is why you never let yourself feel anything. I remind myself. *Vulnerability is dangerous.*

It's worse at The Aria. I can't go anywhere in my room without a reminder of Michael. The shower reminds me of him. The bed smells like him—the pillow still creased where his head laid. Even the small scar on the nightstand from his knife sends a memory searing through my spine, the pain of which forcing me to my knees. I can't look out of the windows, back at the mountains, and I refuse to look back to the city, where he found me covered in blood, surrounded by five dead men.

Hanging alone in the small, mirrored closet is Michael's jacket. I forgot he left it here. I drift over to the closet without meaning to and reach out to touch the sleeve. It's soft and warm, as if he had just been wearing it.

The elbows are worn and the zipper looks broken. The dark brown lining has small blood stains, probably from when he set it over my shoulders the first night he found me. I stare at it for a few minutes, knowing that I should walk away and leave it here. But I can't. It's all that's left of him, and I refuse to leave it alone in this empty hotel room when I leave.

Slowly, I lift the heavy jacket off of the thin hanger and slide the closet doors closed. I fold the jacket between my hands and lift it to my face. The scent of Michael is so powerful I let out a sharp breath. I shove my arms through the sleeves and wrap the thick material around my middle. It's loose, a few sizes too big, but I don't mind. It's as close as I'll get to being held in his arms again.

Before the memories of the other night overwhelm me and leave me paralyzed, standing in the center of the room, I grab the last of my things, shove the leftovers of room service into my backpack, and hurry out of the room. I take one last look back at the unmade bed as I ease the door closed and leave, down the elevator, through the revolving glass doors, and out into the city streets that are just beginning to become busy with early morning commuters.

I don't know where I'll go, but I know I can't bear to stay here. I have to leave the city, leave behind the streets that are haunted by Michael. I pass the alley he kissed me in and the moment rushes back to me—us next to the dumpster, my back pushed against the bricks. I stop in my tracks.

Angry pedestrians run into me, shoving around me, and I stumble into the now bright alley, tripping over my feet and falling to my knees. Each small breath I take snags on my ribs like I am tearing apart. With effort, I grit my teeth, stand up, and run out of the alley and away from the city.

Keep walking, keep moving, keep going.

I can't stop, can't allow myself to relive the small moments we had together. His lips, his hands, his voice, his eyes... If I think about them too long, my feet slow and I freeze, paralyzed just by the memory of him.

When I stop to remember, I'm afraid I'll never move again. I imagine myself pausing to breathe, to remember, and turning into stone. I'd become a statue, like the marble weeping angels of cemeteries, cracked in sorrow. Maybe they lost someone too and paused just a moment too long to mourn, and now they're frozen in grief for all eternity.

I won't let that happen to me. I won't turn to stone.

Keep walking. Keep moving. Keep going.

The bracelet feels heavy on my wrist, a constant reminder that I'm alone. The farther I go, the heavier it feels, but not once does it feel warm. Michael is not near me, not anywhere close.

You're alone.

You're alone.

You're alone.

My hand feels empty and cold without Michael, my fingers twitching from the memory of his hand laced with mine, and I'm furious. I'm haunted by the thought of him. I hate feeling this loss. I hate the fact that I couldn't get through to him, and I hate the fact that he couldn't see that I was telling the truth.

I told him the truth, and he didn't believe me.

He had less faith in me than I thought he did if he was so easily convinced by the lies I fed to Azael. And I hate him for that.

But I don't hate him. I can't, really.

If I were him, would I have been able to believe me?

He woke me up, shook me out of the stupor of shadows I had been living in for so long, and showed me that there was something better waiting for me.

Even as scarred and broken as I was, he found something beautiful within my cracks. For him, I was willing to try. All I had to do was wake up. And I did.

But then he left me here, alone in this new, bright world alone. And now, I'm lost. He shouldn't get to do that—come into my life and then just disappear.

What's worse is that I can't even go back to what I was before he changed me, before he rekindled the fire that had been smothered to embers for so long. He woke me up and now I can't fall back asleep. What I've seen has affected me so greatly that I can't just go back to what used to be. All I can do is adapt to what I now have.

Adapt or die.

My eyes have adjusted to the light, and if I go back into the darkness, I'll be blind again, grasping around me for anyone's hand to guide me. Az will be there, I'm sure, and it would only be a matter of time before I am the demon he's always hoped I'd be. Only the faint glow behind my closed eyes will remind me that there was once any light to see at all.

I can't be blind again. I don't want to go back into the dark. So I have no choice but to stay in the light, to try to find my own way in this strange, new world. I don't owe it to him—I owe it to myself.

I'll find Michael and when I do, I won't just tell him that I'm not lying to him. I won't tell him what he means to me because I'm still trying to figure it out myself. But I can show him I'm better than who I was. I can prove that I don't belong in Hell.

My dagger bumps against my calf, pressing a reminder against my skin. *Not with words alone.*

I'll search the corners of the Earth for him, look as far as I can. Michael kept telling me that I was good even when I didn't want to listen, when I didn't want to hear it. He never stopped telling me I could be something more than darkness, not until I believed him. Then he didn't need to tell me. He never gave up hope that I would wake up and see that. I've lost his faith, but I'll get it back.

I'll tell him the truth until he believes me, show him I am who he once thought I was. I am not my brother and I don't want to go back into the dark. *I will be better.*

For him, at least, I can try again.

CHAPTER 30

DON'T KNOW WHERE TO START LOOKING FOR MICHAEL. I try to call out to him, screaming his name in my mind over and over like a ghostly wail. At night, I look up at the stars and wonder if anyone's looking back down at me. I whisper his name like a prayer, a promise. It's probably pointless. I'm not even sure he's listening.

However we were talking before had to be an anomaly. I can't communicate with anyone telepathically except for Azael. He is my twin, he is my mirror, and our thoughts have always been connected by our blood. But Michael is none of those things, and if he was able to hear me before, it was something he did, not me. And now he may not want to hear me.

But I call him anyway.

Michael, I don't know if you can hear me. I'm sorry.

Michael, I'm not going to give up. I'll find you and show you I'm not lying. You've changed me.

Michael, you woke me up. You can't just leave me alone in this. I need you.

Michael, you can't get rid of me this easily. I won't give up on you.

IGNITE

Michael. Please.
Michael...

My hope of finding him wanes away with each passing day. I'm whittled thinner and thinner with doubt and I wonder how much more I can search. The longer I am without Michael, the tighter I cling to Azael.

I briefly considered destroying my pendant, disappearing from Hell completely, but I couldn't bring myself to do it. I'm not ready to be totally alone. So I don't make any decisions now, not until I know something more from Michael. Not until I'm sure he's not coming back...

Azael or Michael. I know I can't have both. Sooner or later, I'm going to have to make a decision, but I can't just yet. When I think of choosing one over the other I start to spiral into panic.

Could I give up my brother? For Michael, I believe I could. But without him, I couldn't leave Az. He checks in with me frequently, asking if I've seen him. He's antsy, agitated, and needs an answer now.

Pen, has angel boy reared his golden head yet?

No, Az, I sigh.

Well he better hurry up. We can't wait much longer.

I lie to him, reassuring him that everything will go smoothly. *I'm sure he'll be back soon. He probably just got delayed in Heaven for something. Maybe Ariel and Sablo are giving him another horrid history lesson. You know how much they like to talk.*

He scoffs. *History is history for a reason. Let's go on to bigger and better things.*

Azael is growing inpatient, and if Michael doesn't return soon, I'll have to tell him the truth. There is only so long that I can stall him with stories and lies. If it's too much longer, Azael will come up from Hell to finish the job himself. One way or another, he'll find out the truth.

After a few days of silence from Michael, I decide to return to the cave. It's his secret place, the only place he admitted he feels safe and not under the constant supervision of Heaven. If he's anywhere on Earth, he'll be there.

Flying over the thick, green forests of the Pacific Northwest, I feel the first spark of rekindled hope dancing under my skin.

Of course he'll be there! I tell myself. *He has to be there.* I can't believe I hadn't thought to look there earlier.

The tops of the dark pine and fir trees spin past under my feet, and I keep my eyes open for something familiar. I pass over a small patch of large yellow leaves scattered across the ground. Sitting on the leaves is a cropping of white trunks with bare, spindly branches. Aspens, the same ones Michael and I climbed. But now they're bare, all of their leaves having dropped to the coppery pine floor of the forest.

Then I fly over the rough waters of a cold stream, bridged by a mossy fallen tree. I still see a subtle disturbance in the mud of the shore where Michael fell.

I'm close.

I feel a thrill of excitement when a small, glassy pond comes into view. Carefully, I lower myself onto the pebbled bank. It's much colder now than the last time Michael and I were here and the surface of the pond is frozen, covered by a thin sheet of crystallized ice.

The waterfall that once poured into the pond, churning the tepid water, is gone, probably frozen in the shallow riverbed at the top of the cliff. The paper-thin frost is beautiful and delicate, and when I step out on the edge of the pond, I hear it crack under my weight. I spread my wings, fluttering them so I lift just off of my feet as I walk across the pond, following a narrow fissure in the ice until I am below the cave.

IGNITE

The opening of the cave is entirely exposed without the waterfall falling in front of it like a curtain, and its visibility makes me uneasy. Craning my head back, I try to look into the cave from the lake, but I can't see anything inside.

I take a deep breath and call out. "Michael?"

When I spring off the surface of the frozen pond, I break a hole through the ice to the water below. I lift into the air and land noiselessly on the edge of the cave, the light filtering around me in a slanted shadow. The back of the cave is dark but I can see the empty collection of mason jars scattered across the small room. I walk farther back, clinging to a feverish hope that he'll be here hidden around the corner.

Maybe he's asleep.

But when I come to the mouth of the small circular room, that hope disappears.

It's empty. He's not here.

I spin my bracelet around my wrist and it's cold. I didn't notice that it wasn't warm—how did I not notice? I was so sure he'd be here, but I was wrong.

In a surge of frustration, I rip the bracelet off of my wrist, snapping the thin elastic and sending tiny, clear beads bouncing across the cave. I kick out at the mason jars, shattering the thick glass of the containers. The glass rains down around the cave, covering the floor in dangerous, sparkling shards.

He's gone.

With a deep sigh, the anger slips away into despair and I sink onto the hard, carved bench that hugs the perimeter of the room.

He's really gone.

Please, Michael, if you can hear me—just... Just give me a sign. Give me something to hope for. Anything.

I wait in silence, desperately listening for a whisper from Michael. Any hint that he can hear me.

Please. Answer me, please. Please please please, I chant in my head.

Nothing.

The silence in my head seems to grow until it devours me. The quiet sneers at me, mocks me with its emptiness, and I have never felt so deflated in my life. My search for him was pointless. He's not coming back. He doesn't want to come back, and he doesn't want anything to do with me.

Without Michael, I am without hope.

I grab the jagged rock of my necklace and squeeze it in my fist, letting the sharp edges of the stone slice into my palm. *Azael.*

Pen, finally. Have you heard from Michael? Is he ours or is he dead?

I hesitate, looking once more around the cave. *He's gone.*

Fantastic. It looks like Lilith will need to pay up on our bet. Make sure to bring back his heart or head. The choice is yours. But if you do bring back his head, please poke out those horrid blue eyes of his. I don't need them following me around the room like a creepy painting, always watching.

No, Azael. He's not... He's just... He's gone.

There's a sudden angry silence from Azael, and I can feel his fury like an icy burn. *Gone?* he hisses, and I can practically see the letters sliding out from between his teeth.

He's not coming back. My throat feels constricted, like I am being strangled. *Ever.*

And how do you know this?

I just... Trust me. I know. He's gone. As I repeat it, it starts to sink, settling over my skin like a burn. Slowly, I feel the shadows reaching out towards me again, stealing away the last of the light I clung to with all of my strength. I remember what Michael told me, that letting go of what is good is as easy as falling asleep. And I'm so tired.

So he's still alive then.

As far as I know, yes.

Well, that complicates things a bit. He chuckles darkly. *But I'm sure we can exterminate him when the time comes.*

I flinch. *Sure.*

IGNITE

You didn't... His voice fades away. *You sound different.*

I clear my throat unnecessarily. *Different how?*

Upset.

I failed, I answer in explanation.

More than that. He pauses, and while I know he's in Hell, I feel like he's watching me, his eyes probing and skeptical. *It doesn't matter now, I suppose.*

No. It doesn't matter now, I repeat.

I'll see you tonight then. Hell has missed you dearly, sister. It's time you come back and claim your rightful position by my side.

Goodbye Az.

Pen, I'll see you soon.

I let my face fall into my hands as our connection snaps.

It feels like a betrayal to return to Hell, but I have nowhere else to go. I have no one to turn to except for Azael. He is the only one who can fill the hole that Michael has left in my chest. He'll hold me together. He won't know why he has to, but he'll do it anyway. He'll be there for me.

With Azael, I might be able to ignore my memories. I'll be distracted by the war and whatever follows.

I can't afford a conscience when I return to Hell, and somehow I'll have to switch off the small piece of humanity Michael has kindled within me. When I imagine what I'll do for Hell in the upcoming months, I feel queasy. It gets even worse when I think about losing what little good that is left in me.

But this feeling won't last long. After I lose myself completely, I won't hate myself for what I'm doing. It won't bother me because I won't care. I'll feel nothing, be numb to everything. I would do anything to be numb now.

Michael was wrong when he said I am strong. I am not strong. Not strong enough for Michael or Azael and not strong enough to do this on my own.

I cross my arms over my knees and lay my head down, looking out of the mouth of the cave. The misty light of the day is seeping into the graying purple of dusk. I have to wait most of the night until I return to Hell, and I am resigned to let myself use this last moment to mourn. I will stay in this cave, hidden from the stars, as the night deepens into the early hours of the morning. And if my stillness cases me in the cement of a statue, so be it.

After tonight I will have move on, or pretend to, at least, and become the demon my brother believes me to be. I must fulfill my duty as a dark angel. There will be no misguided notions that I am anything but evil, soulless, heartless.

It's foolish to believe I'm something I'm not, and the one person who had faith in me is gone. Maybe Azael was right all along. Perhaps it really is better to reign in Hell than serve in Heaven.

I close my eyes and picture Michael's face. His angular jaw, his wide shoulders, his bright eyes, his innocent smile. I'll never see his face again. At least, I hope I won't, because if I do I know that I'll have to kill him now. I've pledged myself back to Az, back to Hell. I've revealed my location, and what I do from here on out will be seen by anyone in Hell who cares to look. With my failure comes close scrutiny.

If I see Michael again, he will have to die. *By your own hands*, screams a repulsed voice in my head. *You will destroy him.*

Deep within me, I hope he hides during the fighting, that he was telling me the truth that day in the trees when he said he wouldn't fight for either side. I wish for him to stay out of the war so hard that it turns into a kind of prayer. My last prayer.

Stay safe.

The sound of snapping branches outside of the cave breaks me from my thoughts. I open my eyes and sit up straight, looking out of the cave towards the trees that spring up around the pond. Another loud crack reverberates into the cave and I see a body fall out of the sky and land solidly on the hard ground, bringing a few large branches down with it.

Whoever it is—a man, I notice—must be dead. I don't know where the person fell from, but after hitting the ground with such force, I'd be surprised if his neck hasn't snapped or his head cracked open like an egg.

I run to the front of the cave and look out over to the motionless figure.

Lying on the rocky shore of the pond is a lean boy, golden hair pushed in front of his eyes. Two large silver wings are opened below him, spreading wide across the Earth. One of the wings reaches into the shadows of the woods while the other rests on the frozen surface of the pond. A dark red stain spreads slowly over the abdomen of the figure and mats the shiny feathers of the wings, darkening them.

"Michael!"

I'm by his side so quickly my head spins. I kneel down next to him and see he has a bloodied sword gripped limply in a scarred hand. It's the archangel sword, and I gasp loudly, my breath as shaky as my hands that flutter over him nervously, unsure of what to do. I'm not entirely sure this isn't some horrible nightmare again.

Gold hair, silver wings, and red, red blood. The blue of his eyes is hidden beneath his eyelids and I want so desperately for him to open them and see me, maybe smile and tell me he's fine. But he's not fine. I can tell by how much blood there is.

Please be a nightmare.

Carefully, I peel up the fabric of his shirt, sliding it up to his chest and exposing a deep gash in his ribs. The wound is positioned just above his heart. I press my head down on his chest, his warm blood slicking my cheek, and I listen anxiously for a heartbeat, holding my breath.

Silent.

He's gold, silver, and red. A wishing well filled with blood.

I wait, squeezing my eyes shut against this waking nightmare.

"I would wish for you," I say gently. "If I had a wish, it would be for you."

His chest is silent and still for so long that I'm convinced he's dead.

And then, miraculously, I hear one solid beat.

Thump.

Whoever attacked him missed his heart. I'm flooded with relief so overwhelming I struggle for breath. His heart beats again.

Thump.

Thump. Thump.

Thump. Thump. Thump.

It beats once, then twice, and then three times, slowly picking up speed again until it beats normally, without hesitation, without a stutter. I feel his heartbeat echoed in my own chest, and I'm so happy I could cry.

"Michael." I rest my cool hands on his face, leaning down to kiss his lips.

His eyes open slowly, searching through a fog of confusion, and he winces in pain. "Pen?"

I sit back and hold my hand on the gash in his side, pressing his shirt to him to stop the blood from spilling over his tan skin, painting him crimson. "What the Hell happened to you?"

"Is this real?"

"As far as I can tell, yes," I sharply suck air in through my teeth as I feel his hot blood start to slick my hands, rolling between my fingers before sliding down his side faster. I always seem to be covered in someone's blood. "Are you going to tell me what the Hell happened?"

His breath is shallow and labored. "They tried to kill me," he wheezes slowly.

"Who?" I ask angrily, turning away from the wound to look at his face.

His eyes start to lose focus and I press my free hand to his forehead, the cold of my palm acting like an icepack on his hot skin.

"Who attacked you, Michael?"

He takes another shaky breath before he can answer. "The angels."

CHAPTER 31

RAGE BOILS IN ME, HOT AND UNBRIDLED. "*Heaven did this to you?*" I spit.

He nods and closes his eyes, his eyebrows furrowed in agony. All of his muscles are coiled tight and beads of sweat slip down his chest, mixing in with the blood.

"Why?" I demand.

He doesn't answer. His forehead becomes clammy and I feel him go limp, losing consciousness in my arms. The color slips from his skin and he turns white under me, his skin becoming even paler than my own. I need to stop the bleeding long enough for him to heal himself or he could still die. I position myself on top of him, straddling his ribs with my legs. I hover above him, not letting any of my weight rest on his abdomen, and squeeze my legs together to keep the fabric pressed to the wound.

Without having to apply pressure to his ribs with my hand, I am able to rest both of my hands on his face and cool him down. I run my cold fingers over his brow, down his cheek, and across his lips. After a moment, he opens his eyes again, looking confused and dizzy, and tries to talk.

"Shh—shut up for a second," I tell him. "Just breathe. You passed out."

He watches me quietly, shaking under me as his face twists again in pain.

"It's okay. You're going to be fine," I reassure him. "You're just losing a lot of blood. You have to heal yourself."

I take one of his hands in mine and guide it down to his ribs, letting it rest over the balled fabric. I keep my hand against his, making sure he is pressing down hard enough to stop the worst of the bleeding. But his hand doesn't become warmer like it usually does when he heals. It remains cool, clammy, and very still. I look back up at his face and see he is frowning.

"I can't."

"What do you mean, you can't? Of course you can." I look at him, confused. "Just concentrate."

"I mean that—" He shudders again. "I won't."

My eyebrows draw together. "Why the Hell not?"

"I left you," he says pitifully. "I didn't trust you. What Heaven did to me… I—" He breaks off with a ragged breath. "I deserve this."

"Shut up and heal yourself, you idiot!" I snap, pressing his palm to his side harder.

His hand still doesn't move.

Sitting here on the bank of the pond with a dying Michael is too familiar. We've been here before, but he wasn't red. He was gray and his lungs were filled with water. I didn't let him die then, and I'm not going to let him die now.

I turn on him angrily. "Dammit, Michael! Heal yourself!"

He watches me in silence. The blood flows out of him so quickly it slips through both of our fingers and drenches his shirt. It continues to spill across his wings, washing down his feathers and onto the ice. A fissure in the ice fills with his blood and it looks like a frozen vein.

This is what Hell is, I think. Torment—pain I'm helpless to stop—follows me like a shadow, ensuring I'll never be entirely alone.

He still won't move, refusing to heal himself.

I roll my eyes. "For the love of—we can talk about us later, but if you die, then that's it. You are leaving me again." I shake my head, my voice strained. "Don't you dare die here in my arms. You can't leave me like this. I will never forgive you."

For a moment he looks like he is going to blackout again, and I slap him across his cheek, keeping him lucid.

"Do you hear me? I will *never* forgive you!"

Michael grits his teeth and my palm becomes warm. I look down and see that his hand is glowing a soft gold under mine. When he pulls his hand away from his chest, the gash is gone and his skin is unmarked. The blood stops spilling and the color begins to return to his face. It's like he was never hurt.

I let out a relieved sigh, unhitch my leg from him, and sit back on my heels. He sits up stiffly and tucks his wings behind him, hiding the red and silver feathers.

"What the Hell happened to you?" I know I've asked him already, but I don't understand. Why would Heaven try to execute Michael?

"Heaven happened," he says quietly. "They heard rumors that I had a connection with Lucifer. They told me that a small piece of me was left in Hell when I was resurrected. It was a careless mistake they hadn't even realized they made. But this mistake tied our lives together. If I died, Lucifer died."

I shake my head. "No, that was severed a while ago."

"Tell them that." He rolls his shoulders and his face contorts in pain.

The cuts that slice his cheek and curl around his neck slowly fade away, his skin glowing gold as he continues to heal what is broken. I go to reach out and touch him but pull my hand back to me. I won't touch him unless he wants me to.

"So they tried to kill you, to kill Lucifer?"

"That, and they think I'm a traitor. They saw me with you." His voice is bitter. "They thought that my time in Hell had changed something in me. That maybe because I left a piece of myself in Hell, a piece of Hell was in me. That's why they didn't trust me, why I made them nervous. They assumed that you…"

"Were trying to take you back to Hell with me," I finish for him and shrug. "In theory, they weren't too far off. That was what I was supposed to do."

He looks at me for a long while before speaking again. "But you didn't."

"I didn't," I repeat.

"Why?" he asks.

"Because I don't believe in Hell anymore. I told you, you changed something in me." I look away from him, embarrassed.

"I didn't believe you," he says sadly. "And neither did they."

I glance back at him and wait for him to go on.

"They assumed the worst of you and me, and I was sentenced to death." His eyes grow distant. "Ariel and Sablo found me in my room and led me to this great, marbled hall. There were thick, carved columns lining an aisle that ended at an empty golden throne."

I nod. God's throne room. I'm unfortunately very familiar with the space.

"The room around the aisle was crowded with angels, like everyone came to watch me die. Some were even smiling…" He shakes his head, like he's trying to erase the image from his mind. "There were cheers as I was forced to my knees in front of the throne and read my sentence by the executioner. But I had already known. I knew I was going to die by the way the others were watching me."

I bite my tongue. I remember Heaven's executions. They were grand affairs, celebrated with banquets before and dancing afterward. Wine as red as the spilled blood flowed from fountains as we drank to the heavy hand of Heaven's justice being served.

I hated the executions, would bury my head in Azael's shoulder when the sword would come down on its victim. But the others didn't. Azael didn't. They all watched with greedy, excited eyes, breath held only to be exhaled with the falling of the sword.

When Heaven sentenced death, no one questioned it. Heaven can do no wrong, right? If it was Heaven's will, then every death was just.

I remember what Michael told me that first day we met. *No deliberate deaths are just.* I wonder if he still believes that after everything he's now seen.

Michael continues. "I didn't have my sword. One of the angels did—the executioner. All I had was my knife."

"The one with the black handle," I prompt.

"Yes. They didn't see it hidden under my belt. The angel—I didn't see his face—had a white hood drawn low. When Ariel and Sablo stepped back, he struck out at me with my sword. I tried to block the hit like you taught me to, but my blade was too short. He missed my heart, but not by much. He was holding my sword low, so I stumbled to my feet and I rushed towards him. He never saw it coming and I was able to grab the handle away from him. And then I ran. Or fell, rather."

"What did I tell you about never charging someone holding a sword?" I ask angrily.

He chuckles once, wincing slightly at whatever pain still remains. "Of course that is the one part you would chose to focus on." A small, guilty smile spreads across his face.

I soften. "They tried to kill you with your own sword? An archangel sword?"

"Yes."

"And they think *Hell's* filled with vindictive bastards."

He doesn't say anything.

"And that's when you…" I wave my hands up at the trees, motioning to the broken limbs. "You know."

He nods.

"A fallen angel, in every sense of the phrase," I say under my breath.

We both lull into silence. I shift uncomfortably, trying to look anywhere but his face. My pendant hangs heavily around my throat, the sharp stone carefully balanced over my collarbone. Every small movement I make sends it swinging, thumping against my chest. It's my cold, inanimate heart, reminding me of where my loyalties now lie. Where they have to lie now that I have made my choice. *Azael. Azael. Az—*

In a quick motion, he reaches out and takes my hand in his, tearing my mind away from Azael, away from Hell. I sit perfectly still, holding my breath.

"Pen." His voice is warm and sweet.

I can't fight it anymore, and my eyes rise to meet his.

"What I did and what I said are unforgivable." He watches me with large, glossy eyes that I could drown in. That I *am* drowning in. "There is nothing I can say to make it up to you."

I snag my teeth over my lip and stay silent. I don't trust myself to speak.

"I heard you," he continues. "Looking for me. It took all I had not to answer you. Your voice was all around me, and what you were saying—I realized you hadn't lied to me."

He heard me.

"How could I have been so stupid to not see the truth that was right in front of me?"

My voice is so small that I can't tell if he can hear me. "I'm a very good liar. Especially when lives depend on it."

He pauses. "I wanted to call back to you, but it was too late. Ariel and Sablo—angels I thought were meant to protect me—they came to my room and beat me when I returned. They kept me unconscious. I don't know if they were told to do so or if they thought it would be an easier way to keep me… restrained."

I look closer at his face, at his shoulders, and see the shadow of deep bruises. Even after healing himself, the blood is still pooled under his skin in blues, greens, and purples. How many times had they beaten him? How many days was he unconscious?

"For so long, everything was dark. I couldn't hear your voice anymore, and I thought I was dead. I would have preferred to have been dead. But I wasn't. They were still deciding my fate, I guess. No need to rush the decision." He stops and looks at me, his eyes a shade of blue I never would have thought possible. "There were brief episodes when I would regain consciousness, but it was never for very long. I would only catch a snippet of a conversation before the darkness swallowed me again."

"Michael…" I lower my eyes to my lap. I can't bear to imagine him broken and beaten, crumpled on the hard floor of his room. Angels show about as much mercy as demons do. An inflated sense of righteousness is just as dangerous as evil.

"The first time I was conscious enough to stand, they marched me to my death. But even when they were going to execute me, even when I thought I had lost everything, when I wanted to die… I remembered your poetry. I thought of *you*. I suppose I was meant to see my life flash before my eyes, but I had no life to remember. I only had you. You were my life, and the only thing I saw was your face."

He saw me.

"I just wanted to hear your voice one more time, and I remembered how you told me to fight for myself. So I did. I didn't want to die before I had a chance to apologize to you." He leans towards me, his faces inches from mine. "I once asked you to fight for yourself, to wake up and see what I saw in you. And then I gave up on you. But even then, you never gave up on me. I was weak and foolish. *You* were the strong one. You always were."

I chew on the inside of my cheek.

"I don't know how I could have been so blind. It's you, Pen." He reaches out and traps my hands in his. "My heart beats for you. How has it taken me this long to see that?"

"Michael," I murmur, lowering my eyes. I drop his hands and push away from him, standing up.

"Wait!" Michael scrambles to his feet unsteadily. He grabs my hand and pushes it against his chest, over his heart, right where he was bleeding from moments ago. The dried blood stains his chest a strange orange. "Do you feel that?"

His heart beats, strong and steady. I look up at him and nod. "Of course."

"That is not just my heart, not just my soul. It's yours." He pauses. "'Love and harmony combine / And round our souls entwine,'" he quotes. It's William Blake. He found his poetry. "'While thy branches mix with mine / And our roots together join…'"

I pull my hand away from him, leaving a darker red handprint over his heart from my still wet hand, and cross my arms over my chest. "It's not fair to quote poetry at me."

He smiles sadly. "I can't always find the words myself. Poetry has put what I want to say to you in strings of words that make sense. You make it difficult for me to think clearly."

I look away from him, over the icy lake. "I'm not staying here," I say suddenly. My amulet feels bulky under the collar of my shirt.

He's silent for a moment, shifting on his feet. "Where are we going?"

"Where am *I* going," I correct.

He freezes, his gaze meeting mine, searching my eyes and forcing me to look away. "Where are you going?" he asks quietly.

I said my goodbyes to Azael that night under the stars before my world with Michael had crumbled beneath me. But after Michael had left, I clung to the voice of my brother. Even though he was far away, his words, however harsh and crude, kept me sane in my despair. I caught onto him, like the fingers of someone sliding down a sheer mountain side finding purchase on a narrow ledge. He saved me in his own way, just by being himself. He was simply *there*. I promised him I'd see him soon, and I can't take that promise away from him. Not without one final goodbye.

"Back to Hell." I glance at him quickly.

His face falls. "I don't expect you to forgive me," he says softly.

My chest aches, and I tighten my arms around myself.

"I have little hope that I'll ever see you again." His voice is sad and wistful. "But I won't try to stop you, as long as you are doing this because you want to. Not because you have no other choice. Not because of what I did…"

I don't say anything.

"I will let you go, Pen. And I won't follow you. Just promise me one thing."

I look back up at him.

"Stay safe."

It's the same prayer I said for him. My resolve nearly breaks, and I let out a muffled sound like a whimper.

"You need to run," I tell him flatly.

He quirks his head to the side. "I don't understand."

"Run!" I yell at him, backing away and pressing myself to the rough bark of a tree.

He steps forward, a look of concern spreading across his face. "Pen, are you all right?"

"You need to get away from here, away from me!"

My arms are snaked around myself, squeezing so tight I can't breathe. I feel my pendant pulse once and I'm shaking.

Pen, what's wrong? Is that Michael? Azael's voice invades my thoughts. I hear him laugh and it sounds like nails on a chalkboard. *Just in time. Kill him.*

I take the necklace off, throwing it across the shore, breaking our connection. The stone scrapes across the ice and slides to a stop.

Azael knows. He knows Michael is back.

"Please," I scream, my voice high and tight. "Please, run!"

IGNITE

He can still escape. I'll let him run, hurt myself, and tell Azael he put up a fight. He has the archangel sword, and Azael would have to understand. I'll accept whatever consequences his freedom means, even if it's endless torture. It'll be worth it, because killing him would be more painful than anything Hell could do to me. There's still a chance…

Michael freezes, standing perfectly still in front of me next to the bloody sword. In his eyes, I see the light of understanding. "You have to kill me."

Shakily, I take in a gulp of air and nod, not breaking our stare. His eyes hold me captive and I convulse again. *Go!*

He shakes his head. The sun has completely set, and the lake is only lit by the large, low hanging moon. He walks towards me cautiously, his arms stretched out in surrender.

"I won't run."

"Yes you will. You have to." *Please run. Please go.*

"No. I left you once before and it was the biggest mistake I have ever made. I won't do it again, no matter the cost."

"The cost is your life!"

"So be it." He looks at me with a small smile. "If I am going to die, I want your face to be the last thing I see. The real you, not just a memory of you. Even if you are the reason I die, I want you to be with me."

Run—please go!

"I won't live another moment without you."

I shake my head weakly, but he only smiles at me and nods. His eyes shine with unshed tears and his golden hair seems to glow in the moonlight.

"Pen, I understand."

But I don't.

"I am asking you to kill me," he whispers. "It is the only way I can guarantee you'll be safe. I'll give you my life to protect yours."

I'm staring into his bright face. I feel my dagger pressed against my leg, its metal blade cold on my skin. I can't kill him. I won't kill him. I'm going to be sick…

"There's honor in sacrifice."

I want to scream. I told him his life was too big of a burden for me to carry. I need to tell him this, but I can't find my voice. My protests are strangled in my throat. *No.*

"Before you kill me, though, I have one last selfish request."

He looks at me meaningfully and I stare back at him.

"A kiss."

He closes the distance between us in two large strides. Only the smoke of our breath stands between us as he brushes a piece of hair away from my face, curling it behind my ear, his fingers delicate and hesitant. I look up into his eyes and feel a horrible twisting in my stomach.

Slowly, he lowers his mouth to mine, his soft lips hot against my own. A warmth envelops me, swelling up like water, and I close my eyes. I let the feeling pull me under, surrendering to the overwhelming sensation. He whispers his apologies on my lips and places his hand at the base of my neck, bringing us closer together. This kiss is desperate; this kiss is sacred. A single tear falls down his cheek, the saltiness slipping across my lips.

This kiss is a goodbye.

Underneath the sadness, I feel something else. It's something so strong that it crushes my chest and weakens my knees. With effort, he steps back and lets go of me. *Too soon, it's all too soon.*

"Thank you." He turns around and walks over to his sword. He picks it up carefully and turns it over in his hand. With the ghost of a smile on his lips, he extends the handle towards me carefully. "I'm ready now," he says.

Numbly, I grab the sword from him. I'm shaking as I stare down at the sharp tip and the obscured inscription in confusion. I don't understand why his sword is in my hand; I don't understand anything. His blood isn't even dry on the blade yet and he wants me to spill more.

He waits, his arms by his sides and his eyes locked on mine.

I shake my head insistently as panic floods my veins. "No. I can't."

"It's okay," he says as he lowers his chin and stands up straighter. "I'm ready to die. I've already done it once before."

Please run. GO!

"I'm ready," he says again.

"I'm not going to kill you!"

He waits, but I don't. I throw his sword down and it skitters across the ice, coming to a stop next to my pendent. I run towards him and throw my arms around his neck, burying my head against his chest, his heart beating furiously next to my cheek. He catches me in his embrace, unsure and surprised, and circles his own strong arms around my waist. A small word dances on the tip of my tongue.

Love.

As if he heard the word reverberate in my head, he squeezes me to him, his large hands pressing against my back, bringing me closer to him. He leans back and I look up to him. In his eyes shines a fire so bright, so fierce I can feel its heat. It's hope, wild and unstoppable, and he stares at me unbelievingly.

"Pen?" His voice is full of wonder, timid and hesitant.

I can't kill him because I could never live without him. Not now, not ever again. If he were to die, I would die with him. It's like our lives have become inextricably woven, tangled together like strands of DNA. There is no separating us without destroying us, no pulling us apart because we are both unwilling to let go.

"Michael," I whisper back.

I'm sure he can see my desperate need to keep him alive, to keep us together, reflected in my eyes and written all over my face. I'm sure he can hear it in the slight hitch in my breath at his touch. *I can't be without you.* I stand on my toes as he tips his chin down and our lips collide, dancing together dizzyingly. The world seems to be spinning faster around us and I cling to him tighter, as if I'm trying to press us into one being. *I never want to let go.*

His voice is golden and musical in my head, so powerful I feel my knees buckle. *I love you.*

I gasp against him, but don't let go.

He repeats it over and over again. *I love you, Pen. I love you.*

I shiver against him and he opens his mouth to mine. Suddenly, I feel like we are back under the stars again, breathing each other in, starving for the other's air.

It's like the world that shattered after our perfect kiss is being pieced back together, shard by shard, until it is whole again. Until *we* are whole again. The hammer of his heart beats under me, echoing in the empty cavern of my chest. He shares his heart with me just as I share my breath.

I love you, too, I sigh.

Beneath my lips, I feel him smile. He pushes his hands in my hair and kisses me deeper, spreading fire through my veins, searing into my nerves, and melting my bones.

"Thank you," Michael breathes through the kiss.

I pull away from his gentle lips agonizingly and look into his eyes, which impossibly appear warmer and brighter. "For what?" I ask softly.

"For loving me back," he whispers as he pulls me into another deep kiss, his hands resting on my face like a wordless prayer.

CHAPTER 32

"WE CAN'T STAY HERE," I SAY REGRETFULLY, LOOKING BACK over the icy pond to the cave. "Azael knows where we are. Even if the cave is enchanted, he saw... He'll be here soon."

"We'll run." His voice is sure and filled with conviction. "Fugitives from Heaven and Hell. Probably going to cause a bit of trouble down the road."

"Fugitives," I repeat slowly.

Michael takes my hand in his and our bloodied fingers knot together, grotesquely beautiful.

"You didn't try to convince me," he says suddenly.

I look up at him. "Convince you?"

"I am no longer welcome in Heaven. I have nowhere to go, nothing to turn to. The only person I know outside of Heaven is you."

"A demon," I nod understandingly.

"But you didn't try to convince me to fight with Hell."

"Of course not. Just as you know me, I know you. It would have been pointless."

He's silent, listening.

"I don't belong to Hell anymore," I breathe. "The only reason I was going back was because you were gone. And if the only good thing in my life disappeared, I wouldn't have been able to give up my brother. I'm not that strong. He's all I have."

"You're all I have," he whispers, pulling me into him and cradling his arms low on my back.

"Now you're all I have left, too," I say, resting my cheek on his chest. "And I wouldn't trade it for all of the power in Hell."

"But what if you had asked and I agreed to fight with Hell?"

I pull back from him, surprised. Arching an eyebrow, I ask, "You might have said yes?"

"If you had asked me, I might have."

"For me?" My voice is incredulous.

"For you, I would do anything." He brings his hand up to my face again, brushing the pad of his thumb over my cheek. "For you, I would do everything."

I shake my head and grab his wrist, stilling his hand. "Don't. I don't want you to change who you are because of your circumstances. That is not the Michael I've…" *Fallen for.* "I wouldn't want you to give up on all that is good just because Heaven's given up on you. I almost did, and I would have lost myself completely. Giving in like that is like surrendering, letting others tell you who you are and what you stand for." I bring his hand down between us and lace my cold fingers with his again, tying us together. "What's the point of living a life someone else has designed for you? Is that really living at all?"

"But you didn't ask," he says, his eyes bright and smiling.

I twist the corner of my mouth up. "No," I laugh. "I didn't ask."

"So now what?"

I shrug. "Like you said. We run."

"As long as you're next to me, I will run to the ends of the Earth."

I roll my eyes. "Well that's about as far as we'll be able to go, seeing as neither side beyond these ends wants us. Can't go up, can't go down."

A soft vibrating noise sounds from the ice, and I look over and see my pendant glowing. I let go of Michael and tiptoe over the ice, scooping up the cold, black chain of my necklace. Michael follows, picking up his sword and holstering it in his belt. He whispers something, and the blade shimmers once before disappearing completely.

I put the pendent on again, pulling my hair through the chain. The second the stone lands on my collarbone, Azael's voice comes through, furiously screaming, his words as lethal as poison.

PEN! I'M COMING. HOLD THE LITTLE BASTARD DOWN. SAVE ME THE HONOR OF DECAPITATION.

My hands fly up to my head, holding my temples together so my skull doesn't split apart. His voice is sharp and insistent, giving me a sudden migraine that feels like a blinding sunrise in my mind. I can't escape it.

AZAEL! I shout back, trying to stop him. *AZAEL, LISTEN!*

His voice lowers several decibels, but he still is detailing the graphic ways he plans to kill Michael.

Goodbye, Azael.

He stops, his words clipping off mid-sentence. *Goodbye?*

Michael watches me, and I know he can hear what I'm saying, what Azael's saying. His eyes are slightly unfocused, concentrating like our conversation is slightly out of earshot. But he looks sad for me and I know he hears.

I'm sorry, Az. I grip the stone in my hand. *I'm so sorry. I cannot kill him.*

There is no answer.

I love him, and I will *not kill him.*

I feel my necklace become warm, the pendant heating up until it burns my hands. I let go suddenly, pressing my hands together to cool the burn. Michael steps forward and wraps his hands around mine, healing the welt.

"It's okay," he whispers to me encouragingly. "You are not alone in this."

I bite my lip and continue. *I never wanted to hurt you, Azael. And I'm so sorry.*

You think you love him? His voices is low and smooth, sounding like a snake slithering through tall grass.

I do love him.

Well how cute is that? And it explains so much.

I'm quiet.

You don't know what love is, Pen. You are a demon! There is no good in you, no hope for you.

His words knock the wind out of me, and I take a minute before answering. I look up at Michael. *There is always hope.*

Azael laughs condescendingly. *Did he teach you that? Oh, poor naïve sister. I thought you were better than this.*

Apparently I'm not. I squeeze Michael's hands and close my eyes. *If I ever meant anything to you at all, Az, please—let me go. Let us go.*

He doesn't even hesitate. *You think you can betray me and expect me to just 'let you go.'* His laughter is bitter and he chokes on it, his voice hitching at the end with... grief? No Azael has never felt a moment of sadness in his life. *That's just not in my nature. You think you are sorry now, but wait until I destroy everything you love. I'll kill Michael in front of you and make you watch. And then, when you can't take it anymore, I will kill you. Your happiness will burn you in the end. I'll show you what regret truly means.*

Az...

Besides, Pen. You still owe me that fight.

The hair at the back of my neck stands up, and I feel his threat through my bones. I remember him teasing me about this after I attacked him in the soul's memory that one fateful day. It seems like forever ago, but of course he remembers.

IGNITE

You can run, sister, but you can't hide. I'll see you soon.

That was the same thing he said to me earlier, when I told him I was coming back to Hell. *I'll see you soon.* But this time, he didn't sound distracted by war preparations. He wasn't excited to see me again and to fight with me in battle because he won't fight *with* me anymore. He just wants to fight me. This is a promise, and one I'm sure he'll keep.

While this feels like a goodbye, I know it's not. I'll see him again. It may not be soon, but I know we'll cross paths again. He'll even our score, even if it's the last thing he does. This isn't over. It'll never be over until one of us dies.

The thought of killing Azael—my brother, the one constant in my life—makes me ill. We are two halves of one whole; neither of us is complete in the absence of the other. But things have changed.

He doesn't need me anymore. He's the second most powerful demon in Hell now, and no one, not even his sister, will see any mercy from him. I know he won't hesitate to kill me or Michael. So when the time comes, I'll have to kill him. I'll have no choice.

I drop to my knees with Michael clutching my elbows, making sure I don't hurt myself.

"Pen." He wraps his arms around me.

I bite the inside of my cheek, my sharp teeth piercing through the soft flesh until I taste blood. I sit back, open my eyes, and see Michael watching me. I give him a weak smile, trying to reassure him I'm not completely broken.

"I don't think he likes me very much," Michael says quietly, and even though my eyes are welling with tears, I laugh.

"If it helps, he's not too fond of me either. Not anymore."

"Are you okay?" he asks.

"I'll get there." I take a deep breath, clearing my mind. "I knew he wouldn't leave Hell. I just—I hoped he'd let me go."

"He can't let you go because he loves you."

I shake my head and drag the heel of my hand under my eyes. "Azael doesn't love anyone."

"You're his sister. He can't identify what he feels for you, but it's love."

"Maybe, but he doesn't love me anymore. He wants me dead. He wants—he wants to destroy me." I almost laugh, but it sticks in my throat, and instead my eyes well up.

Az and I never saw eye to eye, but we always protected each other. We always valued the other's life as equal to our own. At least I thought we did. Maybe I was wrong…

"I knew I would be on my own. I just didn't expect he would hate me so much."

"Azael doesn't hate you. And you won't be alone. You'll be with me."

"Alone with you," I say with a grin.

"It'll be different on our own," he says softly, taking my hand in his.

"We can't keep a foot in both worlds. Eventually we have to choose, I think. And I choose…" My voice fades. I'm not sure exactly what I choose, but it's not Hell or Heaven. "I choose something my own," I finally say. "Something we will define together, that sees the good in *trying* and accepts people's faults." I look at him meaningfully. "I choose you."

"I choose you, too, Pen." A smile lights his face.

"You see the worst of me, but you love me despite the darkness you've found," I say, incredulous.

"There is more light in you than you think," he replies. "It's just hard to see it when you're so close."

"But you see it?"

"I see it."

I pause. "There's a saying that I used to carry with me when I first fell from Heaven," I tell him. "'All things truly wicked start from innocence.' It reminded me that sometimes the best intentions lead to the most disastrous results."

IGNITE

"I've heard the angels say that. Something about how the road to Hell is paved with good intentions," he agrees.

"I used to whisper it to myself every night when Azael went to bed and I was alone with my thoughts. I used the phrase to justify what I was doing. But I think I may have whispered it too many times, because eventually a human overheard."

"Who?"

"Ernest Hemingway," I smirk. "But I was thinking... Maybe the road to redemption can be marred with a few mistakes? Like an angel and a demon falling in love."

He smiles wider and leans towards me, placing a soft kiss at the corner of my mouth. "We're going to be alone in this," he murmurs against me. "But at least we'll be together."

"Alone together," I repeat, giving him another quick kiss before pulling us both to our feet. "And now we have to go."

"Where will we go?"

"I heard Europe is nice this time of year."

"I've never been to Europe," he says cheerfully. He bends down and swipes up one of the round, smooth pebbles from the bank of the pond and slides it into his pocket.

"A stone?"

"To remember this moment, this place. Where you first kissed me."

"That wasn't a kiss!" I tell him, shoving his shoulder playfully. "I was saving your life."

"And where I told you I loved you, where you said you loved me back," he explains.

"A bit cheesy." I roll my eyes. "You're also forgetting that this is the place you almost drowned, the place you almost bled out. Oh yeah, and the place I almost had to kill you."

"I prefer to remember the better memories." He looks wistfully back at the cave. "Perhaps one day we'll come back here."

I grab his hand in mine and unfurl my wings, watching as his silver wings, still stained with blood, expand as well. "One day," I promise.

A light rain begins to fall from the dark sky, washing away his blood from his wings, his chest, my hands, and the shore of the pond. Together we fly away, slipping farther and farther from the cave and the icy pond.

One day.

CHAPTER 33

MICHAEL AND I FLY EVERY DAY AND EVERY NIGHT, ONLY stopping to rest for an hour at a time. We can't risk Azael narrowing in on our location, so we keep moving. We make our way across the United States so quickly that it makes me dizzy. The states blur into one hazy memory until the land gives way to an expansive blue ocean that deepens into a cold black.

We fly against the sun as it passes quickly overhead, the light of the day sliding across the sky like the hands on a clock as we slip above the water, hiding ourselves in the thick, watery clouds. Eventually, the dark black water of the ocean fades to a deep teal, and the ocean tapers off to reveal the cold and empty coast of England. Waves crash violently against the shore, the water pulling away from the rocky beach like lips curling back from sharp teeth.

"How about here?" Michael shouts over the wind, pointing down at the beach.

I shake my head. "Too isolated."

We'd be too easy for Azael to find and kill. Our best bet is to hide in plain sight, surrounded by crowds. Some place like London.

He nods and we continue on, past the beach. We pass over large gray farms with beige sheep and fading red barns placed on crooked hills. The farther we fly inland, the more populated it becomes.

The rolling farms turn into small, leafy villages, and the villages grow into larger towns, some filthy but all of them overcrowded. We follow a winding road that seems to snake its way straight through these villages and towns until we arrive in the heart of London.

It is a huge city with roads and buildings laid out like a giant puzzle. We fly higher, over large clock towers, stoney bridges, and even a large ferris wheel that rises above the thick mist that clings to the steely Thames river.

"We need to land somewhere crowded, busy," I tell Michael, looking over at him. His cheeks are burned red from the wind and his hair is tossed and tangled. "Somewhere we can get lost and blend in with people. Like…" I think for a moment. "Like a train station."

"Are there any stations around here?" he asks.

"Yeah, just past the park, if I remember correctly. That way." I point back across the river. "We should be able to land on the roof. It's so foggy that no one should notice us."

I take off in the direction of the station with Michael by my side, following the muffled sound of a train that is buried under the louder noises of London. A large, cream and brick building comes into view. The center of the tall, peaked roof of the station is made entirely of glass, and as we fly over it, I can see the crowds of people rushing from one platform to another.

Michael and I set down next to the sloping roof on a small, level landing and tuck away our wings. I hold my hand out and he takes it. We walk forward, looking down to the streets below, and I rest my hand on one of the imposing, carved angels.

IGNITE

Dozens of these angels adorn the station, made of cold, white stone. Their faces are cracked and emotional as they watch over the crowds that come and go through the arched entrance. The small, hard figures are draped around a large, ticking clock. In the dimming evening, several spotlights shine up on the statues, illuminating the faces of the angels in grotesque ways. The corners of the station are decorated with more ornate carvings, strong and curving and unmistakably Baroque.

I pull on Michael's hand and guide us away from the edge and towards a small, metal door that leads down from the roof. Michael reaches out and turns the handle, but it sticks. Without much thought, I step back and kick out at the silver knob, sending the door flying in and revealing a set of steep, narrow steps. I walk in front of Michael down the twisting stairs until we come to a small, tiled room at the bottom. Two rusty blue doors lead out of the room and into a musty hallway of the station.

Victoria Station is the second busiest railway terminus in London. It should be easy for us to get lost in the foot traffic. I brush down my hair anxiously as I step out of the empty hallway and into the crowds bustling between platforms, gripping Michael's hand so we don't lose each other. The station smells hot and dusty, and there is a loud humming sound as the trains slide into the station.

I look over at Michael and see he is staring up through the glass ceiling, completely oblivious to the impatient people that push around him, and I smile. Most people don't bother to look up; only Michael and a few small children, who are pulled fast behind their parents as they point up at the glass, notice the grandeur of the ceiling and the sky that lies beyond. Everyone else is so busy trying to get where they are going that they don't seem to notice the beauty around them.

"This is amazing," he gasps.

"Welcome to London."

We follow the crowd like we are stuck in a tide, being pushed and pulled through the station until the travelers disperse and we spill out onto the street. The humming of the station is replaced by the sound of heavy traffic and the wailing of distant sirens. In front of us is a large court filled with tall, double-decker buses that wait patiently for passengers with their doors open.

I direct us around the courtyard and onto a rickety sidewalk. Dozens of small, squashed black cabs with loud, mustached men sitting at the wheel line the narrow street. One of the drivers waves at us, offering us a ride, but we decline.

We walk a little farther from the station, rushing along the sidewalk until we pass a red phone booth. I pull us around to the back of the booth so we are mostly hidden from the people on the streets. Hedges press up against us, and if I look over the neatly manicured bushes, I can still see the clock draped with the angels of Victoria Station.

"I've never been anywhere like this," Michael says. "So full of life."

"So full of life and so full of filth. It's a bit much if you ask me, but it's the best place for us to hide until we can figure things out." I curl my fingers around the chain of my necklace.

"Can he find you?" he asks, raising his eyebrows.

I know Michael heard Azael's voice ripping through my mind when we fled the cave. He continued his torment as we flew across the globe, his voice raspy and hissing. He threatened me, he threatened Michael, and he detailed ways he would kill me—kill *us*...

I think he talks to me without realizing it sometimes, accidentally leaving his mind open for me to explore. I heard him preparing the army, giving an impassioned speech about reclaiming the throne in the name of Lucifer. He was wonderful, strong, and convincing. I heard Gus talking to him, his voice grave as he fit him for armor. And I heard the moment Lucifer presented him with his sword.

I saw the flat, black blade and the deep violet stone embedded in the shockingly white handle in my mind as clearly as he did. Engraved in sharp, twisting letters along the blade was the quote, "Hail, horrors, hail." A reference to Milton's *Paradise Lost*. Azael probably loves it.

It is a sword made for Hell if ever I have seen one. There was a second twin sword, slightly more delicate looking with a pale emerald embedded in the hilt, that remained untouched in the corner of his room. With an ache in my stomach, I realize it was cast for me.

The last time I saw Azael, we were over the Atlantic Ocean. Azael and scores of demons were leaving Hell, clawing up through ice and speeding into the sky. Dark wings, gnarled and sharp, flapped wildly under armor and an inhuman bloodcurdling scream tore through the pale blue sky that quickly darkened with demons. The sound pierced through me painfully, and I nearly fell from the sky. But Michael caught me and held me up until my vision stopped spinning and I could fly on my own again.

For all I know, Azael could be dead by now, struck down at the pearly gates of Heaven.

But I would feel it if he were dead. Wouldn't I?

"If we stay in one place for too long, or if I don't concentrate on blocking him..." I pause. "Yes. He could find me."

Michael holds my amulet in his palm delicately and studies it with interest, the gradient purple stone bright against his tan hand. "Why don't you get rid of it?"

"I—I can't. Azael and I both have one. We gave them to each other." I pull the stone away from him and tuck it under my shirt. "I know it's stupid. But I can't get rid of it. Not yet. Not until I have to."

"It's not stupid," he says seriously. "I'm sorry, I should have realized how important it was to you."

I shrug. "Do you think—"

Michael lifts one long finger to silence me, his eyes suddenly alert. He takes my hand and pulls me into the middle of the street, which has suddenly gone very still.

The cabs are frozen in place and buses block the middle of the road as drivers and passengers hang out of windows, looking up at the sky. Michael cranes his neck up to the sky, too, and I follow his gaze. The ground begins to shake beneath us and the gray sky suddenly burns a hot red before it begins to melt away.

This is very familiar, I think. *I've felt this before, deep within a memory.*

Screams erupt from the crowds of people behind us and I grab Michael's hand protectively.

He's here. He's safe. He's with me.

The ground continues to shake violently and I hear a splitting sound. I look down and see a giant crack spreading through the street, under the cars and buses. The high whine of car alarms is added to the chaos. Everyone seems unaware of the growing fissure, and I pull Michael over to the sidewalk with me just before the Earth opens, the road collapsing into a massive black pit that swallows up the traffic in the street.

The screams grow louder and more panicked. Blue flames rise from the pit and dance wickedly, licking out at the towering townhouses that line the road. The heat is unlike any I have ever felt before and it throws me backwards into the side of the phone booth, shattering the glass of the door. I cling tighter to Michael's hand, keeping him close to my side, away from the fire. My chest burns, each breath drawing the heat of the fire into my lungs, so I hold my breath.

Michael drags me farther from the road, away from the phone booth and towards thick, green hedges. My eyes begin to water from the heat and smoke, and through the tears I see his lips form my name, but I can't hear him. "PEN!"

I try to yell back to Michael, to let him know that I'm okay, but I can't. The searing heat of the fire burns my throat so severely that I can only manage a horrible croaking sound. I see the concern in his eyes and I want to scream. I look away from him, staring at the leaping flames until I am hypnotized by their bright blue fingers that reach towards the sky, searching for more victims. Only Michael's voice in my head can break my gaze.

PEN!

I look over at him with wide, surprised eyes. *MICHAEL! IT'S FINE. I'M FINE! ARE YOU HURT?*

Our voices are loud and urgent even in our minds.

He shakes his head no. *WHAT IS HAPPENING?*

AZAEL MUST HAVE—HELL MUST HAVE BREACHED THE GATES OF HEAVEN. IT'S THE WAR. IT'S THE START OF THE APOCALYPSE.

Almost as quickly as they appeared, the flames and the pit disappear. The road smoothes over, the pavement stitching itself back together again. There is not a single blemish on the street, only dark scorch marks on the sidewalk and the brick townhouses. I glance back over my shoulder, down the street towards the train station. The buses, taxis, and people that were in the street earlier are gone, swallowed up deep within the Earth, and the stone angels that adorned the clock have vanished.

I look back up into the sky and notice a large, orange sun that sits low on the horizon. That isn't right. It's much too late in the evening for a sun this bright. The sky is still tinted red, and I continue to watch it, thinking I'll see wings again like I did in my mind when Azael led the charge of Heaven.

I expect to see dark wings, white wings, any wings. But the sky is as empty as the streets—eerily empty. I squint up at the strange sun and notice the light is dripping from it. The orange of the sun melts away into a dark violet moon, nearly the same color as my eyes.

My pendant pulses wildly around my throat, faster and more insistent than I have ever felt it before. I trap it in my fist. Next to me, Michael grabs at his chest and falls to his knees. I kneel down next to him.

"Michael, what is it?"

He gasps for breath. "Something… Something is wrong."

I squeeze his hand tighter in mine. "What clued you in?" I try to joke. "Was it the fiery chasm in the middle of the street or the bleeding sky?"

He shakes his head. "No, something beyond this Earth. Something is missing."

I close my eyes, remembering a prophecy I had transcribed for Gus centuries ago.

This world will melt, break beyond repair. The balance between Heaven and Hell will fall. No angel will have a home. They will be stuck in what's left of this Earth, in an unending purgatory.

I snap my eyes open. This is the end of the world, what Hell has been waiting for, planning for.

"Michael," I whisper, knowing he can hear me over the screaming crowds. "The worlds are collapsing."

"What do you mean, collapsing?"

"There is no more Heaven," I say slowly. "No more Hell."

He watches me, clutching his chest, still not understanding.

"The lines between the worlds have been erased. *That's* what's missing."

His eyes grow wide. "And the angels?"

I shake my head. "They'll walk the Earth. Everyone will be trapped."

"Purgatory," he whispers.

I lean forward and give him a desperate kiss, fearing we have little time left together. He twines his arms around me and holds me, tightening his arms protectively around my small shoulders. When we part, I see pale ripples of light sweep across the ground and seep into the dark hedges next to us. Chasing the light is the deep purple shadow of the moon. I place my hand on Michael's chest, and in one heartbeat, we are plunged into darkness and abrupt silence.

Michael's breath hitches in a quick gasp and he grabs my hand. "I remember." His whisper swirls between us quietly. "Pen, I remember *everything*."

IGNITE

Overhead, the sky is black, except for the steely light of the stars and the eery glow of the moon. A deep, icy chill descends and I can feel my breath spill out from my lips in short puffs. If I could see it, I know my breath would be smoke in this frozen air. Michael shivers once under my hand.

Azael was right. The fire was just the beginning; the world will end in ice. As my eyes adjust to the darkness, I can see Michael outlined in front of me. I keep his hand in mine, and I'll never let go.

"I love you, Michael."

"I love you, Pen."

Where armies whole have sunk: the parching air
Burns frore, and cold performs th' effect of fire…
From beds of raging fire to starve in ice
Their soft ethereal warmth, and there to pine
Immovable, infix'd, and frozen round.

—John Milton, *Paradise Lost*

EPILOGUE

Azael

WHEN HE SPEAKS, LUCIFER'S VOICE IS LOW AND EASY, sounding like the sigh a soul makes when it is lifted from a chest. The last exhale of breath before dying.

"You have served me well, Azael."

He is not dressed in stiff, shining black armor as I am. Instead, he is wearing fitted leather gear that is as elegant as it is lethal. I kneel down in front of the golden throne he sits upon.

This is the first time this throne has not been empty. It is always left untouched, reserved for Him, his Father, God, in hopes that He might one day grace the angels with His presence. But no one's ever seen him. Apparently we were all too unworthy.

How can anyone be expected to serve and revere a being no one's even seen? How are we expected to believe that He is even real? The way Lucifer sits in the great throne now, so casually, is sacrilegious, an intentional slap in the face of all angels, all Believers. I smile down at his feet.

There's a line in the human's precious Bible that speaks of Lucifer. *"How you are fallen from heaven, O Lucifer, son of the morning! For you have said... 'I will ascend into heaven, I will exalt my throne above the stars of God.'"* And as it is written, thus it has become. He has become Most High indeed.

Lucifer is real; Lucifer is here. And I will follow and obey.

I place my sword at his feet and bow my head.

"Thank you, sir."

"I cannot say the same for your sister," he snarls, gesturing for me to stand. "She has proved herself to be quite disloyal. It's spectacular that you two can be of the same blood."

I rise and stand in front of him, sturdy, my chin raised and my shoulders squared. I feel my amulet hanging around my throat, the smooth stone cold and heavy against my chest.

Lucifer smiles at me, baring sharp, dangerous teeth. While I know he is one of the oldest angels, the first demon, the way he is draped over the thick, carved arms of the throne makes him appear extraordinarily young. Maybe a year or so older than Gus.

Nothing about him is ordinary or plain. His face is sharp and exact, his elegant features perfectly symmetrical. His beauty is so severe that the longer you look at him, the more grotesque he becomes. Suddenly his nose appears too pointed, his brows too arched, his cheekbones too high, and the sunken hollows of his cheeks are dark and ghoulish. His hair is a shock of white, and he has the same icy blue eyes as Michael.

They are brothers, I remind myself.

His eyes hold a sense of overwhelming knowledge. With just a look, he makes you believe that he knows everything about you. In an instant, he can see your deepest desires, your greatest weaknesses, and know just how to exploit them.

My eyes flick over to his archangel sword, a sword he found in a gilded safe after slaughtering a room of angels. After he fell, Heaven mistakenly cast an extra archangel sword, a great weapon meant for Lucifer. It was a secret guarded fiercely by Heaven, but nothing can be kept secret from the spies of Hell. Not for long, anyway.

When he found out, Lucifer killed the spies who knew, ensuring that he was the only one in Hell aware of the sword. As far as anyone outside of this room knows, Michael is in possession of the only archangel sword in existence.

Lucifer's sword is nearly the same as Michael's. Golden handle, silver blade, but instead of a ruby, his holds a cold sapphire stone. It rests delicately in his belt. I don't think he'll be letting it out of his sight any time soon. He threw down the sword he cast in Hell when he came across his archangel sword and re-holstered this bright weapon in its place.

"She is not my sister any longer," I say, my voice hard and filled with venom.

A corner of his thin mouth quirks up, amused. He tsks me. "Not so fast now. She is still your sister. A piece of her still lies within you, and a piece of you in her."

I'm silent, my jaw set.

"We all have siblings we wish we could forget." He looks away from me, down to his sword as if remembering something. "But somehow they endure, in memory and in life."

Lucifer's voice echoes across the bright, marbled room. It is completely empty except for the throne and several thick columns with fat cherubs carved at the top. He lazily pushes himself out of the throne and glides over to me, his face inches from mine.

"There are ways, however," he says, waving his hand in the air, "that you could get rid of her. It would split you two apart." He leans nearer and his breath curls around my ear. "Permanently."

"I would do anything." A deep burn starts in my abdomen and I recognize it as hatred, disgust. It's not unfamiliar, but I have never before felt it towards Pen. Never this strongly.

"Anything?" he asks, arching a thin eyebrow.

My sister is a traitor. A weak, foolish traitor. I offered her the world, and she spit in my face, turned her back on me for *Michael*.

IGNITE

"Anything," I say again, my voice unwavering.

"Good." Lucifer leans back and smiles sharply. "That's what I like to hear."

In a slow circle, he walks around me, appraising me as the tip of his sword drags across the marbled floor behind him, ringing lightly. When he meets my face again, he leans in close and hisses two words.

"*Kill her.*"

"With pleasure," I answer quickly, my voice thick with anger.

"And if what you've shown me is correct, she will be with my brother." He pauses. "Michael."

I nod curtly. "She claims to love him. Absolutely ludicrous."

"Love is a human emotion, so what she feels is not only false but impossible." He crosses his arms over his dark chest, cocks his head to the side, and smiles. "But it can be used to your advantage. Have you heard of the story *Romeo and Juliet*?"

"I have." Pen used to read it to me. I always thought the story was asinine, but she insisted I listen.

"Two teenagers in the throws of young love." He spins on his heel and collapses dramatically into the seat of the throne again. "Sacrificed themselves for one another in the name of that love. If they could not be together in life, perhaps they could find each other in death. A tragedy, a romance…" A smile creeps across his lips, bending the corners of his mouth into sharp angles. "A story, I believe, that will repeat itself."

I wait.

"Kill your sister. Kill my brother. Or have them kill themselves." He steeples his long, slender fingers under his chin. "I couldn't care less how you do it. As long as they are dead."

I bow low. "It would be my honor."

"And after you reap their souls, bring me their hearts," he adds, as if it's an after thought.

I hesitate, my eyebrows drawn low. "Pen—" I stop and correct myself. "*Penemuel* has no heart, let alone a soul."

"You'd be surprised."

He smiles again, and I see the points of his teeth pinning down his lower lip. He makes no move to explain, so I consider myself dismissed and pick up my sword, turn on my heel, and march out of the room.

"Azael," Lucifer calls out, his accented voice sharp in warning. "Do not fail me. I wish you the best of luck."

I don't need it, I think, walking out of the room.

Lucifer's laugh starts slowly, and by the time I reach the two gnarled Greater Demons guarding the door, his laughter has risen higher and louder, splitting through the silence in a shrill, delirious cackle.

I will find you, Pen. You still owe me that fight.

AUTHOR'S NOTE

Literature holds great significance to Pen. As the demon who was responsible for introducing man to the written word, she has a special place in her heart for literature of all kinds—but a special reverence for poetry.

There are several poems referenced throughout the story, and all are available under public domain. Below is a list of the poems and literature quoted throughout the text, for further reading (and I suggest further reading!):

- "Love and Harmony," by William Blake
- "She Walks in Beauty," by Lord Byron
- "In Neglect," "Fire and Ice," "The Road Not Taken," "Stars," and "Nothing Gold Can Stay," by Robert Frost.
- "Paradise Lost," by John Milton
- "Romeo and Juliet," "Macbeth," by William Shakespeare
- "Gasta," (or "The Avenging Demon") by Percy Bysshe Shelley
- "The Second Coming," by William Butler Yeats

To learn more about poetry, visit http://www.poets.org.

ACKNOWLEDGEMENTS

There are so many people I need to thank. I feel like I should be standing at a podium nervously shuffling index cards. Okay, where should I begin? *Clears voice*

Mickey Reed, my charming, encouraging, eagle-eye editor. I am so happy I found you and I want to thank you for helping me put out the cleanest version of my story that I could. Thank you for reigning in my adverbs. I c0uldn"t have dun it without yew!

Kellie Sheridan, my always enthusiastic critique partner who helped me push my characters—even when they were being stubborn—and challenged me as a writer. You helped me through all of the peaks and valleys that come with writing and publishing a book. Without your guidance, I would have been lost and this book would have been incredibly different. Your feedback was invaluable, and I am eternally grateful for the internet introducing me to you.

The handful of people who gave me early feedback on the early (and rather rough) versions of *Ignite*, especially Alli Kahan and Christine Nelson. Your comments were spot-on and often kept me from losing my mind in an endless cycle of insanity. Which is no small task.

Thank you for Stanislav Istratov for allowing me to use his gorgeous art as the cover for *Ignite*—I could never have dreamed of finding such an awesome image that so accurately represents Pen and her story. http://flexdreams.com.

And, as the say in *Gilligan's Island*, "the rest." This includes my friends and family (I was asked to mention my sister, JESSICA CROUCH, by name, so there it is) who have supported my writing ever since I can remember. From when I was a kid writing hundreds of poems just so I could use clip art, to when I decided to study creative writing in college… It's not always easy to live with me, especially when I'm in my *writing mode*, but I appreciate your patience and support. Ja feel?

Thank you to the earlier reviewers and bloggers—especially Giselle Cormier from Xpresso Tours who helped light the match that sparked the interest of readers and bloggers alike. All the book blogs have been fantastic, not only to me and my book, but for the literary community as a whole. You guys rock!

Last, but certainly not least, I want to thank you, the reader, for letting my story into your life for even just a short time. Thank you for stepping into the pages and joining Pen, Az and Michael as their story unfolds. I hope you'll return for the sequel.

ABOUT THE AUTHOR

Erica Crouch is a 20-year-old living on the outskirts of Baltimore, Maryland. She is pursuing a degree in English & Creative Writing with a specialization in Fiction at Southern New Hampshire University. Currently, she works for a small press in editorial services. She spends what spare time she has reading an overwhelming stack of books, watching an obscene amount of Netflix and procrastinating. *Ignite* is her debut novel and she is currently writing it's sequel along with other future projects.

Read more about Erica and follow her blog on her website, ericacrouchbooks.weebly.com. Find her books on GoodReads, http://goodreads.com/ericacrouch.

UPCOMING TITLES

Entice is an e-novella that prequels Pen and Azael's story in *Ignite*, going back to the final battle of the war and their time in Eden. It will be book 1.5 in the *Ignite* series and is expected to be released November 2013.

The sequel (and final installment of the *Ignite* series) is expected Spring 2014.

Also expected this fall by Erica Crouch is *Cut*, the first installment in the *Undying* series, a New Adult Science Fiction.

For more information, visit http://patchwork-press.com.

Made in the USA
Charleston, SC
13 August 2013